Only One Tear, May Fall

by

Otto Behrman

Bookman Publishing
Martinsville, Indiana

ISBN: 1-932301-73-9

To Linda,

May the road always rise to greet you.

May your days all be good ones, and

may love be the force that guides you.

Grüss Gott

Otto Behrman

To my wife Karen who
is a breath of fresh air
in an otherwise stagnant room

INTRODUCTION

This story is a work of fiction that is based on fact. The basis being a story that was told to me forty-five years ago by one of the women who lived it, and she told it from her perspective.

Verifying the authenticity of a story is a time consuming and very expensive project. I decided to tell the story and not concern myself with whether the story I was telling was the truth, the whole truth, and nothing but the truth. Obviously, the lapse in time invites the interjection of my imagination into what are perceived as facts.

This is the story about a young married woman who was coerced into having an illicit relationship with an SS General. It deals with changing attitudes, morality as it applies to religious principles and morality as it applies to the primal need to survive.

In reality, we all do what we believe we have to do, and that is precisely what Lisa did. What SS Brigadeführer (General) Gerhardt von Leitner ends up doing might surprise us all.

In the upside down world of the Third Reich, the excesses have taken center stage. The stories that are not told are the ones where the worst in times often brought out the best in people.

Such was the case with this story.

This is also the story of Max and Ilsa, two people who would not have met had it not been for the Third Reich. Ilse's husband had been killed during a Nazi purge, and Max was a super intelligent individual with a sense of perspective and the ability to discern. As an SS Standartenführer, he was able to do things he would not have been able to do otherwise.

This is not a story about the Holocaust. It is a story of four people who were inside the Third Reich.......and yet.....they weren't.

In the end, it is only a story.

They were not expected to cry, but when they did, ONLY ONE TEAR, MAY FALL.

One

In the beginning.....there!

1939

When, in the course of human events, it becomes necessary for one group of people to define who they are, it sometimes has a profound effect on the rest of us. Such an event occurred in a place called Germany, and the results of that event are still having their effect on the inhabitants of Mother Earth. It is hoped that the war that followed was of sufficient magnitude to insure that such an event will never visit us again. On the other hand, maybe our descendants will look upon World War II and see it only as a precursor to the main event. Maybe? Maybe not. There is always hope.

Saturday, May 20

The Reichschancellery

Friday was a beautiful day, but Saturday was not. Perhaps, it was an omen, because just before noon, the storm clouds appeared and the heavens opened. Three hours later, it was still pouring.

The occasion was a promotion ceremony in which Gerhardt von Leitner was being promoted from SS Standartenführer (Colonel) to SS Brigadeführer (General). At this time, it needs to be pointed out that senior officers in the SS and Wehrmacht were usually promoted to flag rank without the presence of Adolph Hitler at their promotion ceremonies, but then, Hitler had a soft spot in his heart for Gerhardt von Leitner.

Ceremonies were Hitler's thing.

He loved them. He loved being stage center, and this particular ceremony brought a certain amount of joy to the Führer's heart although it wasn't a particularly joyous occasion for the guest of honor.

Joyous occasions were the exception rather than the rule in Gerhardt von Leitner's life, and it extended all the way back to his childhood. He was the second of two sons that were born to the Baron and Baroness Frederick von Leitner of Vienna Austria, and second sons did not inherit the Entitlement.

They pursued a military career instead. Therefore, in order to give the boy a head start on his career, he had been packed off to a Prussian military academy at the tender age of six.

This wasn't unusual in aristocratic circles, but to a sensitive boy from Austria, the harshness of the Prussian way was tantamount to cruel and unusual punishment, and he often paid the price for his sensitivity until he finally became hardened to the cruelties of life. The last time he had shed any tears at all was at the tender age of seven. Since then——-not one tear had fallen.

He had survived his childhood, the Great War, received a law degree from Heidelberg, became a ruthless and merciless negotiator, but prided himself in having a sense of perspective that relatively few of his colleagues seemed to possess. He often wondered how such men could talk of a Thousand Year Reich without a sense of perspective.. That, he surmised, might be the fatal flaw in the National Socialist movement.

Gerhardt von Leitner was a very impressive looking man, and would have looked good on a poster had one been inclined to use a general officer for a poster model. He stood a little over six feet tall, and had absolutely no fat on his body anywhere. His hair had a natural wave to it, and was light brown in color. His appearance led people to believe that he was much younger than his forty years of age until they looked into his eyes. They were ice blue in color, and *never* betrayed how he felt on the inside.

That led to the belief that ice water ran in his veins.

He was wearing the black dress uniform of the SS, and around his neck was a ribbon that supported the Iron Cross First Class. He was therefore, a hero of *Der Vaterland* (The Fatherland). He had been a hero in every sense of the word.

Gerhardt glanced quickly at his leader and then retuned to his thoughts. He looked upon Hitler with a strange fascination, but stopped well short of venerating the man. Gerhardt von Leitner venerated no man. Neither, did he suffer a fool very well, and with Hitler in charge, he would probably be doing a lot of suffering.

In truth, Hitler was able to charm a snake without a flute. Most of his followers freely admitted to being willing to follow the man to the ends of the earth after being in his presence for less than thirty minutes.

Hitler walked over to his desk, and picked up the citation that elevated Leitner to the rank of Brigadeführer (General). He had no intention of reading it. He was, after all, *Der Führer.* He was the one responsible for this man's promotion. He would make up his own words.

He then surveyed the small group of men assembled in his office. There was Reichsführer Heinrich Himmler, the head of the SS; Martin Borman, the Chief of the Party Chancellery; Josef Goebbels, the Propaganda Minister, and a lowly Sturmbannführer (Major) by the name of Fritz Hoffman.

Major Hoffman was aide-de-camp designate for the new General, and although Majors weren't usually invited to attend these functions, the Herr Major ended up being in the wrong place at the wrong time, and found himself being invited to the inner sanctum by none other than Adolph Hitler himself.

Hitler cleared his throat, and the subdued chatting stopped.

"We are gathered here today to commemorate the promotion of Gerhardt Ludwig Baron von Leitner from the rank of SS Standartenführer to the rank of SS Brigadeführer (General)."

The new General was stunned!

In all of his forty years, Gerhardt von Leitner had never once seen fit to use that title. He was entitled to be called a baron, but not predisposed to being one. He didn't like being a baron. To him, it was the symbol of misuse, abuse, neglect and hypocrisy.

Gerhardt von Leitner rarely saw his parents, and therefore had no affinity for them. Even his brother's death in the Great War had made no dent in his armor. He resisted the call to his so-called family duty by telling his father that honor was as honor did, and since the father refused to honor the son, the son would therefore refuse to honor the father.

Had he been capable of frowning, he might have frowned at Hitler. The Führer, being oblivious to this line of thinking, continued by adding a few more flowery phrases to the illustrious career of Gerhardt von Leitner, and then, closed by saying, "As Chancellor of the Greater German Reich and Führer. of the German people, I affirm your promotion to Brigadeführer."

A smile then came to Hitler's face, "Congratulations, Herr Brigadeführer. I wish you well with your new responsibility. May you continue to inspire those you follow as well as those you lead." They were eloquent words, but then, when it came to the spoken word, Hitler was a very eloquent man.

Hitler offered his hand, and the Herr General took it. One had to be careful never to apply more pressure to Hitler's hand than was being applied by Hitler. The General clicked his heels and replied crisply, "Vielen dank, Mein Führer."

Hitler merely nodded and turned to Himmler who dutifully stepped forward and offered his congratulations as well. Himmler had mixed emotions about his new general, and yet, he seemed to understand Hitler's symbolic kinship with the man.

General von Leitner had been with the SS for six years and had more than proven himself to be a loyal, trusted, and capable man. The simple fact was that Himmler was used to picking his own senior officers and this one had been picked for him.

The Herr General was then congratulated by Goebbels and Borman who both looked like they preferred to be elsewhere, but the congratulations appeared to be sincere.

Major Hoffman, who was very uncomfortable being where he was, decided to wait until later to offer his own congratulations.

General von Leitner also assumed that his part in the proceedings were over and that he would be able to blend into the woodwork.

Wrong!

At that moment, the Führer turned his attention away from Goebbels and directed it toward his newest general.

"Ah - - - General von Leitner?"

"Ja, Mein Führer!" The Herr General replied briskly.

"There is a war coming. Did you know that?"

"We have been on a war footing for some time now, Mein Führer. I simply assumed that sooner or later - - - - it would happen." One of the things that Hitler liked about this man was his candor. The man would always give an opinion when asked for it. Sometimes- - - rather bluntly.

Hitler smiled that smile that only he could smile.

"Tell me, Herr General, if you were planning to go to war, how would you go about doing it?"

It was a question that caught everyone off guard, except the man the question had been directed to. General von Leitner had become accustomed to the unexpected, and simply shifted the gears in his mind to deal with the new subject. He then digested the question although he wasn't a military strategist. He had been trained as a lawyer, not a military strategist, and he was a General in the SS, not the Wehrmacht, but he had spent nine years at a Prussian military academy and that had to count for something.

One could now hear a pin drop. *Very well, Herr Hitler, you like to play this game. We'll see if you like playing it my way.*

All eyes were riveted upon him as he began speaking.

"I know it is your plan, Mein Führer, that we should expand the Reich for the benefit of the German people, and I believe we need to bring the Polish Corridor and East Prussia back into the Greater German Reich. That means that we might have to go to war with Poland." The quiet room became even quieter.

"Of course, we might have to pick a fight with them, but that shouldn't be too difficult. After all, the Poles have their pride too. As for how ....I would simply overwhelm them. They need to be defeated quickly or things could stagnate and turn into a war of attrition. The last war became a war of attrition and that sapped our strength regardless of any opinions and theories to the contrary. We must, at all costs, avoid a war of attrition. I would also expect England and France to declare war in response to our action against Poland. Same rules apply. Overwhelming force, but a caution. We must neutralize England, and that means invading, conquering and occupying them. If we don't, we give their allies a platform from which to stage a counterattack."

Hitler first looked dubious, and then asked, "With France gone, who might they receive help from?"

The General shrugged, "Perhaps America, Mein Führer. After all, they do have enormous industrial capability."

Hitler, drunk with the power that his recent successful gambles had given him, shook his head and said, "Nein Herr General! America has no stomach for war. They are soft and overfed, and their President Roosevelt knows this. No, General von Leitner, America is not the problem you believe them to be, but go on with your scenario."

General von Leitner did just that. "As for the Russian colossus to the north, my inclination is to do nothing about them at all. Leave them alone, but if military action should become necessary, I would try to withhold it until the English matter is resolved. Other military targets of necessity can be sorted out and prioritized only after all of Europe belongs to us."

Hitler bristled. "You persist with this English thing as though it were really important. WHY?"

The General had known Hitler for years, and did not like the man. He never had and probably never would. For that matter, he didn't really know why Hitler liked him unless it happened to be his cross to bear. He finally replied, "Mein Führer, you asked for my opinion and I gave it. Suffice it to say that I am but a lowly General. I will do as I am ordered."

Hitler then asked, "Has anyone else discussed this matter with you?"

General von Leitner didn't even flinch. "Nein, Mein Führer! Since the end of the Great War, I have often wondered how we ended up in those God forsaken trenches, and have just as often asked myself what I would have done had it been my decision to make. As you can see, I have had over twenty years to prepare an answer for you."

It was the right answer and Hitler broke the tension by laughing. He looked at the assembled gathering, and exclaimed, "Good! Good! As you can all see, we still promote the right men to General." Then, he looked at the clock and said, "Now if you will all excuse me, I have another meeting."

Nobody had to be told twice, and the study emptied into a large foyer. The General looked around, and since no one was attaching themselves to him, he sought out Major Hoffman.

At the same time, Major Hoffman sought him out and extended his right hand, "Congratulations Herr General. I am glad to see they are still promoting good men."

Gerhardt couldn't help thinking, *Meaning what, Herr Major?*

The General took his hand and squeezed it warmly. His hands could be warm even if his eyes were not. "Danke, Herr Major. Only it is not necessary for you to be condescending towards me."

The Major just looked at his General strangely. "Begging the Herr General's pardon, but I am not being condescending. I happen to believe you are a good man. If I didn't think so, I would have said nothing."

The General just looked at his aide. No further comment was made.

To fill an acquired void, the major said, "Your driver is waiting downstairs. I hope the rain has let up some."

"If it hasn't, we will simply make do, Herr Major. I never concern myself with that which I cannot control. If it is still raining hard, we will simply get a little wetter."

The Major said nothing. Just looked at his boss before nodding.

They were downstairs slipping into their raincoats when they were joined by SS Sgt. Max Liebert, who took the General's raincoat and helped him into it. Once their raincoats were on, they started in the direction of the exit. They hadn't walked a half dozen steps when they heard the sound of a woman's voice.

"Herr Liebert!"

They all turned and saw the Führer's secretary standing at the bottom of the stairway. She motioned for Sgt Liebert to come with her.

He turned and said, "Obviously, I have been pre-empted. I will be right back."

As Sgt Liebert approached the woman, the General heard the words, "Come with me, Herr Liebert."

It is Herr Liebert NOT Sgt. Liebert, and the lady doing the beckoning is the Führer's private secretary.. How very interesting.

* * * * *

Max Liebert followed Hitler's secretary upstairs and down the hall to the last door on the left. She opened the door and ushered Max inside. It was really a storage room with a table in the middle. No chairs, and storage shelves on two walls. A window was on the far wall.

Waiting for him was Adolph Hitler, a man with a definite flair for the dramatic.

Max stepped inside, clicked his heels and bowed slightly from the waist up. "Mein Führer," he spoke solemnly.

Hitler spoke, "It was good of you to come, Max.?"

Did I have a choice? "A pleasure, Mein Führer!"

Hitler's face clouded ever so slightly. "You used to call me Uncle Adolph."

"I know, but I was fourteen at the time. I was kind of old for such childish nonsense wasn't I?"

"Nonsense?" Hitler's eyebrows went up as he spoke the word.

"Wrong choice of words, Mein Führer?"

"Ja! That it was, my impetuous young friend. I liked being an uncle even if it was only in a symbolic sense."

Max bowed again. "Jawohl.......*Uncle* Adolph."

Hitler quickly appraised him. "You look good in a uniform."

"Danke, Uncle Adolph, but I feel like a fraud."

"Nonsense, Max! A little subterfuge is good for the Reich. After all, there are those who would rob us of our destiny, and how best to ferret them out than by joining their ranks."

When Max didn't respond, Hitler walked over to the table. Laying on the table was a black attaché case. He opened it and took out a black portfolio and handed it to Max. "It is all in there, Max.

Your identification papers and your orders......all signed by me."

The next item he handed to Max was a rather impressive looking wallet. Also, in the color black which, by the way, seemed to be the official color of the Third Reich. It was the type normally carried in an inside coat pocket. Max opened it and looked. Everything was there. The papers had all been reduced and laminated. It was all in miniature. Even he was impressed and Max was a hard man to impress.

Max might have wondered why Hitler himself was taking care of this mundane task rather than his secretary, but he had long since realized there were many quirks to this man who now ran Germany. Therefore, he kept his thoughts and concerns to himself.

Hitler looked at the man before him and said. "I have a lot of faith in you, Max. Perhaps, a lot more than you have in yourself."

"What exactly do you expect of me, Uncle Adolph?"

"You are my personal emissary. Those papers are the passport that permits you to be traveling beyond walls, behind barbed wire fences, into the offices of high ranking officials, and all the lower ranking officials who believe themselves to be important. As my emissary, you represent me.....my interests, and I...in turn bear the responsibility for the interests of the Reich." There was a long pause. An uncomfortable pause for Max. After which, Hitler continued.

"Initially, I wish you to pursue a matter in the Munich area." Then, he turned and faced the window and the waves of rain that were beating against it unmercifully. They were a tonic for him, and for some more very long moments, he stood mesmerized while Max waited. Suddenly, he whirled about.

"We have a financial shortfall. A rather substantial one. . An amount that was donated to our cause by an American financial conglomerate. Do you remember our discussions regarding the international banking community?"

"Ja," Max replied. He had a Masters in Philosophy, a Bachelor's in Anthropology and neither was in economics. Economics had always been a sort of a hobby with Max. Something that supplemented his formal education. Economics and religion had played such a major role in the history of mankind that Max finally concluded that economics played the major role while religion had been the principle beneficiary. Max knew it had always been about money or whatever it was that passed for money at the time. For that matter, the Third Reich was as much about money as any other movement in history, but their true message was hidden in the endless speeches and documents that exhorted the virtues of National Socialism. Again, the message was about change and the fact that National Socialism could affect that change. Unfortunately, it took money for change to happen. Lots of money.

That was the key. Hitler's message not only charmed the German masses to keep them from revolting, but it also charmed the aristocratic elite, not only in Germany, but in the industrial nations as well. His tentacles had touched the people who were so far removed from mundane society that they were no longer in touch with that reality, but they were still in touch with billions of dollars, and that was what Hitler wanted. What amazed Max was that Hitler received the money and still maintained control.

Max's thoughts were interrupted once more by the sound of Hitler's voice. "I won't bore you with the details, because they are in here, " He said referring to a thick packet he held in his hand, "but we believe that Konrad Ruhl, a wealthy Jewish banker from Munich has somehow intercepted the money on its final leg to our bank in Zurich. How it was done still isn't known, but we do have Herr Ruhl in custody. Unfortunately, our normal interrogation processes have not produced any positive results. Not yet, anyway."

"Are we requesting Herr Ruhl's cooperation or just trying to break the man?" Max knew Konrad Ruhl quite well. In fact, there was a side to Max that Hitler didn't know about and hopefully never would.

Hitler's face clouded. Doubtless there were very few men in the Reich who could speak candidly to Adolph Hitler. In fact, Max could actually cross examine the man, but only in absolute privacy. No one else had ever been privy to their conversations.

"We want the money, Max. I don't care how we get it."

"How much money are we talking about?" Inquired Max. Hitler wrote two figures on a slip of paper and handed it to Max.

"The upper figure is the amount in American dollars and the bottom figure is the same amount converted to Deutsch Marks.

Max nodded. He could have figured that out all by himself. It was quite substantial, but Max still didn't register anything. He handed the slip back to Hitler, and Hitler commenced to tear it in many pieces.

"Will the absence of that money drive the Reich to the brink of insolvency?"

"Nein! That it won't, but I fail to see your point, Max.

"My point is this. You have a sizable shortfall, and you *think* you know who did it, but rather than seek the man's cooperation, the man is alienated by heavy handed tactics. Somewhat counter productive isn't it, Uncle Adolph?"

Hitler just looked at his "nephew."

"Very well, Max. You have made your point. You will now have the opportunity to do it your way. "

Max grunted. "You give him to me after torture and expect results?"

"I expect you to try, Max. If you do not succeed, kill him. It should be a public execution to demonstrate that no one can steal from the Reich and get away with it."

Max frowned. "Didn't you tell me that you only *think* he did it?"

"Ja. I told you that."

"Wouldn't executing him be the same as condemnation prior to investigation?"

Hitler's expression clouded over again. "Someone has to pay, Max, and Herr Ruhl is the prime candidate for that honor. He had both knowledge of the procedure and access to the funds."

"But, does stealing warrant the death penalty?"

"Maybe not, but treason does, and the theft of that money certainly undermines the integrity of the Reich and that amounts to treason......*High Treason!*"

"But........?"

"But nothing, Max." Hitler interrupted. "I want verification of the funds or proof that he was properly executed. Do you understand what I am telling you, Max?"

As a very heavy weight descended upon Max's shoulders, he clicked his heels and said, "I will do my best, Mein Führer."

Hitler walked over to him, placed his hands on Max's shoulders, and said, "I know you will."

After that, Hitler walked in the direction of the door. The

meeting was over.

Max picked up the attaché case and walked out of the room. He walked briskly down the stairway and rejoined the other two men.

General von Leitner looked curiously at Max and the case he was now carrying, but said nothing. Instead, he turned and walked out of the front door and into the rain beyond.

Munich

Saturday: May 27

They were just entering the outskirts of Munich. Sgt Liebert was driving, Major Hoffman was sleeping and the General was reading. At least, the General was going through the motions of reading. Most of his thinking was directed toward Munich and his new responsibility. It was hard for him to think well of Munich as he didn't have much of an affinity for the Bavarian capital. For that matter, he wondered if he would be able to even communicate with the locals. He had been there as a stop off before traveling to Garmisch for the Winter Olympic Games, and found it difficult to talk with many of those people. They spoke a different kind of German here.

He then looked at the back of Sgt Liebert's head and wondered if the man might be some kind of spy for the Führer. If so, why? Why would Hitler promote him and then turn around and spy on him? Even a man with Hitler's paranoia wouldn't do that! Or would he? For that matter, he wasn't sure where Major Hoffman's loyalties lie either. Such was the case in Hitler's Germany.

Nobody trusted anybody!

In the driver's seat, Sgt Max Liebert had been in deep thought since leaving Berlin. He had completely digested the information that Hitler had given him and burned any documents that he didn't want to fall into the wrong hands. Somewhere, imbedded firmly in his memory were three account numbers at three separate banks in Zurich. Monday morning would find him at Konrad Ruhl's bank in Munich where he would start to backtrack the route, but first he had to meet with Konrad Ruhl. He would do that tomorrow afternoon. He was only going through the motions, but the meeting with Konrad ought to prove interesting. Very interesting, indeed

Suddenly, he heard another voice. It was the General.

"We are coming into Munich are we not, Herr Sergeant?"

"Ja, Herr General."

"This is a homecoming of sorts for you isn't it, Herr Sergeant?"

"Jawohl, Herr General. I was born in Starnberg and lived there until I was fourteen, and then my father took over a bakery in Munich. I lived there until I went to the university."

The General decided not to pursue the matter further. He laid his head back and closed his eyes, and Max knew that the conversation was at an end. He returned once more to his own thoughts.

* * * * *

When they arrived at the mansion, all were impressed. It was nestled within the wooded forests on the southwest side of Munich. Several acres of forest had been cleared and prepared. The result was about ten acres of beautiful lawn surrounding a large three story house that was built in the style of a Victorian mansion. In the back, beds of roses created a design that, if viewed from the upper floors were like rays of the sun. In the center of it all was a fountain.

It was the sheer majesty of the building that impressed them immediately. Of course, the majesty disappeared with the appearance of the gate. The guard checked their credentials carefully. The General made note of the fact that the guard was Gestapo. That did not please him. There were ways of dealing with that problem without appearing to be an overly high strung SS General.

There was a front entrance to the building, but it was probably never used because there was a covered side entrance. The entrance road actually split three ways at the side entrance. The left split looped to the left and gave access to the side entrance. The center split was an access road to the rest of the property while the right loop emptied into a parking lot and ultimately joined with the incoming leg for the purpose of exiting the property.

It was when the car came to a stop under the canopy, that the General got the first look at his reception committee. The domestic staff was lined up and standing at some semblance of attention.

Standing in front of them was a rather rotund looking man in a black uniform complete with riding breeches and black jack boots.

With the arrival of the car, he snapped to a rigid position of attention. He wore a uniform similar to the black uniform of the SS, but he was a uniformed member of the Gestapo. His rank was the same as the SS ranking for Captain or Hauptsturmführer.

Max exited the Mercedes and walked briskly around to the right rear door, and opened it. He rendered the military salute as he did so. First, the Herr Major Hoffman exited the vehicle followed by the Herr General von Leitner. When both men were outside the vehicle, the Herr Hauptsturmführer clicked his heels and shouted, "Heil Hitler!"

Both SS officers returned the bent arm salute.

"Herr Hauptsturmfüher Zeller reporting to the Herr General, Sir!

The Herr General looked at the man indifferently. Then, he asked. "And, what is your function, Herr Hauptsturmführer?"

The Hauptsturmführer beamed proudly as he said, "I am in charge of the facility, Herr General."

"I see," responded the Herr General dryly.. "And, what does that include?"

"The house, the grounds, everything. .... everything," He gestured wildly as he spoke.

The Herr General then inquired, "Is it your intention to remain?"

"Jawohl! Herr General! I have everything set up, and running well. There should be no problems."

The General might have looked at the man with pity, if he were capable of such a thing, and then figured, oh what the hell. "Herr Hauptsturmführer, your plans are not consistent with mine, and in matters such as that, my plans take precedence. Therefore, since I am now the senior officer in residence, I will assume command of the entire facility which includes the staff needed to operate such a facility. I do not need someone such as you to facilitate the operation as my staff will see to it. What I am telling you is that you are a redundancy that is no longer necessary. I therefore release you so that you can return to your Commanding Officer."

"But, Herr General......!

"This is not negotiable, Herr Hauptsturmführer. You are dismissed!" And he waved the man off like he would have waved off an insect.

General von Leitner then scrutinized the domestic staff. They weren't very precise but then they didn't have to be. They were domestics. After looking them all over, he asked, "Is one of you in charge?"

A man stepped forward and said, "I am Herr General. My name is Erik Halder, and I am the butler."

The Herr General stepped forward and shook the butler's hand. "An honor, Herr Halder. Now then, why don't you dismiss these people and then......you and I shall take a little walk."

Shortly afterward, the two men were walking down a path leading in the direction of the wooded area at the rear of the property. Once they were safely out of earshot of any microphones, the General stopped.

"Tell me Herr Halder, how long have you been here?"

The butler didn't have to think. "I have been for here thirty years, Herr General. I came to work for the elder Herr Ruhl."

"Were you loyal to the Ruhl family?"

"Jawohl Herr General. Very much so."

The Herr General rubbed his chin thoughtfully and then asked, "What was your opinion regarding the Reich's decision to disenfranchise Herr Ruhl and strip him of his wealth, his position and his dignity."

The butler regarded the Herr General quite carefully as he needed to decide if he wanted to answer the question. It was filled with pitfalls, because if he were honest, he might be signing his own death warrant. Then he decided to test the waters, "How should I answer that question, Herr General? I have already told you I was loyal to the Ruhl family. You'll find that domestics are like that. We form a bond with our employers that is much firmer than the standard employee/employer relationship. It becomes a family. Should I then tell you that I found nothing wrong with what the government did to him?"

The Herr General's eyes softened, but it was quite impossible for him to smile. He was far too conditioned against the idea of smiling.

"Very well, Herr Halder. I shall withdraw the question, but in my way of thinking, your loyalty to Konrad Ruhl is to be commended. You did, however stay on after the transition. Tell me.....were you given a choice?"

"Nein.....Herr General."

"Were you treated badly?"

"Jawohl, Herr General!"

"Gestapo tactics?"

"Jawohl, Herr General!"

The General nodded his head, and then asked, "Would you like to stay on?"

"Ja, Herr General. It is what I do. It is what I know. What else could I do?"

Again, the General nodded. "How about the rest of the staff?"

"With a couple of exceptions, they are in the same situation as I."

The General considered what he heard for several long moments before replying, "Let me say this....As a General officer in Himmler's SS, I should be in a policy making position but I am not. I am more like a facilitator. Unfortunately, as a lawyer, I am one of those who is responsible for the Nazi's being in total control. Having made that treasonous comment, I will now go as far as to tell you that you **can** trust me. Maybe I can't trust you, and if I can't, I will find out soon enough. All I really want to know is whether you can be loyal to me?"

The General had already said more than Erik Halder expected him to say, and because of that, Halder was almost willing to trust him completely. Unfortunately, the Herr General represented an organization that had already proven that they were willing to go to any lengths to ferret out traitors. "I cannot give you the same loyalty that I gave to Herr Ruhl."

"I understand that, Herr Halder. After all, loyalty has to be earned and deserved. The point is that we need to function as an smooth running organization and not as a discordant group of functionaries who are afraid of their own shadow."

"Herr General, there is loyalty and there is loyalty. The kind that requires years is quite different from that which is given to an employer we are eager to please. I can assure you, Sir, that just as soon as I speak with the rest of the staff, you will find that we will be quite eager to please you."

"Danke schön, Herr Halder." (Thank you)

"Bitte schön, Herr General." (You're welcome)

"Now then, there is one more matter to discuss. If you feel that any one of your staff should go, tell me and they will be gone. By that, I don't mean that anything bad will happen to them. It means that I only want people that you feel comfortable with. Do you understand?"

"Jawohl, Herr General. I will report back to you."

"Very well! Unless you have another matter to discuss, we shall return to our assigned tasks."

And they did.

Two

Lisa

<u>Sunday: May 28</u>

<u>Southeast of the Village of Berg</u>

"Lisa, why don't you go someplace and compose yourself while I get Heidi ready to go." Anna Rensler was extremely upset with her daughter's mood swings and could honestly say that she didn't look forward to Karl's tour of duty in the army, but conscription was now the law of the land, and that was that.

Lisa looked at her mother as though she had just spoken a foreign language, and then, she sighed deeply. Heidi was still crying, and Lisa seemed unable to cope with the girl or anything else for that matter.. Then, she closed the distance between her and her mother and they embraced.

"Ja, mama, it is best. I will go down by the stream. I am sorry about my outburst."

Anna Rensler would liked to have told her daughter that everything was very good, but everything wasn't very good. In truth, very little was good. Lisa's outbursts were destructive and spiteful, and came completely without warning. They weren't a daily occurrence, but they occurred often enough to upset the usually stable atmosphere in the Rensler home.

Anna pulled a handkerchief from her apron pocket and wiped

her daughter's eye's with it. After that, she wiped her own. Then she reached down and scooped her granddaughter up into her arms. Heidi was a good little girl. She always had been. Unfortunately, Heidi's mother was operating somewhere near the edge, and tended to overreact when the child managed to do something wrong.

Lisa looked at the real life picture of her mother holding her daughter, and decided that it was best that she do as her mother had "suggested."

She walked down the *Deile* or hallway to the rear stairway which was the only entrance used by the people living there. The Rensler family lived in what was commonly referred to as a *Baurenhaus.* The common reference being that throughout *Der Fatherland,* the house and barn were combined into one unit. The house was built over the barn which meant that man and animals shared a common roof. Gus Rensler was a dairy farmer who, in this case, had built his *Baurenhaus* on the edge of the village adjacent to his fields where hay and alfalfa grew. Other *Bauren* or farmers lived in the village as well, but they had to travel a greater distance to get to their fields.

At the bottom of the stairway, she opened the door and stepped into brilliant sunshine. She squinted until her eyes adjusted to the brightness of the day. Then, she turned and looked up into the house where she had grown up. It was typical, but she had gotten used to other ways of living during the last four years in Munich.

The building was a two and one-half story with a red tile roof that had a flatter slope than buildings of the same type in northern Germany. Perhaps, this type of living and working structure best epitomized the utilitarian efficiency of not only the German farmer, but all Germans in general.

Her attention then shifted from the house to the surrounding area, and as she looked about her, she drank in her surroundings. This was where she had grown up, and since she had been the only child, she had explored the surrounding countryside while other girls played with dolls.

Not that Lisa wasn't every inch a girl. No, she had been a very pretty little girl who had grown into a very lovely young lady. The truth of the matter was that she was actually beautiful.

On this particular day, she was wearing a pretty red dirndl

although she rarely wore dirndls anymore. The dirndl was a Bavarian, Swiss or Austrian custom as was lederhosen for men. Northern Germans weren't fascinated by what their "country" cousins down in Bavaria wore. Her husband Karl was one of those northern Germans, and she had been able to pick up a little bit of sophistication during the years spent in and around the University of Munich.

The truth of the matter was that it mattered very little to her. She was basically a Bavarian, and in her way of thinking being Bavarian was a lot better than being German.

Besides, her problem ran a lot deeper than dress styles.

When she reached the bank of the stream, she hugged herself and gulped in a breathe of clean fresh country air. It was warm and sunny, and Lisa really did love this place. She dropped gracefully to the ground by the streams edge. This was where the stream ran downhill thus creating rapids. The water moved over, in, and around the rocks. It acted as though it were in a hurry, and yet it still seemed to be moving very purposefully. She became mesmerized by it once more.

This was her quiet place.....her safe place. Her place of quiet repose. The place she always came to sort things out.

Lisa was twenty years old, and had been married to Karl Mueller for the last four years. She knew that she was a very lovely woman, but it didn't make any difference. She was a married woman and a mother. She would maintain her appearance and continue to make Karl proud of her. Maybe, some day, she would actually learn to love the man.

She was the only child of Gustav and Anna Rensler, and had grown up on this very same dairy farm in southern Bavaria not far from Lake Starnberger. She was a product of the Great War and had grown up in its aftermath.

Like so many German soldiers, her father had come home from the battlefield in a state of complete confusion. It had not been possible for the Fatherland to lose, but there it was for all to see. Germany had lost, and her father, like so many soldiers, began to wonder what losing would end up costing their beloved Deutschland. Moreover, he wondered what would it do to his native Bavaria. In truth, he loved his Bavaria more than he loved that which everyone called Germany. The country, as a whole, contained places and people he didn't care for.

There had been talk about the harshness of the peace treaty, but those discussions had been over the young girl's head.

. Gus loved his only daughter, but he was an overbearing father who mixed Old Testament morality with traditional Bavarian loyalty and kept harping on two main themes: (1) She was a Bavarian girl, and Bavarian girls were always good girls who never brought shame upon themselves or their families, and (2) no sacrifice was too great for the *Heimat,* which in this case, meant Bavaria.

There was very little loyalty for Deutschland or Germany as a whole. Part of Germany was Prussia and the idiots who made up the Prussian state thought they were all military geniuses. He still resented the fact that Berlin, the former Prussian capital, was now the capital of the German Nation.

Her mother, on the other hand, realized that her daughter was still a young girl who needed to grow up as normally as possible, and because of these efforts, Lisa grew up having the normal love fantasies of young girls instead of the Spartan idealism of her father.

, Somewhere around her twelfth year, the rites of womanhood caught up with her and she had her first period, but her first was almost her last. Her body had refused to stop hemorrhaging, and it took all of the skills that a country doctor could muster in order to get it stopped.

A month later, she started again, and this time her body responded the way it was supposed to. The doctor watched her closely for two more months before finally giving her a clean bill of health. It was done so with one reservation ....that she should never have children.

For the next three years, that was no problem at all. She got prettier and more desirable, but her father became the roadblock that stood in the way of any young man's fancy. Things might have been different had it not been for Fritz Lallendorf. He was both good looking and bold. He carried himself with a confidence that was exhibited by so many young men her age. They were following a new messiah. A man named Hitler, and they weren't about to pay for the sins of their fathers. Not when they could commit a few of their own.

Fritz was her first love, but she had to be creative in order to spend time with him. She had always taken long walks, and was still able to do so without raising the suspicions of her father. The only difference being that she was no longer walking alone. Fritz would meet her and they would discover things together. Fritz had given Lisa her very first kiss, and then, he came very close being the first to cross the forbidden threshold that held the magic of her womanhood. The one that only the maiden's husband was ever supposed to cross. Had they been in their favorite meadow on the banks of the lake, it probably would have happened.

What really happened was they had spent the afternoon at the lake, and he walked her home while being careful not to be noticed by her father. They still had some time so they went to what they thought was a private place and began petting. They were about ready to engage in the act when her father discovered them.

She still shuddered when she thought about the scene that followed. He literally ran Fritz off the farm, and then he went back to deal with the daughter who was about to disgrace him. From that point on, he kept a very tight rein on her.

That ended promptly when Karl Mueller came on the scene. Karl was a first year student at the University of Munich who happened to be at Vasser Park in Starnberg one Sunday when Lisa was there and he became so taken with her that he found out who she was and where she lived.

The following Saturday found Karl at her front door, but he did not come to see the fair maiden. He had come to see her father, instead. Gus then, became touched by the respect shown by the young man, and three hours later, Karl Mueller had been granted the privilege of seeking the affections of one Lisa Marie Rensler.

This surprised Lisa because her father was a big man while Karl was slightly built and of medium height. In truth, Karl was the son of a wealthy industrialist from the Ruhr Valley, and a pretty good catch. At least, he was from her father's point of view.

It wasn't that he was a bad looking young man, but he did not fit the mold that she thought her future husband should come from. Fritz did, and that was the reason why things happened between them. Karl, on the other hand, would take some getting used to, and she expressed her feelings to her father while thinking they might mean something to him.

Instead, she had been shocked to learn that her father had

already given his permission for Karl to marry her before her lack of discipline brought shame to the good Rensler name. What followed was the only time she actually came to verbal blows with her father.

She lost.

It was predictable. After all, her father was the boss, and she was expected to do what he told her to do. She would gain no favor from the surrounding community or the legal establishment that governed that same surrounding community, so she resigned herself to becoming Frau Mueller.

His parents actually traveled to Munich to meet with their future daughter-in-law, and were delighted by the beauty and sincerity of this "country girl" from southern Bavaria. Heinrich Mueller was a design engineer who happened to be in right place at the right time and became quite wealthy in the process. He put the icing on the cake by marrying the bosses daughter. The couple had six children, and of those six children, Karl had been the runt of the litter and therefore deemed the least likely to succeed.

It came therefore, as a surprise when Karl decided to study civil engineering at the University of Munich, and it was a further surprise when their son not only found the fair Lisa, but demonstrated that he had the initiative to go after and win her. It mattered not how he did it. Only that it had done.

The last obstacle had been cleared.

Therefore, in 1935, they applied for permission to marry under the "Law for the protection of the Genetic Health of the German People." They submitted to a medical examination to determine if they were disease free, and when it was determined that they were, they were issued a "Certificate of Fitness to Marry."

A month later, they were married, and moved into an apartment near the university. In addition to the money he received from a family trust fund, the Reich needed engineers and since his grades were excellent he also received a grant from the government in order to continue his education. In 1935, Germany was finally coming out of the worst depression in its history.

Once Lisa had accepted the inevitable, She took to marriage with an eagerness she didn't think she possessed. It was something called acceptance. Her father had controlled her life to this point.

Now, her husband did.

The difference being that she now slept with Karl, and found herself enjoying what often occurred when a man and woman slept together. In fact, she found that she really liked sex, and by this time, she had all but forgotten the admonishment not to have children. Unfortunately, Karl's sex drive which was good in the beginning, began to decline some. Between his studies and her, she often came in a distant second. On the other hand, she had no other experience to base her expectations upon, so perhaps this was the way things were supposed to be.

Underneath it all, a feeling of resentment began to surface. Karl had not been her choice. He had been her father's choice. Perhaps, money had changed hands although she did not know that. Her father and Karl had formed an unholy alliance and she was now living in the result of that alliance. In truth, she did not like it. Not one least bit, but these thoughts only surfaced when she was alone. She had found that dwelling on them was bad, so she tried to ignore them.

The good part of university life was that it gave her the opportunity to interact with the university community. While her husband was getting a formal education, she was getting an informal one. Her favorite subjects were philosophy, history, and psychology.

She studied Karl's old books like she was starved for knowledge, and she took every opportunity to enter into discussions. In many cases, her sex barred her.....as in....no women allowed. Sometimes though, she was able to sit in on discussions while at other times she was actually encouraged to voice opinions.

One such group was facilitated by Professor Isaac Nusbaum, a physics professor who had been much revered by his students for his philosophical viewpoints. Physically, he was a ruggedly handsome man in his early forties who was not only opposed to the Third Reich, but was quite vocal in his opposition.

His discussions were lively and soul searching. Unfortunately, he finally angered the wrong people and the Gestapo came looking for him. That would have happened anyway because of his Jewish origin. To avoid arrest, he dropped out of sight and became a fugitive.

* * * * *

Despite the earlier warnings of her doctor, the years had dulled the need for caution and she had become pregnant. It was a mixed blessing, but the news had been accepted and the couple began to plan for an addition to their family.

At the same time, Professor Nusbaum contacted Karl with the news that he needed a place to stay until final arrangements could be made for his departure from Germany. Karl wasn't really keen about the idea, but when Isaac offered to pay, Karl told him that he would consult Lisa.

Karl approached Lisa about Isaac, and since she already knew the man, she said yes, even though she knew that harboring him was against the law. He moved in late one night when he hoped no one was looking.

Professor Nusbaum was a Liberal Jew in that he was part of the reform movement within the Jewish faith. In fact, he could not have been an orthodox Jew any more that he could have been a fundamentalist Christian. His personal philosophy embraced men like the French philosopher Voltaire, and the German philosopher Gotthold Ephraim Lessing. Lessing had become the champion of the jew for works like *Die Juden* (1749) and *Nathan der Weise* (1779).

Lessing sharply criticized the petty intolerance of German society, and so did Professor Nusbaum. If there was one basic ideal in Lessing's philosophy, it was that morality was of greater value than religious dogma. He believed that natural religion common to all denominations was the true religion, and like a seed being planted in fertile soil, that idea became the basis for all that Lisa would come to believe. It would become the anchor for her sanity, and the meeting point between the secular and other worldly parts of her being. If morality was the true basis, what then......was morality? That subject alone provided hours of fuel for their discussions.

It was therefore no surprise to Isaac Nusbaum when the pretty blonde girl summarized one of their discussions by exclaiming, "Isaac! I don't believe that anything done in the true spirit of love will ever put a mark on my soul."

He smiled his approval of her.

Theirs had become a love affair but not in a physical sense. He liked this pretty young woman. More than that, he really liked her, but had taken a paternal attitude towards her. She, on the other hand, was experiencing her second love fantasy and he had become the object of it.

When Karl left for school in the morning, they had several hours before he returned. Even more when Karl went to the library after classes.

Isaac began to busy himself with a book he had been writing more to keep out of Lisa's way than satisfy his own need to write. Unfortunately, the apartment was too small and Lisa was far too pretty and sexy to ignore. Isaac, fearing the inevitable, longed to be able to go for extended walks, but alas, that too.....was impossible.

Newton's First Law of Motion states that *An object in uniform motion will remain in uniform motion until affected by a force.*

The force, in this case, was a very scantily clad Lisa who happened to be leaving her bedroom and heading in the direction of the bathroom while Isaac was leaving the bathroom after having just taken a bath. He was wearing a robe that had seen better days when he came face to face with Lisa who wasn't wearing much at all, and since his robe didn't cover much, he developed an immediate problem. It was one that demanded resolution but he was still too much of a gentleman to make the first move.

That was when Lisa rendered the German equivalent of, "Oh what the hell," and kissed him. What resulted was a passionate explosion of major proportions. Just beneath the surface lurked a wild woman, a woman who Karl had never met, but had been discovered and released by Isaac. In her mind, there were many things wrong with what she and Isaac were about to do, but the wild woman inside of her wasn't concerned with right and wrong.

Isaac had every intention of "doing the right thing" by stopping, but he wasn't able to find the "stop" button. He found the "go" button instead. As a result, they ravished the living hell out of each other, and both found the need of a shower when the passion finally subsided.

When things finally returned to some semblance of order, she felt something strange, and it took her several minutes to figure out that it came as a result of environmental conditioning, and not necessarily the result of moral depravity.

It was guilt.

She would often ponder her guilt, but she decided to live with it, because she made love to Isaac again and again. In fact, his stay extended to five weeks and they had a very hot love affair. A couple of times, they pushed the threshold so to speak, but they always managed to be presentable, and completely disinterested in each other by the time Karl returned.

They managed not to discuss the right or wrong of what they were doing, and by some unspoken agreement, they never bothered to analyze it. Perhaps, it was the danger imbedded in his presence. Perhaps, it was the mutual attraction. Perhaps, it was love.....forbidden though it might have been. Once again, they didn't bother trying to explain something that was much more exciting to engage in. They knew that it would come to an end sooner than they wanted it to, and if anything, each decided to live for the moment.

It wasn't long before Isaac was forced to leave in the dead of a dark night. He didn't say good-bye, and she knew that it was better that way. She never expected to see him again.

Her pregnancy proceeded normally or so she had thought, and it came to pass that on the 3rd day of March 1937, Heidi Marie was born. The delivery was normal. In fact, things were so normal, that she wondered what all the fuss had been about back when she was twelve.

Then it happened.

Thirty days to the day after the birth of her daughter, something gave way inside of her. A glob of bloody tissue. After that, the hemorrhaging began, and they got her to a hospital just in time.

To save her life, a complete hysterectomy had to be performed, and she, like her mother before her, became destined to have only one child. During her period of convalescence, she reflected on her life and especially her affair with Isaac.

In the two years since Heidi had been born, Lisa had done a lot of thinking, but very little talking. Not with her husband, not with her mother, not with a psycho- therapist, or a priest. Her thoughts were for her alone. She had become remote and distant, and no matter what anyone had to say about the matter, she no longer considered herself to be a complete woman.

She had become a woman who only went through the motions of being a wife and mother. She did not love Karl. She never had. She attended to her husband, and responded to his needs primarily because she had been expected to do so. She was a Bavarian woman and was therefore expected to do her duty.

Amazingly, the day came when she actually seemed to enjoy sex with her husband once more. Perhaps, she thought that the ability to enjoy sex had also been removed along with her reproductive organs.

Karl received his degree in January, and on May 15, he had left for active duty in the army. The intervening months had been sometimes strained, and although she had tried to turn his last few days into memorable ones, she didn't know how successful she had been.

Now, as she sat by the rapidly flowing waters, she did something that she rarely did. She thought about the unseen God and wondered if He really existed or if He existed only in the minds of the believers and therefore had no substance at all.

"Lisa!" It was her mother calling from the house.

"Ja, mama," Lisa replied.

"We are ready to go now." They had packed a picnic lunch and were going to Vasser Park in Starnberg for the day.

"Coming mama, " she replied as she picked herself up and headed for the house. She had a date with destiny.

Three

The Converging paths

The same day

Starnberg, Germany

Max Liebert pulled the Mercedes off the road, but did not pull it into a parking place. The black Mercedes was an official SS vehicle used exclusively by a General Officer. These vehicles went where they wanted to go, and parked where they wanted to park. In the middle of the road if that was so desired. They were never parked where other vehicles were expected to be parked.

Max had needed to talk with the General, but didn't wish to do so within the confines of the house. Therefore, he was mildly surprised when he had been summoned to the Herr General's office.

"Herr Liebert, it has not yet been determined what your schedule is to be and more specifically, what your off days are to be, but I need you to drive me someplace today. Can you do it?"

Well, I'll be damned! The man actually knows how to ask.

"Jawohl, Herr General. When would you like to depart?"

"Just as soon as we can," the General replied.

Thirty minutes later, they were speeding south on the Garmisch highway in the direction of Lake Starnberger. Once there, Max was directed to proceed to Vasser Park which he did.

Max had just exited the vehicle, and was in the process of walking around to the right rear door. He was wearing reflective aviator's sunglasses, the kind that seemed to be standard issue for black uniformed SS types, and he attracted more than the usual stares and glances.

When he opened the door allowing the Herr General von Leitner to exit, the same people looked again. This time, they were joined by others. Perhaps, they were waiting for the Gestapo to arrive, and he wondered if they might be disappointed when they didn't.

The General ignored the nervous looks that were coming in his direction. The people who were giving those looks were the types who cowered in their holes, and the General regarded them with contempt. He started walking in the direction of Lake Starnberger, and as he did so, he curled the index finger of his right hand in a gesture that said, "Follow me."

Max followed.

People began moving out of the Herr General's way. In fact, all he had to do was walk in the direction of a group for that group to disappear. After all, public gatherings not sanctioned by the Reich had been outlawed, and although he had no intention of having any of these people arrested, what they didn't know wouldn't hurt them.

Max Liebert caught up with him as they reached the water's edge, and by that time, there was no one within fifty meters. In fact, at least half of them had left. The General found himself respecting the half who didn't leave just because some SS General decided to show up. He wouldn't have left either. He then surmised that the half who left felt the need to return to their holes. *Hitler was right. The people were like sheep. Give them a leader and they will follow.* True statement! Too bad, but true. He found a bench to sit upon, and motioned for Herr and/or Sgt. Liebert, whichever the case might be, to join him.

"Herr Liebert, do you know why we are here?"

"Jawohl, Herr General." Max knew exactly why *he* was there, and the General would soon be enlightened. Until then, the Herr General could be as confused as he chose to be.

The General now looked at his driver curiously. Something had just changed, and then he realized what it was. The servile nature of this man was changing, and that gave the General cause for concern, but not for alarm.

"You may or may not know, but indulge me if you please,

Herr Liebert." Then, he paused for affect, "There are two reasons, " he said while holding up two fingers. "The first, of course, is that this is a pleasant place to be." He then held up two fingers. "The second reason being there are probably no listening devices anywhere near this location." He paused for affect, and then he added pleasantly, "Do you think this might be a reasonable assumption?"

Liebert made no effort to get up and check the area. Instead, he replied, "I definitely believe that might be a reasonable assumption, Herr General."

"Good," replied the General. The General's mood concerned Max slightly, because he was being quite congenial, and Gerhardt von Leitner was not known for being the epitome of congeniality.

The General was gazing out upon the waters as though he might have been mesmerized by the sun's reflection dancing upon the choppy water. Then, he turned his head slowly and said, "Let us now discuss a matter that might be of great interest to both of us."

"And what might that be, Herr General?"

"You."

The General let that sink in for several long moments before continuing. As he watched Herr Liebert, he was amazed at the man's ability to control his own emotions. Whatever he was, he was a very cool customer. That made him a dangerous one as well. The General decided to begin with a question. "You have two college degrees, is that correct?"

"Jawohl, Herr General." Max was also watching the sunlight dancing upon the water. It had a hypnotic affect upon him..

"And if my memory serves me correctly, they are in philosophy and anthropology. Is that also correct?"

Not knowing where the General might be headed, Max dutifully replied, "Jawohl, Herr General."

"Why did you choose those two fields?"

That was an easy one. "Because I happen to like them both. I have always been interested in the science of man. His relationship to physical character, distribution, origin, classification, and the relationship of the races. The study of philosophy sort of goes hand in hand with this. Philosophy deals literally with the love of wisdom, and how the secular world relates to the non-secular one. The other world so to speak. I have also extensively studied the idea of a singular god in the universe, and whether this god has any anthropomorphic or human qualities."

"Did you come to a conclusion?" Inquired the General more out of curiosity than anything else.

"Not one that I wish to ever have published, but in truth, we seem to have created a god in our own image, and then we elevated him to the position of Supreme Deity." He was watching the General closely and waiting for some sort of reaction, but when none came, he continued, "I base my assumptions on a basic principle which states that belief in anything.....anything at all.....will give it form and substance. We therefore believe something into existence, and in the process, it is we who became the creator and not this Deity."

The General was fascinated, and wished to continue this conversation but at some other time. "I am very interested in what you are saying, but right now, I have another matter to resolve. To come to the point, do you know why a man with your educational background is the driver of my personal vehicle or does it now require a man with your educational background to drive a vehicle that carries a General officer?"

Max now knew where the General was going, and wasn't surprised. After all, he was an intelligent perceptive man. Why should he be fooled? Hitler wasn't being very realistic when he suggested this charade, but then, Uncle Adolph could never be accused of being realistic. It was now time to amend the script to fit the facts. For some reason, he trusted this particular General, and trust was not something that was being promoted in the Third Reich.

He reached inside of his tunic and produced a leather wallet and handed it to the General. The General opened it. After two or three minutes, the General laid it on his lap and said, "Very impressive! You are therefore, a free agent, ja?"

"Ja."

"This still doesn't answer my original question. It tells me only that you can do whatever you want to do as long as you can convince the Führer that what you are doing is the right thing to do, and in the best interest of the Reich. On the other hand, I doubt seriously that he will ever comment about your comings and goings. He has other matters to attend to. Therefore, I will ask one more time......why are you my driver."

Max took a deep breathe and exhaled audibly. "You are wrong, Herr General. The Führer did send me, and it was he who suggested that I arrive in Munich as your driver. It would be less conspicuous that way."

"Why?"

"It concerns the matter of Konrad Ruhl."

"The deposed Jewish banker? The one who used to own the house we now occupy?"

"Ja," Max answered quietly.

"Again, I ask why?"

"There is a small matter of quite a few million American dollars that have somehow become lost, misplaced, misdirected or stolen."

The General whistled softly, and then looked as squarely as he could at the man who sat next to him. "Is Herr Ruhl guilty of this crime?"

"He had both access and the ability to commit the crime."

"It doesn't matter. You are assuming facts not yet entered into evidence. My question therefore remains the same......did he do it?"

"That question has been rendered a moot point, Herr General. The Führer wants either the man's head or the money. Sometimes, I think he wants both. He has left no room for debate on the matter, and as we both know, Rule of Law is a matter that Herr Hitler considers to be a discretionary prerogative. Namely, his prerogative."

"Have we completely set aside the idea of justice in this country?" Then, as soon as the question escaped his lips, the General knew that he had temporarily lost control.....a fatal flaw.....one that he would have to correct.

Max was just looking at him. The General said, "Never mind. I already know the answer. I helped make it possible." The General was as close to showing emotion as he had been in thirty-four years, and he struggled to maintain his air of detached indifference.

The General stood and walked near the water's edge. He was agitated, and took two or three deep breathes before looking back at *Herr* Liebert.

The General spoke clearly and distinctly, "I have been no different than anyone else in this matter. I helped draft the document that turned Herr Hitler into a dictator, and for some insane reason, I expected a different man to emerge at the end of the process than the one who entered it."

Under the current rules, his comments had become treasonous. That was, of course, if Max had the desire to pursue the issue. The truth was that Max had no intention of pursuing anything of the kind. Instead, he decided to extend the conversation with a few treasonous comments of his own.

"We can hope for anything, Herr General, but we are best advised to expect the worst especially where Uncle Adolph is concerned."

The General became puzzled. "Uncle? I didn't think his sister had any children."

"She doesn't. At least as far as I know, she doesn't. I first met him when I was fourteen. It was at my papa's bakery here in Munich."

The General digested this bit of information since he must have missed it when he was reading Herr Liebert's dossier. Either that or it had been omitted from his dossier.

"Your papa......is he still living?"

"Ja....." Then he paused long enough to develop a frown. "Unfortunately I haven't taken the time to see him yet?

"How about your mother?" The General asked with genuine interest.

"She died when I was twelve. That is why papa purchased the bakery in Munich. Starnberg reminded him of mama."

The General nodded his understanding.

The General then felt a slight twinge of guilt although he didn't show it. "Would you have visited him today?"

Max shook his head first, and then he said, "Nein, Herr Gerneral. The matter of Konrad Ruhl has the greater priority. "

"Well Max, if you don't mind my addressing you by your given name, since you are not really an SS Sergeant, what do you propose doing about Herr Ruhl, and that brings up another matter.....Where is he?"

"Dachau."

Just the mention of the name invoked a shiver in General von

Leitner. Of course, the shiver was only an inner one, but it was a shiver none-the-less. To make it a little more frightening, Dachau came under his jurisdiction. He hadn't visited Dachau yet, but he had a funny feeling that he would be going to Dachau before he really wanted to.

"So......what do you propose, Herr Liebert."

"I will change into a good civilian suit, and find someone to drive the two of us to Dachau. After meeting Herr Ruhl, I will make a decision."

The General found himself liking this man who had somehow found the balance between sanity and insanity in an insane world. He felt that it might serve them both in the coming months. Unfortunately, there was still the question of status. Should Herr Liebert continue to function as an occasional subordinate whose real function was to do the personal bidding of one Adolph Hitler, *in absentia,* or should he just designate the man as what he really was. Namely, the personal emissary of *Der Führer,* and not part of the local chain of command.

"One more question, Herr Liebert. What is your real relationship to our beloved leader?"

He needs to know thought max. *I'd need to know too if our positions were reversed. The last thing he needs is for me to undermine his command.*

Max smiled as he began to speak, "He was everything to a fourteen year old boy who had become disillusioned with the Fatherland and its leaders. Papa never liked him. Thought he was a blowhard, but not me. I idolized him. Talked to him every chance I got. Believed in him. He once told me that I had a brilliant mind. One that was too good to waste, and because of that, he sponsored my education. Not that he paid for it or anything of the kind, but it happened that one of the party members was a college dean of admissions." He stopped and shook his head. "They paid for everything. Tuition, room, board, books.......everything, and I tried not to waste my opportunity."

This time, the pause was longer before Max spoke again. Waves were gently lapping against the shore adding to the peaceful tranquillity of the park. It was only an illusion, he knew, because within the framework of this illusion lived a people who no longer trusted love. Max was a right-brained person who just happened to be living in a world controlled by left-brained people. His attention returned once more to the General. "You wanted to know my real relationship with Adolph Hitler..........he is my benefactor and regardless of whatever happens.....I shall never betray him." Max was only saying what he thought the Herr General might want to hear. It was much to soon to bear his soul.

The General looked at Herr Liebert without seeing him. His attitude was a noble one, but would that be his defense for looking the other way while Hitler raped his country? Then the General wondered what **his own** defense might be.

This was the moment of compelling attraction, when two points converged. The moment that called for something to be done, and in this case the only something that could be done was talk. Words had to be spoken

His eyes met Herr Liebert's as he spoke softly, "That is a noble concept, Herr Liebert, and I commend you for having it, but I often wonder when our loyalties to individuals might give way to the preservation of the German state. We cannot continue our present course of action with impunity. If we intend to wage war on those who would oppose us, sooner or later, the rest of the world will oppose us, and they will demand accountability. Even if our initial actions meet with tremendous success, the tide will ultimately turn against us. Why? Because our cause is not just. We cannot justify aggression for the need of *Lebensraum*(Living Space)." Their eyes locked as Max considered the words.

"I ask you not to betray your Führer, Herr Liebert. Nor, do I ask that you betray yourself. I ask only that you be true enough to yourself to see the greater truth and what it represents. After doing that, you need only to ask yourself what you can do to make the picture look better." His eyes left Max's eyes long enough to drift over the water that still glittered from the rays of the mid-day sun.

"The words I have spoken could be looked upon as treason by those in control, but as a lawyer, I respectfully submit that the present regime is an illegal one. I know that, not only because I am a lawyer, but because I helped create it. You may, if you wish, take this conversation to___"

He didn't finish the sentence because Max interrupted him.

"This conversation will go no further than the two of us." Max was tempted to tell the Herr General about his organization, but too much was at stake to be overly trusting, and although his instincts told him that he could trust this General, his survival instincts told him otherwise.

"Danke shön (Thank you very much)," replied General von Leitner.

Max clicked his heels and replied, "Bitte shön (Your very welcome), Herr General."

The Herr General had just gone far out on a limb. Much further than he had ever gone in his life.. Gerhardt von Leitner definitely needed a diversion from the trying moments of his job.

He didn't know it yet, but such a diversion had just arrived in a strange looking truck.

Four

The diversion

Still the same day

Max and the General were still standing at the water's edge when the truck pulled into a parking space. When the General saw it, he almost laughed out loud. Germans were well known for their ingenuity, and the owner of that particular vehicle was ingenious to say the least. Whoever it was had taken an old truck and modified it. It looked like he had salvaged the cab, then extended the frame to accommodate a larger truck bed. After that, he enclosed the bed, and when he was done, he painted the whole thing field gray. The same color that military vehicles were painted. The only thing missing were the black crosses on the sides. That was what struck the General as being funny.

Max was the next to see it, and when he did, he asked, "I wonder who that belongs too?"

His question was immediately answered as a fairly good size man opened the driver's side door and got out.

"Gustav Rensler!" Max exclaimed.

"Who?" Asked the General.

"You forget that I used to live here, Herr General. The man is Gustav Rensler. He has a dairy farm down by the village of Berg."

The General digested that bit of information while wondering how important it was when compared to the price of tea in China. At that moment, the rider's side door opened and someone else emerged.

A very pretty someone else.

For a few very long moments, the General had become entranced by the young lady in the red dirndl with the flowing and blowing long blonde hair. Then, he saw the little girl, and once more, had he been capable of frowning, he might have done so.

Gus Rensler had just gotten out of his truck and was stretching his large frame in order to loosen up after the drive. He looked over at the black Mercedes with the Nazi flags that were fluttering in the breeze and wondered who the big shot might be. Gus might have placed Bavaria first in his loyalties, but he was also a loyal German and therefore felt that he had nothing to fear from those people.

Lisa had already gotten out of the other side followed by little Heidi. His wife Anna was now emerging.

Gus announced rather loudly, "I will take the picnic basket,. Why don't you women lay claim to that picnic table over there before someone else grabs it."

Anna replied, "Ja Gus. I will do that," and to Lisa, she said, "Come with me......please?"

Lisa dutifully picked up her daughter and followed her mother. A brisk late morning breeze had developed and whipped her blonde hair around vigorously. Her mother had a table cloth which she unfolded and shook out. Lisa placed her daughter down and helped her mother place the cloth on the table just in time for Gus to arrive with the basket which he used to weigh the cloth down so the wind wouldn't blow it away.

No one noticed the two SS officers who were approaching.. Max had recognized both Gus and Anna Rensler, and although he didn't know the young lady, he had good reason to believe that she might be the daughter of the older couple.

The General had told him, "Let us not assume anything, Herr Liebert. Instead, let us go and find out."

Something about the young blonde woman had gotten his attention, and he needed to be closer to her. For what reason, he did not yet know. She was obviously the mother of the little girl which meant the possible existence of the child's father somewhere. It would violate quite a few principles for him to intrude upon her life. On the other hand, he never told anyone that he was a man of principles.

As the two men approached the table, the pretty young blonde was placing plates, silverware and drinking glasses on the table while the older woman was placing containers of food on the table.

Gus was the first to see them, and exclaimed, "Guten tag (Good day)!"

Both men touched the bills of their caps and responded in kind. Gus knew the ranking system in the German military, and realized that the SS used basically the same system except with different names. The one man wore the rank of a sergeant while the other wore the rank of a General. He then associated both men as the occupants of the black Mercedes. The next question that came to mind was, what did they want with him?

The sergeant removed his sunglasses and his hat before asking, "Do you recognize me, Herr Rensler?"

Gus took a closer look and said, "Ja, Ja, I believe I do. You are Fritz Liebert's boy, Max, ja?"

"Jawohl, Herr Rensler. You have a good memory."

"Speaking of your father, young Max. How is he? I haven't seen him in ages."

"He is fine. He now has a bakery in Munich."

Gus shook his head, but made no further comment on the matter. Instead, he looked squarely at the SS General.

Max finally remembered his manners. "Herr und Frau Rensler, allow me to present General Gerhardt Ludwig von Leitner."

The General removed both his sunglasses and cap before clicking his heels and saying. "It is an honor to meet you both, " He said while looking directly at the young woman whose name hadn't been mentioned yet.

As if on cue, Gus said, "This is our daughter Lisa Mueller and her little daughter Heidi."

The General was about to inquire if there might be a Herr Mueller lurking around somewhere in the cosmos when Gus volunteered, "Lisa is married to Karl Mueller. He just left for the army. 6th Panzer I believe."

"Ach, Heinz Guderian's division if memory serves me correctly."

Gus shrugged, "Ach, I don't know `bout those things, but I

know `bout medals. That's the Iron Cross First Class you are wearing, ja?"

The General shook his head yes.

Gus might not have been the swiftest dog in the pack, but he knew that the Iron Cross wasn't handed out like prizes at a summer picnic. It was given for acts of extreme bravery.

"I seen a man do what it takes to win the Iron Cross, but he wasn't alive when they gave it to him."

The General wasn't interested in discussing his or someone else's acts of bravery. He was only interested in Lisa and how he might become part of her life. What he really wanted to say was, "Excuse me, Herr Rensler while I take your daughter to someplace where I can ravish her completely and thoroughly." Instead, he could think of nothing worthwhile to say. How could he ever hope to make an impact upon a married woman? Religion might no longer be a dominant force in Nazi Germany, but adultery was still the primary grounds for divorce, and adultery was based on a religious concept.

Max had nothing to say, and he guessed that the General was delaying his departure because of Lisa. That would create an interesting problem, if he were correct.

It was an awkward series of moments that were finally broken by Gus Rensler, "It is a good thing that you are doing, Herr General."

The comment caught the General completely off guard, "Er..Ah...what good thing am I doing, Herr Rensler?"

"Ridding the country of the vermin that is infecting it."

The General was still confused. "I still don't understand."

Rensler became pious as he spoke, "You know, the Jews, the Communists, the Freemasons, the queers, and the rest of the misfits who would drag our country down the way they did during the Great War."

Lisa had been somewhere else in her thoughts and her attention returned once again to this General who wore the black uniform of the SS. He was one of those who made it impossible for Isaac to continue living in his homeland. Whatever the General wanted to accomplish by meeting this girl was being undermined right before his eyes. Her eyes didn't speak softly of a clandestine lover's rendezvous. They spoke only of hatred and loathing, not for something he himself might have done, but for the institution he represented.

Ja, he thought, *you......my dear, are the real Deutschland (Germany). Too bad there aren't more like you. It might be a better country. I will get to know you whether you wish to know me or not. Of that, you can depend upon.*

To her father, he said, "I don't think I wish to take credit for that. Now, if you will all excuse me." He returned his hat to his head and his sunglasses to his eyes. He clicked his heels and rendered them all a smart military salute. After that, he wheeled about and walked quickly to the car.

In his wake, Gustav Rensler didn't know what the General meant by his final remark, and all that Lisa could do was despise the man for what he represented. Anna, who hadn't uttered a word, saw something in the General that even the General didn't see in himself. That was compassion, but it was deep....very, very deep.

Inside the car that was now speeding away, General Gerhardt von Leitner lay his head back on the seat cushions secure in the knowledge that he had made an impression even if it were a negative one. He could handle hate. It was indifference that he could not tolerate. Now, he would be able to deal with the woman.

That afternoon

Dachau

Sgt. Erik Grimm had been drafted to drive Max and the General to the concentration camp that was located at the northwestern outskirts of the city.

SS Standartenführer (Colonel) Reinbolt, the commandant, was not on post, but it didn't take long for him to appear, and give a proper welcome to the Herr General although he inwardly didn't appreciate Generals who didn't know that Sunday was supposed to be a day of rest.

"I did not come to see you, Herr Standartenführer. Herr Liebert here," he said while indicating in the direction of Max, "Is the personal emissary of *Der Führer,* and as such, wishes to speak with a prisoner by the name of Konrad Ruhl."

The flurry that followed was almost comical. Fortunately, they hadn't beaten the man lately, but they still had to clean him, polish him, and make him presentable for their distinguished visitors.

A comfortable room was chosen for that purpose. In fact, the room chosen was the Commandant's office, a fact that didn't particularly please the Commandant, but he knew better than to object. In fact, what he said was, "Jawohl, Herr General," and backed graciously out of his own office.

Ten minutes later, there was a knock upon the door after which a guard ushered Konrad Ruhl into the office. Max Liebert was seated behind the desk while General von Leitner lounged on the black leather couch. The fact that Liebert was seated behind the desk indicated that he was senior to the General, a fact that might have confused the prisoner except for the fact that the prisoner and Herr Liebert knew each other quite well.

Signals passed between the two men, but if anyone were watching, they would have been hard pressed to see anything that was unnatural. Max signaled Ruhl that everything was as it should be and that he might just get out of this alive. He also signaled that the SS General was not privy to anything meaning that the interview was not being staged strictly for the benefit of the microphones.

On the other hand, Ruhl knew that he had been careless or he would not have been in this position in the first place.

A black leather upholstered chair was placed directly in front of the desk, and Herr Ruhl was told to be seated in that chair.

Max now regarded the man seated before him.

Ruhl was a tall man with graying hair who bore a dignified bearing even after suffering the depravities of captivity. Max felt a lot of respect for the man who suffered and very little respect for his tormentors.

Then, after several long moments, Max opened the black portfolio laying on the desk before him, and extracted the letter from Adolph Hitler granting Maximilian Liebert the right to act in his behalf. It was fully laminated in plastic.

He handed it to Herr Ruhl who took it and carefully read the document. When he finished, he handed it back to Max. In reality, Ruhl was quite impressed.

Max began speaking. "I am Maximilian Liebert, and this

gentleman," he said indicating the General, "Is the Herr Brigadeführer Gerhardt von Leitner. He is the Herr Commandant of the Munich Military District." He didn't bother explaining what that meant, if anything.

"I will not banter with you, Herr Ruhl, nor will I threaten or attempt to intimidate you. Instead, I will simply ask what you know about the missing transfer of American money."

His letter placed him somewhere near the right hand of Hitler, and yet he was an unpretentious man. In the years that he had known Liebert, Konrad Ruhl found Max Liebert to be a rare combination of intelligence, courage, and humility. He was a man who would be counted upon. Now, all he had to do was play the game as best he could and trust that Max would be able to get the job done without rising suspicion.

Ruhl began speaking. "I received a telegram from Berlin telling me that the money was going to be sent. I even received a telegram from New York that it had been sent, but when I contacted the bank in Zurich, it had not arrived. Berlin kept asking for confirmation, and I couldn't give it. Finally, they sent a courier with a threatening letter, and in its wake, I was arrested the same day."

"Your position therefore is what?" Asked Max.

"The **truth** is that I don't know where the money is."

Max mulled that over in his mind for what seemed like an eternity.

"Can you tell me the route the money was supposed to take?"

Ruhl then looked at his inquisitor strangely.

The question implied knowledge that nobody other than a banker needed to know. "I can give you the information you have asked for, but what good would it do you? The international transfer of money is a complicated process that involves certain knowledge that you may not fully understand." Once again, the words spoken were for the benefit of both, the microphones and the Herr General.

Max then took the next fifteen minutes and gave the banker a tutorial on the International Banking System in general and the transfer of capital in particular. When Max finished, the banker reached for a pad and pencil and started writing.

When he finished writing, he pushed the pad toward Max. After reading everything, he looked at Herr Ruhl. The banker had written everything out thus depriving the hidden microphones the benefit of the valuable information.

Max then said, "Danke! I will conduct my own personal investigation after which I will return and we will talk again."

"Does that mean you believe me?"

"Nein Herr Ruhl! It means that I am willing to investigate the facts rather than believe what I want to believe. It is only fair to inform you that the Führer wants either your head or the money?"

"What if I can't produce the money?"

Max cocked his head and just looked at the man. He was not about to restate the obvious.

Max picked up the telephone receiver. After a few moments, he said, "The prisoner is ready to return to his cell." Then, he hung the phone up, clasped both of his hands in front of him on the desk, looked Ruhl right in the eye, and rethought the idea about restating the obvious. Then, he spoke again for the benefit of the microphones, "Do not misunderstand me, Herr Ruhl. I can still sign your death warrant, and if I don't come up with the money, I will. Why? It's not that the loss of the money will bankrupt the Reich. Certainly not!" Then, after a long pause, he said, "It's all a matter of principle, Mein Herr. We do not tolerate stealing from the Reich, and we have a very good circumstantial case against you. Therefore, Herr Ruhl, think hard about your situation, and if you have additional information, contact me. I will be located somewhere near General von Leitner's office."

There was a knock on the door.

After the guards had left with Konrad Ruhl, Max and the General departed for a walk around the grounds.

After several minutes of quiet reflection for both men, the General finally broke the silence, "For what it is worth, I approve of the way you handled things back there."

Max shrugged. "Ruhl knows the rules of the game. He also knows that he was very careless or he wouldn't be in his present situation."

Gerhardt didn't know what to say, so he said nothing. Something told him that what he just witnessed might have been staged, and if it were, what then?

He stopped long enough to notice that the beautiful sky of the morning had now turned into the dark and foreboding clouds that were rolling in as the advance guard of a storm. Then, he saw lightning flash in the distance followed by the low rumble of thunder. As the wind picked up in anticipation of the approaching storm, he immediately wheeled about and with Max in tow, headed for the car.

He set a brisk pace, but managed to ask the inevitable question, "So what are you going to do now?"

Max ignored the ominous clouds and stopped. "For what it is worth, Herr Ruhl is lying. He gave me information that no innocent bystander would have knowledge of., but unlike those who surround Uncle Adolph, and for that matter, Uncle Adolph himself, I do not enjoy killing. Furthermore, when I look at men like Ruhl, I do not see a Jew. Instead, I see a man. Just a man. Perhaps, you as a General in the infamous SS will be better able to sign his death warrant that I can." He paused for effect. "You can, if you wish, report me as a spineless traitor."

"I will do nothing of the sort!" The General replied indignantly..

Max looked at him and shook his head just before laughing. In fact, he laughed quite hard for a few minutes.

Gerhardt looked confused and remained that way until Max finally stopped laughing, and then he inquired, "What is so funny?"

Max was still grinning as he framed his reply. "Look at us, Gerhardt. We are inside of Dachau in the middle of misery personified, and neither of us has the stomach to sign a death warrant for just one of the prisoners housed in this facility." At this moment, Max was only betraying his own feelings. The movement was still safe inside his head, and a false compartment in the heel of his shoe held the capsule that would end his life and deprive the Gestapo of being able to torture him.

Gerhardt asked, "So where does that leave us?"

"In the end, I will probably to go through the motions of having him transferred to Gestapo Headquarters in Berlin for final disposition, and although the word execute will never be used, the Gestapo knows exactly what the words "final disposition" mean. That means that we will have to conjure up what our Russian friends call a Maskirovka."

The General looked puzzled and Max explained it to him.

The General liked what he heard. He too, didn't like murdering people whose only sin was being born into the wrong religion. If there really was a God in his universe, maybe He would allow Gerhardt von Leitner's life to finally mean something. No greatness.....just a simple atonement process to rid him of the evil spirits that had infected him. No...that was not correct. He still had to deal with Frau Mueller.

<u>Friday, June 16, 1939</u>

The General was reading his copy of a report Max sent to Hitler outlining his progress, and he came to one inescapable conclusion. Max Liebert was an excellent fiction writer. More importantly, he was able to write fiction that was interwoven enough with fact to be not only believable but quite impressive.

The General noted that Max had targeted the following Friday for a final decision unless Hitler overruled him. The General also understood that typical Nazi thinking, if there was such a thing, could very easily conclude that the whole thing was a Zionist attempt to undermine the Reich. Then, he placed the report in a special file folder to be placed in his secure file.

Ja, Max Liebert is a very good man. I hope he survives.

At that moment, his attention drifted to another file folder laying on his desk. The name on the tab read, MUELLER, Karl Ludwig.

On the inside of the folder itself, the following was listed: FRAU: Lisa Marie KINDER: Heidi Marie (no others)

All of the data pertinent to the three individuals thus named followed the title page. In fact, the first three pages elaborated on the dry statistical data. It also reflected the redundancy in German record keeping. *Better to know too much than too little.*

Karl was the son of Heinrich and Maria Mueller of Dusseldorf in the Ruhr Valley, and the General knew exactly who Heinrich Mueller was. So did a lot of other people. The hard to believe part was that they actually approved of his marriage to the daughter of a Bavarian dairy farmer. The General wondered why?

Then, he began to find out for himself. His parents approved of her, but not necessarily him......their own son. He was a maverick with a mind of his own and had his own idea about how he wanted to live his life. The report went on to explain how he had lived his life, his goals, his ambitions, and more important to many who read this report, his political reliability. Even rumors and gossip were included, because although redundant and possibly superfluous, it did make the creating of a profile more possible. The epitome of German efficiency.

Then, he came to Lisa Marie Mueller, the object of his research. She too, had her own file, as well as being in each of her parent's file. That was much too redundant for him. To save time, he chose the husband, and was able to research the rest of the players as well.

Along with the large single portrait of her, several other photographs of the lady were displayed and some of them were of her and her husband together. In one picture, they were both dressed up. She was especially lovely, and although she had been dressed tastefully, she was an extremely sexy woman.

Like most men, he had gone to the pictures first, and since they didn't render the desired result, he went to the biography, and found that she had been born in 1919 which made her twenty, but that she had been married in 1935 when she was only sixteen.

Why?

A woman who looked like her could have had her pick of the current herd of wild stallions. When she finished with one of the stallions, all she had to do was go to the door, and shout, **"next,"** and men would die in the stampede.

He continued to read and found that shortly after her daughter had been born, severe complications had developed and she had to have a complete hysterectomy.

Hmm, he thought, *too bad for someone so young, but youth has its resilience. On the other hand, the fact that she is now barren might become a deterrent. After all, the SS Reichsführer would like the men of the SS to impregnate as many of the young ladies of the Reich as possible. Marriage was not a prerequisite. The children were to be raised as wards of the state. Therefore, the information about Lisa would somehow have to be kept from prying eyes or she might find herself becoming a whore for the Reich.*

It was when he got to the investigator's report that a few

truths seemed to emerge. The first truth being that her father was an overbearing sort. The General could believe that. The man combined Old Testament morality and Germanic mythology with emerging German Nationalism and created the concoction that conjured up Hitler. Gerhardt noted sadly that there were a great many men just like him.

The next truth that emerged was the circumstances of her betrothal to Karl Mueller. It had been an arranged marriage. Rumor had it, if rumors could be believed, that Papa Rensler had caught Lisa and a neighborhood young man in a compromising position, whatever that was, and ran the young man off the property. After that, he castigated the girl for being the kind of Jezebel who could promote that kind of behavior. Not long thereafter, she had caught the eye of Karl Mueller and the rest was history. That fact that he was Heinrich Mueller's son probably weighed heavily in Papa Rensler's decision.

According to the same rumor, she kicked and screamed upon learning of her fate, but in the end, she walked meekly down the aisle.

There was one final report. A short one by a Gestapo inspector who had been investigating a group that met regularly at the University. Its purpose wasn't clear, and the Gestapo never found the real purpose for the group's existence, but Lisa Mueller was one of the participants. She had been linked with Isaac Nusbaum, a former professor at the university, and a man still wanted for crimes against the state although he hadn't been wanted at the time of the group meetings.

He was a Jew.

In conclusion, her political reliability hadn't been compromised and no one had been able to link her romantically with him or anyone else since her marriage to Karl Mueller. The fact that she wasn't an important personage might have limited the investigation, but Gerhardt rather doubted it. Once again, German efficiency would have dictated they be as thorough with her as they had been when they investigated him. Therefore, with the lack of smoke, they hadn't bothered to look for a fire.

He closed the file, and laid it on the corner of his desk.

Good, he thought. *I love the Fatherland enough to commit treason, but I don't have the good sense to leave this lovely young lady alone. Well, I shall have her and that will be that. Hopefully, she will gain through the experience, and if she doesn't..........I will.*

SUNDAY, JUNE 4, 1939

Starnberg

General von Leitner had planned on driving himself to Starnberg, but Max got wind of it, and insisted on driving even though he was no longer the General's driver. Max had an idea as to what might be on the Herr General's mind, but since the Herr General had not confided in him, he wasn't able to know for certain.

Max parked the vehicle in the same approximate location as the previous Sunday, and started to exit the vehicle when the General said, "Never mind, Max. I can handle it myself this time.

Max didn't argue.

The General was disappointed. He didn't see the homemade truck, a fact that greatly diminished her chances of being in the park. He sighed deeply.

Well? What did you expect, Herr von Leitner? What kind of fool are you? Do you think, perhaps, that she might know what she is supposed to do without ever seeing the script?

He was wrong.

Lisa *was* there, but she was alone. Her depression had gotten worse, and her mother had taken her to a friend in Starnberg for the weekend. It had been hoped that a change in scenery might lift up her spirits. So far, it hadn't worked.

According to Newton's First Law of Motion, *an object in uniform motion would remain in uniform motion until affected by a force.* Whether she knew it or not, she was about to meet that force.

She was standing by the water's edge when the General saw her and his heart skipped a beat. He had written the script and therefore knew the all the lines. Which direction he took now depended entirely upon her response, but he did not know her circumstances. She began walking in his direction, and when she got closer to him, he saw signs of recognition in her eyes.

It is that SS General again. He must really like this place, because he always seems to be here. Doesn't he have anything else to do?

The General was wearing his cap and his sunglasses. He touched the bill of his cap in a salute and said, "Guten morgen, Frau Mueller."

She forced a smile and replied, "Guten morgen, Herr General," and continued walking. She had only gotten three or four steps beyond him when she heard him say, "Stop!"

She did! It was an instinctive, knee jerk reaction. After that, she turned in his direction.

He motioned to her and said, "Come!" Not please or the German word "bitte" but "come." Blindly and dumbly, she did as she was told like a lamb being led to the slaughter.

The General removed his sunglasses, but his cap remained on his head. He might have tried to soften his gaze somewhat, but he was not successful. She waited patiently for him to say something.

"You are an extremely lovely woman, Frau Mueller. Do you realize that?"

She felt the color rise to her cheeks and she politely answered, "Danke schön, Herr General."

He clicked his heels, dipped his head, and replied, "Bitte schön, Frau Mueller."

"Ja, you are very lovely, indeed." This time, she said nothing. The alarm bells began ringing, and she didn't care for the direction he was heading.

He had just abandoned the script and began to ad lib.

"To be truthful, Frau Mueller, you are not only an extremely attractive woman, but you are quite desirable as well."

She remained silent, but her eyes began to betray the loathing she was feeling for the bastard.

He proceeded mercilessly down the primrose path. "In fact, I fully intend to have you."

"Well!" She replied indignantly. "You **can't** have me! I am a married woman. Besides that, I have a two year old daughter!"

She looked into his eyes and saw nothing .... nothing at all to betray what he might be thinking. Instead, he looked at her coldly and inquired, "Is there a point you are trying to make, Frau Mueller?"

All further protestations died somewhere in her throat. She was totally exasperated with the breed of human being that was being represented by this man.

He spoke distinctly and dryly. "Let me explain this to you in a manner that you might find easier to understand, Frau Mueller. (Pause) If you value the lives of those you love, you will cooperate with me fully. (Another pause) I hope I make my intentions clear. My driver will call upon you within the next few days with further instructions. Until then, I bid you Auf Wiedersehen."

He saluted her, clicked his heels, and marched purposefully to the car, after which, he got in and the car moved swiftly away from the park.

In his wake stood Lisa Mueller, a woman who was no longer depressed. She had become furious instead.

Five

Water under the bridge

<u>Wednesday May 31, 1939</u>

<u>Munich</u>

The General was unable to concentrate on his new duties.

Reinhard Heydrich, the number two man in the SS, might have been considered by many to be a genius, but he was also a flaming idiot.

SS General Gerhardt von Leitner was probably an enigma to a man like Heydrich, because he was not Himmler's man. Instead, he was Hitler's man. Rather than anger *Der Führer,* von Leitner, an AllgeMein SS General, was sent to Munich with administrative control over six concentration camps and the local Gestapo.

This was unheard of since the Gestapo had been designed to operate as a totally independent police agency.

They were actually above the law.

In addition to this, he also had responsibility for the rail system in Bavaria plus the main line which ran to Vienna. The command structure had been loosely defined by Heydrich, and it would most certainly cause trouble in the future. When, the General didn't know and until the unknown became known, he wouldn't concern himself with it.

There were two known factors in his life right at that moment.

The first was Max Liebert, the man with degrees in anthropology and philosophy, an expert's knowledge of economics, and the ability to pass himself off as an SS sergeant while actually being a special emissary of the Führer.

He liked Max, but liking someone was a luxury he seldom indulged in. So, why then, did he become involved in Max's activities? What the hell was going in his head? Did he really want to get hung on a meat hook in the basement of Gestapo Headquarters in Berlin?

The second factor was Lisa Mueller. The ultimatum he gave her ran contrary to who he was and what he stood for. Without realizing it, Gerhardt von Leitner had passed beyond being a paradox. He had now become an enigma.

His personality had been forged by the rigid upbringing of Sturnberg Military School, the fiery violence of the Great War, and then, honed to a fine edge in the hallowed halls of Heidelberg's College of Law, but more than anything else, it was the direct result of a man he always referred to as *The Baron.*

Sturnberg stood on a bluff overlooking the village below like a fortress that was bold and imposing. For over two hundred years, it had trained the sons of the Prussian elite. The village, of course, was nestled in the valley, and standing on the ridge opposite from Sturmberg was a castle that belonged to a very wealthy but eccentric baron. A man whose father had been a close personal friend of Otto von Bismarck, the Iron Chancellor, and founder of the Second Reich.

Gerhardt's beginning had not been good, and for almost a year, he had paid the price for his sensitivity. That was when he met The Herr Baron.

Every Saturday, after inspection, the boys who passed were allowed to go to the village below, and there was a bus that made continuous round trips every thirty minutes until 1830 hours. Anyone who missed the final bus was faced with a long walk back. In this case, young Gerhardt had to get away from the school even if he had nothing to do once he got there.

It was on one such Saturday that he had been sitting on a bench quietly sobbing to himself when he heard a voice asking, "Do you really think that crying will solve whatever it is that you think is worth crying about?"

It was the beginning of a friendship. One that that had

endured until The Herr Baron's death in 1936. Simply stated, each filled a void in the other's life. The Baron was the father he had been denied, and he was the son the Herr Baron never had.

It was The Herr Baron who had underwritten his education, and more importantly, it was The Herr Baron who told him that fear was a slow acting poison that would kill as surely as a bullet. It was better to die than to live in fear. The Baron also told him that a human being could never be owned by anyone, and that no document could ever sign title and deed of one person to another even if that document happened to be a marriage license.

Perhaps, the most valuable lesson came in the form of a warning. *Do not ever accept anything simply on authority.* The only true authority was vested in one's self, and blind obedience to a cause, any cause, was a fool's errand. That, of course, was in direct violation of what it meant to be a true Prussian. To obey was the prime directive.

Even the Bible told him to *Render unto Caesar that which was Caesar's, and render unto God that which was God's.* In this case, Caesar occupied a office at the Reichchancellery in Berlin. These days, he was called Hitler.

So, how did this all relate to Lisa Mueller? It was simple. Something told him that he needed to know her, and this was the only way he knew how to go about doing that. Convention certainly would have prohibited any approach save the one he took. If he became a bastard in the process........so be it!

He had altered the script to fit the facts.

The phone rang.

The General picked it up and said, "Leitner."

"Ah, General von Leitner. I'm glad I caught you. Chief Inspector Zimmel here. I am sorry that I haven't paid my respects to you as of yet, but I have been very busy. Do you have a few moments?"

The illustrious Gestapo Chief has just been heard from.

"I have a few moments," replied the General with a certain amount of ice in his voice.

"A matter has come to my attention. It concerns a Hauptsturmführer by the name of Reiner. Wilhelm Reiner. Do you remember him?"

"Ja, what about him?"

"You relieved him of his duties. Can you tell me why?"

"I don't believe I have to justify my actions to you, Herr Chief Inspector."

"That is true, Herr General, but the Hauptsturmführer was appointed to his position by me prior to your arrival. I placed him directly under Inspector Gottlieb on the organizational chart. Because of that, I would have hoped that you might have coordinated any changes with me before you implemented them."

"Is **that** so?"

This time, the Herr Chief Inspector kept his mouth shut. This Herr General was reputed to have ice water running in his veins instead of blood.

After a few awkward moments, the General began speaking. "Let me make myself clear, Herr Chief Inspector.......I will not.....**repeat.....**not seek your approval in order to conduct my life or do my job. Do you understand me?"

"Jawohl, Herr General."

"Now then, the Hauptsturmführer is not my type of officer, and I dismissed him without prejudice." After that, he decided to soften his stance somewhat. "It goes without saying that you and I need to communicate, Chief Inspector. Perhaps, we will do a better job of it in the future." The meaning was clear. It was incumbent upon the Chief Inspector to communicate with the General. Not the other way around.

"Very well, Herr General. Perhaps my schedule will be clear enough to make a courtesy call on you Friday afternoon."

"No, Chief Inspector, I will be in your office tomorrow afternoon. Make room for me on your schedule."

There was a long silence followed by, "Jawohl, Herr General!"

The line went dead.

Thursday, June 1

Gestapo headquarters - Munich

Gestapo headquarters was cold, efficient, and antiseptic much like the rest of the National Socialist world. After a brief military style ceremony, Max and the General were being ushered into a conference room.

The General considered the Chief Inspector briefly. The man had opted to wear the uniform of a SS Srandartenführer (Colonel) instead of the plain clothes that Gestapo officers were allowed to wear. No one else wore a uniform. The General thought it strange, but simply filed it away.

This brought up a question of protocol. The Herr General, being the senior SS officer present would naturally sit at one end of the table with Chief Inspector Zimmel occupying the seat at the other end. That is until one took into consideration the fact that Maximillian Liebert bore the credentials of a personal emissary of Der Führer himself. Herr Liebert, therefore could not be expected to sit on one of the sides with the rest of the underlings. According to Chief Inspector Zimmel, Herr Liebert was, in fact, the senior man present.

The Chief Inspector was in hopes that the Herr General might have been willing to relinquish his position thus saving face for the Chief Inspector, but the Herr General was not predisposed to do such a thing. He remained seated while the Chief Inspector took his place with the rest of the underlings. Thoughts of a slow death being administered to the Herr General danced in the Chief Inspector's head, but the smile remained on his face.

The Herr General ignored him. Instead, he looked first at Max, and then opened the portfolio laying on the table in front of him. He smiled slyly and then looked at the man whom he had usurped. This *was his* turf, and normally he would have facilitated this meeting, but then the Chief Inspector had no idea what the agenda was.

The General cleared his throat and began, "Gentlemen, for those who don't know me, I am General von Leitner, and as of 0845 this morning, when a courier from Berlin handed me this dispatch from the Herr SS Reichsführer, I became the commander of all SS forces in southern Bavaria."

He held the dispatch up or all to see, and then passed it around the table. Nervous glances were being discreetly cast about.

"I have no idea what this news means to any of you, because, as of right now, nothing changes. I will still refrain from direct involvement with Gestapo activities. Matters involving policy will still be handled through whoever commands this post."

Zimmel did not look up. The meaning was clear. *Whoever commands this post.* He burned inwardly at the thought, but what he didn't know was that the Herr General had already declared Zimmel to be *Persona no Gratia.* The General did not mess with anyone who openly questioned or defied his authority. He knew the value of authority. It was blind obedience to it that he resisted. He knew what he was part of, and that he might stink with an odor that could not be removed by a thousand baths, but he was not following them blindly. That was the basic difference between he and Zimmel and the rest of his Gestapo cronies. He knew exactly what he was doing and they didn't.

The General then directed his attention to his immediate left. Seated directly across from the Herr Chief Inspector Zimmel was the Herr Inspector Heinz Gottlieb.

The quiet buzzing of conversation filled the gap in conversation until the General cleared his throat, and attention once more returned to him.

"The second item on my agenda concerns the matter of Konrad Ruhl." He paused expectantly, and not to be denied, Chief Inspector Zimmel blurted out, "The wealthy Jew banker?"

The General regarded the man once more. "Ja, that is the one, and while your are at it, Herr Chief Inspector, what is our interest in the man?"

The Herr Chief Inspector shot an anxious look at his nominal superior wondering if he should divulge what might be esoteric knowledge to unenlightened ears. The General only said, "Well Herr Chief Inspector, I am waiting."

"Herr Ruhl is suspected of misappropriating an unspecified amount of American dollars that were intended for the Reichsbank."

"And what have you found out so far during the month that you have been in charge of the investigation?"

The Chief Inspector dropped his head, and said, "Nothing."

The General was astounded.

He expected lies, deceptions, half truths, and accusations. Instead, he received the truth. For what reason, he did not know. Perhaps, the Herr Chief Inspector had some redeeming qualities, and perhaps the truth was a smoke screen. He decided not to judge. Instead, he would acknowledge the truth by saying, "Danke, Herr Chief Inspector .... Danke."

The General's eyes then drifted all around the table. "Gentlemen. Herr Liebert," he said while indicating to Max at the other end of the conference table, "Is now in charge of the Konrad Ruhl case. He was given that responsibility by the Führer himself. I now direct this organization to give Herr Liebert all the assistance and support he requires." He stopped abruptly while looking once more at the assembled bodies. "Let me make this point clear. The operative word in my previous statement was, "requires." Give him only what he needs and asks for. I want absolutely no over-zealous sherlock to go out on a tangent of his own choosing. Some very sensitive international relations are at stake here. If you have pertinent information, give it to Herr Liebert. He will know what to do with it. You won't. Understood?"

Nods of agreement came from everyone but Chief Inspector Zimmel. So much for redeeming qualities. He would deal with Zimmel when the time comes.

"That is all I have on my agenda," the General said. "Unless someone has something of interest to the group as a whole, I will consider this meeting adjourned." No one even moved.

"Dismissed!" The General said as he hit the table lightly with the knuckles of his right hand. The men all stood up and gave the stiff armed Nazi salute.

In unison, they all said, "Heil Hitler!"

The Herr General responded with a casual bent arm salute of his own followed by the perfunctory, "Heil Hitler!"

After that, the Gestapo staff officers moved in an orderly manner through the door. Chief Inspector Zimmel remained behind.

"May I have a moment of the Herr General's time?"

The General replied tersely, "As you wish." The Chief Inspector noticed, with dismay, that Herr Liebert also remained. He hadn't uttered a word, but his presence had been felt.

When only the three men remained, the General said, "Close

the door!" There was no doubt as to who was supposed to close it. The Chief Inspector did so, and turned to face the General, but there was an awkward pause.

Finally, the General said, "The time is yours, Herr Chief Inspector. How do you wish to spend it?"

"I wish to protest, Herr General. The Ruhl case has been taken from me, and I want to know why?"

"Because you bungled it!" The answer came not from the General. It had come from Herr Liebert instead. For some reason, the Chief Inspector was ready to argue with his nominal commanding officer. After all, the General was still within the structure of the SS/Gestapo organization. Herr Liebert was not. The Herr Chief Inspector didn't know how to go about disputing things with this Liebert person, and here he was accusing him of bungling the case. The Chief Inspector just looked at him.

Max continued. "I don't suppose that it has occurred to you, Herr Chief Inspector, that many methods are available to us other than torture and threats of death. Don't you realize that death is a welcome release from torture? Do you know how to go about finding that much money?"

The Chief Inspector still couldn't answer. He simply didn't know. He had used the only methods he knew, and didn't even think to find out if other methods were available.

Max pressed forward. "In the New Order, Herr Chief Inspector, there is failure in lack. The New Order will not tolerate your lack, Herr Chief Inspector. Of that, I can assure you! Auf Wiedersehen, Herr Chief Inspector," and Max left the room abruptly.

In his wake, the Herr General regarded Zimmel disdainfully. "I have nothing to add to what Herr Liebert has already stated unless you do." The Chief Inspector shook his head no, and the General departed without further comment.

Plan "A" had just been placed into effect.

Six

The rendezvous

Friday, June 16

Southeast of Berg, Germany

If it hadn't been for a man by the name of Isaac Nusbaum, Lisa didn't know how she would have been able to handle this latest development in her life.

She had been taught a brand of Old Testament morality mixed with German nationalism and mythology to the point where it was a little too rigid for her to handle.

This was the same moral code that demanded absolute virtue from a woman, while at the same time, men were guilty of racial and religious intolerance. Lisa instinctively knew there was something wrong with that picture, but it wasn't until Isaac had come into her life that she had been able to place these issues into a broader perspective. One that examined **all** the facts.

Until this happened, she would not have been able to have an affair with any man. Not that her broader perspective gave her license to commit adultery. That wasn't the case at all, but she wasn't about to justify her actions.....even to herself.

Her broader perspective examined all the facts while the best any earthly judge could do was make a judgment based on the facts they knew. If anything was wrong with religion, especially the Christian religion, it was that religious people tended to make judgments without any of the facts. They operated strictly on rumors spread by gossip. God supposedly has all the facts and He still loves us. If this Jesus told us not to judge, why then do his followers do so?

SS General Gerhardt von Leitner tells me that I am lovely to look at. Does that give him the right to order me to sleep with him? Don't I still have the right of selection? I selected Isaac. I did not select this SS General. He has selected me, and if I don't cooperate, great harm could come to my loved ones. Then she came to the great realization that she hadn't selected her husband either. Someone said some words, sprinkled holy water, and she was married until death parted them.

She then turned and saw her reflection in a mirror. She was wearing the white dress that he had sent her, and she was thankful that it was something she could actually wear in public. He also sent her a pair of high heeled shoes and although she wasn't used to wearing high heels, she would wear them anyway.

If he allowed her to do so, she would submit to him with grace. That was who she was. She would not beg, cry or grovel at his feet. What he was doing was the same as rape. Maybe there was a special hell for a man such as him.

She glanced at her watch and said good-bye to her mama, her daughter, and her tight lipped papa.

He had pressed her as to why the Reich needed her to the point where she finally became exasperated and cried out through great wrenching sobs, "Papa! You have always preached that no sacrifice is too great for the Reich, and now that I am required to make that sacrifice, you tell me it is too great. In the name of everything that is decent, will you please make up your mind.?"

She had just stepped out of the back door when a black Mercedes appeared around the corner. Max Liebert stepped from the vehicle. He was not wearing a uniform. A fact that puzzled her. She wondered why, but would not ask.

He moved with a beauty and grace not normally associated with a man as he first opened the rear door, and then guided her gracefully into the vehicle. Then, he picked up her overnight bag and set it on the front seat beside him. That having been done, he restarted the engine and backed out of the driveway. Lisa waved to her mama and her daughter as a tear escaped and started its trip down her cheek.

Max observed this and wondered what her real thoughts were. He didn't approve of this anymore than she did, but so far, he was powerless to do anything about it. He would have bet money that Gerhardt was above this type of activity, but then, the Nazi's had a way of corrupting everything they touched, and good people were often the first to go.

* * * * *

Gerhardt von Leitner was seated in his study staring off into space. He should have been happy, but happiness was not to be on his agenda. Not this night anyway. Why he had taken this tactic with this woman was still beyond him. He didn't have to coerce a woman into sleeping with him. Of course, if he wanted this particular woman to sleep with him, coercion had been necessary.

As a lawyer, he knew that his actions were illegal even in the Third Reich. He knew only that the invisible tentacles that reached out and grabbed him were strong. Very strong indeed, and her effect upon him had been immediate. Someday, he might be called upon to defend himself in a court of law, and he didn't have the first idea as to how to go about doing that.

Case in point: What did he expect from this woman other then obedience? Could he expect love and affection? More than likely, he would get submission. After all, he had threatened the lives of her family had she chosen not to cooperate with him. What kind of a man had he become?

* * * * *

At the same time, Max was pulling into to the side entrance. When the vehicle came to a stop, the entrance door opened and another man wearing the dress uniform of an SS officer opened the rear door.

"Good evening, Frau Mueller. I am Major Hoffman, Aide de Camp to the Herr General von Leitner. Allow me to assist, if you please."

Once she had exited the vehicle, he extended his arm which she took and said, "Come with me, please." She did.

They entered the building and he walked slowly and purposefully across a large receiving hall, and down another hallway into a small sitting room.

"Please make yourself comfortable, Frau Mueller. I will notify the Herr General that you are here." She smiled weakly as he left.

What am I supposed to be feeling.........Joy, privilege, luck? Maybe I will learn something. Maybe I will somehow enjoy this. Maybe........Oh, what the hell, just maybe! She was on the brink of tears, but so far none had fallen. Then she felt something wet on her cheek. It was one tear......one tear had managed to fall.

* * * * *

Major Hoffman knocked lightly on the door frame and then stepped into the study. "Herr General, Frau Mueller is waiting for you in the small sitting room."

The General smiled and said, "Danke schön, Fritz. That will be all for today."

"Bitte shön, Herr General. I'll see you in the morning." Gerhardt nodded and the Major departed.

* * * * *

Gerhardt stopped just short of the doorway and took a very deep breathe. Was he in charge or was she? *If she only realized how much power she has over me.* He took another deep breathe. At that moment, he knew that he was not going to force her to do anything she didn't want to do. He would simply let her off the hook.

Well, here goes nothing.

Lisa was startled as Gerhardt von Leitner walked into the small setting room. He walked to within a respectable distance of her and stopped, bowed slightly, and said, "Good evening, Gracious Lady. Welcome to my home."

Did I have a choice? What she really said was, "Danke."

Just then, a wine steward came in with a tray and two glasses of wine. They each took one, and Gerhardt raised his glass. "To you." She nodded and sipped from her glass.

My God, this woman has class....real class.

Gerhardt took a seat and made an attempt at conversation although he was severely restricted by things he could talk about, and she was actually enjoying his difficulties until he surprised her, "Your husband is an engineer is her not?"

"Ja."

"University of Munich?"

"Ja."

"6th Panzer division?"

"I believe so, why?"

"They inducted him as a private soldier?"

"Ja, and again, I ask...why?"

"He should have been commissioned as an officer."

"Oh?"

"Ja. I think I can correct the oversight."

Lisa looked at him sharply. "*Really*, Herr General. Do you really care about him? For that matter, do you really care about me? We are but pawns on the giant chess board of life. That makes us expendable, doesn't it? You brought me to your house for your sexual enjoyment and whatever goes along with it. Don't insult my intelligence by pretending that you care."

He was very happy about her outburst, because it was sobering. "Very well then, Mein Frau, I will not insult you. I especially will not insult your intelligence ....but, you are wrong. I do care about what happens to your husband. I may well be the only General in the whole damned SS who really gives a damn about anyone but himself, but when it came to you, I was presented with a dilemma, and I handled my dilemma the only way I knew how to do so. You are here right now because of the way I chose to handle it, and if you believe that I am going to grab you by the hair, throw you to the floor and ravish you, you are wrong..........Dead wrong!"

He had become very furious with her and yet he never lost control. There was something strangely fascinating about this man. He was very dangerous and yet....he wasn't.

She was about to speak when he decided to finish what he had started to say. "At the very least, Frau Mueller, you and I should try to behave and get along with each other. Be civilized! It is really quite simple, Mein Frau.....I really do want you. The simple fact is that I need you and for the life of me.......**I really don't know why!!"**

His head shook giving extra emphasis to the last phrase. The silence that followed was so abrupt that it startled her more than the words he spoke.

Then, he continued. "Without realizing it or even wanting to, Mein Liebe, you have made a lasting impression upon me, and because you are a married woman, you are the forbidden fruit. Well my dear, I am going to partake of that forbidden fruit whether you like it or not, and my best advice for you is try and enjoy it."

Lisa remained silent.

Another steward came and announced that dinner was being served. Gerhardt escorted her to the dining room where dinner was going to be served in ten courses. During dinner, Gerhardt made another attempt at conversation, and this time he succeeded. He immediately got the impression that she did not approve of the Third Reich, but she was smart enough not to come right out and say so.

Besides politics, the subject of philosophy fascinated her, and Gerhardt surprised her by saying, "You need to discuss that subject with Max Liebert. He has a Master's Degree in philosophy. More than that, he has his own ideas about how the universe is put together. He told me about a philosophy professor at Marburg University. A man who was an excellent teacher, but because of his religion, is no longer at the university."

She colored and began to speak, but Gerhardt held his hand up. "A word of caution. Frau Mueller, I never say anything to anyone that I would be afraid to have played back to me someday. " A look of gratitude came to her eyes, and he continued, "You see, we of the ruling class are so paranoid that we don't even trust each other." She smiled.

That loosened the emotional log jam that had existed between them, and the conversation became lighter, more humorous and more free flowing. Somewhere, between the sixth and seventh course, she actually found herself beginning to like the bastard. When desert had finally been polished off, Gerhardt pushed his chair back from the table and stood up.

"Would you like to take a walk, Frau Mueller?"

She stood and said, "Maybe I need a walk just to settle things. You need to tell your chef that he is excellent. The dinner alone was worth the trip."

He looked at her strangely as though he were searching for her meaning and then, she added, "There is one thing we need to do before we do anything else, Herr General."

"What is that?" He asked.

"When you consider my real purpose for my being here, Frau Mueller sounds a little too formal. Why don't you loosen up and call me Lisa."

He smiled again. It was becoming easier. "Very well, Lisa it is then, but only if you call me Gerhardt." They actually shook hands.

* * * * *

The moon was rising as the sun was setting, and it was a little on the cool side. Lisa had neglected to bring a wrap, but Gerhardt improvised by going into a bedroom and returning with a light coat that fit her perfectly.

"There! It was made for you."

"That brings up another point. The dress that I am wearing fits me perfectly and the shoes fit me perfectly. Are you perhaps, clairvoyant?"

He didn't want to get into the subject of the previous occupant and his very young "house guest," but he had to tell her something, and by employing the circular reasoning of the Third Reich, a half truth was much better than a lie. "The previous occupant had a house guest, and you are wearing her clothes."

He couldn't see her face, but he could sense that she was frowning. He then placed a hand on each shoulder, and spoke softly. "Lisa, I am an SS General. I was promoted by the Führer himself, and I don't like the way things are going in the Fatherland. Maybe someday, I will get a little backbone and do something about it. Until then, I keep the faith and do what I am told."

"You know the Führer?"

"Ja, I know him. Better than I want to know him, but I do in fact, know the man." This was the real Gerhardt. A man who was able to express feeling and compassion. She had almost forgotten the threats he had made against her family. The man who made those threats was an entirely different man than the one who stood before her in the moonlight.

It was an awkward moment. One that silently spoke of similarities rather than differences. *Why* was she there? She had forgotten the *why*. The *what* seemed to be all that mattered now.

"Do you dance?" He finally asked more to break the silence than the desire to dance with the woman. On the other hand, it would definitely solve the problem of when and how he was actually going to touch the woman..

"Not very well," she answered.

"Let us go and struggle through a dance or two."

They returned to the house, and found their way to the large receiving hall. It was lighted but not by the glaring lights she was used to.

He removed her coat and hung it on a hall tree that was located near the rear entrance. Then, he walked in the direction of a panel. She watched in fascination as he touched something that made the panel door slide open. After that, he pushed some buttons and returned to her.

A few seconds later, music began pouring softly from the hidden speakers. They just looked at each other.

"What is the music?" She asked softly.

"The artist is an American by the name of Glenn Miller. The music is something called *Moonlight Serenade*."

"It is beautiful."

"You are beautiful, " he added as he took her in his arms and began dancing. He might have chosen one of the several Strauss waltzes on the machine, but this kind of rhythm didn't require skill. Only the ability to sway back and forth to the music. The Americans had the right idea.

This was it, she thought. *I wondered how he might handle it. I don't know what kind of a man he really is but I like the man he has become tonight. I hope he is a good lover.* Her body moved closer to his and told him precisely what he needed to know. He tightened his grip on her.

The dance was about to end when his lips found hers. It startled her. Not that she didn't expect a kiss, but when it happened, she shuddered. He drew away slightly. His eyes caught hers in the dim light. Their lips met again and this time, there was welcome in the intimate touch. It was a quiet understated kiss. One that spoke softly of sweetness and light. She initially responded in kind, but in the process, her body informed her of a need, a physical need, and the man with the ability to fill that need just happened to be kissing her. All she had to do was let it happen and maybe help things along a little.

It was time..

Seven

The morning after

<u>Saturday June 17</u>

The phone rang.

Somewhere, at the edge of her consciousness, a phone was ringing. *Why doesn't somebody answer it,* she thought.

Then, she heard Gerhardt's voice, "Ja?"

There was a short pause which was followed by, "Sehr gut, danke." (Very well, thank you) After that, she heard the sound of the phone receiver being returned to the cradle.

Lisa was still located somewhere in the pre-dawn of consciousness and although she registered and identified sounds, the conscious Lisa had not asserted herself yet.

Then, her eyes popped open.

It was light outside, but she had no idea what time it was. She looked to her right and saw the form that was Gerhardt, and then she remembered. Last night, somehow as if by magic, he had been transformed from a toad into a handsome prince who made love to her several times. She did not count, but he seemed to savor her and that pleased her. They had even found each other in the night and made love. If it were magic, she wondered how she might transform him back into that handsome prince or did the magic only work at nighttime?

Gerhardt stretched his long frame and looked at her. The softness that had appeared in his eyes was still present, but the phone call had apparently heralded the need for him to become the Herr

General (also known as "the toad") once more.

"That was the gate sentry telling me that it is now 6:30 and I have a ten o'clock meeting this morning."

"It's nice of them to call you and tell you that," she answered.

"It's their job," he replied curtly. *Ja, he was the Herr General once more.*

Then, he hauled his body out of bed and walked in the direction of the bathroom. He was still naked. A few seconds later, she heard the sound of the toilet flushing. A little later still, he came back out of the bathroom, and said. "Come with me please?"

She dutifully did as she was told. She was still naked and didn't appear to be embarrassed by her nakedness as she followed him into what she discovered was another bedroom exactly like his.

He gestured with his left hand while he spoke in a matter-of-fact tone of voice, "This is what the rich, privileged, and pampered often refer to as the queens chamber. It is the private bedroom of the lady of the house. Apparently, after a while, some married couples decided they can no longer stand each other, and the rich were the only class able to afford the luxury of this duality of bedrooms." How true is was, she thought, as she remembered she and Karl in the space of four short years.

Gerhardt continued, "This room is now yours."

Lisa did a double take. She no longer had to inquire as to how long her relationship with the Herr General was supposed to last. It now looked like it might be a permanent one.

The general began speaking once more, "Anytime you are in this house, you may use this room. It is the one place you can go in order to be alone."

He stopped again, and his look became pensive. "I have not yet deluded myself into thinking that I can be ever anything special to you. I am still the man who forced you into being here." There was a perceptible pause followed by, "Right now, I believe we might be feeding a mutual need, and maybe that will be as good as it will ever get. In the meantime, this room is your place of privacy. There are two doors, and both have locks on them. Both doors can be unlocked from the outside, but I will impose the following restriction. No one.....I mean.....**no one** may come in here without your permission and that includes me. Anyone who forces entry will have to answer to me."

He let that sink in for a few moments and while he did, he quietly appreciated her, and appreciate is exactly what he did. They were both stark naked and, in her case, she wore it very well. She was an exquisitely formed woman who looked good regardless of what she was wearing even if she were wearing nothing at all. In short, she looked good with her clothes off, and It was amazing that she apparently was not aware of her beauty. Her husband had gotten himself quite a catch. Gerhardt wondered if the man realized his good fortune.

At that moment, his penis decided to grow. It did so on its own, because he was only appreciating her.....He was **not** coveting her. He was, of course, thinking about her and that might have had something to do with it. For some strange reason, his erection embarrassed him, and she became inwardly amused by his dilemma.

As if he were trying to get his mind off of his continuing problem, he walked over and opened a sliding door. The closet was a large walk-in, and the selection was huge. There were gowns, dresses, coats, all kinds of negligees, garter belts, and an enormous selection of shoes. Someone apparently had done their shopping in Paris....... perhaps at a brothel. Then, she saw that the other half of the closet contained dresses that were actually suitable for wearing in public.

"The clothes in this closet now belong to you."

Lisa was somewhat overwhelmed by the gesture and didn't know what to say so she said nothing at all. She did, however manage a slight smile.

By this time, Gerhardt's problem had become more apparent, and Lisa was tempted to ignore it. She didn't know if toads made love during the day or if they had to wait for nightfall so they could turn into handsome princes once more. She glanced at her own private bed and then back to Gerhardt. Obviously, he was waiting for her to initiate something.

The temptation was overwhelming, but somehow, by a mutual consent that remained unspoken, they decided to elevate their relationship to a higher level by not giving into their animal instinct to mate anytime they happened to be in heat. They opted to get dressed instead.

Thirty minutes later, they both emerged from their respective bedrooms cleaned, polished and ready for the new day. He was resplendent in his black uniform and she was wearing a pretty black dress with matching heels. The dress had lots of lace on it, and was quite feminine. She didn't really approve of the manner in which she came into this large wardrobe, but she wasn't about to say no to it either. Lisa was learning how to compromise her principles simply because *higher authority* had made it possible for her to do so.

There was admiration in his eyes as he offered her his arm and said, "Come, let us go to breakfast."

* * * * *

She recognized the main dining room from the previous evening. She especially remembered the table which was long but not too long, oval in shape and beautifully decorated. Already present was the man who had introduced himself as Major Hoffman. As she and Gerhardt entered the room, he rose to his feet, clicked his heels, bowed slightly, and said,

"Herr General.....Frau Mueller."

"Good morning, Fritz. Be seated, please" Fritz returned to his seat while Gerhardt seated Lisa. Then, he went to the head of the table where he took his own seat.

The Herr General looked squarely at the Herr Major with a puzzling look on his face. Then, he spoke quietly, "Ah.........Fritz, there is a matter that requires some attention." Then, he looked at Lisa and said, "Would you excuse us for a few minutes while I have a brief discussion with my Aid-de-Camp?"

She began to stand up when The General said, "No, Mein Liebe, remain seated. The Herr Major and I are the ones who will be leaving the table." She smiled slightly and the General motioned to the Major and said, "Come!" The Major did as he was told. As soon as they reached a place of privacy, the General turned and faced his Aid.

Fritz looked at his general in anticipation

"I received your dossier by courier yesterday, and made an amazing discovery when I read it." He stopped and looked his Aid-de-Camp squarely in the eyes.

A shadow came to the Herr Major's face as he asked. "And what is that, Herr General?"

"The question, Herr Major is......namely.....how is that I have a psychiatrist for an Aid-de-Camp, or does the Reichsführer now feel that I am need of psychiatric help?"

Major Hoffman scowled at first and then sighed. "If it pleases the Herr General, I am.....in fact......a psychiatrist."

"How in the hell did you manage to become an Aid-de-Camp to a General officer in light of that fact?"

The Herr Major conjured a slight smile as he answered. "We are well known for our efficiency, but when we *do* manage to screw up, we do a *really* good job of it."

"Meaning?" The Herr General inquired.

"I was brought into the SS as a psychiatrist, and became part of the medical staff at Sachsenhausen, but then.....last year......there was a general staff shakeup and I found myself at SS Headquarters in Berlin with nothing but time on my hands. That was when I discovered that my records had somehow been lost and someone, somewhere was in the process of reconstructing them. I was reassured that reconstruction was possible, but that such matters took time, and they would find something to keep me busy." The Herr Major frowned. The Herr General frowned in sympathy.

Major Hoffman continued, "They were certain that I was a Major, but they were certain of nothing else, and I was in the process of doing something meaningless like counting paper clips when I found out that you were going to be promoted to Brigadeführer. I knew that I could perform the functions of an Aid-de-Camp with nothing more than my good looks and some common sense. Therefore, I asked to be assigned to your staff as your Aid-de-Camp." He stopped talking.

The General was tightlipped as he exhaled through his nose. "You know that the Reichsführer will not allow you to continue in your present capacity, don't you?"

Major Hoffman nodded first, and then said, "Jawohl, Herr General."

"Well, Herr Major, Since I am supposed to be a capable and responsible administrator, I will be forced to notify Berlin of the error."

"I understand, Herr General."

"In the meantime, Herr Major or maybe I should address you as Herr Docktor, you are an excellent Aid-de-Camp, and you may continue in that capacity until you are re-assigned."

"I would like that very much, Herr General."

After that, they returned to the dining room and the puzzled look of Lisa Mueller. Gerhardt noted her look but said nothing. She did not have a need to know. Not right then anyway.

Stewards brought in pots of coffee, biscuits, butter, honey and an assortment of jams. One of the stewards asked Lisa, "Would the lady prefer tea to coffee?"

Lisa replied with a smile, "Nein, danke." (No, thank you)

The steward then clicked his heels and replied, "Bitte." (You're welcome)

Soon, Max Liebert arrived..

"Good morning, Max," replied a good spirited Gerhardt. "Find yourself a place to sit." Max did, and soon, all were buttering biscuits and drinking coffee. Strangely enough, none of them smoked at a time in Germany's history when smoking seemed to be the thing to do.

The biscuits were followed by eggs, sausages and potatoes. Conversation was sparse and limited to requests to pass something. Otherwise, the order of the day was to eat.

Lisa was amazed at how well these people lived. During the hardest of economic times, her family ate well down at the farm, but farmers usually did eat well. City people didn't and many got used to being hungry. That was how she might have experienced life in Munich had Karl not been the son of a wealthy man.

Of course, by the time she had married Karl, things were a lot better in Germany, and most people gave the credit to Adolph Hitler. They called him the savior of the German people. Maybe she would have too, but that was the benefit of the years spent in the university community. Most twenty year old German girls didn't know this, but the vast majority of the gross national product was based on war production, and in order for this war production to become consumable, it was necessary to wage war. No, she thought, Hitler was not the savior of the German people, but they did not know that. Not yet anyway.

Gerhardt waited until everyone had finished eating, and were in the process of enjoying a cup of coffee before he started speaking.

"First of all, allow me to welcome everyone to the oval table. Our benefactor and beloved SS Reichsführer Heinrich Himmler is rumored to be enthralled by the famous Round Table, and might become envious of this table.....if he ever heard about it."

"Next item......Max, do you have anything planned for today?" This had been pre-arranged, so the question was being asked for Lisa's benefit.

Max replied, "Nein! My day is completely clear."

"Good!" Gerhardt replied. "I have a favor to ask of both you and Lisa."

Lisa's head came up.

Gerhardt looked very serious as he said, "I don't know how to ask this, but I have a very important meeting this morning. The Gestapo is bringing a prisoner here at 1000 hours, and I would rather the two of you not be here at the same time he is here."

Lisa looked dubious, but for some reason, she doubted that Gerhardt would kill the man here. There were other places more suitable for killing. Then she asked, "Where would you like me to go."

"I would like Max to entertain you for a few hours. Perhaps lunch and whatever it takes to while away the afternoon." Lisa looked at Max and smiled. This was turning out differently than she had expected. She had somehow expected that she might be kept in seclusion as a love slave waiting only for Gerhardt to seek her for the satisfaction of his needs. She now looked at the handsome Max who smiled at her in return. She returned her attention to Gerhardt and smiled at him as well.

"I'd be delighted. It might be fun."

That was when Max asked, "Have you ever been to the Hofbräuhaus?"

The Hofbräuhaus

At 10:30 on a Saturday morning, the Hofbräuhaus was already fairly crowded with people. Max guided Lisa into the courtyard and found a table. He noticed the appreciative glances in Lisa's direction, and wary glances in Max's direction. In his dark suit, Max seemed to represent something official. The Nazi's had done a fairly good job of impersonating a legitimate political party, and now that they were in power, they did an even better job of keeping everyone off balance. A waitress appeared and Max asked Lisa, "Is it too early for you to drink bier?"

Lisa grinned broadly as she said, "My husband Karl told me it was never too early to drink bier?"

"Truly, a wise man," Max said thoughtfully. Then, he inquired, "Do you have a bier preference?"

"Nein. I normally drink what is ordered for me."

"Very well," Max answered, and promptly ordered two light Pils beers served in Litermass or large glass steins.

When the waitress returned with the beers, Lisa's eyes grew big, "Ach, du Lieber! They are huge!"

"If you are not used to drinking this much beer, take your time. No hurry at all. We won't eat here. I know a really good restaurant out by the university....if they are still open. In the meantime, enjoy the atmosphere."

A few minutes later, several men in black entered the establishment and began a random check of the occupants. He was fairly certain that if he had to show anything at all, his ID would probably impress the hell out of them. It was signed by Adolph Hitler.

This was the Nazi method of crowd control. Those who had been staying away from the scrutiny of the law, probably felt there was safety in numbers, but not so. The Reich really didn't like the idea of crowds, and large crowds were not desired at all, but rather than disbursing them, they hassled them instead. People could be seen sneaking toward the toilettes or the exits, but no one got away as officers were stationed at all exits and those who sought refuge in the toilettes found Gestapo officers waiting for them when they came out. Some were taken away, and the rest were visibly shaken by the experience. A woman at a table next to them started screaming as two officers started taking her away.

Suddenly, a very large man in the rear corner of the garten stood up, raised his litermass and shouted, **"Dir dies glas, Bavaria!"** (To you this glass, Bavaria!)

It surprised everyone including Max and Lisa. He remained standing and a few seconds later, he raised his litermass again, and shouted, **"Dir dies glas, Bavaria!"**

The third time, a few people from around the room joined him in the toast and it kept building like a tidal wave until almost all the men in the room were standing with their steins held high and shouting,

"Dir dies glas, Bavaria!"

"Dir dies glas, Bavaria!"

"Dir dies glas, Bavaria!"

This continued over and over again.

Max and Lisa were perhaps the only ones not standing, and it made the hair stand out on the back of their necks.

The Gestapo officer in charge, a uniformed Hauptsturmführer (Captain) looked at the man who started it all with a certain amount of menace in his eyes.. He might have considered arresting the man, but the sheer size of the man had to be a deterrent. Besides, the Gestapo lost a lot of its effectiveness in large crowds. Their chief tactic was to isolate and terrorize. People were supposed to be kept cowering behind closed doors waiting to see if their turn ever came. In this group, men might decide to become heroes.

The Herr Hauptsturmführer then looked as though he had come up with a better idea, whirled about and walked purposefully around the corner and out of sight.

Max looked at Lisa who looked back at Max. Each guessed what the other was thinking. Was the regime bold enough to ban the biergartens? After all, each Bavarian considered it to be his sacred right to drink whatever he wanted to drink, whenever he wanted to drink it.

Suddenly, there was a drum roll followed by the clash of symbols. After that, the band began playing, *Das Lied der Deutschen* the German National Anthem, and everyone began singing the words:

Deutschland, Deutschland über alles
Über alles in der welt,
Wenn es stets zu Schutz und Trutze
Brüderlich zusammenhält,
Von der maas bis and die Memel,
Von der Etsch bis an der Belt-
Deutschland, Deutschland über alles
Über alles in der welt.

When it was over, a singular voice spoke loud and clear,

"ein Volk, ein Reich, ein Führer." (one people, one empire, one leader)
The speaker repeated the phrase again, and this time, more people began shouting the chant. It continued for a few more minutes until everyone was chanting it, and then, another singular voice rose above the melee with a single word:

"Sieg!"

The crowd responded with, "HEIL!"

The voice: "Sieg!"

The crowd, "HEIL!"

The voice, "Sieg!"

The crowd, "HEIL!"

It was over and order had been restored once more. A simple interjection of German Nationalism replaced local Bavarian loyalty and reminded everyone who was really in charge. Perhaps the Gestapo Captain should have been commended for his resourcefulness. The majority of the officers then departed the establishment leaving two officers behind to provide a "presence."

Max looked at Lisa and said, "Come Lisa, let us go someplace where there is not so much atmosphere." She smiled weakly and took the hand he offered her.

The mansion

For the previous six years, General von Leitner had been walking a fine line between the "right way of doing things," and the needs of the SS as directed by Heydrich and Himmler. The general might have been born in Vienna, Austria, but he had been programmed as a small boy to think and act like a Prussian Junker. The needs of *Der Vaterland* (The Fatherland) were therefore uppermost in his mind.

He could not contradict the orders of Himmler or Heydrich, but he would attempt to modify them in the best interest of the Fatherland. Militarily speaking, it was called an oblique movement. He wasn't sure how long he would be able to walk this fine line between "the right way" and "the SS way," but he would walk it as best he could for as long as he could. Today was the most extreme test yet. For that matter, today could well be the last day of his life.

At precisely 10:00, a sedan rolled to a stop at the side entrance. Chief Inspector Zimmel, and a sergeant emerged from the sedan followed by the prisoner Konrad Ruhl.

Erik Halder, the butler was standing along side General von Leitner and the light of recognition flashed on the faces of both Erik Halder and Konrad Ruhl, his former master.

Chief Inspector Zimmel looked expectantly at the General.

Gerhardt then looked at the small group, but addressed only Konrad Ruhl, "Come Herr Ruhl.....Let us take a walk. I need to decide what to do with you, and that will be more up to you than me."

The Herr Chief Inspector protested, "Herr General, one of us should accompany you for safety's sake."

The General seemed to be preoccupied as he answered, "Ja, of course. Either you or the sergeant may follow us at a discreet distance, but I need to talk to this man in private."

"Jawohl, Herr General!" The Herr Chief Inspector was clearly not in agreement, but still willing to submit to the general's authority. The men of the Reich understood authority, and would do whatever authority dictated, but deep down inside, it was not authority they wished to submit to. It was authority they wished to exercise over others. Everybody wanted to be the man in charge. *Well, Zimmel is in charge of his own domain. Unfortunately, for him, this is my domain, and here, I command!*

"Walk with me, Herr Ruhl," the general said as he headed toward the wooded area immediately to the west of the grounds. Ruhl followed obediently and walked erect as only a proud man could do.

At the edge of the woods, the path changed from concrete to a dirt path, and they had walked about one hundred meters into the wooded area when Gerhardt stopped. Ruhl stopped along side of him, and Gerhardt noticed that Zimmel was still about 50 meters back. His pistol was not drawn but his flap was unhooked and folded back against his tunic. *Sloppy.....very sloppy.* Gerhardt decided to ask, "Are you..... perhaps..... wondering what is going to happen now?"

"Ja....but I am equally certain that you will tell me, Ja?"

"Ja, that I will, but all in due time. In the meantime, I will allow the Herr Chief Inspector back there to stew in his own juices." This time, Ruhl cast the General a puzzling glance.

Gerhardt von Leitner was considered to be a master negotiator in that he never showed his emotions. He had showed them to Lisa last night, but she was the lone exception. Today, Gerhardt was back in full control, and Ruhl was unable to read him.

Then, all at once, out of the blue, the general spoke, "We have recovered the money. Did you know that?" Gerhardt suspected that Ruhl was in league with Max, but in what way, Gerhardt did not know. He also did not know that the role he was playing had been set up by Max who realized that Gerhardt didn't have a need to know. It was a simple roll of the dice, and Konrad Ruhl's life hung in the balance. Max was gambling that some how, Gerhardt would make it possible for Ruhl to escape.

As a reaction to the question that the General had asked, shock managed to register on Konrad Ruhl's face. "No....er...ah...how could I have known that? After all, I have been in prison, you know." Disbelief now replaced shock on Konrad Ruhl's face.

A smile was necessary and Gerhardt managed to conjure a

small one up. "Of course not. How could you have known?"

The general's smile remained regardless of the expression on Ruhl's face.

Konrad Ruhl remained both mute and motionless.

Gerhardt knew little about the esoteric aspects of large amounts of money. Only that they were necessary for the continued stockpiling of the weapons of war. During the months leading to Hitler's rise first, to chancellor, and then to dictator, he had spoken often of his dream. A dream that Germany would expand its borders to make more room for Germans at the expense of those who already lived there, and once that had been accomplished, the population would be purged of the vermin that infected it. He actually believed everything he was saying. Each time he heard the story, Gerhardt would shiver inwardly, but instead of walking away, he joined with others to make sure this strange little man somehow found his way to the top of the heap. Hitler was capable of charming a snake.

Gerhardt now regarded the banker and the question he had just asked. "Herr Ruhl, you people tend to venerate the institutions you serve as though they were religious icons. We all do it. It appears to be a human trait. I am a lawyer, but let no one delude you into believing that our first responsibility is to those we represent. No, our first responsibility is to the judicial system without which we could not function. That is our icon. We worship it as though it were a god."

Konrad Ruhl wasn't quite sure where the general was headed, and then he realized that the general's mind was really quite sharp and orderly. Wherever he happened to be in the back channels of his mind, he was never out of sight of his objective. Did the Nazi's have many like this general? If so, the rest of the world might be in trouble. Real trouble! Maybe to save the world, men like this general had to die, and that was when he realized that the general would probably outlive him. He, Konrad Ruhl, would probably not survive the next few minutes.

"Are you still with me, Herr Ruhl?"

Ruhl blinked. He had actually been lost in thought. Not very orderly at all. "My apologies, Herr General. No, I don't believe any of my problems have been solved."

"Do you wish to live?"

Ruble looked at his inquisitor. Did the man think that he was suicidal? "JA, Of course I wish to live."

"I won't ask if you deserve to live. Perhaps, none of us really deserves life. We just happen to be in possession of it. Therefore, I will not pass judgment on that." He reached inside his tunic and withdrew an envelope, which he held up high enough even for the Chief Inspector to see. "Inside this envelope is a simple document. This document directs the local Gestapo to transfer you to Gestapo headquarters in Berlin for *final disposition.*" The lawyer in him stopped long enough to allow the words to sink in. "Make no mistake about it, Herr Ruhl, the Führer wants you dead, and I am in no position to argue with the Führer. My next move is to take you to the Herr Chief Inspector along with this document and watch the Herr Chief Inspector and his guard take you away. They take a perverse kind of pride in this type of activity...........I don't."

Puzzlement registered on Ruhl's face.

"Herr Ruhl, if you could have ten seconds alone with the Chief Inspector, do you think that you could manage to work it to your advantage?"

Killed trying to escape were the thoughts swimming in Konrad Ruhl's mind, and then, in the space of a heartbeat, the panic ceased. *Yes, death by gunshot in the place I love is far more desirable to anything the Gestapo might dream up for me.*

Gerhardt had watched panic turn into calm acceptance. *Good,* he thought, *the next five minutes will become critical.* "The truth is, Herr Ruhl, that Herr Liebert is not a killer, and signing your death warrant makes him as much of a killer as the man who actually executes you." Ruhl just looked at him. The general then reached for the Iron Cross that hung around his neck. "I have killed many men, Herr Ruhl. In fact, I won this medal during the Great War in an action against armed and trained British soldiers, and during that battle, many brave British soldiers died by my hands, but again, I emphasize that they were trained soldiers not unarmed civilians. I do not kill unarmed civilians."

Somehow, Ruhl believed him. Why, he didn't know, but he did. Did he have a chance? If so, he would take it no matter how slim it was.

"Listen to me very carefully, Herr Ruhl. I am going to walk you back and turn you over to the Herr Chief Inspector. If he decides to handcuff you, then all bets are off, and you will have to do what you believe you have to do. I can't blame you, but you will probably end up dead. For that matter, I don't even know if the man has handcuffs. Men in his position don't usually carry them. It's simply a contingency I need to point out. On the other hand, if he doesn't cuff you, he will have you proceed him as you walk to rejoin the sergeant. Once this happens, you are definitely a dead man. Understand?"

Ruhl nodded his understanding.

"I don't know how you are going to do it, but I would bet my life that you can somehow overcome him, and maybe even relieve him of his revolver. Once you do that, you will need to make it to that pile of leaves about thirty meters to right in that clump of trees. From there, you ought to make it out of here in the confusion."

Thoughts crowded against Ruhl's mind like an out-of-control mob. He managed to nod briefly, and then, the general said, "Come! We can delay no longer without drawing suspicion." And then he said something that was completely out of character for an SS General ...."God be with you."

They walked toward Chief Inspector Zimmel.

When they were abreast of the Chief Inspector, the General handed the envelope to him and explained, "The envelope contains the order remanding custody of Konrad Ruhl to the Gestapo for final disposition."

The Chief Inspector smiled thinly and said, "Danke, Herr General, " and to Ruhl, he said, "Take the lead, Herr Ruhl, and begin walking."

Gerhardt breathed a sigh of relief, and wondered if Ruhl did likewise. He watched them walk away from him and wondered when Ruhl would make his move, and then he couldn't help wondering how well the sixty-one year old man would do. Was he giving the man a chance or just sending him to his death.

Konrad Ruhl was not a religious man even though he had been a Jew all his life. He therefore did not usually seek God's advice and counsel prior taking on difficult tasks, but this time was different. He went deep within and suddenly a vision came to him. It was that of a twelve year old boy in a ballet studio. His mother had insisted that he take ballet lessons, and he did so until he finally convinced her that he was better suited for something else.

The vision was of a boy completing a spin kick. *My god! I haven't done that in fifty years. How can I possible do it now?* Then suddenly, he knew.

Suddenly, Ruhl stopped, and with a blinding motion, his body began to spin to the left as he brought his left leg up in a kicking motion that connected with the Chief Inspector's chest and sent him sprawling to the ground. Ruhl was surprised that it worked but he didn't have time to celebrate. Zimmel was also surprised. So much so, that he did not reach for his weapon, and that was his fatal error. Ruhl, on the other hand, did not squander the opportunity. He knelt down, extracted the Luger and with one swift motion, pointed the weapon at the Herr Chief Inspector Zimmel and pulled the trigger. Zimmel's body lurched and then fell limp.

Ruhl didn't bother to tarry any and he rose to start running, but first, he aimed the weapon at the General and pulled the trigger. Gerhardt had less than a second to react and began to dive to his right when a hot burning was felt in his left shoulder.

His own revolver was now in his hand and he aimed at the now moving target and pulled the trigger. He was a crack shot, but this wasn't a shooting gallery. It never was. That was how life was.

He then became aware of another presence. It was the sergeant. "Herr General! Herr General! The Herr Chief Inspector.....I-I believe he is dead, and the prisoner has escaped, and now you are wounded. What do I do? Tell me.....what should I do?"

"Call for help," was the only answer that Gerhardt could give as darkness claimed him.

Lake Starnberger

They had found a spot. A perfect spot. A place they might have come to had they been lovers, but alas........Max and Lisa were not lovers. Maybe someday they would become lovers, but for now, they had simply decided to enjoy some part of nature that man had not yet soiled with his petty intolerance's and ambitions.

Both Max and Lisa had grown up near the banks of this huge lake, and both had learned to love the quiet serenity of its more remote locations.

Max had fully intended to eat at Augie's Restaurant near the university, but when they got there, the windows were all boarded up. They were both disappointed as Lisa and her husband had often eaten there. Lisa couldn't believe what she was seeing and wondered why. She decided to find out what she could about what happened, and went into many of the shops, but each shop had people who could see no evil, hear no evil, or speak no evil. She was usually told to mind her own business.

Rather than retreat to the safety of the Mercedes, the admonishments from those who decided to remain blinded to the obvious only served to strengthen her resolve, and she finally found a woman who was not afraid to talk to her.

Augie's Restaurant had been attacked on November 9, 1938 during a night which had become known as *Kristallnacht* or the Night of the Broken Glass. It was the night when the Nazis systematically smashed the store windows of Jewish owned businesses throughout the German Reich.

Again the Jew had been blamed for whatever problems that might have infected the Reich. The woman, who was quite elderly and probably didn't care what the Gestapo might do to her, told Lisa that Augie and his wife finally realized that the Nazis would not only destroy their business, but would ultimately destroy them as well. Consequently, they decided to see if it were still possible to leave Germany. The woman reported with pride that she had received word that the couple had reached safety. Their ultimate goal being the United States of America. The woman then spoke with pride when she told Lisa that good people still lived in Germany. Unfortunately, they were not in charge.

When Lisa returned to the car, she suggested they stop at a market and buy some cold meat and potato salad, and when they had done so, find a quiet spot by the lake to eat it.

"What has happened to our country, Max?"

"Are you just waking up, Lisa?"

"No, but I didn't realize how bad it had gotten."

"I won't taunt you, Lisa. You are much too intelligent for that, but I dare say that Germany has not yet seen how bad it will become. Our country has been known by a lot of names, but the words *Nazi Germany* will become indelibly stamped in our nation's soul if, in fact, our nation manages to survive the Nazi era."

It was a warm day and Lisa shivered.

"You make it sound hopeless, Max."

"Hopeless Lisa? Nothing is hopeless. Nothing."

"So, enlighten me. What brought us here, Max."

Max sighed deeply. "I really don't know for certain, Lisa, but if I were to hazard a guess, I would say that along with being a very industrious and hard working people, we are also a superstitious lot and tend to believe the myths that make up our heritage. Uncle Adolph has used these myths and legends to make us believe that he was somehow called to lead the German people out of the wilderness, and that his way is the only way.

Lisa looked strangely at Max and his reference to *Uncle Adolph.* Then, she said, "You just referred to the Führer as *Uncle Adolph.* Surely, you are joking."

"Nein, Mein Frau. To his face, I call him Uncle Adolph," and then rather than keep her dangling on a string, he told her about his real relationship with Adolph Hitler.

Her expression was wistful as she digested what he had told her. Perhaps, she was looking for part of Isaac in the man. For some reason, she never looked for Karl in any other man. The truth be known, she knew not what she was seeking. It then became her turn to sigh deeply, and then, without thinking, she said, "What profit a man to gain the whole world, and yet.....lose his soul."

Max looked at her sharply. She was quoting the Bible. Did she know that?

He didn't ask, but had he done so, she would have told him, "No."

Max pulled a handful of grass and stuck a blade into his mouth. He wondered if he might be dealing with two Lisa's, and then, as if he were, he decided to address them both, "It's not just the Jews. It's the communists, the homosexuals, the free masons, the elderly, the chronically ill, and whoever else might be considered by the Nazis as cancerous growths within the national body. Of all that I have mentioned, the Jews are considered to be the consummate enemy, but you can be certain that very few people will stand with the Jew, the Communist or the homosexual. In fact, Germany cannot take care of its elderly and chronically ill and still produce the weapons of war. No! It's a lot easier to let the government take care of these problems in their own way as long as they don't tell the people how they are doing it. The people just don't want to know or it might affect the national conscience, but in truth, if they did know they would still do nothing. This would allow pangs of guilt and nobody likes to feel guilty."

Lisa looked downcast. "You paint us as though we are callused and uncaring."

"It's not that we don't care, Lisa. Unfortunately, we feel that if we don't see, hear or speak evil, that it doesn't exist, and by the time we do care......the government has organizations like the Gestapo to tell us to mind our own business, and stay out of theirs." The downcast eyes now had tears in them.

Max continued, "Lisa, it's not just Germany. It's a human problem. It's people everywhere. We'll be the ones under the magnifying glass, and people will point fingers at us, but those who point fingers need to remember that when one finger is pointed at another, three more are being pointed back at the one doing the pointing. Therefore, instead of pointing, we need to find a mirror."

Lisa was warming to this man. She didn't know what it meant, but she was warming to him.

"Max?"

"Ja."

"I slept with an SS General last night."

"I know that."

"What do you think of me?"

"It matters not what I think. It matters only what you think.

"Maybe so, but what you think is also very important."

"I do not do moral judgments. Therefore, I do not judge you. You are quite lovely and desirable, and I wouldn't say no to you, but that is as far as it goes." Max stopped short of saying what he was really thinking.

He fondled another blade of grass and started talking again without looking at her. "I only know that you slept with him. I know nothing else, but that doesn't make you a bad girl. It makes you a practical one. As far the act of sexual intercourse is concerned, it is first and foremost, a physical act and no physical act will ever fill an emotional void. I do not believe that the act itself is any more sacred than this blade of grass." His eyes now gazed intently into hers.

"Lisa, I really do like you, and really did not intend to start preaching. Nothing you do with Gerhardt von Leitner or any other man, for that matter, will ever affect how I feel about you." *And I could very easily fall in love with you, and if I don't watch myself, I will.*

Lisa had spent hours discussing the idea of marriage with Isaac, and anytime the idea of marriage had been presented apart from religious injunctions on the subject, it lost a lot of its luster.

The idea of God still made Lisa itch in places she couldn't scratch in public and still be considered a lady. It simply didn't make any sense for this God to create man, give him freedom of choice, and then turn around and tell him that something was verboten. All because this God supposedly can't abide sin.....whatever that means.

It was scary to her that so many people accepted this idea without question. Max was right because these very same people accepted the Third Reich and its policies without question. Then, this very same God not only banished Adam and Eve from the Garden but many generations later, He further complicated matters by creating The Ten Commandments.

Once again, God had supposedly created the species and granted them freedom to do whatever they wanted even if it happened to be wrong. Maybe this same god was jealous because they didn't choose him. If that were the case, then this god was also fickle and untrustworthy.

Lisa knew what Max meant, and yet Max was giving the male point of view. Maybe she needed to make love to Gerhardt. Maybe she needed to make love to Max. Maybe she needed to know that life and love didn't stop simply because they had to remove the organs that made it possible for her to have babies.

Max had been doing some thinking of his own. Maybe he had been reading her mind, but whatever this woman did while she was alone with a man, would always be between her and that man unless she wished to confide in someone else. It would always be important for her to at least give the impression that she was a lady.

He would grant her that. Whatever this complicated woman happened to be, she was definitely a lady.

A few minutes later, they returned to their feet, brushed the grass off their clothing and drove back to the mansion.

* * * * *

The trip back to the mansion was made in relative quiet, and when they arrived, they received extra scrutiny from the gate sentry. Once he had been satisfied, they were granted entrance to the property.

Something was different. Very different. Max already had an idea what it was. Extra guards were now patrolling the grounds. All the sudden, Max became very nervous. What if something had gone wrong?

At that moment, Major Hoffman came out to meet them.

"Max.....it is good to have you back. We had a major problem this morning."

"As in what, Fritz."

"First of all, the prisoner escaped, but before he did, he took the Herr Chief Inspector's revolver and killed him. Then, he shot the general in the shoulder."

Both of Lisa's hands went to her mouth. She didn't realize that she cared. Max noticed her reaction and inquired, "Where is the Herr General?"

"He is lying down in the parlor."

"What is the current situation, Fritz?"

"The Herr Inspector Gottlieb has taken command of the local Gestapo, and so far, has taken everything at face value. He has disputed nothing. I guess it might have been a disaster except for the fact that The Herr General had already gotten the location of the missing money and the Swiss bank account number from Herr Ruhl.

Max tried not to show any emotion.

Fritz went on, "Apparently, Herr Ruhl felt that he was trading the money for his life and The Herr General decided to turn him over to the Gestapo instead. Inspector Gottlieb then felt that Herr Ruhl was probably desperate enough to make a last ditch attempt to escape, and it worked."

A slight smile came to Max's face. Lisa saw it, and then.....she knew. It was nothing more than a perception, but she knew. *Well, I'll be damned. The man who threatens the lives of my family makes it possible for a Jewish banker to escape and no one is the wiser except for Max Liebert and myself. Will the real Gerhardt von Leitner please identify himself!*

Fritz didn't notice anything at all. Instead, he said, "Come, let us go pay our respects to the Herr General."

Eight

Karl

Wednesday June 21, 1939

The 6th Panzer Division

"Panzerschülze Mueller!"

Karl snapped to attention, "Jawohl, Herr Sergeant!"

"You are to report to battalion headquarters immediately!"

"Jawohl, Herr Sergeant." He then took off at a slow trot in the direction of battalion headquarters while wondering what in the hell battalion wanted with him, a lowly panzerschülze. He had found out rather quickly that the army didn't agree with him, but he had managed to stay out of trouble. He had completed his basic training and was transferred to the 6th Panzer Division without benefit of any leave. Something was up. He could feel it, but everyone was being close mouthed about everything. There were rumors, but then........there had always been rumors.

He was running easily, and that was something he couldn't have done before entering the army. No, he couldn't have run anywhere. He had lived the life of a married college student with a wife who, to his surprise, was a very good cook. She was also very beautiful, and that had been the primary attraction. The good cook part came with the package and turned out to be a serendipity.

Suddenly, he turned the corner and found himself in front of battalion headquarters. He stepped inside and waited until for the clerk to acknowledge his presence. When the clerk finally looked up, Karl made his announcement:

"Panzerschülze Mueller reporting to the battalion commander as ordered."

The clerk eyed him curiously before standing up. He then walked to the inside door that separated the battalion commander's office from the outer office. He knocked twice before entering. A short while later, the clerk returned with the terse announcement, "OberstLieutenant (Lt. Colonel) Heilman will see you now."

Karl found himself standing in front of a very stern looking man. Karl rendered the standard military salute. He had been surprised to learn that the Wehrmacht did not salute the Nazi way. The Battalion Commander just sort of waved at him in return.

"Stand at ease, Mueller." Karl did as he was told.

The commander had a sheet of paper in front of him, and he read it again and again while Karl was kept waiting. It was as though he didn't believe what he was reading and figured that if he read it often enough, the words might change. After a while, he finally grunted his acceptance and looked up at Karl.

He pointed to a chair, and said, "Be seated, please." Karl was puzzled but did as he was told. Battalion commanders were not interested in his comfort. He had just spent three months learning that the German army was very strict, sometimes cruel, and so far, they hadn't "asked" him to do anything.

Once seated, the commander relaxed a little and formed a steeple with his fingers, "This document tells me that you are from Munich."

"Jawohl, Herr OberstLieutenant!"

The commander nodded and went on, "It also tells me that you attended the University of Munich. Is that correct?

"Jawohl, Herr OberstLieutenant!"

"It further tells me that you graduated with a degree in engineering. Is that also correct?"

"Jawohl, Herr OberstLieutenant!"

"You certainly have that line down pat. Why don't we just settle for a simple Ja and nein. I like discipline but too much discipline might just impede the progress of this conversation."

"Jaw——. Er..Ja."

"Sehr gut," replied a happier commander. "We like officers who are still teachable."

"Sir?"

"Oh........I forgot to tell you. Either that or I was waiting for the right moment, but as of this moment, you have just become an instant officer, and you have been promoted to OberLieutenant (First Lieutenant). They even bypassed Lieutenant. You must be really special."

The words had a sledgehammer effect on Karl's mind..

"I-I don't understand."

"You are not supposed to, but prior to this troop buildup, I might not have understood either. The truth is that the needs the needs of the Fatherland do come first and the Wehrmacht is the protector of the Fatherland."

He then held up a paper. "According to this paper, an SS General in Munich has discovered that you possess a Bachelor's Degree in Engineering, and because of the needs of the Wehrmacht, the Oberkommando (High Command) der Wehrmacht has decided that you are to be transferred to the 357th Engineering Battalion as a commissioned officer." The commander waited for that information to settle some before continuing.

"How the Herr SS General obtained this information or why he acted upon it is beyond me, but he did, and that is that!" His head nodded to punctuate what he had just stated. "Therefore, you are to become an instant officer just as soon as we swear you in. After that, you are to get new uniforms, and then, you will go to your former company and pick up your personal belongings. Once that has been completed, you are to return here for transport to your new battalion. They will be advised of your pending arrival. Do you have all that, Herr OberLieutenant?"

Karl's head was swimming, but he managed to say, "Jawohl, Herr OberstLieutenant."

The clerk returned with several documents that required signatures, and once everything had been signed and witnessed, Karl raised his right hand and swore the Loyalty Oath to Adolph Hitler, the German Reich, and the Wehrmacht.

* * * * *

Three hours later, after a lot of problems incurred while obtaining the right uniforms, newly appointed OberLieutenant Karl Mueller stepped into his former tent. Hans Kuhlman, one of the other five men in the tent saw the rank of an officer and shouted, "Achtung!"

Four men snapped to attention before Hans saw who it was and said, "At ease, gentlemen. It's only Karl." To Karl, he said, "Why are you impersonating an officer? You can get into a lot of trouble for doing that."

"Make jokes if you wish, Hans, but someone found that I am a graduate engineer and made me an officer. Turn me in and we will find out who gets in trouble."

They all returned to attention and saluted him once more.

* * * * *

For the second time this day, Karl found himself at the entrance to a battalion headquarters. Prior to entering, he had to decide just how a German officer would report to a new assignment. Would he be cocky and arrogant, loud and boisterous.....what? Then, Karl decided that he would be a sincere, no nonsense officer who had something to offer other than a loud mouth and an arrogant attitude.

He stepped inside.

The clerk saw him and immediately snapped to attention. He wore the rank of a Unterfeldwebel (Junior Sergeant).

"Good day, Herr Unterfeldwebel. Ober Lieutenant Mueller reporting to the commanding officer as ordered."

The clerk clicked his heels and entered the commander's office. Shortly thereafter, he returned with the terse announcement that the Herr Major had been expecting the Herr OberLieutenant, and that he should go right in.

When Karl reported, he stood at attention and rendered the standard military salute. This commander was a major who had thinning hair and a jovial expression on his face. It made Karl wonder if he were still in the German army.

The Major returned Karl's salute smartly, and then leaned

back in his chair and scrutinized the new officer.

After a few seconds, The major stood up and offered the OberLieutenant his hand. Karl took it. It was warm and firm.

"Have a seat, Herr OberLieutenant." Karl took his seat and managed to sit in a modified position of attention.

The major noticed it and decided to ignore it for the moment. Instead, he said, "I bid you welcome! I am Major Wilhelm Schmidt, and I happen to command this engineering battalion. Again, I welcome you to my battalion." He picked up a pack of cigarettes, took one and offered one to Karl who declined with thanks.

Major Schmidt chuckled. "Another evangelist?"

"Nein, Herr Major. Until a few short months ago, I was a college student with too much to do and not enough time to do it in. Smoking was simply a habit I never bothered to acquire. Nothing evangelistic about it at all, Herr Major. Just a matter of preference.

"Sehr gut!" The major said and leaned back, "Now then, do I understand correctly that you are an instant officer?"

"Jawohl, Herr Major!"

"You must have friends in high places, " he mused, and then added, "Normally, I am not in favor of that sort of thing. Things that don't have to be earned are usually not appreciated. On the other hand, you have earned a college degree, and you have learned how to become a basic German soldier. That has to count for something. Therefore, I accept the edict of the Oberkommando der Wehrmacht without adding my own personal prejudice to the equation." He stopped talking long enough to rub his chin and then decided to ask, "Now then, what is your conception of how an officer is supposed to act?"

"Er...I don't know, Herr Major."

"Based on the circumstances, that is good. That which you don't know, can be taught. It is much more difficult to unlearn something."

The next hour was spent with Karl learning how he was expected to act as an officer is the 6th Panzer Division. It was a basic crash course. There would be other instructions, but this was the beginning. At the conclusion of that hour, he was turned over to Captain Reinhart whose job it was to find out if this new officer knew anything or would just be taking up space.. The Captain was pleasantly surprised with Karl's knowledge and quiet approach to what being an engineer was all about.

Their battalion's primary function was the support of the 6th Panzer Division through the building of roads and bridges, and for some strange odd reason, both men had been trained to build roads and bridges. They were actually going to do what they had been trained to do. Both men looked forward to the day they could be building them as civilian engineers, but until whatever was about to happen was over and done with, they would build bridges and roads for tanks, trucks, and soldiers.

* * * * *

That night, as Karl lay in his bed, he reflected on the day, and what a day it had been. He had not looked forward to his life as an infantryman. Life in the army was harsh and sometimes brutal, and yet, men seemed eager to suffer these hardships for the sake of the Fatherland.

Each man seemed to embrace the work he had to do as a soldier. Work seemed to be the right tonic for men like him, and Karl had no doubt that the men in the engineering battalion would do no less..

That was when his mind drifted to his wife, Lisa. He had obtained a real jewel when he married her, but he often wished that she loved him as much as he loved her. Perhaps maybe.......that might be asking too much.

No, he reasoned, she might never love him, but had their marriage been any different than so many others? After all, it was the duty of the woman to be subservient to the man. This was the custom and it was much more defined in Lisa's Bavaria than it had been in his native Ruhr Valley.

And now, mandatory military service had separated them. Would their marriage survive the separation? Karl hoped that it would, but then.....there was always hope. Without hope, what was the purpose of living?

With that final thread of optimism, OberLieutenant Karl Mueller drifted off into a dreamless sleep.

The Mansion

It was early Sunday afternoon and the small party of four had just retired to the front sitting room in order to settle their meal. Major Hoffman was wearing his uniform, Max was wearing civilian trousers and a white shirt, Lisa was wearing a pink dress with matching heels, and Gerhardt was wearing his uniform trousers, and a black shirt open at the collar. It was a couple of sizes larger than he normally wore in order to accommodate the bandages that covered his chest and left shoulder. Occasionally, his eyes would grimace in pain, but as a general rule, he bore it well.

Lisa looked at the three men she now sat with. Forty-eight hours ago, she would have shook her head in disbelief at the prospect. Now, she registered only a quiet acceptance. It was as though she had embarked upon a great adventure, but she was still saddened by the methods employed by Gerhardt von Leitner. It demonstrated a ruthlessness on the part of the SS general. A feeling that the end would always justify the means.

Therefore, the "rightness" of the adventure was still in question, but she no longer felt manipulated She could not have explained the disparity of her conflicting emotions had her life depended upon it.

When she first saw Gerhardt yesterday afternoon, she had been shocked. Somehow, she had pictured him as being bulletproof, and the fact that bullets did not bounce off of him was rather disquieting. Of course thoughts of that nature tended to be amusing, and his wound was definitely not a laughing matter. Not at all.

When she had walked in on him, he had been wearing only his trousers and shoes with his upper body being naked except for his bandages. She remembered his sheepish smile. It was as though he was embarrassed to have actually been in the way of a bullet. That was when she found out that he had gone through some very intense fighting during the Great War and had never been wounded, not even a scratch, "and now this."

Later, when they had retired to his bedroom, he looked at her and said, "Well, Mein Schatz, you have a reprieve for tonight. I hurt much too badly to indulge in any kind of carnal activity. If you wish, you may sleep in your own bedroom." She nodded and went into the bath in order to ponder the offer.

But when she had emerged from the bath, she crawled in beside him. He looked at her curiously, but said nothing. She didn't say anything either. The next thing she discovered was that the condition of his shoulder had nothing to do with his sexual arousal. She kissed him and he kissed her back. He might have wanted to take a pain pill and go to sleep, but her gentle caresses were making him forget about the pain. More important issues faced him at the moment. He then wondered if she might only be teasing him. Would she be that cruel? Then, he remembered the methods he had employed to bring her here in the first place. The thought had actually occurred to Lisa, but she dismissed the idea. She decided not to reduce herself to his level. What she was doing, she did for her benefit only. He was on his own.

Her aggressive behavior took him completely by surprise, but he was able to adapt to new circumstances in a heartbeat, and he accepted her advances. Of course, when it came time to consummate their passion, he was unable to assume the dominant role so she assumed it instead.

A few wild minutes later, Lisa lie beside him on the bed. Her body was glistening with sweat. His good right arm was around her, and when she raised herself to look into his eyes, they were filled with a cross between love and gratitude. Lisa didn't know where one left off and the other began, and smiled inwardly to herself.

After several long moments, Gerhardt whispered, "Vielen dank, Mein Schatz (Thank you kindly, my treasure.). You didn't have to do that, but I am very glad you did."

She touched a light kiss to his lips, and went into the bathroom to clean up. When she returned, Gerhardt had already fallen asleep. Lisa climbed in beside him and within two minutes, she was sleeping also.

* * * * *

Now, as she looked at the other three men relaxing in the parlor with her, she wondered what it all meant. She, the mother of a two year old girl, and wife of a German soldier, found herself consorting with the enemy. Men who were of the Third Reich but not necessarily......the Fatherland. She very easily discerned the difference. The Third Reich was a reference point. A name given to a specific point in time. The Fatherland was forever.

Max looked at her thoughtful expression and wondered what she might be thinking. He correctly guessed that she might be wondering just who these strange men were that now influenced her life.

Conversation was non-existent. Each seemed immersed in his or her own private thoughts.

At that moment, Eric Halder, the butler, walked into the parlor, and stood at a proper and respectful position of attention.

"Herr General! My apologies for the intrusion, but the Herr Inspector Gottlieb is here to see you."

"Ah yes, the Gestapo has arrived. Show him in, Eric.....Please?"

Eric clicked his heels and replied, "Jawohl, Herr General... ...right away!"

No more than a minute had passed when Chief Inspector Heinz Gottlieb walked into the parlor and stopped abruptly. His tall body stood erect and he cradled his hat between his left arm and his side. His bearing was military, and yet, there was something else about him. Something close to the surface and yet ....still hidden from view. Something a person could feel long before it could be seen and identified. Unlike his predecessor, the Herr Inspector preferred dark civilian clothes to the wearing of a uniform.

The new Gestapo Commander looked directly at his nominal superior while ignoring the other two men in the room. The woman, on the other hand, was rather difficult to ignore.

"Herr General," he said with the proper amount of respect in his voice. It was a deep baritone voice. Pleasant sounding to Lisa's ear drums. "My apologies for this interruption, but I have just completed a long telephone conversation with the Herr SS-Gruppenführer Heydrich in Berlin concerning the Konrad Ruhl matter. He expressed joy at the recovery of the money, and a certain amount of sadness at the death of the Herr Chief Inspector Zimmel. As for the escape of Konrad Ruhl, the Herr SS Gruppenführer is naturally disappointed but appears to understand the circumstances and the desperation on the part of Herr Ruhl. The Herr SS Grappenführer was actually surprised that you not only managed to get a shot off after you were wounded, but that you actually hit the man."

THAT surprised Gerhardt. This development had not been mentioned yesterday. Gerhardt now regarded the man carefully. Very carefully. Yes, he would have to be careful. Inspector Gottlieb was not the political hack that the late Herr Chief Inspector Zimmel had been. Gottlieb had been a police officer in Berlin prior to becoming a member of Himmler's secret police. Gottlieb would therefore approach all investigations in the cool manner of a professional investigator. Did the man smell a rat? If so, he didn't show it.

Gottlieb also regarded the Herr General. There were unanswered questions in his mind about this case. The first and foremost being why the Herr General had insisted that Ruhl be brought here in the first place. Unfortunately, he would have to tread lightly because the Herr General was very close to Adolph Hitler. That caution had come direct from Himmler himself through Heydrich.

According to the Sergeant, who was the only other witness besides the General and Ruhl himself, everything happened much too quickly for there to have been a conspiracy. It all appeared to have depended upon time and chance.

The incredible fact that Ruhl managed to knock Zimmel down, take his weapon and shoot the man still astounded Gottlieb. The fact that the shot killed Zimmel was probably luck, but when a man is shot in the heart, he dies. What really surprised the Gestapo chief was that Ruhl had the presence of mind to take a shot at the General. Then the general managed to shoot Ruhl after being shot in his own shoulder. The Herr General's record indicated that he was a expert shot. A man who generally hit what he was shooting at, but was his action a reaction or a planned event? If it were a reaction, then the Herr General was definitely a man to be reckoned with. Unfortunately, he doubted that he would ever know.

He took another look around the room, and no one seemed to be nervous about his presence. Gottlieb's thought processes bothered him, and yet, they were proper for anyone in his position. An investigator was supposed look for what didn't seem to be there. He was supposed to search for the hidden piece to the puzzle, but the professional part of him needed to know when he was beating a dead horse. When all was said and done, he needed to close the book on one case and pick up another book.

Of course, in the wake of the incident, the entire property had become a crime scene and all of the people, whether they were part of the incident or not, became possible suspects and were interrogated accordingly.

He had met with his investigators that morning and they all came to the same inescapable conclusion. No one......absolutely no one acted nervous or out of the ordinary, and based upon the conclusion that Konrad Ruhl, who acted out of a sense of desperation and completely on his own, simply got lucky. Unfortunately, he had disappeared without a trace. A complete search of the entire wooded area had turned up nothing. Absolutely nothing. It was as if Ruhl had disappeared into thin air.

It still came back to why the general had him brought here in the first place, and then, he decided to at least ask the question, "Forgive me, Herr General, but there is one question that keeps nagging at me, and I would like to ask it."

"And, what is that, Herr Inspector?" The General's

"May I speak to you in private?" After a brief .nod from Gerhardt, the other three left the room. Just as soon as they left, Gottlieb closed the French doors and returned to his position of standing in front of the Herr General. The Herr General never did offer Gottlieb a seat.

Gottlieb sighed and asked, "Why did you have the prisoner brought here?"

Gerhardt had anticipated this question. It would have been the first question he would have asked had their positions been reversed. He actually managed to force a slight smile. "Call it a humanitarian gesture if you will. The man used to live here, and I knew that he might like to see the place for the last time. Call it an act of compassion if you will. I also knew that the private talk along the trail was a less threatening atmosphere than a Gestapo interrogation room. He needed to realize there was no tomorrow. I had already signed the order, and he was going directly to Berlin."

"Did he seem to be frightened?" Asked Gottlieb.

"I think resigned might be the better word."

"Why did he give **you** what we weren't able to persuade him to give **us**?"

"He didn't."

Gottlieb looked strangely at the man who was his nominal

superior, but wasn't able to say anything right away. After several long moments, he finally was able to say, "But, I thought......" And then he stopped.

Gerhardt decided to elaborate. "I will be honest with you. I might have considered setting the man free had he given me the correct account numbers, but it was only a consideration, and in light of the facts, it was the wrong consideration. Herr Liebert had already figured it out, and when I showed the numbers to Herr Ruhl, he turned white. He was a very poor actor, and I wasn't about to set him free under those circumstances. I never told you people that Ruhl was the one who gave me the account numbers. Only that I had them. My only option therefore was to remand him to your custody for final disposition."

"But how did Herr Liebert figure out the Swiss account numbers? Those are carefully guarded secrets."

"Suffice it to say, Herr Inspector, there is absolutely nothing under the sun that is impossible, and Herr Liebert lives by that philosophy. I grant you that luck is no small factor, but luck usually occurs when opportunity meets preparation. Wouldn't you agree?"

"Jawohl, Herr General." What else could he say? The road out of Germany was not a paved highway that traveled through check points. He would give this investigation another week, and if nothing significant came to light, the book on this one would be taken off the front burner and placed on one of the rear burners. It would remain inactive unless Herr Ruhl happened to be captured alive and that had a very remote chance of happening.

Gerhardt replied, "Danke." Gottlieb then walked over and opened the French doors. The other three returned to their seats.

Once everyone was situated again, Gerhardt addressed the still standing Gestapo Commander . "Before you leave, I need to mind my manners." He then gestured in the direction of the other three, and asked, "Do you know these people?"

Gottlieb looked at Major Hoffman and said, "I met Major Hoffman, yesterday, but I have not yet had the pleasure of meeting the other gentleman or the lady.

"Very well, the other gentleman is the infamous Max Liebert. He refers to our beloved Führer as Uncle Adolph." Inspector Gottlieb stepped forward and shook Max's hand, and said, "Herr Liebert," as he shook his hand.

He held Max's hand for a few seconds longer than necessary as he looked closely at the man who had been able to perform the impossible.

After Max, Inspector Gottlieb shifted his attention fully to the pretty young blonde in the pink dress. Miracle workers were oddities, but lovely ladies were a delicacy to be savored. Gerhardt also smiled at the thought of Lisa. It was becoming easy to smile at Lisa, and for a man like Gerhardt von Leitner, the act of smiling was a major accomplishment.

"And this gracious lady is Frau Lisa Mueller."

The Inspector took her right hand in his and surprised her by kissing it. "To look into your lovely eyes is to behold a second sunrise. It is indeed a pleasure to meet someone who is as lovely as you, Gnädige Frau (Gracious Lady)."

At the touch of his hand, she felt a warming sensation course through her veins. She had been flattered by his words and the eloquence with which he had spoken them. She smiled warmly at him. She couldn't help it. She seemed to be aware of who the man was and what his capabilities were, but that didn't deter the feeling of warmth that surged though her. What it meant was a matter to be determined at a another time in another place if......if it still mattered. Her answer to him was simple and direct. "Vielen Dank (Thank you kindly), Herr Chief Inspector."

He clicked his heels, and rendered a military salute, "Bitte shön (Your welcome), Frau Mueller."

At that moment, he realized that his visit was at an end, and he addressed the General, "If there is nothing further, Herr General, I shall be taking my leave now."

"Auf Wiedersehen, Herr Inspector."

Gottlieb saluted and left the room.

In his wake, a vacuum ensued and since Mother Nature abhors a vacuum, something will always take its place. In this case, three people began speaking at once.

Gerhardt held up his good right hand. All quiet ensued. "Now then," He began, "Perhaps you gentlemen will yield to the lady."

They nodded their acquiescence.

Lisa took a deep breathe. "Just who was that man?"

Gerhardt instinctively understood that she wasn't inquiring

about his name. "Lisa, that man is in charge of the local Gestapo. He assumed command yesterday when his commander was killed."

"But what is his relationship to you?"

Gerhardt contemplated that one for a moment before he answered, "This is where it gets complicated, Lisa. I am SS and he is Gestapo, but if you look at the Table of Organization, the Gestapo is part of the SS. I, as an SS-General, definitely outrank him, but I am only his nominal superior, and from an administrative standpoint only. The Gestapo is a police organization, and I do not participate in police matters." He looked at her before continuing. "Is any of this making sense to you?"

"Well.....I guess so. I was surprised to find that he would be able to interrogate you like anyone else."

Gerhardt made a face that passed for a half smile. "That is because he **can** interrogate me like anyone else. Being an SS-General doesn't exempt me. For that matter, he can arrest me like anyone else. He had better have a good case, but he can do it. You see, I was party to two crimes committed against the Reich yesterday. The first being the murder of Chief Inspector Zimmel and the second being the escape of the prisoner. He can....in fact.....he **must** interrogate me in order to reconstruct what actually happened, and learn the truth." What remained unsaid was the fact that truth remained an illusive element within the Gestapo organization. Truth was as it was perceived to be, and then it became what it needed to become in order to fit the National Socialist agenda.

Lisa also wondered what the truth was. This man was not the inhuman brute she initially perceived him to be, and yet his mannerism still frightened her at times. He could be tender and loving, and then turn around and become cold and indifferent. Still.....since that day in the park, he had not mistreated her at all. He obviously intended for their arrangement to continue or he would not have given her a room of her own, but how was she going to manage it? She looked at the men who were now engaged in a conversation of their own, and since she wasn't interested, she immersed herself once more in her own thoughts.

In her own mind, she couldn't stay at her parents home and commute back and forth to the mansion on weekends. It would attract attention, and cause people to speculate about that which they knew nothing about. It was better not to give them reason for speculation, but she did not know how to convey that message to Gerhardt?

After about an hour of quiet chatter, Gerhardt looked at Lisa and said, "I think that this light conversation has go on long enough. Come Lisa ......you and I need to have a meaningful conversation."

And so, he took her by the hand and he led her out of the side door into the brilliance of the outside world. There wasn't a cloud in the sky, and Gerhardt had to wonder what had kept them inside for so long. He guided her into the main rose garden where the fountain was located. Here, there were four stone benches equally spaced around the fountain, and Gerhardt motioned for her to have a seat on one of them.

She shook her head first before saying, "No, I would rather stand."

He nodded, but didn't begin speaking right away, and in the absence of the spoken word, she began to think. It had been an interesting weekend. Not one that she would treasure always, but interesting none the less. In fact, this whole situation had been good for her. She was no longer immersing herself in self-pity. Instead, she had allowed her anger to flare at the obstinate arrogance of this SS General. In the end, she accepted it because she had no other options He had threatened the lives of those she loved, and she would **never** forgive him for that. She would peacefully coexist with the man, and sexually gratify him, but she would not forgive him. Now, she wondered what was on his mind?

Her thoughts were his cue to begin speaking, "I am sure that you have already come to the conclusion that I wish to continue *our arrangement.*"

She pursed her lips and replied dryly, "Ja......I gathered that."

He was usually a very proper German General who was the master of the outward form, but this time, he uncharacteristically jammed his hands in his pockets and walked toward the fountain. He had intimidated her once, but he never intended to intimidate her again. *How the hell do I place a gun to her head, and then come at her with words of tenderness and caring. Can a man with a gun ever become a nice person or will he be forever remembered as the man with the gun?*

Suddenly, he whirled about and said, "I need to be more aware of your needs, Mein Schatz (My treasure)." He had a excellent command of the language, and yet.......he was groping for the right words.

She sensed this and part of her was enjoying the spectacle

while the rest of her felt compassion for his difficulties. He cleared his throat. "Maybe it took a bullet in the shoulder, but It finally dawned on me that appearances might be important to you. Very important, and the most important of these appearances **would be the appearance of respectability.** "

She nodded. He was right, but what was the alternative?

"Therefore," he continued, "I recommend that I hire you as my private and confidential secretary, and since you don't have transportation to and from your father's farm, It would be necessary for you and your daughter to move into the mansion." He paused for a moment "This would give you a legitimate reason for being here, and of course, it would naturally give me greater access to you, but I would also grant you the Right of First Refusal."

"What does that mean?" She asked quietly.

"I am a lawyer, and I always seem think in legal terms." He paused momentarily. "To me, it means that I never intend to force myself upon you. (Pause) I want you and the more I know you, the more I want you, but my ability to force myself upon you has its limits." Another pause. "You need your space, and I intend to give you as much as you need."

She just looked at him. His proposal was an answer to her earlier concerns, and it would definitely solve the problem, but more importantly, he was asking.........not telling.

"I don't expect an answer right now." He said as though he had read her mind, and then he added. "Perhaps, you can give me your answer next weekend."

She numbly nodded her head. It was *her* choice, but what if she declined? What then?

He looked at the water that was cascading down the small mountain of rocks in the center of the fountain for the longest time before looking back at Lisa. "You will think about what I said, Lisa?"

She managed a small smile and said, "Ja."

He took her hand, and they returned to the mansion. An hour later, Max drove her back to the farm.

Nine

It all had to start sometime.

Saturday September 2, 1939

Munich

Gerhardt and Lisa were having breakfast alone this morning and Lisa had become pensive. This thing of theirs had been going on for several weeks, and she now had a hard time remembering when Gerhardt had not been a part of her life. She had gotten past the righteous indignation of the beginning, and her life had become one of quiet acceptance. She still bristled occasionally, but she had quit placing herself in the role of a martyr.

If anything, she had been a rebel. A woman who had allowed herself to resent the customs of her community, but she, like everyone else, did not know any better when she was a child growing up. She simply obeyed. It was when she began to read about customs in other lands that she began to dream about true love, and the handsome princes that were associated with true love. She had never dreamed that she would not be allowed to find her true love. Therefore, she had born a real resentment toward her father for insisting that she marry Karl, and yet, it wasn't the German way for parents, especially fathers, to cater to their children. That didn't stop her from resenting her father. Nor did it give her the ability to love her husband.

If anything, it gave her the ability to accept the duality of her existence.

When Gerhardt offered her the position as his secretary, she really didn't have to think about the idea. After all, appearances **were** important. Especially, the appearance of respectability. In truth, living at the mansion did solve a problem for her, and it was nice having her daughter with her, but she didn't want to appear to be too eager.

In truth, her life had become a paradox.

Now that she had found her way into his bed, she had found that she was not a prisoner. In fact, nothing could have been further from the truth. She had been granted the freedom to move about the local Munich area........... within reason, and that was as good as it got for any local German citizen. Checkpoints had been set up in order to restrict travel, and curfews had been established to keep people off the streets at night.

She was free to visit her parents or to go to the market or to a cinema or to a Biergarten or shopping or wherever. She was also free to receive guests at the mansion. The truth was that Gerhardt treated her with the utmost respect, and she couldn't help wondering how a man who could be so cold, distant, and remote some of the time, could be so loving and caring the rest of the time.

Lisa was even enjoying her daughter. She no longer blamed Heidi for being the reason why she was no longer able to have children. Her body had been the reason, but she had been in denial. Now, she calmly accepted the way things were. Of course, it helped considerably when Gerhardt had thought to engage the services of a nanny.

Brigitte Gunderson was a lively young woman not much older than Lisa who had a natural gift of being able to relate to young children. She was unmarried, but she was betrothed to a young man who, like Karl, was in the army.

Then, there was her work.

That was another matter entirely. Being a secretary was something totally new to her, but learning wasn't. She had been totally immersed in learning while Karl was at the university, but she never received a degree for her efforts. She soaked up knowledge like a sponge soaks up water, and now, she approached her job in the same manner. Only, this time, she was being paid for what she did.

Unfortunately, her life was still a contradiction.

She was the product of strict upbringing coupled with four years of having been married to a man who was not her choice. Even now, she was living a life that had been forced upon her., and although the act itself didn't really bother her.......It was what it was. A physical act that resulted in a physical release. There was nothing emotional involved in the process. Most of the time, she enjoyed it, and when she didn't, she always pretended that she did. She had also come to the realization that her rebellious nature could be self defeating if she didn't learn how to control it. That meant that she had to compartmentalize her life by placing Karl in one compartment, and Gerhardt in the other.

The truth of the matter was that she was tired of having things forced upon her. Maybe someday.......she would be able to live the life she wanted to live. In the meantime, she had a better situation than she had at the farm. She had learned to live with it. She would make the most of it.

Suddenly, the door opened and Major Hoffman entered the room with a yellow piece of paper in his hands.

"An important teletype message for you, Herr General."

The General read it and laid it down, his eyes staring off into space. Lisa violated both protocol and security by walking around and reading it for herself.

She shivered inwardly as she read that on September 1st, in response to provocation's brought forth by the Polish government, three Army Groups of the Wehrmacht had crossed the Polish frontier and nothing less than full victory was anticipated. It ended with the terse announcement, "Heil Hitler."

Then, her hands came to her face and she cried, "Karl!" It was an uncharacteristic reaction from a woman who didn't really love the man whose name she had just spoken.

Gerhardt came out of his reverie, bolted to his feet and embraced her, not as a lover but, as a man who was giving comfort to a good friend who was in distress. He read the dispatch one more time and realized the reason for her outcry. Lisa's husband had probably gone in harm's way, and she feared for him.

Without intending to or, for that matter, wanting to, Gerhardt had read one of Karl's letters to Lisa. Karl had spoken of his promotion to Oberlieutenant and his feelings, but more than anything else, he professed his love for the woman he called his wife. The woman who bore his child at great risk to herself. Then, he told her that he loved her more than life itself, and hoped that his love for her might somehow protect him from whatever dangers that awaited him in the unknown world that existed just around the next bend in the road.

He concluded by telling her that it was his fervent hope that someday, she might love him as much as he loved her.

And now Gerhardt held that very same Lisa in his arms. As he did so, he came to an important realization. He now had something in common with Karl Mueller. He too, was in love with Lisa Mueller, and Karl Mueller had a greater right to her than he did.

Lisa broke away from his embrace and tearfully cried, "Oh Gerhardt, what can we do?"

He shrugged helplessly. "I don't know, Lisa. I am certain this is only a preamble to that which is to follow. I am also certain that the Führer will settle for nothing less than the entire European continent. Tomorrow or the next day, Britain and France will declare war upon us, and the domino effect will begin. The iron boot of the Prussian warrior will stomp on anyone not quick enough to avoid being stomped on."

"You're a lawyer, Gerhardt. Is it all legal?"

Gerhardt looked at her strangely as he mouthed the word. "Legal?"

Then he said it again as though it were some unknown word in his vocabulary,

"Legal?"

It took a while before he finally began speaking. "When have legalities ever mattered? The Romans didn't seek legalities when they invaded, pillaged and plundered. Neither did Attilla the Hun, Napoleon or any other invader. Maybe we should ask the American Indians if the Europeans who invaded their homelands bothered to obey their laws?" He shook his head. "No my dear, the German Reich will conquer all that it sees and wants without any consideration to the sovereign rights of those who are indigenous to the countries that are being invaded. Sorry Europe, but you have to move over. Deutschland (Germany) is taking over."

"Oh God!" She cried in exasperation. "Why is this happening now?"

Gerhardt only held her. He had no answers. Only Questions.

* * * * *

The news rolled over Germany like a shock wave. People were not overjoyed at the news, and perhaps in the privacy of their own homes, many reacted the same way Lisa did.

* * * * *

Thursday September 7, 1939

The events of time and circumstances always have ways of turning minor incidents into defining moments, and such a moment was about to happen to Karl Mueller.

The invasion of Poland did not come as a surprise to OberLieutenant Karl Mueller. For example, he knew that the Führer intended to take the Polish Corridor and East Prussia back into the Greater German Reich. By force if necessary. This was the area that had been ceded to Poland after the Great War., but they were ethnic Germans, and Hitler decided they should be part of the Reich once more.

What Poland did or did not do prior to the invasion became a moot point. The invasion had been a pre-planned event, and the only thing that could have forestalled its coming would have been the total capitulation of Poland, and no one saw that as even a remote possibility.

What Poland didn't know was that they were about to be hit by a new kind of warfare. It would be called Blitzkrieg or lightning warfare. It was the combining of air power with fast moving tanks and other armored units. Even the infantrymen were transported in armored personnel carriers called Sud Kampffashrzeugs. These were abbreviated down to SdKfz. In that manner, the infantrymen were able to keep up with the fast moving Panzer regiments.

One of the principal authors of this type of warfare was GeneralOberst Heinz Guderian. He remembered well the stagnation of a protracted war. The Great War had been like that. It resulted in a

German defeat, and Guderian, like so many other senior staff officers, vowed not to let it happen again.

Some members of the High Command who did not like the idea of Blitzkrieg claimed that the flanks were exposed when the Panzers moved too far, too fast. Guderian, who had a quick wit, countered that a fast moving Panzer had no flank. The whole idea was to crush the opponent, and not give him a chance to regroup.

Karl's moment in the sun began almost routinely. He had been placed in charge of a bridging platoon that traveled in two of those SdKfz's while their bridging equipment was being transported on Opel 3 ton trucks. His unit had not been tested under fire yet, but he was confident that it would perform well. Karl might have been a dove at heart, but he was still a German officer and he now wore his rank with pride. He tried to instill that same pride into his men. For some unknown reason, his men liked him. They had adopted the motto, *The hell with it...Just do it!*

For the invasion of Poland, GeneralOberst Guderian took command of the XIX Army-Corps, and Karl's Engineering Battalion went along with him. From Karl's perspective, this war was going to be over very quickly. The High Command had presented Poland as the major opponent they weren't. The lightening assault upon Poland had been designed to keep the Polish armed forces continuously on their heels. They would be unable to dig in defensively and make a stand. Many a Pole tended to look to the heavens for a miracle. Something that might give them some measure of pride.

That was when a suicide squad went to a river and blew the bridge. It's name is not important. Suffice it to say that it was too minor to appear on any maps, but it was deep and wide enough to stop the leading units of the advancing German army column until they could build another bridge, and with Polish sharpshooters picking off the bridge crews, maybe they could delay things for a while.

They were situated on tree covered hill over looking the position where the Germans would be building their bridge. Six Polish sharpshooters had volunteered, and had taken positions in the trees.

The time was mid-day when the radioman interrupted Karl's half slumber with the terse announcement, "The Herr Major wishes to speak with you, Herr Oberlieutenant."

Karl took the radio, and said, "Ja, Herr Major."

The major wasted no time, "Take your platoon to the river directly in front of you, and build a tank bridge. Take the best time you had in practice, and cut it in half, Karl. The Herr General wants it finished by this time yesterday."

Karl sighed and acknowledged his commander and then barked out some orders of his own. Shortly, his platoon had arrived at the river bank.

His Chief Engineer, Oberpioneer Dieter Krenzler, looked at the blown bridge and considered the size of the stream. After a couple of minutes, he said, "No problem, Herr OberLieutenant, I will take care of it. Consider it done." and started barking orders at his men.

As equipment began rolling off the lead truck in the proscribed order, Karl became filled with pride. He didn't know it yet, but his unit was being observed by none other than General Guderian himself.

Soon, the lines had been drawn to the other side and the pontoons were being put in place. The Chief Engineer was standing on one of the pontoons directing the activity when all of the sudden, his body became rigid, and his body turned slightly and fell into the water. The shot was heard a half second later. Karl immediately went into the river after his sergeant, and six other men followed. Karl reached him first and with help from the other men, they got him to the riverbank, but it had all been in vain as the Chief Engineer was dead.

OberLieutenant Mueller was enraged but not enough to do something stupid, and since he had the firepower of the tanks of the XIX Corps behind him, he took the radio and requested that the grove of trees on the small hill be surgically removed from the face of the earth. The ensuing bombardment was so devastating that he didn't think anyone could have survived it, but just as soon it stopped, the snipers seemed to mock the Germans by downing another of his men.

The MP4D sub-machine gun was still laying where his Chief Engineer had dropped it, and an enraged OberLieutenant Mueller picked it up and said, "Heilman, take the first four men you see and go around to rear of that knoll, and to the next three men, he said, "You three, follow me. The rest of you, wait until we get to the other side, and start firing on that hill."

By this time, his men might have followed him to the gates of hell and back as they had just seen their officer dive into the river to rescue the Chief Engineer.

Through his field glasses, General Guderian saw the drama unfolding before him. The engineering officer had lost his Sergeant, tried to rescue him, called in the heavy guns which had failed to remove the snipers, and he was now attempting to take out the snipers on the hill with his own men. Engineers were not infantry, and he could ill afford to lose the engineers. Guderian, a master planner, decided that someone had overlooked the simple fact that engineers would be needing infantry to supply covering fire. It was something he would not overlook in the future.

Karl and his men had reached the other side and fanned out. Karl now realized that he had three regiments of tanks behind him, but no one ever seemed to ever think of the simple things. Besides, he didn't know where his other men had gone.

Karl gave the advance signal and started up the hill at a crouch until a hot poker entered his left shoulder. He immediately lost his footing and rolled several meters downhill.

The private who found him first, put some packing in the wound and wrapped it tightly before saying, "Come, let us get you out of here."

"Do you think they will just let us walk out of here?" Karl asked.

The private apparently hadn't thought about that possibility, and just looked at his officer dumbly.

If it is to be, it is up to me thought Karl through a mind that had become just hazy enough not to be afraid. Then, throwing caution to the winds, he stood up and fired three bursts in to the trees and began his solo assault of the hill. Soon, he was joined by his three comrades and the polish sharpshooters started falling. The two men who were left decided to retreat, and ran into the other group of Germans coming from the rear.

End of skirmish.

It looks like it's over, thought Guderian, and then he saw the lieutenant coming down the hill. The whole left side of his body seemed to be red with blood.

Guderian ordered his driver to advance to the river bank.

When Karl reached the river bank, he saw the Major standing on the other side, and might have deferred to the senior man, but he thought, *the hell with it. It's my job and I'll do it!*

"Achtung! Achtung! Fun's over. Let's get this damned bridge built!"

After that, he passed out.

The same day

Max leaned back in his seat waiting for the Gestapo to complete their inspection of the train. Things were getting old fast, and the war was only a few days old. Max had been summoned to Berlin by the Führer so that he could be decorated for his part in recovering the missing money. To Max, it was a whole lot about nothing. Just another occasion for Hitler to feel important. Not that his Uncle Adolph needed occasions like that in order to feel important. He was, after all, the absolute ruler of the German people.

Max had made this trip from Munich to Berlin and back many times, but this trip was the worst yet. To his way of thinking, it could only get worse.

Then, his eyes focused upon the woman who was sitting in the seat directly across from him. Her name was Ilse Heinrich, and she was a widow who had lost her husband during the *Night of the Long Knives*, an event that occurred on June 30, 1934 when Hitler and his men purged the Sturm Abteilugen otherwise known as the S.A. Of course, the real target of the purge had been Ernst Röhm, the leader of the S.A. and one of the original supporters of Hitler during his rise to the top. His problem was that he didn't have the grace to step aside. He was the original Brown Shirt, and he kept threatening the established authority (namely Hitler) with his power. In this case, Hitler had bent under pressure from the military, and since he wasn't firmly entrenched just yet, he yielded to that pressure and purged the S.A.

According to Ilse, her husband had been targeted for assassination for a reason that she was unwilling to discuss. Unfortunately, regardless of the reason, her husband was just as dead.

She was pretty, but not drop dead beautiful. She wasn't a lump of coal either. Her hair was dark brown with wisps of light brown Her eyes were the required color...... namely blue. Anything other than blue prompted an investigation for the existence of Jewish blood in one's ancestry.

Max and Ilse drifted together at the Berlin train station and just kind of stayed together for the trip. From Ilse's perspective, Max was not only a high ranking SS officer, but he was also a nice looking man. He was also a very nice man, and once again from Ilse's perspective, the word "nice" did not normally apply to an SS officer.

Max smiled at her, and she returned it.. The seat next to her had become vacant, and so Max moved to sit next to her.

"Max?"

He had allowed both his eyes and his mind to wander, and when he heard her speak his name, he focused back on her and said, "Ja?"

"Do you have any idea how many more times we will be checked before we arrive in Munich?" It was a rhetorical question. She didn't expect him to know or, if he did, to impart that information to her.

He only shrugged, "Ach! I wish I knew, Ilse. It seems like we have spent a lifetime on this train."

Actually, she was only making conversation. She didn't really care. They would get there when they got there. The Gestapo had already checked this car, and had a man stationed at each end to make sure no one was able to come or go without their knowing it.

Ilse Heinrich was a twenty-eight year old woman whose angular face beheld a loveliness that made a quiet statement, and Max really did not know how to deal with her.

She had gotten up to walk to the other end of the car and back just for exercise. Without wanting to, he had observed her from the rear, and began to realize just how well put together the woman was. She wore a plaid skirt and a white sleeveless sweater and low heeled shoes. Several men stopped what they were doing and watched her. On the way back, he got a very good look at her bust line as well as her face. She noticed him watching and smiled.

He, like a fool, blushed.

Finally, the car lurched forward and steadily began moving once more. They were underway again. Two hours later, they were rolling through the outskirts of Munich and it looked as though it might be the parting of the ways. Conversation had become strained sometimes simply because Max had not known where he wanted to go with Ilse or, for that matter, if he wanted to go anywhere at all.

Once they finally stopped at the Munich station, he accompanied her off the train and was getting prepared for another of those sticky uncomfortable good-bye's when she surprised him by saying, "We will have to part company here, Max." Then, before he could say anything, she reached into her bag and withdrew a pencil and paper upon which she scribbled some numbers. She handed it to Max, and asked, "Can you read those numbers?" He nodded, and she added, "It is my phone number. Will you call me, please?"

He smiled and said, "Ja. I will call you."

* * * * *

Karl looked at the ceiling that now replaced the canvas roof that he had become accustomed to. He sighed deeply as the doctor entered his room.

"Good morning, Herr OberLieutenant, how do you feel?"

"Sore," was Karl's only response.

"Does that mean you can tolerate visitors?"

Karl looked surprised. Who would be visiting him?

Then the doctor decided to add, "Of course, I wouldn't deny one of the visitors. He is a GeneralOberst (Four Star General). I just came to see if you were awake. I'll send them in."

Them? Karl wondered who the other man was? At that moment, GeneralOberst Guderian walked in accompanied by Major Schmidt. It made Karl wonder who was tending to the war.

General Guderian stepped forward and extended his hand. Karl took it and General Guderian exerted just enough pressure so that Karl knew that his hand was being gripped.

The GeneralOberst said, "I wanted to meet you, Herr OberLieutenant. I observed your actions, and admit they were quite heroic. Unfortunately, they were more of an emotional response as opposed to being well thought out prior to execution."

Karl looked up at his General in amazement. *You are a hero, Herr OberLieutenant. Unfortunately, I am going to court martial your ass right after I pin this fucking medal on it.* That was when training took over. One did not challenge Higher Authority. Not in the German army, one didn't. When it was raining shit, one had best be prepared to smell like shit.

Guderian continued talking, "Again, it is unfortunate that we cannot always control the actions of our soldiers. Some become cowards and run while others, like you for instance, say, `The hell with it,' and charge the angry lion. I admire that characteristic, Herr Oberlieutenant."

Karl was now confused and decided to wait for whatever was coming next.

"Some will say that what you did warranted the Knight's Cross of the Iron Cross while others will say that you were impetuous and got lucky in the process. What say you, Herr OberLieutenant?"

Karl sighed. "Begging the Herr GeneralOberst's pardon, but I will readily admit to being impetuous. That I was, but I did call for tank fire prior to my action. When I found that the snipers had survived the shelling, I saw red. How dare they kill my sergeant and interfere with my work. I am sorry, Herr GeneralOberst."

"Don't be sorry, son." He said as he touched Karl affectionately on the arm. "Pain has a way of educating us, and even though we decorate our heroes, heroism is still classified as a form of insanity. Your not alone though, son. I too, have had my moment of insanity. Fortunately I, like yourself, survived the experience."

He reached for the small box in his jacket pocket and handed it to Karl. "It won't take away your pain, Herr OberLieutenant, but every time you wear it, you will always remember what caused the pain." He opened the box, removed the Knight's Cross and pinned it to his pillow.

"Wear it with pride, Herr OberLieutenant. It signifies that you are the best of the best." He offered his hand one more time. Karl took it, and after the handshake, Guderian left the room.

The Major, who hadn't opened his mouth yet, also shook Karl's hand, and then, he added, "Get well soon, Karl. We miss you." Then, the Major left the room to join his General.

* * * * *

"Karl's coming home, Gerhardt."

"Ja, that I know."

"What should I do? " she asked.

"You should be with your husband," replied Gerhardt sincerely. "I will miss you."

"You want me to be with him?"

"You obviously don't know me yet."

"What does that mean?"

"It means that you should be with your husband, and I will neither object nor will I interfere." He turned as if the subject were closed. She wasn't finished yet.

"You once told me that if I valued the lives of those I loved, I should cooperate with you."

"I said that."

"But, did you mean it?"

"I remember the first night you came to me as though it were yesterday. I also remember deciding that I wasn't going to force you to do anything you didn't want to do."

"But.....you...never...told...me...that."

"You were still willing."

"Only because I decided that it was better to enjoy doing it than hate doing it."

"Are you telling me that you would have left had I given you a choice?"

"Quicker than you can say my name, Herr General."

Her whole attitude took him back, and he looked at her again. This time he looked at her not as a lover, but as a man who failed to look beyond the beautiful woman he had made love to. Lurking within was a real woman. Her basic need was to present the illusion of being a lady, and as long as higher authority had mandated her participation in illicit sexual activity she had become a willing and eager participant. Make it a volunteer effort and she would drop it like a bad habit.

"Very well. Do you wish to stop seeing me.?"

"Jawohl, Herr General" she answered and Gerhardt's heart sunk, but then, he did something he seldom did. He smiled.

"Frau Mueller, I hereby grant you your freedom, but there is something that you need to know and understand. You and I, Mein Schatz, are from the same cut of the cloth. We know and understand each other far more than we know and understand anyone else on this planet. So far, our relationship has been a combination of the carnal and the practical, but I have not enlisted you as my love slave. We have gone from the confining aspects of the Third Reich to the unlimited aspects of our senses, and we have yet to find out where our sensual limits are located if, in fact, they exist at all. You can walk away from that, but can you stay away?"

Lisa just looked at him.

"I needed to get your attention, and I got it the only way I knew how. German officers are supposed to be honorable, and when I coerced you into becoming my mistress, I was not being honorable. I therefore apologize for the anxiety it caused you, and leave it entirely up to you as to whether you wish to renew our relationship after your husband leaves." He paused then for what seemed like an eternity.

"I will leave you now with one final thought.........I care for you more than you can ever imagine, and if I can ever do anything.....anything at all for you, don't hesitate to call upon me."

Her eyes watered as she looked once more at the man who had brought her so much pleasure. There was a real depth of perception to this man and she still had the feeling that somehow they might team up and make a difference to someone. Maybe a lot of someone's.

She resisted the temptation to embrace him. Instead she whirled about and walked purposefully out of the study and out of his life.

Then, something formed in Gerhardt von Leitner's eyes. Something that hadn't been there since he was eight years old.

It was a tear, but there was only one. Only one was capable of forming. Therefore, only one tear could fall.

Ten

The changing face of life.

October, 1939

Munich

The fall chill was definitely in the air as the small crowd of people gathered at the Munich train station. There was even a military band to entertain those who waited with traditional German military marches.

Lisa stood next to her parents. She held Heidi in her arms. She faced what was coming with both pride and trepidation. She was proud of Karl, but he might have just as easily been killed. And, what about her feelings for him? Would they ever improve or would she always be going through the motions? She had decided one thing though......She would get through this life the best way she knew how, and she would never divorce him. He might end up divorcing her, but she would not divorce him.

Suddenly, a train appeared and before she knew it, the train had come to a halt. People began spilling out of the cars and many of them looked in surprise at the assembly of people that were waiting.

Then, he appeared.

Karl Mueller, wearing the field gray uniform of an officer in the German army, stepped down the steps to the platform, and broke into a big grin. At the same time, Lisa took her daughter, and literally ran to his waiting arms...correct that, arm (singular as the left arm was still in a sling).

It was quite a scene as husband, wife, and daughter all embraced tearfully before the assembled body which now included SS General Gerhardt von Leitner. He had arrived quietly without fanfare, and remained at the edge of the small crowd. In truth, he was uneasy with the knowledge that the only people who actually knew the lieutenant were his wife, daughter, and his wife's parents. The rest of this group had been organized by the SS at the behest of the propaganda minister. Such was the nature of this group that now ran Germany. They feared any crowd not controlled by them and the crowds feared them.

Motion picture cameras recorded the event for propaganda purposes, and within a few minutes, the whole event would pass into history.

Gus and Anna had already gone to the truck, leaving Karl and Lisa to meander on their own. Gerhardt was tempted to approach them, and congratulate him, but Gerhardt now saw the man as a competitor, and that would never do.

Besides, Karl Mueller still had proprietary rights to the woman, and that made Gerhardt von Leitner the interloper. Gerhardt returned to his car unseen by either Lisa or her husband.

Max, now wearing the uniform of an SS Standartenführer, had come to stand by his side and immediately felt an empathy for the man. It had to be terrible to be on the outside looking in, but Max had to admit that the Law of Cause and Effect was an absolute that lacked moral judgment. It reacted to both good and evil with equal discernment.

Gerhardt, who had used fear to gain advantage and favor with the lady, was now paying the price. The cause which has not had its effect was an event not yet completed, and it must be completed for that is the Law. Max Liebert was a very deep thinker.

As he returned to the car, his chauffeur opened the door and the General got in, followed by Max.

"Back to the mansion, Fritz

"Jawohl, Herr General."

* * * * *

Karl spent a total of six weeks at home which was an eternity for the young officer, and he tried not to waste any of it. He loved his wife and he loved his daughter, and even though he knew that Lisa didn't really love him, she was careful not to show that side of her nature.

Karl had developed a greater need for the sexual side of marriage and Lisa had been only too happy to accommodate him. She now needed that part of Karl. Perhaps, more then any other part.

A friend of her father's owned a cabin on Lake Starnberger, and he loaned it to the couple. It became well used during the six weeks.

The one thing that hadn't been discussed was her relationship with General von Leitner. Essentially, Karl didn't have a need to know. Perhaps, no husband ever had a need to know that his wife was having an affair.

Ignorance could be bliss.

Karl had his feelings and suspicions. He wasn't stupid. He had suspected that something might have been between Lisa and Isaac when he stayed with them, but he also realized that without something concrete to go on, he would have been chasing shadows.

This time, there were only vague innuendoes and references that were made during the course of conversations, but the Germany he had been born into was gone and had been replaced by Hitler's Germany. People who normally gossiped, now did so with great care. People were more apt to keep their nose to the grindstone, and not concern themselves with what their neighbors were doing or not doing.

The fact that Lisa now lived at the headquarters of an SS General, was something that Lisa had informed him about, but it was only a brief comment in a letter, and the sentence immediately following had been deleted by the censor. He wanted to know more, but Lisa told him that very little could be said because of the confidential nature of her work.

That frustrated Karl, but there was little he could do about it. He wasn't even sure if he could tell her not to go back to this General after his leave was over. On the plus side, she was more relaxed now. She was even a better lover which meant that maybe he should count his blessings and not ask silly questions.

Of course, some people would gossip regardless of who might be in control, and he had heard rumors. Things that were said when he was in listening range of a conversation. People talked about beautiful women who were known to consort with high ranking officers and government officials. Karl didn't do anymore than listen at the time, but it did manage to register, and if these people were talking about his Lisa, Karl was relatively certain that she would not have entered into that kind of relationship voluntarily.

Other than that, he didn't concern himself with suspicions. If Lisa had been experiencing the affections of another man, it wasn't affecting their personal relationship in a negative manner. Instead, she had become an aggressively passionate woman. Maybe he should thank that other man, if he existed at all.

Now, it was mid-November and they were standing on the platform at the Munich train station once more. The train was about to pull out and Karl had already said his good-bye's to Gus and Anna. He would have liked to have held his daughter in his left hand while holding his wife with his right, but alas, his left shoulder was still tender although he had discarded his sling. Therefore, he had held Heidi close to him for several long moments before putting her down and reaching for Lisa.

"My heart will ache for you, Lisa."

"As will mine for you, Karl."

That was when Karl took their last minutes together to a new level of honesty. "Lisa, I have always loved you more than you have loved me. I know that and I accept it. I just want you to know that I appreciate the time we have spent together, and hope that we will spend a lot more time together."

She looked at him affectionately and placed her hand on his cheek. "Life is an illusion, Mein Liebe. It is only what we perceive it to be. Be not dismayed by what you see or should happen to hear. Things can always happen but they are not really real nor do they have to be permanent. Understand only that, in my own way, I do love you, and if we should ever separate permanently, it will have to be you who separates us, for I shall never leave you."

Karl looked at her strangely for the longest time before he kissed her hungrily. The train whistle blew for the final time, and Karl jumped on board as the train began to move.

He watched as she receded from view but the taste of her lips lingered and her words still rang in his ears. This time, it would be hard to stay away from her, but if he did manage to come home and surprise her, what might he find?

Lisa purposefully walked down the platform to a pay telephone. She dialed a number and waited. She didn't have to wait long.

"Ja?" The voice belonged to Gerhardt.

"Do you still want me?"

"Does the sun still rise in the east?"

"I will be at the farm."

"I will send Fritz," he answered, and they both hung up.

As she returned to her father's truck, a strange feeling came over her. She had just gone from being a conscript to being a volunteer.

* * * * *

Max made a mad dash from his car to the front door of the bakery. He was trying to keep from getting soaked. As he arrived at the door, it opened and he almost collided with the woman who was coming out just as fast as he was going in.

He stepped back immediately and upon seeing who it was, he exclaimed, "Ilse!"

She registered as much surprise as he did, and then, she exclaimed, "Max!"

They just stood there, half in and half out of the bakery shop. He was standing in the rain, and she was standing in the shelter of the doorway. Somehow they seemed to be frozen in place, each staring into the eyes of the other.

From inside the shop, a male voice could be heard, "The next time someone wants to know if my son knows enough to come in out of the rain, how should I answer?"

That broke the spell, and Ilse stepped back thus allowing Max to enter the shop. He answered his father by saying, "You may tell whoever might be inquiring that not only does your son not know enough to come in out of the rain, he doesn't even know which end is up."

At that moment, Fritz Liebert came around the counter and embraced his son. It was a totally non-Bavarian thing to do, but Fritz

Liebert took special pains not to do what was expected of him. Max had visited his father several times since his return from Berlin and each time, his papa greeted him like a long lost son. Max had long since ceased to be embarrassed by his papa's actions. He was thankful that he still had a papa who could hug him.

Ilse stood watching the scene that played out in front of her with a strange fascination. She had been a customer of Herr Liebert's since her return from Berlin, and she had never placed Herr Liebert and Max Liebert together as perhaps being father and son. Maybe it was because Herr Liebert was a fun loving man who loved to joke and tell funny stories and Max seemed to be a typically stiff SS officer. Nice.......but stiff.

Max remembered that Ilse was supposed to be standing there and turned around to make sure she hadn't walked out. For some reason, that had become very important to him, and he noted with relief that she was still standing in the same place.

Fritz backed off and he too looked at Ilse. "Tell me Frau Heinrich, do you know my son, Max?"

She blushed slightly. "Ja? I met him on the train from Berlin."

"Ach! You didn't tell me you had made the acquaintance of such a lovely lady."

'Er..." Max began with a stammer, and Ilse interrupted his train of thought with an accusing statement, "You didn't call me."

Max also became red faced, "I-er-ah."

"Spit it out, Max," Fritz interrupted. "Did Frau Heinrich ask you to call her?"

"Ja, but...."

"But nothing! Did you tell her that you would call her?"

Ilse, not wanting to cause a rift between father and son, protested, "Please......Herr Liebert, if Max doesn't wish to call me.....?

"That doesn't matter, Frau Heinrich. I raised Max to be polite and considerate. If he doesn't keep his promises, he is being neither polite nor considerate."

The shock of the last few minutes had finally subsided and Max finally got it together. "Papa?" He said....his voice firm and even. "I love you but I don't need an arbiter. I might need a keeper, but I don't need an arbiter." Ilse almost laughed at his humor, and Max continued, "What I would like to do is take Frau Heinrich someplace where I can apologize to her, and if she will forgive me, maybe we can have a meaningful conversation."

"Good," his father replied. "I will see you when you come back....whenever that might be."

Max didn't bother to ask Ilse if she wanted to go anywhere with him, but when he offered her his hand, she took it. The rain had let up some when they got outside and Max guided her to his car. He opened the door and she got in. As soon as they were underway, Ilse said, "I accept your apology, but why didn't you call me?" She knew that she had been much too forward, but she had felt the need to be forward with this man. More importantly, she felt the need to be with this man.

Max didn't drive far. Maybe only a couple of blocks, and then, he pulled into a parking place, and turned off the engine. He looked at her appraisingly, and said, "Indeed, why didn't I call you?"

"No fair. I asked first."

"I don't know why. I just know that I didn't." The truth was that he thought about calling her several times, but lack of courage stood as his primary reason for not doing it. Dare he tell her that?

Her face became quite serious now. "Max, I am sorry that I am putting you on the spot about doing something you obviously didn't want to do. I guess I wanted something out of you that you don't want to give." She paused long enough to search his face for something. Instead, she saw nothing. "I am guilty of trying to force a relationship, and I have been told that trying to force a relationship is like pushing a string. It just doesn't work." She shook her head with the last statement and her eyes began to water. "Damn!"

Max knew exactly why he hadn't called her. First of all, he was smitten with a woman he couldn't have, and because of that, he had excluded all others. Secondly, he now wore the uniform of an SS officer, and an involvement with him might suck her into all of the nefarious activities of the SS. It would be the splatter effect. Finally, he didn't deserve her............or did he? It was her idea to give him her phone number, and he had been willing to bet that he would never see her again had it not been for their chance meeting in his papa's bakery......if....it was a chance meeting. If it wasn't a chance meeting, that would mean that forces outside of two of them were involved in this undertaking. Maybe it was meant to be, and if it was, he had to explain a few things to her.

"Illse, I feel the need to explain something to you, and when I am finished, you will need to decide if I am still worth the effort," and he spent the next forty-five minutes explaining "things" to her. At the end of his dissertation, he smiled weakly at her and said, "That is it, Mein Schatz (my treasure)"

It warmed her to have him refer to her in this manner. She finally admitted that she had fallen in love with Max Liebert from the first moment she saw the man and yet, she hadn't even admitted it to herself until that very moment, and if he wasn't in love with her, she could accept that. She would try not to be bothered by the fact he was infatuated with another woman. A married woman. A woman that he couldn't have even though this General......General von Leitner didn't seem to be bothered by her marital status. Not in the least! This only meant that Max had character enough to leave her alone......a fact that only served to intensify the feelings that she felt for the man. He was waiting for her to say something.

"Thank you for telling me, Max. I don't feel quite so rejected."

He placed his hand on her shoulder, and spoke softly, "You don't have to feel rejected at all, because I haven't rejected you. I only felt uneasy about moving closer to you. Perhaps, you are God's gift to me."

"I didn't know that you believed in God."

"I'm not sure I do, Ilse. Part of me still holds fast to the idea that maybe we are the ones who created God in the first place, but the better part of me realizes that there might be a God in the Universe. Perhaps, it is the perception of this God that we are responsible for."

"Very interesting," was her only comment. It was only a passing interest on her part. Nothing that she wanted to pursue any further....not right that minute anyway. She really shouldn't have pursued the matter at all. She wasn't interested in what form God took or why.

"So what do you wish to do, Max?"

"I would like to get to know you better, and see where it goes from there."

Now, we are getting someplace. "How do you propose doing that?" She asked.

"Why don't I start by taking you to dinner tonight, unless, of course, you have something else planned."

She smiled a very relaxed smile. One that lit up the interior of the automobile. "I would be delighted to have dinner with you tonight, Max, but rather than go out and spend money, why don't we have a quiet dinner at my apartment. Do you feel comfortable going there?"

He was silently thankful for what was happening within him, and he answered her by saying, "I am quite comfortable being with you. I would like it to become habit forming."

She responded by moving closer to him, and he responded by placing his arm around her shoulders and drawing her even closer. She did not resist, and the kiss that followed was as natural as the two people who were doing the kissing. It wasn't a long kiss but it did pave the way for the others that would follow. They were finding sweetness and light in a world that could be a very dark and dangerous place to live.

* * * * *

Illse's apartment was only a short walk from his father's bakery, and since the rain had stopped completely, Max parked his car, and paused long enough to tell his papa that he was going to Ilse's for dinner. His papa was overjoyed. It was about time his son paid attention to the opposite sex. For that matter, it was long past time for his son to be married. He would pray to God that his son didn't mess this thing up. Max took Ilse's hand in his and off they went.

Ilse's apartment was an easy walk up to the second floor. When they arrived at her door, she fumbled nervously with the key. Max finally took it from her and opened the door. She was red faced.

He held her key up and she took it. "I'm sorry Max. I don't know what came over me."

Max smiled at her and said nothing in reply. Once inside, Max also became nervous. It was then that he decided to bury a ghost if such a thing were possible. "Ilse, I wish to understand something, and I need your help in order for that to happen."

Ilse looked at him warily, but said, "If I can, I will."

"On the train, you told me that your late husband was a casualty of *The Night of the Long Knives*, but you declined to elaborate. I can understand that line of reasoning if I were only a casual acquaintance, but I appear to be more than that." He paused long enough to allow that to sink in. "That be the case, Liebchen, would you do me the honor of telling me why he was marked for assassination?"

Tears came to her eyes, but she did not cry. She swallowed hard and began. "Karl was one of the original Brown Shirts. He was close to both Hitler and Röhn, but only in a professional sense. He didn't like either man, but felt that Germany's destiny might be in their hands. You might say that he was very loyal to the cause, but he resented Hitler's decision, once he became Führer, to cast aside men like Röhn and the SA in favor of Himmler and the SS." Her eyes were quite dry now. And a new resolve seemed come over her.

"We didn't know that Hitler was planning to purge the SA, even though repeated warnings had been directed to the men of the SA and Röhn in particular. I had warned Karl, but like most males, he considered my warnings to be no more than the ravings of a hysterical female, and he totally discarded them. Therefore, on what has become known as *The Night of the Long Knives*, Karl and I were home. I remember being in the kitchen when there was a knock upon our door. Karl told me that he would answer the door, and I didn't think anymore about it until I heard the shots. I believe there were three of them. That brought me running to the sound of the shots like the fool that I am. Lucky for me, the assassin had already left, but in his wake, Karl's body lie in a pool of blood. On the floor beside him was a note telling me that Karl Heinrich was not only a traitor to the Reich, but was also a practicing homosexual. The note also told me that this method was a better alternative to the public disgrace of a trial, and that I should be thankful that my life had been spared."

"When I became a widow, my parents wanted me to return home, but I was an adult and not inclined to return to my papa's authority. They were unhappy with my decision, but were glad that I escaped the fate that visited my husband."

Max was aghast.

"I'm sorry, Ilse. I don't know what else to say except to

repeat that I am sorry."

"Danke schön, Max.

Max took a deep breath. He had stayed away from the matter of Ernst Röhn, but he was curious about the tendencies of Karl Heinrich. "You were his wife, Ilse. Do you believe he was a homosexual?"

"It came as a complete surprise. I found out later that it wasn't really true, but, at the time, I didn't have that information. I had to deal with it, and I felt shame. I felt that Karl and I had a normal enough relationship. We weren't really in love, but we got along reasonably well."

"You weren't in love?"

"Nein."

"Why did you marry him?"

"It was an arrangement between our parents."

"Ach! I did not know that," he replied. Then added, "Where are you from?"

"Here."

Max shook his head and swallowed hard. She, like he, was a Bavarian and in Bavaria arranged marriages were not only customary, but legally enforceable. His own father did not believe in such things, and for that matter, Max himself did not believe in them. Perhaps, that was why he was still unmarried.

"If you were to get married again, would you like to do it for love this time?"

"Ja! I would like that very much." There was no shame in what she had revealed. Instead, her eyes gleamed. She had allowed herself to hope that she might just have a relationship with this man, but she now knew that Max needed to know the kind of woman she was if she was to have any kind of relationship with him at all, but that would come later.....if she could muster enough courage.

Max smiled and Ilse said, "I invited you to dinner. Perhaps, I had better prepare one."

He nodded and she retreated to the kitchen.

She kept forgetting that food was rationed, but performed wonders with small portions of meat, dumplings, and potatoes with apple strudel for dessert.

"You are a wonderful cook, Ilse.

She beamed and he started to help her clear the table.

She looked alarmed and said, "Nein! Nein! Please go sit down. I will finish."

Max understood, and met her alarm with a smile. A nice loving smile. One that Ilse had never experienced before. "I want to help you because I want to be with you, and I can't be with you while I am sitting in the living room waiting for you to finish. Besides, it doesn't make me any less of a man because I desire to help you."

She walked over and gave him a long, enticing kiss. It took him completely by surprise, because it invited intimacy and spoke of things to come. He was exhilarated by the warmth of her presence. Her smell! The essence of her being. They worked well together, and the male invasion of a previously exclusive feminine domain no longer bothered her. Soon the last of the dishes had been washed, dried and placed in its proper place..

She poured them each a cup of coffee and they retired to the living room. It was time to talk but Ilse still lacked courage, so they engaged in small talk. After about thirty minutes, Ilse looked him and said, "Max, I need to tell you something else. Something very important." She sat on the couch while he occupied the soft easy chair across the room from her.

He looked at her strangely, but said nothing.

She started out slowly and softly, "My husband's death did not pay the price for his disgrace. I did." She paused then for what could have been called, a dramatic pause and then she continued. "I received a letter, a train ticket to Berlin and some money. The money was definitely welcome, and the letter was on the official stationary of the Housing Ministry.

After reading it, I realized that the letter was a summons and not a request. More troubling yet was the fact that it didn't state the reason for my summons, and since I did not wish to return to the authoritarian rule of my parents, I took its arrival as a reprieve. You see, Karl's death left me in a financial vacuum, and I was ready to return home." She sighed heavily. "I also bore the shame of his homosexuality alone, because I hadn't mentioned it to either his parents or mine."

She went on to tell him about an affair that lasted just a little over four years with a man who had been well placed in the Nazi

Party. A man she had met during the early years. A man who had finally decided he must have her at all costs, and he wanted her bad enough to make sure that Karl Heinrich was on the list of those to be disposed of.

She called him Otto, but she also told Max that Otto wasn't his real name. When she first met him, he took her to dinner, and told her that the Party had no interest or desire in creating problems for the families of Party members who required discipline, and because of that, provisions had been made. She would be provided with an apartment, ample ration coupons, and a position in the Housing Ministry. She was grateful to Otto, but she didn't yet know just how far that gratitude had been expected to extend.

She blended into life as a Berliner, and it was almost three weeks before she heard from Otto again. It was dinner again. This time, at one of Berlin's finer night clubs. Otto even bought her a nice gown for the occasion. By this time, it had become very apparent that Otto had a eye for her. She was also attracted to the man enough to accept his overtures. What she did not plan for was the full extent of those overtures. The full extent being that she was seduced, not once but several times by Otto. Each time it happened, she felt as though she might be consorting with the devil and yet she had become unable to resist the man. The woman who had been raised as a strict Roman Catholic became unable to discern between license and constraint, and she finally ended up attempting suicide, but she chose sleeping pills and was discovered by Otto who rushed her to the hospital.

Otto knew her religious beliefs, and had used them against her. Suicide was a mortal sin. Homosexuality was also a mortal sin. Should she not cooperate with him, he would have made public the sins of Karl Heinrich, and she would have suffered public disgrace. At that point, she surrendered completely, and the days turned into weeks that turned into months which turned into years until he finally found himself in trouble too deep to weather the storm and ended up sticking a Luger into his own mouth and pulling the trigger.

Ilse couldn't have wished for a more fitting end for such a vile and evil man. He had one redeeming quality. That being a confession that he was the one who had marked Karl for death. He had also fabricated the charge of homosexuality against Karl.

She didn't elaborate about the intensity of the affair except to say that Otto had an enormous sexual appetite. Max didn't have to guess what she was talking about. His imagination was perfectly capable of picking it up and going from there.

Max listened intently to what she was telling him and doing so with a strange clinical sense of detachment. Max was not a moralist and therefore rendered no moral judgments. He was interested only in what she was right then and not what she had been before he came into her life.

The crux of her story was based on the age old story of what happened to women who were subjugated under the iron boot of authority. If he were to reject her, it might have a devastating affect, but he was a Bavarian male, and men like him were more likely to reject her as not.. She was therefore taking a tremendous risk.

No....He was not like a lot of Bavarian men. He would not reject her, but he was perceptive enough to realize that four years was a long time to be engaged in something that one utterly despised. No, that wasn't it. He believed that Otto was not a very nice man, but it wasn't the man. It was what he did to her and for her. Strange, he thought, that she was able to detest a man while savoring the affect he had upon her. It would have been extremely paradoxical. The next item that Max's orderly mind processed was what she might not be telling him. Namely, that there might have been others or at least one other man. He decided that he would not press her about that issue. Perhaps someday, she would tell him, but until then, he would be satisfied with what she had shared.

Therefore, the sum total of her disclosure was that she was an experienced lover. Was that bad? The sexual union was one aspect of human behavior that left no apparent physical scars. Emotional scars, maybe, Therefore, a man's search for feminine purity had to be based upon how he perceived her.

Men often sought women of purity when they married, but sought the tarnished variety when the time came for wild oats to be sowed. His Masters thesis in philosophy had been entitled *The Eve Syndrome*, and it dealt with the two factors that were absolutely necessary for Christianity to work as a religion regardless of how it was being presented.

Namely, the existence of an Evil Force i.e. Satan AKA the Devil. The second factor was The Fall from Grace, and virtually everyone knew that the Serpent induced Eve to eat of the Forbidden Fruit in direct violation of an injunction given by the Lord God himself.

The next thing she did was convince Adam that he should share the guilt by partaking of the Forbidden Fruit himself, and being the prototype for all gullible males that followed, set himself up by doing what she asked him to do. When God found out, Eve did everything but claim responsibility for her actions, and ended up paying the price in a rather big way. In the process, she pulled Adam down with her.

In any respect, that was the story that gave Christian leaders the elements needed to convince the faithful that God had a plan of salvation, and every time Max looked at this plan, it reminded him of a bad melodrama. *Good God! Do people really believe this nonsense?*

That brought him to the part of his thesis that was germane to the issue at hand. All women had been affected by the actions of their earliest ancestor, and were greatly inhibited by the influences that society had placed upon them. Max then conducted a study that included all women on campus who would fill out a anonymous questionnaire and return it to him. He remembered that he had been overwhelmed by the response. Perhaps, young German women were sick and tired of the chest beating of their brothers. After all, they had lost the Great War. You would have thought that they had won the damned thing.

Anyway, he had used their responses to expand on the theory that virtually **all** women had hidden desires that, given the proper stimulus, would be acted upon. They were all sexual in nature, and when a woman didn't have to identify herself, she could be quite explicit.

Now....as he looked at the lady herself, he might have been looking at one of the women who filled in one of his questionnaires. Was she beautiful? Was she pretty? What was she? Was it fair to say that she was "almost pretty? He knew that looks did not necessarily create the feminine allure, but they factored into the equation. . No, he reasoned, the male attraction to her was really quite simple. Those who were attracted to her might just go to any length to have her, and in the process, she would be able to become her *Secret Self.*

He could well understand how this Otto person would have resorted to almost anything in order to have her. For that matter, *he* was attracted to her. In truth, the longer he was in the same room with her, the more he wanted her.

Isle was observing the blank expression on Max's face and having misgivings about telling him anything at all. It was a lot for a man to understand, but she reasoned that it was better to tell him than have him find out later......if there was to be a later for them. She was about to break the eerie silence when Max cleared his throat.

A half smile then came to his face as he said, "Why are you such an easy woman to love?" The question startled Ilse. For that matter, it even startled Max.

"Er....what was that?"

"I just wondered why you were so easy to love. Don't you know that you are the paragon of virtue in the eyes of any man who loves you? I am grateful that you chose to tell me, but it doesn't change the way I feel about you."

"I don't know what to say, Max........." and then she allowed her words to drift into nothingness as she found herself in his arms.

Max, being a true genius, found it difficult to be forward with a woman. One of his philosophy professors had actually tested his IQ and found that it was so high that so-called normal people might tend to distrust him. He was therefore advised to act as normal as possible. A couple of months later, he found that he could be quite normal where the opposite sex was concerned. Now, he was finding that he was quite capable of falling in love with a woman without attempting to analyze it.

His lips met with hers and he marveled at all the things that were happening within him as a result of that singular contact.

"Do you mind?" he asked.

She swallowed hard and replied, "Nein...of course not. I want you to."

"Mien Schatz (my treasure), I too, have had some experiences with a woman, but I have never been married, or for that matter, engaged to be married. I have three college degrees and one of them is a Masters. I have an extremely high IQ which pleases Uncle Adolph, but he still thinks he is smarter than me, and that pleases him. One should never be smarter than one's Führer, and for the record, I do address our leader as *Uncle Adolph*, but he is not my real uncle. It's a long story that I will tell you someday when we have nothing more pressing on our agenda."

Ilse's eyes sparkled with the realization that Max was moving forward and didn't seem to be stumbling and tripping over her past. He was now seated beside her and she was in his arms.

The only reason that she shared her past with Max was to accelerate things dramatically. He would have either gotten up and walked out in disgust or taken her in his arms, and from her point of view, it was worth the gamble.. If she were to have a life with Max, she didn't know if they would have days, weeks, months or years? If they only had days, there was no time to waste. They had to get started right away, and if they were to be blessed with weeks, months or even years, they would still be glad they didn't waste any time.

Max had just placed his left hand softly on her right cheek and caressed it gently. "Ilse," he whispered softly, "As smart as I am, I don't understand what has come over me. Maybe I can see all the way to your soul, and if what I feel is really and truly love, then I love you." Further talk then became unnecessary. Except the question he found time to ask her. The one she eagerly said "yes" to.

He didn't want to waste any time either.

* * * * *

The next afternoon, they drove to The Mansion, and Ilse was quite impressed when she found out how the other half lived. Max pulled into a parking space near the side door and went around to open the door for Ilse. She made no attempt to hide how she felt about Max. If anything, their night together served to prove an important point. That Max Liebert was a very special man indeed.

Max still hadn't sorted everything out. He only knew that his place was with her.

When they approached the side door, they were greeted by Erik Halder, the butler.

"Good day.......Herr Standartenführer. It is good to see you." Herr Halder was still trying to discern the variations of attire having been worn by Herr Liebert. He had gone from being an SS Sergeant to a civilian and was now wearing the uniform of an SS

Standartenführer (Colonel). Max had never bothered to explain it.

"And a fine day it is, Erik." He placed his right arm around the small waist of Ilse and proudly stated, "Allow me to present, Frau Ilse Heinrich. Ilse, this is Erik Halder, our butler."

Erik clicked his heels in classic Prussian style and bowed from the waist up, "The pleasure is mine, Frau Heinrich."

She curtsied and blushed at the same time. "The privilege is mine, Herr Halder." Herr Halder nodded again. *What a lovely woman* He thought. *And there is absolutely no doubt about how she feels about Max. He is a lucky man indeed."*

Max swallowed hard at the scene he had just witnessed. Without knowing anything about what Erik was thinking he too had come to the conclusion that he was a very lucky man. *Ach du lieber...Ist gut, ja?*

"Is the Herr General in residence?"

"Ja," answered Erik. "I believe he is in the rear parlor."

"Danke," Max said and then inquired, "And Frau Mueller? Is she also in residence?"

"Ja," replied Erik. "I believe she is in the third floor nursery with her daughter."

"Ach!" replied Max. "Then, we shall pay our respects to the Herr General first. Perhaps then, the lovely Lisa will have decided to join us." They removed their coats, handed them to Erik and started in the direction of the rear parlor.

* * * * *

Gerhardt was seated on a couch reading when Max and Ilse entered the parlor. He looked up first in surprise and then he showed pleasure. After that, he showed the breeding of a gentleman by rising in honor of the lady's presence.

"Ach! Max my friend, it is good to see you, and I see you are accompanied by a lovely member of the fairer sex."

Max was in full uniform while Gerhardt was wearing a pair of black slacks and a white dress shirt that was open at the collar. Ilse was wearing a plain navy blue dress and medium blue heels. With the gleam in her eye, she presented a very pretty picture indeed. Max took her hand and closed the distance between the two of them and

Gerhardt.

"Gerhardt, I would like to present Frau Ilse Heinrich. Ilse, I present the Herr General Gerhardt von Leitner."

Ilse extended her hand and it was taken by Gerhardt who bowed deeply and kissed the lady's hand.

To her, he said, "It is an honor and a privilege, gnädige frau (Gracious Lady)."

A blush came to her face as she replied, "I too, am honored to know you, Herr General."

"Max," Gerhardt began, "You are to be complimented in your choice of women." Ilse blushed again as Gerhardt continued. "And where, pray tell, did you manage to find her?"

"We found each other, Gerhardt, but had it not been for the persistence of this lovely lady, we might never have gotten together. Now, as I stand in the presence of you, and the blessed object of my affection, I tell you truly that I love this woman." Max took her hand and she glowed as she had never glowed before in her life. Gerhardt observed this spectacle with a certain amount of awe. NO woman had ever looked at him like Ilse was now looking at Max.

At that precise moment, Lisa entered the parlor and beheld the spectacle as well.

"Max!" Lisa exclaimed happily, and Max walked over and embraced her vigorously. Then, he proceeded to introduce her to Ilse. Once, the introductions had been made, Max and Gerhardt took their leave, leaving Lisa and Ilse to get acquainted.

Max and Gerhardt walked to his study. Gerhardt closed the door, and turned to face Max.

"Lovely lady, Max."

"Ja, that she is. Very lovely indeed." He placed his hands together in the small of his back, and walked over to the window to watch the last of the leaves wrestle free of the force that bound them to the trees and float softly to the ground. It was a gray overcast day with a threat of rain.

Max turned to face Gerhardt, "It is always nice to hear one's lady being complimented for her looks. It tells us that we chose well, and that others approve of our choice. That would be good if I were looking for approval which I am not. I love Ilse for all of the really important reasons and the way she looks is way down on the list of things I consider to be really important."

"Max," Gerhardt began in protest, but Max waved his hand to silence him. Max could do that with Gerhardt, and he could also do it with Adolph Hitler. Max was that kind of man. He had the force of personality that would actually surprise people because they weren't offended by the action. He would have been the perfect politician. It was too bad Max Liebert wasn't the Führer. The world would have been saved a lot of pain, but the world had never heard of Max Liebert while that very same world would never forget the name of Adolph Hitler.

"Gerhardt.....I am not rebuking you. After all, you are only human. You see only the packaging without knowing the nature of the contents, and that is the way it is supposed to be in polite society. I, on the other hand, know the nature of the contents and like what I see and what I have found. I like what I feel. I like what I know."

At this point, Max paused momentarily, and then he spoke, his voice clear and strong without being loud. "Gerhardt.....I wish to marry Ilse."

The man who could command leaders with a solitary gesture, had learned how to ask, and Gerhardt considered his request. Of course, Max and Ilse could marry, but they had to meet the requirements of the Reich first. On the other hand, could it be that his friend was being premature?

"This is rather sudden is it not, Max?"

Max snapped to attention and replied, "You are NOT the one who should be questioning sudden impulses, Herr General." There was a decided edge to his voice and his eyes had changed from sky blue to steel gray in the space of a single heartbeat

Gerhardt nodded. "Touché. Your point is well taken, Herr Standartenführer."

"Danke schön, Herr General," Max said with a slight bow. The edge in his voice was still present.

"Bitte schön," The general replied with a nod.

"Where were we?" Max asked. The edge had now left his voice.

Without hesitation, Gerhardt replied, "We were discussing the upcoming marriage of SS Standartenführer Max Liebert to Frau Ilse Heinrich. Nice couple.....Do you know them?"

"Only by reputation, Gerhardt. I have not had the pleasure yet." The bad moment had passed.

"When would you like to marry?"

"Just as soon as we clear the obstacles, and gain permission."

"Have you considered that The Führer might wish to come to your wedding, Max?"

"Nein! Our marriage will be a simple affair, and the Führer's presence could turn it into a state sponsored circus. Besides, Ilse has been married before, and given the circumstances of her husband's death, certain people might not be welcome at her wedding. If need be, I'll simply go to Berlin and explain the facts of life to him."

Gerhardt began to chuckle and shook his head in amazement, "You are something else, Herr Liebert. No one else in the entire Reich would have guts enough to do that, and you would *simply go to Berlin and explain the facts of life to him."* Gerhardt wanted to ask about the circumstances of her husband's death, but he didn't want to upset Max again.

Maybe Max read his mind, because he voluntarily gave Gerhardt a brief resume of the last ten years of Ilse's life, and Gerhardt listened thoughtfully. When Max finished, Gerhardt told him, "I'll simply request her file. It will tell us if she has any problems. Unless she turns out to be politically unreliable, her only problem would be the existence of Jews in her family tree."

Max shook his head. "I inquired about that, and her family is very catholic."

"Very well," Gerhardt said. "We shall see what we shall see. In the meantime, she could move in here without a *Certificate of Fitness to Marry.* It is one of the benefits of *Lebersborn.*

"Danke, Gerhardt, but I am not interested in pollination. Ilse is quite enough for me. "

Gerhardt nodded in agreement. "Very well. Let us now return to the ladies."

* * * * *

When they returned to Ilse's apartment that night, they were a couple. They belonged together, but if Ilse had not had her experiences, it would have been awkward. The passion level this evening was every bit as high as the previous evening, but this time, no questions had to be asked, no explanations given, and the talk that would be generated by her neighbors about the SS officer who came to the young lady's apartment would continue without explanation. None had to be given. None would be given. Max would present the idea of her moving into the mansion.

Just before sleep claimed her, Ilse thought back to her conversation with Lisa. Both women had so much in common. Their husband's were both named Karl, and each had been conscripted into a "love" relationship by a man who was "in authority." The only difference being that Lisa's husband was still alive while Ilse's Karl had died first. Now, for the first time in a long time, Ilse was reflecting on her relationship with Otto.

It was not only tolerable but at times, it was quite enjoyable. A woman became a woman when she was capable of having a baby. A woman's first sexual experience was then supposed to be with her husband on their wedding night.

When she married, there was the "thrill" of being Frau Heinrich. Unfortunately, it became routine much too soon, and Karl was not the kind of man to experiment. When Karl was "done," it was over, and it was time for sleep.

She had been raised in a strict home, and because of that upbringing, she never complained to anyone. A Bavarian wife was a good wife because she knew her place was in the home and secondary to that of her husband. She had wanted children because they would further define her and give her life greater purpose. After a year or two, she and Karl both knew that something was wrong, but Karl's political ambitions were greater than his ambition to become a father. Besides, everyone in his family had been quite fertile. Therefore, the fault had to be hers.

As the years rolled by, she knew that questions were being asked but none to her face. She and Karl had ceased to discuss the matter. They had celebrated their sixth anniversary just two weeks before Karl had been killed.

Thus ended the era of Karl and after a short period of time, the era of Otto began.

This was an entirely different relationship. First of all, it was illicit as far as the church might have been concerned, if in fact, they knew about it. They never did as she had not gone to confession since moving to Berlin.

Otto was a stiff Nazi everywhere but in her company. With her, he had been casual, witty, and sexually proliferate. He had been perfectly capable of taking her to the heights and keeping her there for a while. He also liked to dress her up as sexy as convention allowed and take her to places. Nice places.

It didn't take long for her to realize that, through the perverted efforts of, Otto, she had been able to become her secret self.......the woman of her fantasies.

It was at one of those nice places that she had met Heinz Gottlieb. He had been a Gestapo Captain at the time, and because of his connections, managed to find out where she lived, and made a surprise visit to her apartment. She found him to be attractive, but that was as far as she wanted it to go.

Unfortunately, she hadn't been able to tell him that she wasn't that kind of girl, and he wasn't in the mood to accept rejection. So, he proceeded as though she had granted her consent. He "forced" himself on her in that he had ways of touching and caressing her that were "different." The intellectual part of her told him no, but her body told him yes. Her body won out, and she surrendered to "the thrill of it all." For that matter, she continued to surrender, because she resisted him each time he showed up on her doorstep. Not that she didn't want him, but because she liked what he did to "persuade' her.

Heinz Gottlieb played it fast and loose in Berlin because he had been a police detective there, and had several women "stashed" around the city. Each time he called upon Ilse, he had the uncanny knack of knowing that Otto wasn't going to be there. After a couple of years, Heinz stopped coming. She never inquired about him to anyone, but she had to admit that she missed him.

Of course, Max changed everything, but then, Max knew about Otto, but nothing about Heinz. Pangs of guilt began to appear, and Ilse fell asleep wondering if she should make a full confession.

Eleven

The day of reckoning

Mid-December 1939

Berlin

Gerhardt had been summoned to Berlin by the Herr SS Gruppenführer Reinhard Heydrich himself, and since Heydrich was the number two man in the SS, it was a command performance.

This time, Lisa was accompanying him to Berlin.

Lisa was still uneasy about her role in whatever was happening, but regardless of her uneasiness, she always looked forward to their lovemaking as a child looked forward to Christmas. She only wished for their relationship to have greater meaning. Otherwise, she was only sleeping with a man other than her husband. That turned it into a cheap affair.

Her return to Gerhardt actually defied logic. She was still able to pretend that she was being forced or coerced into being his mistress, but that had become a lie, and the one person she was unable to lie to was herself.

In truth, a strange force had drawn her back to him. Perhaps this was the same force that "compelled" him to intimidate her in the first place. A sort of, "The devil made me do it," kind of situation. On the other hand, the idea of being "forced" was not a strange concept because Karl had been forced upon her.

As a lawyer, Gerhardt never allowed himself to be concerned about the more ethereal aspects of life. He was much more pragmatic than that. He knew that his relationship with Lisa was an illegal one, but then the German government was an illegal government which of course rendered the SS to be an illegal organization since it operated within the framework of the German government. In truth, it was all a house of cards that might just fall down at any moment.

As for the matter of Lisa, there was an overriding feeling that they somehow belonged together. For what reason, neither knew, and until then, there could be no resolution.

At the end of this dark tunnel stood the figure of her husband Karl. She may have married him for all the wrong reasons, but the fact remained that she had married him. Therefore, she owed him honesty, and yet she didn't know how she would ever be able to give him that. She didn't know it yet, but the wheels were turning inexorably in that direction.

* * * * *

Gerhardt's orders were to appear in Berlin on 15 December 1939. It was a Friday, and since Lisa had never been to the capitol city, this would give Gerhardt a chance to show it to her.

The black Mercedes was moving slowly toward the SS Headquarters on Albertstrasse.

In the back seat, Gerhardt was wearing a black greatcoat that covered his dress uniform.

Lisa had chosen to wear a long sleeve black jersey dress that hugged her body without being overbearing about it. . Her stockings were silk and her shoes were black patent leather high heels. She was very pretty, quite elegant, and sexy. She was also wearing a short black wool coat.

Gerhardt looked approvingly at her. She returned his look. Both smiled.

"So this is Berlin," she uttered. It might have been a very large city and the German capitol, but a pall kind of hung over it. On the surface, it was a subdued atmosphere.

He shrugged, "Ja, this is Berlin." He knew her thoughts and made no attempt to rebut them. It was still a very interesting city and underneath the dark pall existed a world that would amaze her.

She laughed at their feeble attempt at conversation, and she asked, “Is this the best we can do?”

“Apparently so, Leibchen,” he replied good naturally. Lisa was good for him. She made him feel good. He winked at her. “Maybe it’s this meeting with Heydrich. It makes me uneasy.” She snuggled closer and squeezed his right arm.

“We don’t have to talk,” she answered, “but you might not wish to meet your fearless leader with lipstick smeared all over your face.”

“We could always place your lips where the evidence will not be seen.”

She grunted. “Nice try, Herr General. Nice try.”

“I’ll try to look forward to it anyway, “ he replied dryly.

She elbowed him and he grimaced.

* * * * *

Two other men were in Berlin for the weekend. Two officers in the German army who sought to lose themselves in the vastness of the city and maybe partake of its delights. So far, they weren’t very impressed and were out for a walk to nowhere in particular and everywhere in general when they turned right on Albertstrasse and found themselves approaching a large building . One that wouldn’t have interested the two officers otherwise, but the comings and goings of black uniformed officers caught their attention.

. “What is it, Karl?” Inquired Oberlieutenant Thomas Kranz.

“I believe it is SS headquarters,” replied Oberlieutenant Karl Mueller.

Both men were still short of the building when a black Mercedes pulled up to the curb and stopped. Both men stopped walking. They were both curious, but not *that* curious. After all, this was *SS* headquarters. Therefore, both men decided to observe things from a discreet distance. Karl would be very glad they did.

The driver a tall man who wore the black uniform of a chauffeur but not an SS uniform, walked briskly to the right rear door and opened it. Out stepped a tall general, but instead of walking briskly to the building like these SS types usually did, he turned and assisted a woman out of the car.

When she emerged from the vehicle, Karl just stared!!!

He didn't believe his eyes. *Can it be? Could it be? Oh my God! It is her. Lisa? My God, it IS Lisa.*

Every instinct told him to go and claim his right to his legally wedded wife, and yet, he remained rooted to that spot. *Not here,* he thought. *These people don't play fair.* He looked at her again. *My God, but she is lovely. Did I ever realize just how lovely she really was?* She hadn't looked in his direction at all. Instead, she looked at the general and smiled warmly. He gave her his arm, which she took, and they started up the steps to the front door with a chorus of "Heil Hitler's." echoing off the buildings. When they reached the top, the doors were opened and the General and Lisa disappeared from view.

For the first time, Thomas noticed that his friend had turned white.

"Karl......what is wrong?"

Karl didn't reply. He couldn't. He wouldn't say anything to anyone. He was only thankful that Thomas did not know Lisa.

Wait! Do I know that it was my Lisa? It looked like her, but was it really her or am I just too lonely and too ready to jump to conclusions? After a few seconds, he concluded that.....yes.....he really did know his wife when he saw her.

He looked to his comrade who happened to be waiting for a reply and said, "I-I-I don't know, Thomas. All of the sudden, I just don't feel well." That, at least, was the truth.

"Sorry to hear that, Karl. Would you like to go and lay down for a while?"

Karl said yes, and they returned to their hotel.

Once Karl had been deposited in their room, Thomas told him, "I hope you don't mind, Karl, but while you are resting, I am going to get a few biers. Should you wake up and decide to venture out, I'll meet you in the lobby at six."

Karl agreed, and Thomas left.

* * * * *

At SS headquarters, Gerhardt had taken Lisa to a special lounge, got her something to drink, made sure she was comfortable, and said, "This should only take two hours." She nodded to him and he went to his appointment with Heydrich.

Just as soon as Gerhardt left the room, a young lieutenant entered, and poured a cup of coffee. After that, he sat at the table next to her table. They were the only two people in the room.

The lieutenant smiled. He was struck by her loveliness, and being one of the pretty people himself, he was taking the first steps necessary for establishing his claim on her. In his mind, they belonged together, at least for the coming evening. Women, especially the pretty ones, rarely said no to him.

She returned his smile, and noticed how handsome he looked, but other than making that simple observation, she had no interest in him at all.

"Good day, my lady," he said.

She replied, "Good day."

"I have not seen you here before. Do you perhaps work in the building?"

She shook her head, "Nein. I am here with General von Leitner." She silently reprimanded herself for voluntarily offering that information.

"Ach! That accounts for you being in this room rather than the cafeteria. It also explains your dress."

I do not have to explain anything to you at all, Herr Lieutenant.

She didn't say anything, but he was undaunted. "Are you perhaps, the general's daughter?"

Again, she shook her head, and replied with a simple, "Nein."

The lieutenant was handsome, well built and virile. Under normal circumstances, if such a condition still existed in her country, she wouldn't have even been in Berlin let alone this building. Whatever he was attempting to do was therefore doomed to failure.

* * * * *

Heydrich had a male adjutant bearing the rank of Hauptsturmführer seated at a desk in his outer office when Gerhardt entered the Herr Hauptmann's domain. The Hauptsturmführer looked up expectantly, and Gerhardt said, "General von Leitner to see the

Herr Gruppenführer."

The Hauptmann consulted an appointment book for a few seconds before looking up and announcing, "Yes, Herr General. Allow me to announce you to the Herr Gruppenführer."

He stood and entered Heydrich's office. After at least three minutes, the Hauptsturmführer returned. "You may go in now, Herr General."

Gerhardt was then escorted to the inner sanctum.

* * * * *

The Lieutenant was still trying to make headway with Lisa when a Hauptsturmführer (Captain) walked into the lounge. Seeing that she was the only woman, he walked to her table and said, "Pardon me, Mein Frau, but would you happen to be Frau Mueller?"

She replied, "Ja."

"I have a message from the Herr General von Leitner. He wanted me to tell you that his meeting with Gruppenführer Heydrich will last until six o'clock. He is sorry, but it cannot be helped. Would you like me to provide transportation back to your hotel?"

She was aggravated by the news, but what could she do about it? She was about to accept the Hauptsturmführer's invitation when the Lieutenant spoke up, "Pardon my intrusion, Mein Frau, but my vehicle is parked around the corner. I would be more than delighted to drive you to your hotel."

The Haupsturmführer was about to speak, but Lisa silenced him with a gesture. She looked once more at the Lieutenant. He had an inflated opinion of himself, but other than that, she decided that he might be pleasant company. "Ja, Herr Lieutenant, I will accept your invitation."

The Lieutenant beamed with self satisfaction and the Haupsturmführer bowed and departed. The Lieutenant helped her with her coat and they left.

* * * * *

Heydrich had greeted Gerhardt and told him to take a seat which Gerhardt did. Heydrich's mood was hard to gauge

Heydrich continued to shuffle some papers on his desk. He appeared to be gathering his thoughts.

The blonde beast! The nickname had already been given to this fool, and he deserved it. Gerhardt wondered where this conversation might be headed once it got started in earnest..

"Tell me, Herr General, where exactly do you think you fit into the New Order?"

"I am not an idle dreamer, Herr Gruppenführer. I am a trained lawyer, but a law degree can lead in many directions. One such direction, is the direction I am headed right now although I will be the first to admit that I am uncertain as to what my function really is."

Heydrich admired both the bluntness and the coolness of the Herr General. Maybe the man did have ice water running in his veins, but there was something he needed to settle his mind on before allowing his admiration to cloud his judgment.

"Tell me something, Herr General. Where do your loyalties lie? I sometimes get the impression that you only tolerate the party. Am I wrong? And if I am right, what then?"

I see that we have just reached the critical point in this conversation, Herr Heydrich and it took less than ten minutes.

When all else fails, tell the truth.

"Herr Gruppenführer, I don't know if you can ever have a minimum level of loyalty to a specific cause. Not one that is shared by all the people. Rather, I would think that loyalty to the greater cause, or in this case, the Reich, might be of greater importance. There are many Germans who would never betray the Reich, not because they are good Nazis, but because they are good Germans. I may have been born in Vienna, but I haven't lived in that city since I was six years old. Therefore, I am a German. I like to believe that I am a good German that will always do right by Germany regardless of who happens to be in power. Now that I have said all of that, I do believe in the twenty-five points of National Socialism, and maybe I should remind you that I was one of the framers of the Enabling Act which gave *Der Führer* the power he enjoys today.

His answer was the right answer for that particular moment, but it was not the right answer. Being a good German was not tantamount to being a good National Socialist, and Heydrich decided to accept von Leitner's position without further question or comment.

Gerhardt later surmised that Heydrich wanted to see past the General's loyalties all the way to his real abilities.

Gerhardt knew that he was a master negotiator, and some day, Germany might need his services. That is if Hitler had the vision to realize that not every goal could be reached through conquest.

What Gerhardt didn't know was that it had been decided that the Reich would be better served with Gerhardt von Leitner out of the way. On ice, so to speak. He could be called upon for his real purpose later if and when it was really needed.

Heydrich had taken a calculated risk in transferring von Leitner to the Munich area, and with the exception of Dachau, it was working out. The local Gestapo was out of his direct control but Dachau wasn't. Oh well, he would allow things to play out and see what further steps needed to be taken.

Heydrich then leaned forward and began speaking. His face bore the strain of intensity as he spoke. "And now, Herr General, I am going to explain our plan for *lebensraum* (The plan for expanding the boundaries of the Reich to accommodate the growth rate of the German people), and the decontamination of the infestations of those who now reside in the conquered nations."

Gerhardt took a deep breathe and hoped that he would be able to survive the next few hours.

* * * * *

Karl had indeed returned to his hotel room and laid down but that was not what he needed. He wasn't physically ill. No, the act of seeing Lisa with that SS General was what had upset him, and laying in that bed looking at the four walls wasn't going to help a thing, so he got up, dressed, put on his heavy coat to protect against the cold, and ventured out once more. Before he did, he left a note for Thomas telling him of the need to walk and not to wait. Karl apologized for abandoning him, but there were things that needed to be sorted out. He gave the note to the room clerk and ventured out into the mid-December cold that had settled in and around Berlin.

As he walked, he remembered that day just a short month ago when they stood on the platform at the Munich train station. *Had it only been a month? Maybe, it was more like a lifetime.*

Then, he remembered her words, *Life is an illusion, mein Liebe. It is only what we perceive it to be. Be not dismayed by what you see or hear. Things can always happen but they are not really real and because of that, they don't have to be permanent in our minds. Understand that, in my own way, I do love you and if we ever should separate permanently, it will have to be you who separates us, for I shall never leave you.*

In a way, they were comforting words, but the stark reality of actually seeing her with the General was almost more than he had been able to bear.

He continued walking and for some reason, he was becoming stronger with each step. Her words **were** a tonic for him, but it was not the words. Rather, it was her meaning. Isaac had always told him to seek the meaning first and not to own the words.

After what seemed like the endless walking, he finally became weary and sought a place where he could rest and renew.

* * * * *

The Lieutenant, who had introduced himself as Josef Hauser, judged correctly that the lady was angry with the Herr General, and the Lieutenant, always the ladies man, knew exactly how to use her anger to his own advantage.

Lisa was only too happy to accept the handsome Lieutenant's invitation for a drink, and they rode in silence as Josef negotiated the streets of Berlin. It wasn't long before he pulled into a parking lot of an establishment called:

Rudy's

By his watch, he had five hours to accomplish his mission and return her to her hotel before the Herr General returned. Five hours was a lifetime. When they entered the establishment, he guided her to a booth in a dark corner that was not visible to the bartender. Trudi Wilder, a part time waitress, shared a look with the bartender. Lieutenant Hauser was a regular, and he seldom, if ever, brought the same woman twice. Trudi had to admit to herself that the man was good. Damn good! He always rented one of the rooms in the back and she could never remember any time that he didn't use the room. He never failed. Therefore, the pretty young lady had to be the latest burnt offering to the *Goddess of Sexual Fulfillment*. God help her!

She looked up and saw him approaching the bar.

"Good day, Mein Liebe. How is the prettiest waitress in Berlin." Trudi was pretty, but she was also on the plus side of forty. Where exactly was a fact that she kept to herself. She was a good example of the old saying, "You don't get older. You only get better."

"Come now, Josef," she replied. "I know you tell that to all the waitresses."

"Jawohl, Mein Liebe, but only to those who appreciate being told the truth."

He gave her a kiss followed by a loving pat on her rump. Then, he got serious. "I will need two schnapps, and the key to a room. Give me five minutes and bring a bottle." He took a folded bill out of his pocket and tucked it into the bosom of her low cut dress. "This is for you." He winked at her as he gave her another bill. "This one is for the schnapps."

When Josef returned to the booth, Lisa smiled at him.

He returned her smile, and set the drink down in front of her. He scooted in beside her and handed her a glass. He raised his own glass and spoke, "Here is to you, Lisa Mueller. May you always be as lovely as you are right now."

She liked his toast and she drank it eagerly. It was peppermint flavored, and it warmed her all the way down. It felt good and she wanted another. As if on cue, a nice looking waitress approached their booth with a bottle in her hand. "May I pour another, Mein Frau?" Lisa nodded and Trudi did the honors.

Rudy's

Karl looked at the sign blinking on and off and decided to stop. As he entered the establishment, he observed only a few patrons. There was a man behind the bar and two women, one sitting and one standing. The one sitting was a lovely woman while the one standing was only average looking and was probably the waitress. What he didn't know was that the pretty one was also a waitress, but because of the lack of business, she had been given the night off, and decided to stay and drink and chat, and whatever......

When Karl walked into the establishment, Trudi observed him carefully and although he did not have the impressive persona of a man like Josef Hauser, he was a nice looking man and seemed to have a quiet dignity about him. Besides, he wore the *feldgrau* (Field gray) uniform of a soldier and not the black uniform of the SS. He also wore the *Knight's Cross* a medal he had to have won in Poland. She became intrigued and saw a way in which the excitement that Josef had stirred within her might be satisfied. Karl bought her a drink, and with it, he bought a lot more than he expected.

* * * * *

Karl had no way of knowing that his wife was seated in a booth in the dark corner of the adjacent room of the same establishment. She was presently engaged in a passionate kiss with SS Lieutenant Josef Hauser. In fact, it was more than passionate. It was downright lewd as the young Josef had taken considerable liberties with the young lady. Liberties that were very exciting for the young lady. She was now taking liberties with the Lieutenant. What she was doing was something she never would have done back in Munich. Karl, who had to use the toilet, passed within ten meters of his wife and didn't know it.

Josef was moving rather quickly not only because of the presumed time constraint, but he did not believe that the meek would inherit the earth. Rather, he believed that the providence to rule belonged only to the bold. In that matter, he was a perfect SS officer.

He used alcohol not to ply but to relax. A drunken woman was a poor lover whereas a relaxed and stimulated one was potentially a great lover especially when she was mated with a man who knew how to appreciate that quality. Therefore, Josef proceeded forward boldly knowing that if she had objected at any point along the way, he would simply return her to her hotel room and stop wasting energy on a lost cause. Josef Hauser would not have bothered with the raping of a woman when there were so many willing ones available.

What he didn't know was that Lisa had made that decision

during her long appraisal of the him prior to her acceptance of his invitation. When she told him yes, she had been telling him yes to everything. *Wherever he wanted to go, and whatever he wanted to do.*

By the time Karl had left the toilet, Josef and Lisa had left the booth in favor of the privacy of Room #1. It wasn't long before Karl and Trudi were heading toward the darkened booths as a prelude to their going to Room #2.

In the meantime, Lisa and Josef had removed all their clothing and were heavily engaged in passionate sexual activity.

Sometime later, Karl and Trudi found their way to Room #2, and a married couple managed to find sexual fulfillment that night, but not in the arms of each other.

* * * * *

It was a little after five o'clock by the time Josef and Lisa could pause in their lovemaking long enough for him to discover that he had to return Lisa to her hotel before the Herr General arrived. When he informed her of his intentions, he found that she had no such desire. She intended to stay as long as he had anything left in him. Then and only then, would she return to Gerhardt. Perhaps, this was her declaration of independence.

* * * * *

It was a little after six when Gerhardt returned to the main floor of SS Headquarters. He checked with the duty desk and found that his driver was in the cafeteria and that the lady had left the building as per his instructions but not with a staff driver. She had left with a young SS Lieutenant instead.

When he returned to the hotel, he checked with the desk and the spare key was still in the box. Lisa had not returned to the hotel, and it did not require the services of a genius to figure that she had gone someplace with the Lieutenant. Her actions were out of character, but she obviously had been upset with him. After all, she had been ready to see the sites and his message told her that he would be tied up the entire afternoon and her only option was to return to the hotel room and look at the four walls.

He could not have said no to Heydrich, but he should have prepared for that contingency. The Lisa he knew had obviously taken advantage of an available opportunity. The next question was obviously how long would she be gone?

He sighed heavily and sat down at the desk, and wrote her a note on the stationery that was provided by the hotel. When he finished, he placed it into one of the envelopes and wrote Lisa's name on it. After waiting until seven, he shrugged back into his greatcoat, and went in search of a place to eat right after handing the envelope to the room clerk.

Two hours later, he returned to the hotel, and found his note was still in the box along with the extra key. Disappointment weighed heavily upon him as he considered how he might spend the rest of the evening.

* * * * *

Sometime, in the late evening hours, Josef began to run out of gas, and for that matter, so had Lisa. Never, in her entire life, had she experienced what she had been experiencing for the previous nine or ten hours. He was definitely not the run of the mill male. She had read about satyrs and suspected that Josef might be one them. Gerhardt had been her best, but even Gerhardt was not in the same league with Josef. If a woman wanted to keep her sexual batteries charged, she might be advised to schedule a weekend every year with this man for that purpose and that purpose alone.

He had already informed her that she was "among" his best. It was "comforting" to know that she was probably in the top five or ten. No......she definitely would not fall in love with the man, but as much as she felt the need to return to Gerhardt, she wasn't ready to leave yet. About an hour later, he awoke and things began all over again.

* * * * *

The sun had returned to Berlin by the time Gerhardt finally woke up. A look at the clock told him that it was ten in the morning, and since he had closed the hotel lounge the night before and didn't have anything on his schedule, he wasn't upset by the late waking hour. He wondered if he would have a hangover and decided that he would find out just as soon as he decided to move.

About that time, he heard a sound coming from the outer room. It sounded like a key in the lock which meant that it was either the maid or Lisa had decided to return.

The clicking of heels on the hardwood floor told him that it was probably Lisa since he doubted that the maid would be wearing high heels. She appeared in the doorway, and just looked at him. For the first time in their relationship, he was unable to read her. She just looked at him.

"Guten Morgen, Mein Schatz," he said hoping that he had friendliness in his voice and not irritation.

"Guten Morgen," was her only greeting.

He managed a weak smile and said, "I am happy that you decided to return. I was told that you left with a Lieutenant and because Berlin is such a large city, I decided not to conduct a search."

She bristled immediately, but held her tongue until she regained control of her emotions. Once that had been accomplished, she began, "Gerhardt, I am not crawling back to you on my hands and knees. I did not come to you voluntarily in the first place, but I do come voluntarily right now. What I did yesterday, last night, and this morning, I did for me! I apologize for not telling you where I had gone and what I was doing, but not for doing what I did. Knowing what I know now, I would do it again."

Gerhardt swallowed hard with the knowledge that the young Lieutenant was probably very proliferate in the art of lovemaking. More so than he, and Lisa's attitude was telling him something he didn't want to hear.

"Do you wish to be with this man on a permanent basis?"

For the first time, she began to pace back and forth. As she did, he observed her very closely. Her coat only half covered the snugly fitting jersey dress she was wearing. It revealed her hips, shapely calves, ankles and high heels. Regardless of the gravity of this situation, he was becoming aroused, and he was glad that the blanket covered him. Suddenly, she stopped pacing and walked over and sat on the bed beside him.

"My answer is no, I would never in my wildest dreams consider trying to tame Josef. He is not a one woman man, and he would surely wear me out before I ever got close to taming him. Had I not been brought into your life so abruptly, I might have spent the rest of my life with Karl and never knew that men like Josef actually existed. Now that I have compromised whatever moral principles I had, I found that it was actually easy to go with him and become a willing participant."

His desire began to wane in light of what she had just told him. Instead, he asked, "Why did you return to me, Lisa?"

She didn't delay this time. "You represented a part of me that I only had a vague memory of. You see Gerhardt, you were not my first venture into forbidden territory. I almost ventured there before I married Karl. In fact, that was the reason my father arranged the marriage in the first place. Had he discovered us five minutes later, he would have caught us in the act, and I would have no longer been a virgin. Then came Karl. He is a good man, but he is plain and without imagination. Then, after I became pregnant for Heidi, a man came to live with us for a short period of time, and when Karl left for school, Isaac and I were left alone and to make matters worse, I was attracted to the man. We behaved for only about three days, and then things happened. They kept happening until Isaac finally left. I haven't seen him since." She stopped speaking as though she needed to collect her remaining thoughts.

Gerhardt decided to ask, "Isaac......The name sounds Jewish. Was he?"

"Ja," she answered quickly. "Being Jewish didn't make him unattractive or impotent. In fact, many Jewish men are quite attractive.

He smiled and she continued. "Then, after Isaac left, I became despondent and stayed that way until Heidi was born, and a month later, I almost died. To save my life, my female organs had to be removed. I became even worse mentally until Karl had been inducted into the army. Shortly after that, you came into my life, and although I was furious, I accepted your intrusion into my life because I had no other choice. Then, to my surprise, you treated me with loving affection and that bothered me." She paused again, and Gerhardt just waited this time. "Anger has a therapeutic affect on me, Gerhardt. It allows me to do things I normally would not or could not do. When you told me that I was free to go, I was relieved, and was able to be a wife to Karl for as long as he was home. After he left, I didn't want to go back to my parents farm, and so here I am."

"Are you telling me that it was only a job and a way to avoid boredom?"

"Nein! I came back because of you."

"I am confused, Lisa. Because of me, you were able to compromise your moral principles, and because of me, the man who compromised your principles, you came back to me. Conversely, you were able spend the better part of a day and night with this Josef, a man who might just be the ultimate lover. Tell me, Mein Schatz, where do I really fit into your life, and should I feel good about it?"

She shook her head and smiled as she did. "You silly man. I care for you as a man. Under normal circumstances, I could fall in love with you. For that matter, maybe I have and have not yet admitted it. You might be a lot older, but you do know how to treat a woman, and I have learned to appreciate that. I also appreciated Josef. I hope you can appreciate what I have just said because I don't think I could repeat it. "

He sighed. "I just felt an emotion called jealousy, and I seldom feel emotions. See what you have done to me."

She stood up long enough to remove her coat and hang it up. He looked appreciatively at her figure and things began to happen to him again. Visions of her in various stages of undress came to him along with visions of her being ravished by this Josef person. There was no doubt that she would spend time with him again if the opportunity presented itself. For some reason, the idea no longer bothered him. He would talk to her about the virtue of telling him about future encounters.

In the meantime, she had returned to the bed, kicked her shoes off and lay there beside him. He rolled over and met her lips. Lisa had risen to a new level, and would never return to the lower level again. When finished, she reached for his blanket and removed it from him. He had risen to the occasion and she increased the intensity of her kiss.

The defining moment of her life had come and gone, and memories of the previous twenty-four hours receded into the back channels of her mind. Her thoughts were only of Gerhardt.

As for him, the reason he had cut her loose was really quite simple. He had fallen in love with her, and he decided the best he could ever do was love her and take care of her. He would do that in spite of Karl, in spite of Josef or anyone else who came along. He would just love her.

He could do no better than that.

* * * * *

That evening

Munich

Fritz Dorfmeier was pacing nervously in his study. The oldest of his four children and only daughter was coming home for dinner and she was bringing a young man with her, an SS Standartenführer by the name of Max Liebert.

Herr Dorfmeier was a man of medium height who was battling a weight problem that accompanied him into middle age although he was not what one could call obese. He had a middle age paunch. His eyes were the required blue, but his hair was a dark brown. He had a thin line of a mustache and what one might be inclined to call a stern look on his face.

He was nervous because this Liebert happened to be the choice of his daughter and not his choice. Not that Ilse didn't deserve to have a choice of her own. After all, her late husband Karl had been too close to Ernst Röhn and gotten himself killed for his efforts.

To make matters worse, Ilse did not come home after Karl's death. A good daughter would have, but she resisted, and told him that she had been summoned to Berlin. She had to go. That was four years ago. Four Years! What good could have come to a young widow in that terribly sinful city? No doubt she had been forced to submit to some Nazi or many Nazis, and now she was consorting with an SS Standartenführer (Colonel) of all people. After all, weren't they were all a pack of gangsters and thugs? Good people no longer ran Germany. The gangsters did.

Well, he would be a good papa and meet this Herr Standartenführer Liebert, and then, at a later date, he would have to talk her out of marrying this man.

Just then, he heard the door knocker. If he were a little further up the pecking order at the bank, he would be able to afford a housekeeper. As it was, he answered his own door.

He opened the door to Ilse and her SS Standartenführer. She smiled and said, "Good evening, papa. I am glad to see you."

He stood there stiffly for a long moment before breaking into a genuine smile and reaching for his daughter. They hugged and she cried for what seemed like an eternity and then, when it all seemed ready to die down to a dull roar, her mama arrived on the scene and it started over again. When the dust finally settled, she looked nervously at her parents and said, "Mama, papa, allow me to introduce the Herr SS Standartenführer Maximillian Liebert."

Then to Max, she said, "Max, allow me to introduce my mama and papa, Herr und Frau Dorfmeier."

Max took the hand of Frau Dorfmeier and kissed it, "The privilege is all mine, Frau Dorfmeier," and then, to her papa, he offered his hand and said, "It is an honor and a privilege, Herr Dorfmeier. I have been looking forward to this meeting."

Fritz Dorfmeier took the hand offered by Max Liebert and squeezed it firmly. Fritz found strength in Liebert's hand and the two men's eyes met and held. He had just met Max Liebert and he already felt there was something genuine about the man. It was a quality he had found missing in every Nazi he had met so far. It was something called sincerity.

He finally said, "The honor is all mine, Herr Standartenführer."

Once the introductions had been made, Frau Dorfmeier announced that dinner was ready and they retired to the dinning room.

Even though Herr Dorfmeier felt that Liebert was a sincere man and therefore the genuine article, he was still an SS officer. Conversation was guarded and questions were asked about Max and his background. Both Herr und Frau Dorfmeier were surprised that Max had lived in Munich. They were especially surprised when they learned the extent of his educational background. Going to college in post-war Germany had been a privilege of the elite, and they were curious as to how a baker's son had been able to enjoy that privilege. They asked and he told them. After he did, Herr Dorfmeier became even more wary of the man.

After dinner, Max and Herr Dorfmeier retired to the study for an after dinner schnapps. It was over this and a few more schnapps that Herr Dorfmeier learned the full extent of Max's education. The young man's knowledge of banking and finance rivaled his own, and all of the sudden, Herr Dorfmeier remembered why the name, Max Liebert, sounded so familiar.

He had recently taken a trip to the Reichsbank in Berlin and while he was there, he heard about the legendary exploits of a certain Max Liebert who had actually compromised the Swiss banking system. Curiosity might have killed the cat, but he had to know.

"Ja," Max answered. "I am the guilty party."

"But how?" Asked a puzzled Herr Dorfmeier.

"I just got lucky, that's all."

Dorfmeier knew that luck existed only in the minds of men. The reality was that luck only seemed to occur when opportunity met preparation, and he told Max as much.

Max replied, "Well....actually, Herr Dorfmeier, one also has to believe that nothing is impossible. Every armor has it's chink. Every chain, it's weak link. Find the weakness and the impossible not only becomes possible but extremely probable."

Fritz Dorfmeier was perplexed, "But you haven't told me anything."

"I don't intend to," Max answered. "With all due respect, Herr Dorfmeier, a secret ceases to be a secret when another person is made privy not only to its existence but also its substance. Therefore, I choose to keep this knowledge to myself. I am sorry for the need to speak so bluntly, but we need to understand each another.

Herr Dorfmeier was tight lipped, but he seemed to understand. He had just come to realize that having Max Liebert as a son-in-law was a tremendous asset to his career. He would move up the ladder more rapidly now.

His respect for Max Liebert had multiplied many times what it was before the night began. He no longer regarded Max as an opportunistic interloper. Herr Dorfmeier had become the opportunistic interloper instead..

When he and Max finally rejoined the ladies, he had not only given his blessing to the proposed marital union, but offered to help expedite the necessary bans and approvals needed by the catholic church.

When Max and Ilse finally said good night, Fritz Dorfmeier was inwardly proud of his good fortune. He was especially glad that he had the good sense to recognize good fortune when he saw it.

Had he been able to read Max's mind, he might not have felt so confident. Max had been able to see through the facade all the way through to Herr Dorfmeier's frustrated ambitions. It wasn't that Max didn't wish to help his future father-in-law's frustrated ambitions, but no matter how Herr Dorfmeier happened to be dressed, he would still only be a lackey, and an ambitious one at that. Unfortunately, untalented ambitious men were not to be trusted. He would do his best to protect the man from himself, but that would be the extent of what he would do. He looked at Ilse and was thankful that he had her. She would understand, because it was she who briefed him about her father in advance. After that, he simply observed and played it by ear.

Twelve

Innocence lost

1940

Mid-February

A strange pall had settled over the European continent. War was raging in the Atlantic. The Russians were fighting the Finns, but the main event had not yet started. It was called the Phony War.

In Berlin, Hitler was smug as he looked at the map of Europe. He could now envision the entire continent under German domination, and from his perspective, that was a good thing, and well worth the price he would pay in terms of lives lost and equipment expended.

Hitler had proven that he could be brave in battle, but in truth, he had a fault. One that he was unable to deal with even if he had been able to recognize it. Basically, he was unrealistic in his expectations.

War had become an abstract reality to him. In truth, brave men were often incapable of managing a war. To Hitler, it had become like a game. War had become magnetic pieces that could be moved about on a map. The Austrian Corporal had become a Field Marshal with none of the training or experience needed to perform the job, and no one would ever be able to tell him that he was not equal to the task. To make matters even worse, those who were closest to him were as unrealistic as he was.

He had unleashed his war machine against the Poles, and had

won decisively. Now, he was preparing to unleash the Wehrmacht once more against the rest of Europe, and he would crush them all like the piece of paper he now crumpled and threw into the waste basket.

In February of 1940, the man whose realizations would ultimately fail to meet his expectations, was now ready to sacrifice the whole of humanity in search of something that did not exist.

* * * * *

Munich

The expansion of the Reich would just have to wait.

The first order of business was the wedding of Max Liebert to Ilse Heinrich. After the thorough, but rapid investigation of Ilse's background and a physical examination of both Ilse and Max, approval had been granted. The speed of the approval surprised Gerhardt until he saw that the approval had been granted by none other than Adolph Hitler himself.

A note from Hitler came with the approval informing Max of his desire to see Max married, but he regretted that pressing matters of state precluded his attending. Max observed dryly that since *Der Führer* had not been invited, his regrets were not necessary.

The other potential obstacle, namely the church, proved not to be an obstacle at all. The church, which understood authoritative rule quite well, was still trying to find an identity within the structure of the Third Reich and the Reich wasn't being very cooperative. Virtually the entire hierarchy was made of Roman Catholics. Hence, in this case, they went out of their way to please.

Therefore, on Saturday, March 9, 1940, Max and Ilse were married in the church chapel rather than the main sanctuary. In attendance were Fritz Liebert, father of the groom; Herr und Frau Dorfmeier, parents of the bride, Kurt, Richard, and Thomas Dorfmeier, brothers of the bride, The Herr SS General Gerhardt von Leitner and Frau Lisa Marie Mueller, friends of the groom.

Gerhardt stood up for Max and Lisa stood up for Ilse.

It was a pretty wedding despite the fact that it was March, and after the wedding, a reception was held at the mansion. Other close friends and relatives that weren't invited to the wedding were invited to the reception, and after the reception, Max and his new bride were going to fly to Vienna for a short honeymoon.

This was a gift from Adolph Hitler who realized that the couple would not be able to go anywhere because of the travel restrictions imposed by the Reich. Therefore, he decided to combine business and pleasure by having Max to act as a courier between Berlin and Vienna. Two days before the wedding, a special courier arrived from Berlin carrying a diplomatic pouch which was to be delivered to the Reich Main Office in Vienna. Along with the diplomatic pouch was a detailed set of orders authorizing Herr und Frau Liebert to travel via air (special Plane) to Vienna for a week, and their return airplane trip to Munich. Max and Ilse were both grateful to *Der Führer* for his generosity.

It was obvious that someone in Hitler's office had to have diverted their energies from the affairs of state to the task of planning this trip for Max and Ilse. It was complete right down to the fact that Ilse's personal documents had the new name she would be assuming with her marriage to Max.

Thus, after a reception and wedding dinner hosted by the staff at the mansion, Max and Ilse were taken to the airport to meet the flight to Vienna which was scheduled to leave at 7:20 PM. They didn't even have time to get comfortable on the airplane before it was announced that the plane would soon be landing in Vienna.

As an official representative of *Der Führer of Das Reich, ,* Max and his bride were met at the airport by the Military Governor himself.

Vienna, the Imperial City, had once been the seat of a large empire. Then, after The Great War, it reverted to simply being the Capitol of Austria, and then came the Anchluss where it ceased to be Austria's capitol. In fact, Austria had ceased to exist as a nation.

It had now been absorbed into the Greater German Reich, and had thus lost its autonomy. It was now the Province of Ostmark a fact that relegated Vienna to being a provincial capitol.

During the week that he and Ilse stayed in Vienna, he found that many residents had not yet come to terms with this fact. It wasn't anything they came right out and talked about.. Rather, it was the pain he could see in the eyes of many of its people.

Adolph Hitler, an Austrian, was a man who now stood at the pinnacle of power in the Greater German Reich, but when he had lived in Vienna, he was so low that he had been almost a street person. The pendulum had swung from one extreme to the other.

Sunday, Monday, and Tuesday were filled with banquets, sightseeing and balls. Despite the fact the Germany was at war, Vienna was still Vienna, and Vienna would not be Vienna without the *Karneval* season. Unfortunately, the restrictions of the current regime made it impossible for all but the top balls to be held, and Max and Ilse attended the ones that were held while they were there.

Nothing was scheduled on Wednesday which turned out to be a beautiful day, and after a leisure breakfast, they decided to take a walk around the Ringstrasse. That was when he noticed the looks that he was getting from passersby. They tended to make him a little uncomfortable.

Ilse also garnered a few discreet glances, a fact that that made Max feel a little better. It told him that Viennese men weren't so obsessed with their resentment of the heavy handed Germans that they couldn't still appreciate the loveliness of a lady. About lunch time, they found a quaint little place that was run by a Greek couple and decided to have lunch there.

Ilse happened to let it slip that they were newlyweds and the couple went out of their way to please the young couple.....not because Max Liebert was an SS Standartenführer, but because the idea of being newlyweds still seemed to bring out the best in people. The Greek couple was no exception.

Max and Ilse were seated in a small alcove that gave them privacy from other patrons, and Max, who had already finished eating, was savoring both the wine he was sipping and the wonder of the woman who was now his wife. How did he get so lucky? What a difference a day made.

She seemed to appear out of the blue and now, she had become a fixed part of his world.

She became aware of his gaze and raised her eyes to meet his. They often did that. Neither would say anything, but they would continue looking into each other's eyes. At moments like this, he knew they were communicating in a language that could not be spoken. The language had to be God's language, if in fact, there was a God. He surmised that if this God were the Creator of the Universe, he wouldn't need words..

Those who sought this God would always know how to find Him. They wouldn't need a path to show them the way. Unfortunately, those who sought this God had to be very small in number. The rest of the population probably couldn't find their collective arses with both hands and a road map.

His thoughts of God dissolved once more into thoughts of Ilse. His precious Ilse. The woman who might have been places and done things that could still make a harlot blush, but to him, she possessed a purity of spirit that seemed to transcend the temporal human part of her.

She finally decided to ask, "What, pray tell, are you thinking about, Mein Liebe?"

His serious look became a broad smile, and he said, "Well, Mein Schatz, you might be surprised to know that I was thinking of you and God."

She just shook her head. "You have me in good company. A little too high maybe, but good."

"Why not? Are you trying to tell me that you are not good enough to be in the same thoughts with God?"

'I have never given it much thought."

Max laughed at her choice of words. "Actually, Liebchen (sweetheart), I have placed you on a fairly high pedestal."

"I wish you wouldn't do that. I am only human, you know."

"Ja, and a very nice human if you don't mind my saying so. Actually, the only reason I would ever place you on a pedestal is so I could look up your dress."

She colored and said, "Oh...you," and then she playfully slapped him on the back of the hand. "Actually, you don't have to go to all that trouble. Just ask me, and I'll take my dress off for you."

"You are much too willing, darling."

Their eyes met and with their eyes their hands touched. "For you, Max, I think I would do anything."

"Anything?"

"Well......anything within reason."

"That's my Ilse." Then, his smile dissolved into a serious look, and Ilse became concerned. "Max, what is wrong?"

"Nothing is wrong between the two of us, Liebchen. . We are newly weds. People like us look with hope to a good life. One with a minimum amount of challenges."

"There is nothing wrong with hope, Max, but let me remind you that regardless of the holy vows we took about forever and ever, the only time we will ever have is right now."

Max cocked his head and just looked at her for the longest time. "That is a lovely thought, Ilse, and I think you would be right."

She placed her hands on his again. "Max, my darling, I harbor no false illusions about where we live and what goes on here. I only have to remember what happened to Karl in order to return to that reality. I love you, Max. I love you very much. Sometimes, I love you so much that it hurts, and I don't want to lose you. Yet I know that if I ever want to keep you, I have to be willing to let you go. Does that make any sense to you?"

Amazement registered on his face. "Jawohl, Mein Schatz!"

She got serious again. "Max, I never told you everything about me, and I have something you need.—-???"

Max held his hand up and she stopped in mid-sentence. "No, Ilse.....Maybe some bright day tomorrow, or any one of the bright tomorrow's in our future, we may once again hold true confessions, but in the meantime, I don't care if there were one hundred lovers in your past. It doesn't matter. I don't have a need to know. Not one least bit. I love you far too much for it ever to matter. We all have feet of clay. Therefore, Mein Liebe, do not fret about a past that matters not."

Tears were flowing freely now, and Max reached for his handkerchief and handed it to her. She dabbed at the tears and blew her nose. It took a few minutes, but she finally composed herself, and returned the handkerchief to her husband.

"Max, what did I ever do to deserve you?"

"I don't know what you did, Liebchen, but I am thankful that I finally did something right.."

"Now that we have said all of those flowery things about letting each other go with grace, do you mind if I am selfish enough to want to just hold on to you?"

He smiled. "Nein, Mein Schatz.....In fact, I would encourage it."

"Too bad we can't have a baby, Max."

"Oh I don't know, Mein Liebe. Maybe it just wasn't your turn yet. Or perhaps you didn't have the right partner."

"Thank you for that, Max, but again, I don't harbor any illusions."

"Let me be the one who harbors the illusions in this family, Ilse. I have more than enough for both of us."

* * * * *

The next day found them at the townhouse of the Baron and Baroness Frederick von Leitner, the parents of Gerhardt. Gerhardt didn't know about the visit and probably would not have approved of it had he known, but Max, who had a very good relationship with his own father, decided that if he ventured nothing, he would gain nothing.

He contacted the baron through an intermediary, and was surprised by the quick acceptance. Therefore, the Herr und Frau Liebert were received at the townhouse at two o'clock in the afternoon on Thursday.

The visit lasted only two hours, but during the visit, Baron von Leitner expressed a profound sadness about the way in which he and his wife had treated their second son. It was his profound desire to finally mend the fences, and Max promised the baron he would do what he could just as soon as he found a way to tell their son.

The baron was happy to know that Gerhardt was in Munich and would have traveled there to plead his own case, but the travel ban now made that difficult if not impossible.

Munich

Lisa was seated in Gerhardt's office going over some manifests when Max knocked on the door jam.

Gerhardt looked up and exclaimed, "Max! Welcome back. Come in" He only saw Max, and was pleasantly surprised when he reached back with his right hand, and Ilse materialized at his side. *I wonder how they did that.*

Lisa was only about a half a second behind Gerhardt, and she exclaimed both names, "Max....Ilse," But she went to embrace Ilse first. The two not only became good friends, but each had become the sister that neither had, and that made them very special to each other. After embracing Ilse, she embraced Max and while she did, she whispered, "Are you taking good care of Ilse, Max?" He held her at arm's length and replied tenderly, "I can do no less than my best, Lisa. I love her too much to do otherwise." Ilse's eyes gleamed.

The ladies went up to the third floor to chat while the men decided to take a walk. Once they were outside and away from any intruding microphones, Gerhardt asked, "How was Vienna, Max? How are they holding up in the wake of Anchluss?"

"Not very well, Gerhardt, but Vienna is a proud city with a proud past. On the surface, they are doing quite well, but that proud exterior hides a lot of pain, and the fact that Hitler is an Austrian doesn't do anything to help matters."

Gerhardt considered what Max had just told him with a pensive expression on his face and he might have kept his thought to himself but Max was too good a friend not to tell him what he was thinking. "Back in 1933, when we were seeking a way to make Hitler's power absolute, he and I had several meaningful conversations about Austria in general and Vienna in particular. I had mixed emotions about the city while Hitler had only loathing for it. I found it strange that he would hate the place where he failed rather than himself for failing."

"Actually Gerhardt, he doesn't look upon it as a personal failure. He looks upon the Vienna Academy of Fine Arts as an institution of narrow minded fools who lack the ability to truly appreciate art."

Gerhardt chuckled. "Have you ever seen any of his paintings?"

Max replied, "Ja, I have had the privilege if you could call it that."

"My sentiments exactly," agreed Gerhardt. "But, then, neither of us is an art critic."

"Enough to understand the basic nature of our leader, Herr General."

"Very well, Max. Where are we going with this?"

"Actually, it was you who wanted to know how Vienna was, and although I cannot give you a definitive answer, I can give you a glowing report about how Frau Ilse Liebert reacted to the Imperial City."

"And........"

"She loved it. Wishes to return, and most of all, she loves me. Is good, ja?"

Gerhardt had nothing in reply to that, and since he didn't, Max decided to fearlessly go where angels might have feared to tread, "Gerhardt.......I am not trying to interfere in your life, but I gave into a temptation while we were there. I....we....Ilse and I went...to see.....your parents."

The change in Gerhardt was immediate, but instead of bristling, he withdrew into his famous shell. Words formed in his mind but not on his lips. Hostile retorts formed but did not materialize, and he finally realized that Max was Max and as such, he would not berate his friend for meddling, so instead, he said, "You did?" He also refrained from asking all the questions that might have placed Max on the defensive. Instead, he asked, "How are they?"

"They are well as far as I can determine. I didn't know how well I would be received if, in fact, I would be received at all. Your father wanted to know if you had knowledge of my visit and when I told him no, he sighed heavily. Then, he wanted to know why I came, and I told him that I knew the pertinent facts, and simply wanted to meet with he and the baroness. Now that I have gone out on a limb, I am very glad I did."

"What does that mean, Max?"

"I means that nothing ever stays the same, Gerhardt. Your father has reached the age of remorse. In fact, he reached it several years ago but pride held him back. He still has the same pride, but he was trying to conjure up enough courage to somehow bridge the gap between the two of you. That was when I came forth and gave him the opportunity."

"So what does he want, Max?"

"A son, Gerhardt."

"He has one."

"But, he wants a relationship with his son."

"If he wanted that, he shouldn't have shipped me all the way to a place called Prussia in Northern Germany and forgotten about me."

"He knows that."

Gerhardt made no sound at all.

Max vowed not to argue the point with Gerhardt. He wasn't about to try pushing the string. The herr baron was perfectly capable of pleading his own case. The herr baron knew that fact and accepted it. Max would ask only one more question, "Gerhardt, if your father contacted you, and wished to talk with you, would you?"

"Ja. I would talk. I will probably be civil to him. I might even be nice."

"One could ask for nothing more. I will relay that information to him."

"Very well," Gerhardt answered. "Next item of discussion."

"What's that," inquired Max.

"I have a letter signed by SS Reichsführer Heinrich Himmler considering your status with the SS."

Max was very interested only because he wanted no part of the SS command and control structure. He felt that the SS would ultimately come to no good and being a part of this group of no goods would probably be a death warrant to all the principles especially when Germany lost the war they were about to wage.

He was not a defeatist.....he was a realist. No matter how easy it might look in the beginning, if Hitler did not fight it the way Gerhardt suggested that Hitler fight it, Germany would ultimately lose. Max looked back at Gerhardt, and said, "So what did the Herr Reichsführer have to say?"

"He has defined your purpose to me and in doing so, has let you off the hook, so to speak." Max Brightened. "He has designated you as an Ad Hoc member of the SS who has been assigned to the SS purely as a means of assigning everyone to an organization. You can assist me in the performance of my duties, but cannot take part in any of the special projects that are being contemplated by Heydrich and that is good, Max. That man is insane. Totally insane, and he is good at hiding it, but not for very long."

Max just looked at Gerhardt. He hadn't talked to Heydrich yet. He knew that Hitler liked him and within the Reich that was all that mattered.

Gerhardt continued, "In any respect, I want you to have a

photo copy of the letter. Keep it someplace where it can't be found." He paused briefly and swallowed hard when he did. "Max, I need to tell you something that is very treasonous. I believe that I can trust you implicitly, but if it turns out that I can't, I will not fear the consequences. I will not live my life in fear. Therefore, I will now come out of the box."

Max did not give him words of reassurance. They were not necessary. He just waited.

Gerhardt sighed heavily, "Max, within the next few days, Germany will wage a war of aggression against its neighbors. We will probably overwhelm them. After the small countries are defeated, we will invade France, and the stupid French believe that the Maginot Line will be a deterrent to German aggression. **It will not!**. We will ignore it. The shortest route still goes through Belgium."

"But, the Belgians are neutral."

"They were in the Great War, and Belgian neutrality won't mean anymore to us now than it did then."

It was Max's turn to sigh now.

"Max, Germany has to lose. Somehow, we have to lose."

Max gulped when he heard what he heard.. "But how, Gerhardt? Good God, you know how these people think."

"It is because I know how they think that I say what I say. I don't know how I will manage it, but I have to try. It is important that we do not win."

"But how.......?" Max let his sentence drop into nothingness.

"There has to be a way, Max. I don't know how yet, but there has to be a way."

"Very well, Herr General, and as long as we are dealing with treasonous talk, allow me to tell you a story about what I have really been doing these last seven years," and he did. The time had been right to bring Gerhardt into the Legacy.

When Max finished, Gerhardt looked at his friend with renewed respect. For the first time in years, Gerhardt began to see a way to atone for all that he had done wrong starting with the Enabling Act.

Death might be all that waited at the end of a long dark tunnel, but when it came, maybe they could cheat the executioner by doing their own way.

Maybe they would even live.

Thirteen

The real war begins

April 7, 1940

German naval units carrying troops and equipment left from German ports to begin Operation Weserübung which covered the invasion of Denmark and Norway. The British countered by mining Norwegian waters in preparation for British and French landings.

The Danish army did not oppose the invasion. Thus on April 9, German forces occupied the whole of Denmark while naval and parachute troops landed at several Norwegian locations. At sea, the German cruiser Blücher was sunk by Norwegian coastal batteries, and the cruisers Königsberg and Karlsruhe were sunk by British naval units.

On April 13th, a fierce battle between German and British naval units was fought in Jössing Fjord that resulted in the loss of ten German destroyers. The next day, the British and French landed troops near Namos and Narvik in Norway. They fought well but their efforts were only an exercise in futility as they had to be evacuated on April 28, 1940.

On May 10th, at 5:35 a.m., the Wehrmacht began the invasion of Holland, Belgium and Luxembourg. They called this Operation Yellow. The operation employed Army Group A and Army Group B with Army Group C which was held in reserve. In addition to the three army groups, three Panzerkorps were included. This constituted close to 2500 tanks and they struck with lightening like speed.

Hitler spoke to his troops in the field and told them that the battle that was beginning that day would decide the fate of the German nation for the next thousand years. For the record, the battle was successful....highly successful, but the Reich only lasted for twelve years. But then, Adolph was very adept at making the gross overstatement.

Operation Yellow did manage to resolve a lot of things, not the least of which was the downfall of Neville Chamberlain, the British Prime Minister, who resigned later that day. He was replaced by Winston Churchill.

By May 12th, French forces withdrew behind the Meuse river. This withdrawal, like most withdrawals, had strategic implications, but it was all for naught, because the very next day, May 12, the two German Panzerkorps of Heersgruppe (army group) B, emerged from the Ardennes forests and advanced to the same Meuse river and established multiple bridgeheads on the other side. What they accomplished was ripping a 50 mile gap in French lines. The 7th Panzer division commanded by Rommel was the first division across.

This was the action that precipitated Churchill's famous "Blood, sweat, and tears," speech to the British House of Commons. It did look bleak from the Allied perspective, while from the German point of view, things were looking, "wunderbar!"

On May 18, the XIX Panzerkorps under the command of Guderian had managed to rapidly advance to the English Channel. By the 20th, Guderian's XIX Panzerkorps had captured Amiens and then moved to the Channel coast at Abbeville. This action separated the British Expeditionary Force and the Belgians from the French in the south.

An ill-fated attack was made by a French brigade under General de Gaulle against Rommel's 7th Panzer Division. Then, to make matters worse, the French Ninth Army was surrounded and destroyed. Its commander, General Giraud surrendered.

Perhaps the greatest victory in German history became tainted by a strategic error on the part of the Leader of the German people. He had halted the advance toward Dunkirk, a spot of beach whereby the defeated British Expeditionary Force was trapped between the bluffs and the waterline, and in defeat, the British demonstrated their own tenacity by commencing Operation Dynamo.

This was the operation whereby every thing that would float and had a means of power was dispatched to the beaches of Dunkirk in a bold attempt to rescue their troops.

Once again, *Der Führer* did not unleash his armies in an effort to halt the evacuation. Instead, he sent the Luftwaffe to handle the problem.

They didn't.

By June 3, 1940 218,226 British and 120,000 French lived to fight another day.

On June 4, German troops entered Dunkirk and captured 40,000 French prisoners.

Munich

On the night of June 4th, 1940, the air raid sirens sounded for the first time during the current war. It would not be the last. The residents of The Mansion found shelter in the sub basement. The bombers were French, and the damage to Munich was minimal.

As far as Gerhardt was concerned the greatest damage was inflicted by Adolph Hitler when he allowed a third of a million Allied troops to be evacuated from Dunkirk.

The Battle of France

June 5th, 1940.....This was the beginning of Fall Rot or Operation Red of the second stage of the invasion of France. A huge conglomerate of German military power, part of which was Heersgruppe (Army Group) B was unleashed against the Weygand Line.

On June 10, 1940, Norway surrendered, and on June 11, in France, German forces captured Rheims which forced the French government to leave Paris for Tours.

On June 12, 1940, General Weygand, the French Commander-in-Chief ordered the troops opposing Heeresgruppe A to withdraw to the south.

On June 14, 1940, German troops entered Paris which had been evacuated of most of its inhabitants. At this point, German troops prepared to assault the Maginot Line. This was the line originally designed to keep the Huns out of France. It didn't. Obviously no Frenchman expected Germany to attack from the west. By June 15th, units of the 7th Armee broke into the Maginot Line and took Verdum.

On June 16th, German forces continued to attack the Maginot Line on a broad front with units of Guderian's XXI Panzerkorps reaching the village of Besancon on the Swiss border. This action prompted the resignation of the French government of Paul Reynaud. It was replaced by a government led by Marshal Petain.

From that point on, France fell quickly under the iron boot of the German Juggernaut. On June 22nd, an armistice between France and Germany was signed at Compiegne. The terms were read out loud, and they called for the occupation of most of northern France including the entire coastline, the industrial areas, Alsace-Lorraine. The majority of southern France was to remain unoccupied with an interim French government at Vichy.

On June 25, 1940, all acts of war between German and French Armed Forces ceased officially.

June 26, 1940

Munich

Six people now shared the dinning table for each meal. Namely, Herr und Frau Liebert, the Herr General von Leitner, and Frau Lisa Marie Mueller In addition to these four, Bridgette Gunderson and Erik Halder also took their meal with the Lord and Lady of the Manor.

On this particular morning, The Liebert's were late coming to the table, and although German efficiency dictated punctuality, Gerhardt wasn't pre-disposed to have someone go and check on the couple. After all, they hadn't been married all that long. Perhaps, they had found an "urgent" matter to attend to. If not, they would arrive sooner or later.

About then, Max and Ilse arrived. Both looked like they

were about ready to burst.

"Guten Morgen," said a jovial Max. Gerhardt looked first at one, then to the other and back and forth several times before finally looking at Lisa. They both shrugged. Then Gerhardt answered Max's greeting with, "Guten Morgen, Max, and tell me.....what pray tell, has gotten into the two of you."

Max looked at Ilse who looked at Max who looked at Ilse and then, Ilse finally said, "You tell them, Max. After, all you are the man of the family."

"Tell us what?" Inquired an nearly exasperated Gerhardt.

"I am truly sorry for the evasion, but when I married Ilse, I never expected to become a father. Now, she tells me that the reason she has been going to her mother's so often is to see the family doctor, and.......... well........she is pregnant."

Confusion reigned for a few minutes as back slapping, hugging and tears of joy seemed to be the order of the day,

After everything died down to a dull roar, they all sat down to breakfast amid excited chatter. Suddenly a man appeared at the doorway to the dining room. It was a messenger carrying a teletype message. Gerhardt motioned for the man to enter. After he signed for the message, he promptly read it. All chatter stopped while he did. Then, he laid it down and looked up.

"As of 1:35 AM yesterday, hostilities have officially ceased between the German Reich and the French Republic. The Wehrmacht has completely and thoroughly defeated the French." He closed his mouth and exhaled from his nose. Ever mindful of the two "hidden" microphones, he raised his coffee cup as in a toast and said, "To the Thousand Year Reich!"

The two women looked at each other but neither said anything. The happiness of the news about Ilse's baby had just been upstaged by the Greater German Reich.

* * * * *

Later in their own quarters, Ilse began crying and Max realized her need to cry. He also recognized her need to be comforted, and he held her until her crying finally abated. It was through sobs that she finally asked, "Why Max, are we bringing a child into such a world?"

Max, who was much wiser than his thirty years might have indicated, replied to her inquiry, "Ilse, Mein Liebe, I don't believe it was our choice. God knows and God understands. God is life and God is hope. That is why I look forward to this coming son or daughter with great anticipation. Life is sacred, Ilse....Maybe that is why we are being blessed with it."

Max Liebert was the man who had doubted and even scorned the idea of a God until lately when he began to embrace the idea of a God.

She held him tightly. Maybe someday, she would also embrace his idea of God. Until then, she would embrace him.

* * * * *

There was celebrating. Especially in the Biergartens that were filled with Germans who celebrated the quick defeat of the hated French, but by and large, those who were out and about walked taller and straighter. Gone was the bitter taste of defeat that Germany suffered in the wake of the first war. This time, The Fatherland had literally smashed the opposition. On that day, Adolph Hitler looked very much like a savior indeed.

Unfortunately, some of the population were not celebrating. Instead, they were mourning, because the defeat of the French, the Dutch, the Norwegians, and the Belgians among others did not come without a price, but to the High Command and more importantly, *Der Führer,* the price in German lives given was a manageable number and the families of those who sacrificed were reminded that no sacrifice was too great for the Fatherland.

In Munich, some people actually found their way to the Horst Wessel monument. Why, was not known. Of all the people who might have died to advance the cause of National Socialism, Horst Wessel's death might have been one of the most ignoble, but in the topsy turvy world of the Third Reich, things did not always add up.

* * * * *

Lisa had been concerned about Karl, and Gerhardt tried to

assure her that no news was good news. Still, the not knowing was a little maddening. She could not have explained her feelings even to Karl had he been there to ask. She had a very hot and passionate love affair going with Gerhardt, and still she felt something of a longing for her husband. Something deep inside of her was allowing her to love two different men. Something that defied logic.

It was these thoughts that happened to be rattling around her mind when Erik Halder, the butler stopped in front of her desk and bowed slightly,

"I beg your pardon, Frau Mueller, but there is an officer courier from Berlin waiting in the sitting room. His name is Hauser, Josef Hauser. He is a Hauptsturmführer, and he has a package for the Herr General. I told him that I would inform the Herr General's secretary of his arrival."

Lisa started to thank Erik, but she stopped at the sound of Hauser's name. She flushed and her body began to react in a strange way. It was something she didn't like, but something she seemed powerless to do anything about. She hadn't even seen the man yet, and already, her body seemed to be saying yes to something that her mind was already rejecting.

Erik noticed her difficulty and inquired, "Are you all right, Frau Mueller?"

She took a deep breathe and replied, "Ja....Erik....I am good....I think. You see, Josef and I are old friends. Danke shön. I shall see to him immediately."

Erik bowed and said, "Bitte shön (you're welcome)," and left.

Lisa stood up and realized that she was wobbly. *My God, what kind of power does this man have over me?* Fortunately, she wasn't experiencing feelings of love. She did not know very much about love, but she was willing to wager that sexual intercourse had very little to do with love. It had everything to do with having sexual intercourse..

She entered the large entry hall and started to head in the direction of the sitting room when she caught sight of her image in the large full length mirror on either side of the door. She was dressed tastefully in a navy blue sheath dress. Gerhardt always told her he liked it because it hugged her in the right places. As she appraised her image, she wondered what Josef would think of her in the dress. Doubtless, he would like it also. Then, she took another deep breathe and walked purposefully in the direction of the sitting room with the clicking sound of her heels clicking echoing all about her.

She reached for the doorknob and opened the door gently. Josef who was seated on the couch, rose to his feet, and smiled in recognition.

"Lisa!" He exclaimed. "I was hoping that it might be you, but it seemed to be more than I had any right to expect, and now.........here you are."

Wunderbar!

He closed the distance and took her hands in his, "Jawohl! It is good to see you again."

Wunderbar!

That was the only thought she was capable of having. Otherwise, her mind had gone blank on her. So far, nothing verbal was coming forth. Then, as if by magic, she calmed down enough to respond. "It is good to see you again, Josef. How have you been?"

He clicked his heels and replied, "Very well, Danke."

"I understand that you have something for the Herr General."

"Jawohl, but I have to give it to him personally. Is he here?"

"Nein. He is on an inspection tour. I don't expect him until tomorrow afternoon."

"That means that I will be here until I can have him sign for it. Does the local SS have facilities for transient officers?"

She knew that having Josef in the same house with her was a bad idea, but she had no other choice. It had been decided that the house had too many rooms not being used to justify the expense of a downtown hotel. Even after providing living quarters for Max and Ilse, there was still an abundance of rooms.

Lisa decided to answer, "Ja, I will have Erik show you to your room. Do you have any baggage?"

"Ja, it is right here," he said pointing to a small suitcase.

"Good," she answered. "I will tell Erik to come and direct you."

He clicked his heels and thanked her once more.

The afternoon dragged by and she hadn't seen Josef since early afternoon. For some reason, she believed that her mind might be winning the battle with her body. She had not been preoccupied with Josef. There were times when she had thought about him, but it was no longer an obsession. It would be easy to surrender to her body's basic need, but was that who she was? Max had once told her that she would never find out who she was until she found out who she was not. Well.....who was she really? She had license to go to bed with Josef or anyone else she wanted to go to bed with, and now that the fruit was no longer forbidden it had lost some of its flavor.

In another part of the house, Josef was starting to wonder if he and the fair Lisa were going to get together at all. He had reason to believe that everything might be going his way and then, all of the sudden she had changed. He had so looked forward to a good romp with her. Well, dinner would be served at seven. He would check her attitude then.

Josef arrived at the dinning room at 6:55 and discovered that another couple were already seated. The man was an SS Standartenführer, a fact that unsettled Josef. As an SS Hauptssturmführer (Captain), the SS Standartenführer outranked him by a considerable margin. He greeted the Herr SS Standartenführer and his lady, and then he noticed a card laying on one of the plates. It had his name on it, so he seated himself. The other couple were conversing quietly without regarding him at all.

"Hello Max! Hello Ilse! Hello Josef!" The voice belonged to Lisa who stopped to give a quick hug to the Standartenführer who now had a name.....Max, and the lady, who was obviously Ilse. Lisa did not give him a quick hug, but Josef refrained from making a comment.

Without being directed to do so, Josef stood up and seated Lisa. She thanked him and then directed her attention to Max. "Max, Gerhardt called just before I left the office and told me that he finished earlier than expected. He should return in late morning.

Then, she turned to Josef, "That should be good news for you Herr Haupsturmführer Hauser." Then she snapped her fingers, "Have you met the Liebert's, yet." Josef said no, and she did the honors after which the kitchen doors opened and the stewards began serving the evening meal.

When dessert had been polished off, Josef remarked, "You people eat well here."

Max answered, "We have no complaints, Herr Hauptstumführer. It comes with the territory."

In an effort to make conversation, Josef inquired, "Is the Herr General inspecting concentration camps?" The question was directed at Lisa who was taken back by the question, and didn't know how to answer it. That was when she noticed the signal from Max.

Max regarded the young man evenly. "My dear Herr Hauptsturmführer, perhaps some bright day tomorrow, you might become privy to the Herr General's itinerary. When that happy day arrives, you may have all the information you need to know. Until then, you do not have the need to know anything at all." He met Josef's eyes and held his gaze until Josef dropped his.

Josef was taken back by his rebuke, but he promptly acknowledged, "Jawohl, Herr Standarten führer!" Then after a few moments, he asked, "May I be excused please?"

Max nodded and Josef left the table.

Lisa watched him leave, and for some reason, she felt sorry for the man.

Max looked at her strangely. Started to say something, and then he decided not to. After that, she stood up and started after him.

She decided that if she were rebuked like he had been that she might want some air so she went outside. He was standing not ten meters from her. She walked over and stood behind him.

"I'm sorry, Josef."

He turned and looked at her. "I was hoping that it might be your footsteps that I was hearing. I guess I made an ass out of myself, ja?"

"You asked the wrong question, that's all. Max is not your standard Berlin type SS Officer, but anytime a Berliner stops and stays for a while, they all manage to incur his wrath."

"I am not the only one?"

"Certainly not! Max went to a lot of trouble to recover a considerable amount of money for the Reich, and then the underlings in Berlin, the ones who like to prove how important they are, send couriers like you all over the Reich with multitudes of redundant documents."

"What if the documents inside my packet prove to be important?"

"It will be the first time, Josef. You forget that I am the Herr General's secretary. That which he has to sign for, will be read by me. I have been cleared for the highest security in the SS, and I can read all documents."

"Then, what are you saying, Lisa?"

"It's not what I say or do not say that is important. What is it that you want, Josef?"

"You." He was blunt and to the point.

She regarded him closely. He was no longer the cocksure man he might have been earlier.. All of the sudden, she realized that whatever power he had over her had vanished. He was still a very desirable man, but she felt no compulsion to have him, and since the compulsion had gone, she decided to ask, "Why?"

"You are the most desirable woman I have ever met. Would you be surprised to know that I have dreamed about you?"

"Ja....that I would."

On impulse, he took her in his arms. Then he backed off slightly. "I am sorry, Mein Liebe. I became too excited. You are too close, and I am too vulnerable to your charms. I must leave soon."

"My God, Josef. Who do you think you are talking to? A child? Don't you give me credit for anything? I didn't want to have to make love to you because my body told me to do so. I could do it only if I had a clear choice in the matter."

He embraced her again, and kissed her. The nervously compulsive male became one with a purpose once more.

Watching from the window were Max and Ilse.

Max said, "I do believe the lady knows the gentleman."

Ilse answered, "Ja, one could say that by observing their behavior."

Max patted his wife's behind gently, and said, "If you were to ask me, I do believe that she has him right where he wants her."

Then, the kiss ended as Lisa pulled away.

Back outside again, Josef asked, "What is wrong, Lisa?"

Lisa became agitated and walked about three steps and turned to face him. "Its this whole damned seduction game! That's what is wrong! You men think about it all the time, and between you and Gerhardt, I am thinking about it all the time, but I will not become like a cat in heat. I will not bare my naked arse to any man who manages to conjur up an erection. It is not who I am. In Berlin, you caught me at the right time. Maybe you will catch me in that mood again someday and maybe you won't. As for tonight, Josef.........I'm sorry."

"I'm sorry too, Lisa. I thought you and I had something going."

"Maybe we still do, Josef, but not right now."

"Lisa I have learned that I can never seduce a woman with my intellect. Seduction has nothing to do with intellect. It has everything to do with chemistry. If it isn't there, words won't make it so. Maybe we should say goodnight."

She bid him goodnight and gave him a goodnight kiss. Then, she went back inside and found Max kissing Ilse.

Lisa actually blushed.

Max broke away from his wife and said, "Things looked promising out there for a while. Care to share what happened?"

"I don't really know who I am yet, and I am reluctant to continue doing what I might not be. Because of that reasoning, I will probably spend a frustrating night, and if what I saw is any indication, you two should be well on your way to having a really marvelous night."

Max drew Ilse close to him.

Lisa smiled and said, "Good night," and retired to her bedroom.

* * * * *

Lisa tossed and turned for what seemed like forever, and sleep still didn't come. Finally, in frustration, she reached over and turned on her bedside lamp. Anytime Gerhardt was out of town, she slept in her own bedroom. The two mattresses were virtually identical so it didn't matter which one she slept on.

She looked at the clock and discovered that it was only midnight. She sighed heavily. Reading looked like an option, so she got out of bed and walked over to her chair. She turned the reading lamp on, but after a half hour had gone by, she couldn't find anything to hold her interest.

She rendered a large sigh and walked over to the hook that held her robe and peignoir. The peignoir was long and sheer. It was a match to the negligee she was wearing, so she reached for the peignoir. She had just decided that the night was probably warm enough for her to go outside. Then, she looked at her slippers and decided against them. They were high heeled slippers. The kind that men loved for women to wear, and she was probably not going to meet any men, so she decided to remain barefoot.

She let herself out of the bedroom and went to the back stairwell. The house was quiet except for the strange settling noises that houses seemed to make at night.

When she reached the backdoor, she opened it to a brilliant full moon. Without the floodlights, the shadows caused by the moonlight cast an eerie glow.

Prior to the termination of hostilities between Germany and France, the French actually mounted an air raid against Munich. It was ineffective, but the message was clear. Don't give an enemy a target. Therefore, the flood lights had been turned off permanently.

Lisa stepped off the sidewalk and walked barefoot in the grass. She felt like a pixy and began to whirl round and round until she became dizzy and stopped. About that time, she heard the water in the fountain, and began walking in the direction of the sound.

As she got closer, she saw something or someone and stopped. It was the glow of a cigarette. She wondered who it was and almost turned around and returned to the house. Instead, she became a little braver and decided to investigate.

With the brilliance of the moonlight, she got close enough to make out the fact that it was a man, and he too was wearing a robe. He was also barefoot, a fact that calmed Lisa's nervous anxiety. Men in bathrobes were usually not the menacing type. The only thing that was less menacing was a naked man. He was exciting, especially if he was aroused.

Lisa decided to announce her presence by clearing her throat.

She still startled the man, but he recovered and turned to face her.

It was Josef.

"Lisa!" What are you doing here?"

"I couldn't sleep. What is your reason?"

"The same, and tossing and turning is not how I wish to spend my nights"

He seemed rooted to the spot where he was standing so Lisa decided to move closer.

"Do you have any idea just how beautiful and desirable you look right now."

She managed a smile although she was sure that he could not make out her smile. "I don't really know, Josef. I have been told that I am lovely, pretty and beautiful, not all at once but at different times by different men most of whom had designs on getting me out of my clothing and into a more favorable position."

He chuckled. "Then, why are you standing here right now?"

"I also find you to be beautiful and desirable, and my body keeps asking my intellect why I made the decision I made earlier."

"And?"

"Josef, regardless of the reason, I am here. A man like you knows perfectly well how to take advantage of that kind of situation."

"Jawohl, Mein Schatz. You are right, but in your case I have learned to be cautious."

"Josef, stop talking and kiss me."

He did exactly as he was told. He started out with a kiss that he might have given to his sister, but Lisa's kiss was sufficient enough to tell him that he was definitely **not** kissing his sister. In fact, Lisa began to really apply the heat, and when her body touched his body, she found that he had risen enormously to the occasion.

She pulled away suddenly and surprised Josef in the process.

He managed to stammer, "What is wrong?"

She stepped back and said, "Nothing is wrong, Mein Liebe," and she removed first, her peignoir followed closely by her negligee. She let both garments fall gracefully to ground. Then, she walked up to Josef, who was drinking in the loveliness of her nakedness, and removed his robe and let it fall to the ground. Having done that, she took him by the hand and led him in to the shadows of some rose bushes. "A now, my lovely man, let us do what we both really want to do."

She slid gracefully to the ground and assumed the position. After that, Josef came down on top of her with equal grace and gentleness. Additional preambles were no longer necessary. This love dance had gone on long enough. Therefore, she took his wonderfully hard member and guided him into her.

* * * * *

It was a very tired but refreshed Lisa who took a bath the next morning with the realization that she still wasn't finished with Josef. That somehow, she still needed him, but was her need real or was she simply taking a special license.

When she dressed, she dressed tastefully in a sleeveless yellow dress with a tight bodice and a full skirt. She wore matching yellow heels and went to rejoin the other members of the house.

When she reached the dinning room, Josef was already there, and he smiled at her as she entered. Greetings were exchanged, and Lisa smiled brightly at everyone especially Josef. Then she walked over and kissed him in front of the knowing looks from Max and Ilse.

She had made that decision while combing her hair. She wasn't about to spend the night with her legs wrapped around the man and then turn around and ignore him.

After breakfast, she returned to her bedroom. About five minutes later, she heard a light knock on the door and went to let Josef in. She often dressed with easy access in mind, and she noted with irony that the men in present day Germany had a lot more clothing to remove than the ladies.. She only had to remove her dress so that it didn't become wrinkled and soiled.

Then, she set the alarm clock for eight forty-five. After all was said and done, she looked at the aroused and ready Josef who only lacked an invitation. She opened her legs and held out her arms. That was the only invitation he needed.

* * * * *

Gerhardt arrived at eleven o'clock and went straight to his office. After a few minutes, he called Lisa in to discuss what had transpired in his absence. As she spoke, he noticed a slightly different demeanor about her. Then, she mentioned that SS Hauptstumführer Josef Hauser had arrived the day before with a packet from Berlin.

The name immediately registered with Gerhardt, who, among other his other attributes, had a photographic memory. His memory had always served him well, and he had continued to develop it. In this case, he had bothered to inquire as to the name of the man that Lisa had spent twenty-four hours with during their stay in Berlin. The man's name was Josef Hauser, but he had been an OberLieutenant at the time. He had obviously been promoted. So what did this development do for their relationship, if anything?

He looked at the woman, but could not do so with anything that even remotely resembled detachment. He was in love with her, but he couldn't help wondering why he wasn't jealous. Another look at her told him that he would do anything to protect her and do his best to make her happy. Even if it meant that she continued to have romantic interludes with men like Josef Hauser. He reached out and clasped his hands together. Then, he got an idea.

"Lisa, would you bring Josef Hauser and his packet to me please?"

She nodded, stood up and went to fetch Josef.

When they returned, there was an obvious "something" between them, and it appeared to be growing stronger.

The Herr Hauptsturmführer snapped to attention and rendered the standard military salute. "Hanptsturmführer Hauser reporting to the Herr General as ordered, Sir!"

Gerhardt regarded the man as he would have regarded any competitor. His idea would be a bold stroke, and one that might be rejected by her, but he rather doubted it. He returned the salute and stood at attention. "Stand at ease, Herr Hauptsturmführer," said a soft spoken Gerhardt Then he offered the Herr Hauptsturmführer his hand, an act that surprised Lisa. After doing that, Gerhardt said, "Have a seat, Herr Hauptsturmführer." Josef sat in a chair next to Lisa.

"First of all, the packet that brought you to Munich in the first place."

Josef, who had the packet on his lap, took it and handed it to the General along with the receipt that Gerhardt needed to sign. Gerhardt picked up a fountain pen, signed the document, and handed it back to Josef. Josef returned to his chair and glanced sideways at Lisa as he did. Lisa flushed, and Gerhardt, being the astute observer that he was, noticed it.

He inhaled very deeply. Then, he exhaled through his nose.

He rubbed his chin and looked at Josef. "Tell me Herr Hauptsturmführer, what are your orders?"

"I have them inside my tunic, Herr General, and you may see them if you wish, but I am to deliver the packet to you, and return to Berlin within 72 hours of my delivery. They further tell me that I am authorized to travel by rail."

Gerhardt nodded, "I don't need to see your orders, but I did need to know how much time they allowed you to return." Josef nodded and Gerhardt turned his attention to Lisa. "Lisa, during my inspection tour, I spoke with the SS Reichsführer who indicated that he wanted all secretaries within the SS to come to Berlin for special instruction. It would last for thirty days, and you would be housed in a hotel with room, board, and travel expense, all to be paid by the SS. The Reichsführer knows and understands the circumstances concerning your daughter and will not force you to attend, but regardless of your decision, you will need instruction. It will be much easier to give you that instruction in Berlin. So, what are your thoughts?"

She hadn't brightened at the prospect of spending a month with Josef. Instead she looked at him thoughtfully. Finally.....she said, "May I speak to you privately, Gerhardt."

Gerhardt answered, "Ja," and then to Josef, he asked, "Will you excuse us please?"

Josef was puzzled. The Herr General was giving he and Lisa a perfect opportunity. Was she questioning it? Whatever it was, he was in no position to question anything. So he stood up and left.

Once the door had closed, Lisa asked, "You know don't you?"

Gerhardt looked at her evenly. There was a time when he would have said or done anything at all just to have her. Now, he would not lie to her even at the risk of losing her. "It's my memory, Lisa. It's too good. I remembered his name from when you told me about him in Berlin. The rest was simple deduction."

She smiled at his directness. She had no doubt that this man would never lie to her again, and neither would she lie to him. So she recounted the events of the previous day and he listened with fascination. She talked about her restraint which was later followed by frustration that ultimately led to their "chance" meeting by the fountain, and finally the explosion of merging passions.

He became aroused by just listening to her, and then, he pushed those thoughts aside. It was time to meet the dragon head on.

"Lisa, I violated my cardinal principle. Call it the prime directive if you will, but I lied to you about Berlin."

She became puzzled, and so, she asked. "You weren't going to send me to Berlin?"

"Oh, I was going to send you there all right. That much was the truth, but not for training. You could stay in a hotel if you wished or his apartment if he has one. The reason that I gave was necessary in order to give it dignity and purpose. It might have sounded better to your convoluted sense of logic than the real reason. I am sorry that I found it necessary to fabricate a story, but I'm not sorry I did it. I love you far too much to play games. If you want to be with Josef, I won't stand in your way. To prove it, I will ask Josef if he would like to be my aid-de-camp. That way, you wouldn't have to move." *What I didn't tell you, Lisa is that Josef is only a courier, and couriers don't have much value to Himmler except that they are probably good Party hacks, but I won't cast aspersions on your young man if you really want him.*

"Lisa, I now ask you......what do you want?"

Time became elongated as Lisa seemed to be mired in deep thought. Her eyes never left his during this entire thought process. Finally, she smiled, and Gerhardt allowed himself to relax slightly.

Lisa began with a sigh. "Gerhardt, I do believe that I love you, and that creates a dilemma in my mind because I also love Karl."

Gerhardt smiled as Lisa continued. "I don't love Josef. I only desire him. So intense was our first encounter in Berlin that my body probably craved a repeat performance. I don't know if that makes any sense to you, but I think that is what happened. At least, that is the way Max would probably explain it. Would I do it again? I don't know, but I have to believe that I might. The problem with Josef is that he is superficial. He doesn't really have a lot going for him outside of the bedroom or wherever we decide to make love. I have a better future with you or with Karl.....maybe both."

He laughed heartily. "Danke shön, Mein Schatz. I will keep my own observations about Herr Hauser to myself, but I doubt if he will go any higher than where he is right now, and now Mein Liebe, what is your pleasure? I refuse to assume anything. Not where you are concerned."

She stood up, walked around the desk, turned his swivel chair so that he faced her, sat on his lap and kissed him passionately.

Afterward, a visibly shaken Gerhardt said, "I guess it means you don't want to go."

She stood up and said, "Jawohl, Herr General. I wish to remain with you, and now I had better break the news to Josef."

Thirty minutes later, Gerhardt's driver took Josef to the train station in the Mercedes. Josef wasn't happy but he seemed to be satisfied by Lisa's admission that she might still need his services in the future. That was when he began to wonder if women like Lisa only saw him as a means of satisfying their lustful urges and nothing more.

Fourteen

Secrets

Lisa wasn't quite ready to charge her lustful experience off as "growing pains." Once again, she was tripping over the idea of morality, but if that were the case, her entire experience with Gerhardt was a wrong one, and in order to clear her mind and whatever conscience she still had, she sought the knowledge, wisdom and experience of Max Liebert.

Max probably knew Lisa as well as any man. At least as well as any man not sleeping with her. Perhaps that privilege was not to be his destiny although he was not complaining. After all, he was married to the fair Ilse, and when he took off his blinders, he had to realize that more men wanted to sleep with Ilse than with Lisa.

It was an unexplainable phenomenon. Lisa actually dazzled them while Ilse didn't, but Max had to admit that men seemed to dwell more on Ilse then they did on Lisa. Still water ran quite deep.

Anyway, this conversation wasn't about Ilse. Lisa wasn't actually feeling *guilty* about her experience with Josef, but in a repressive society, and Max guessed that Hitler's Germany was about as repressed as it could get, women were made to feel guilty when just *thinking* about sex unless they were having sex with a Nazi.

In that case it was okay.

The fact that German males seemed to be as fiesty as any other male tended to confuse matters. Then......along came men like Gerhardt who told her to jump into their bed *or else*. It was enough to confuse any maladjusted female. The fact that men like Gerhardt actually ran the country didn't help matters any.

Lisa seemed to be seeking absolution without the aid of a priest while, at the same time, disdaining the idea of the need for absolution in the first place.

As he listened to her concerns, he couldn't help but admire her. He also desired her, but he imagined that any man who was not a neuter probably would. In Max's non-judgmental view of the world, such desires were normal and should not be repressed. After all, desire was only desire. Sometimes desires were made manifest. Other times, they were not. He often wondered if the taboo created the priesthood or if it was the priesthood that created the taboos?

When it came Max's turn to react to what Lisa had told him, he was a mite perplexed. Then he smiled and shrugged. "I really don't know how to react. After all, you already know that I don't think like the rest of the herd." He smiled mischievously. "That doesn't mean that I don't have the same desires, but I like to think that I am more civilized than the rest of them." Lisa smiled.

"Actually Lisa, I think you are better adjusted than the rest of us. If anything, you seem to be operating in the shadow world that lies between *license* and *constraint.* It might tend to give you an occasional headache, but I wouldn't worry your pretty head about it if I were you.." He shrugged again.

"In truth, Lisa, you are chewing on the subject of morality as though it was synonymous with spiritual law, when in fact, it only deals with accepted rightness." She looked up sharply when he said that.

"In other words, when you made the decision to copulate with Josef, it was only between you and him. The rest of society wasn't involved. They didn't have a need to know. They probably wouldn't have approved even if they did know. Don't ask them. Just be discreet, and don't let the rest of the flock know you are different."

She kissed him......the conversation had ended.

* * * * *

Ilse and Lisa lived in two entirely different worlds and in contrast to Lisa, the world of Ilse seemed to be a less complex place to live even though they had experienced many similarities.

While being attractive in an understated way, Ilse had an

appeal that naturally attracted males, but until she married Karl, no man had crossed the threshold of her femininity, and during her six year marriage to Karl several men expressed more than a passing interest in her, but only one man had made any serious overtures and he might have succeeded had he obtained access to a secure location, but he lacked both imagination and initiative Therefore, he was unsuccessful.

In truth, Ilse did not care if her looks were understated, overstated, or simply not stated at all, because none of this kept her from having secret thoughts and desires. She had disdained all the fairy tales about being the pretty princess that would be rescued by the handsome prince. No! Once she had reached maturity, any decent looking well endowed male would have sufficed, but those thoughts remained buried just below the surface. In addition to that, her world consisted exclusively of Bavarian men, and the idea of a greater Deutschland was still foreign to many Bavarian folk even though it had been that way since the 1870's. Bavaria was still the *Heimat.* The place where she was from.

Bavarian men were.......well...they were Bavarian men! What else could be said about them? Besides, she surmised that men were men regardless of where they came from.

After Karl's death when Otto had intruded into her life, she had been amazed at how easy it had been for Otto to crack her veneer. He didn't even have to threaten her. He was both sympathetic and loving. More importantly, he made her feel like a desirable woman. She felt wanted, and when he seduced her in front of the fireplace on a cold winter's evening, she had put everything she had into pleasing him.

Of course, when the novelty wore off and she tried to break with him, he had other ideas and coerced her into continuing the relationship.

At least that was what she told herself. Good Bavarian girls didn't do this and good Bavarian girls didn't do that when in truth, the word *good* was a relative term that applied only to the majority opinion.

She finally realized that no one knew what was going on behind closed doors and that was when she took a perverse kind of pleasure in each of their couplings. Her secret self had emerged.

The "X" factor in the equation had been Heinz Gottlieb. His appearance had been sudden and everlasting. He was the man who knocked on her door and not ten minutes later, they were horizontal and superimposed.

It was like that with him. She never knew when. Only that when he did show, the fireworks display lasted for as long as he was there. He had been her phantom lover and anytime her life hit a low ebb, he would magically appear and lift her spirits along with everything else.

There had been other times when she dressed respectably and went to a cabaret all alone, something that she wouldn't have done back in her native Munich. In Berlin, she felt a sense of freedom that she never felt anywhere else.

She found that women who dressed like sluts attracted men, but the quiet, well dressed, and respectable young lady attracted a better quality of man. Although she hadn't done it very often, she did it just often enough to allow her secret self to come forth behind the closed door of wherever it was that he decided to take her. She never took a man to her own apartment. Some of her wildest flings came when she coupled with those men, but the wildest of them all happened with Heinz Gottlieb.

In spite of all that has been said, Ilse remained a very quiet woman. She was a good friend to all who knew her, and was a wonderful companion for Max, but she usually held back in conversations and tried not to upstage her husband. In that, she was not only a good Bavarian wife, but a good German wife as well. She was completely non-confrontational.

If Josef was Lisa's nemesis, Heinz Gottlieb was therefore Ilse's nemesis. It had been a long time since she had seen him, but his memory never completely faded from view. Now, they were both in Munich but neither knew about the other even though he was head of the local Gestapo and she was the wife of a high profile SS officer.

Gottlieb's name had not even come up in a casual conversation, and since she really did love Max, Gottlieb seemed to be relegated to a forgotten spot in Ilse's memory. She was married to a really good man and was carrying his baby. How could life be any better? She was about to be introduced to a man by the name of Murphy.

Murphy was an Irishman, and any good German will tell you

that Irishmen are not reliable since they are not serious individuals. They drank far too much and tended to get carried away with their mouths..

In any respect, Murphy had a law. Everyone called it Murphy's Law and one part of that law stated that when things tended to go bad, and they usually did, they would do so at the worst possible time.

Ilse's time came during a dance held in honor of something or someone that no one would ever be able to remember. Such was the nature of the Third Reich where even the redundant types were remembered in song and an occasional ball or two.

It gave men a chance to dress up and show their women off or go off chasing after another man's woman. It was all good sport, and although both Gerhardt and Max felt no small amount of trepidation about subjecting their ladies to what could end up becoming a drunken brawl, they had been duty bound to attend.

When they arrived, the foursome did a wonderful job of circulating and since Gerhardt was the senior ranking SS officer in the Munich area, junior officers seemed to come in endless numbers in an attempt to gain a small amount of favor.

Suddenly, another male voice, one with confidence spoke up but not to Gerhardt. "Hello, Ilse.....what a pleasant surprise. I didn't know you were in Munich?"

Max regarded both Gottlieb and Ilse for long moments. Her reaction was one of initial shock followed by something he couldn't define.

She quickly composed herself and replied, "Hello Heinz, this **is** an unexpected surprise."

The fact that Ilse and Gottlieb knew each other filled a blank in Max's mind. He had suspected that his wife had a man or men she chose not to share with him, and Heinz Gottlieb was either that man or one of the men. Why she had chosen to keep quiet about the man was a mystery, but many women had secrets they kept from their husbands. It heightened the allure, the anticipation, the desire. It also made him wonder why Ilse would omit her experiences with Heinz when her experience with Otto had been on the wild side. Was it because Otto was dead and Heinz was still alive? Was it because Heinz might still be able to light the fire within her? If that were true, was Heinz a threat to him?

Suddenly, as if hit by a bolt of lightning, Max remembered that she had tried to tell him something when they were on their honeymoon in Vienna. He also remembered that he silenced her by telling her that it didn't matter if she had one hundred lovers. he would love her anyway. That was what he said and that was what he meant. End of that debate.

Heinz replied, "Surprise **is** the correct word isn't it?"

Ilse wanted to say, *you never came back! You didn't even call. Why?* In Ilse's mind, abandonment was the same as rejection. Now, he appeared out of the blue with no fanfare whatsoever. Why?

Instead, Ilse responded with, "Surprise is the right word. Are you now living in the Munich area?"

"Jawohl! I am the head of the local Gestapo, and you?"

She took Max's hand and said, "I am now married to Max Liebert."

He bowed slightly, "I know your husband, but I didn't know he was married to you."

She chuckled. "You see.....there are some things the Gestapo doesn't know."

He shook his head. "Not so, Frau Liebert. Ignorance is always temporary. Sooner or later, we always find out, ja?"

A vacuum ensued, and it was Max who said, "Well, if you will excuse me Herr Chief Inspector, we must be rejoining the Herr General and his lady. Perhaps you two *old friends* can get together soon."

Heinz took Ilse's hand and kissed it. Ilse would not tell her husband how her body reacted to that simple gesture. Instead, she took her husband's arm and they walked away. She felt his eyes on her as they walked away, but she was sure she was imagining it and then, she gave into the impulse to look.

He was.

When they returned to their table, she sat down and realized that she was aroused. So aroused, in fact, that she was uncomfortable and she fidgeted for a while before Max asked, "Is something wrong?"

She answered, "Ja, I need to go to the toilette."

He nodded while knowing full well that the toilette was on

the other side where they had just come from. She arose and walked away, and as she did, he tried to observe her the way another man would. He knew that he was blinded by love for the woman, but as she clicked away she was slightly unsteady on her feet. Her wobble was only slightly perceptible, but it was still there. Her black chiffon dress was exposed in the back and the hem line fell just below her knees. Her black matching heels made her look quite alluring..

Any man would appreciate that feature in her, and she might just find herself in another man's bed whether she wanted to be there or not.

By some strange coincidence, similar thoughts were going through Ilse's mind. She had often turned to find a man looking at her, but she never bothered to think about what it might be like to be with that man. She wasn't mentally wired that way. Being a sex object might have been a secret desire, but it was still strange territory regardless of her experiences in Berlin. She normally didn't think that way. In fact, only two men ever caused her to become aroused by just thinking about them and she happened to be married to one of them. Now that the other man was here, what was she supposed to do?

She felt a deep sense of love for Max, and she felt that she knew Max's personal philosophy, but that didn't give her the license to have sexual relations with Heinz, if for that matter, Heinz still desired her?

When she entered the toilette, she found a stall and closed the door. Then she lifted her dress and removed her underwear. Her standard underwear had been garter belt, stockings, and panties, and since sex for she and Max was fun, her panties were easy to remove.
This time was no exception.

She wasn't even bothered by the conventional fear that if she ever took sick, the medical people would know that she wasn't wearing underpants and surmise that she was an easy woman. She reasoned that sick women weren't sexy and didn't care.

Once removed, she looked and saw a place near the base of the stool where she could stuff them. She didn't care. She had plenty. Then, she wiped herself off, and left the stall. After washing her face and hands, she left the toilette.

She started walking in the right direction but she felt the grip of a hand on her arm and felt herself being guided in the opposite direction. With a mighty effort, she managed to stop.

She looked and saw it was Heinz.

"What are you doing, Heinz?"

"I need you and I want you!"

"Your forgetting something, aren't you?"

"What is that?"

"I am married to Max!"

"So?"

"I am also pregnant with his child."

"I am happy for you, Ilse, but what has that got to do with me?"

"I am not the same woman you knew in Berlin."

"No Ilse, you are not. You are even more desirable."

"But, if you cared, why did you stop coming?"

"I was sent away for special training, and I couldn't come."

"You could have called."

"Could I? How? You had a special number. One that I didn't even know. When I finally returned to Berlin, Otto was dead and I didn't know how to find you."

She sighed heavily. "So what do you want?"

"You!" .

"What about Max?"

"He already has you. I only want part of you."

He had been steadily guiding her and they were now moving down an intersecting hallway. They came to a door which he opened, and she was guided inside.

Ilse knew exactly what was in the offing. She wanted to resist, and yet she didn't. In the dim light, Heinz's face was very close to her face, and then, he kissed her lightly. She broke away and pleaded, "Please Heinz......don't."

"Very well," he said. "Tell me that you don't want me. Do so....be convincing, and I will leave you."

She became quiet.

Stillness can be maddening especially when you know that stillness should be filled with words of denial, but regardless of what it should have been, stillness remained.........still..

This time, Heinz covered her mouth with his and her mouth

opened to receive his tongue. Somewhere, in the back channels of her mind, there were reasons why she shouldn't be doing this, but she couldn't think of a single one.

He raised her dress and discovered that she wasn't wearing underpants. After that, he laid her down on a pile of quilts, and removed his own clothing while Ilse lie there torn between the need to leave and the overwhelming desire to stay.

It was her indecision that doomed her if doom is the proper word to use, for nothing really bad happened to her unless the idea of having sex was considered to be bad. In the world of police matters, Ilse was about to be raped, and yet what Heinz found waiting for him was a fully aroused woman, and from his perspective women who about to be raped were terrified. They were definitely not aroused. They did not kiss the rapist eagerly with each passing second encouraging the rapist to greater heights.

A fully aroused Heinz Gottlieb now hovered over his *prey* and caressed her feminine parts which took her to even greater heights.

Then, he entered her and stopped.

He had never done that before. He just considered her for long moments before the ride began, and for as long it lasted, it was the wildest of her life. The kind that could confuse a woman, and make her long for something she didn't have, didn't want, didn't need, but would long for anyway.

Even after he had spent, he wasn't finished, and she held on to him tightly as they traversed the roller coaster of ecstasy one more time together.

Then, it was finally over.

There was an afterglow, a need to kiss and to caress, but soon, a sense of urgency came to her, and this time, he didn't stand in her way. She was disheveled and disarrayed, but she was still fully clothed, and she smoothed herself as best she could and moved rapidly in the direction of the toilette.

She was finally put back together and leaving the toilette only to see that Max was waiting for her.

He looked at her anxiously and asked, "You took a long time! Is anything wrong?"

She really wanted to be honest with him and say, *"I'm sorry,*

Max, but Heinz and I are old friends and we...er...well...we went someplace and ravished each other. I hope you don't mind." Instead, he had inadvertently given her a way out, and she said, "I became sick. I hope I didn't worry you." It might explain her still flushed appearance.

Max said, "I am sorry, dear. Do you feel all right, now?"

She replied, "Yes, I feel better now. It must have been something I ate."

There were flaws in her story. Flaws that could not have gotten by someone as perceptive as Max Liebert. Flaws like a wrinkled dress. Flaws like a red mark that was beginning to rise on Ilse's neck. No, he didn't think she had been sick. Not at all, but he would not make an issue of it. Not yet, anyway.

Later, when they were alone in their apartment, Max was seated in his favorite chair reading while Ilse was taking a bath, and getting ready for bed. Actually, Max was thinking. The book was only a prop.

Ilse dried off and looked at herself in the mirror. That was when she noticed the red mark. A love bite. Heinz had been sloppy. Her passion had carried over and she wanted to finish it with her husband, but now......???

She slipped into something that Max always liked but there was nothing really sexy about it. It covered everything but the love bite. She sighed and went to join her husband.

She walked into the stube and sat across from Max who looked up and regarded her warmly and yet there was something, and then she thought about the red mark and she instinctively knew that Max had seen it.

She prefaced what she was about to say with, "Max, I have something to tell you," and ended up telling about her encounter with Heinz. She told him exactly how it happened, and when she was done, she stopped talking and dropped her eyes from his.

When she looked up and saw that he was smiling, she realized that she had been holding her breathe. He got up, walked over and sat down beside her. He placed his arms around her, drew her to him, and they kissed passionately, wildly, madly. Max was on fire and he transferred his fire to her. Before long, they were rolling on the floor, with clothing being magically removed from their bodies.

It was as if a secret storm had generated mighty waves that

moved relentlessly toward the rocky shore, and when the first wave broke, it pounded that same rocky shore with all its fury, and each succeeding wave kept pounding the shore thus driving the water even further inland until the ocean had finally spent its fury and the water receded once more to the depths from whence it came.

They lie quietly in each other's arms.

Sooner or later, they would find the energy to struggle to their bed. In the meantime, they lie quietly. Neither felt the need to go anywhere.

It was Max who finally managed to utter, "What manner of woman are you, Ilse Marie, that you are able to drive two men to the ultimate of their abilities, and manage to do so with both men in the same evening."

She only managed to kiss him as the ability to talk was still beyond her ability to accomplish.

Later, much later, they struggled to their feet and finally made it to their bed. The tenderness that followed their bout of sexual violence gave Max an even greater philosophical spin on life, *Why dost thou struggle for Heaven, my love, for the real Heaven resideth within.*

It was Ilse who finally managed to say, "I am not certain what love really is, but if I had to make a guess, I would say that it is the way I feel about you right now. There is a rightness about this place....this time....you and me."

Max made it impossible for her to say anything else until he stopped kissing her, but then, the kiss didn't stop until the miracle of love happened once more.

Yes that is correct.

At a time when doing anything at all seemed to be at the end of endurance, they made love, and this time it was gentle and loving.

At its conclusion, they disengaged and fell into a deep lover's sleep.

In the morning, they arose fresh and rested. Not much was said about Ilse's encounter with Heinz except that its telling seemed to be the catalyst that impelled them into their sexual odyssey.

Later.....much later, when the subject came up again, Max informed her that he had absolutely no feelings about Gottlieb whereas he had all kinds of feelings for her. Maybe, their odyssey had been better primarily because it was nature's way of asserting the natural partners over the unnatural partners. For the man who had all kinds of theories, he offered no other.

For some reason, Ilse seemed to think that Gottlieb's hold on her might have lessened somewhat. Max told her that it didn't matter what happened between she and Heinz Gottlieb. It mattered only what happened between she and Max Liebert.

* * * * *

Ilse had also been granted permission to operate somewhere in the same shadow zone between license and constraint that had been granted to Lisa The sanctity of the marital institution was not an issue. In a way, it took their marriage to a new level. One that allowed latitude within reasonable limits.

Max had always viewed the story about the Garden of Eden as fiction and not very good fiction at that. In his view, the plot was flawed. He reasoned that any God powerful enough to create a vast universe in which everything moved in perfect synchronization and symmetry would not have created a flawed human being.

The story also told us that sin was introduced to the world when Eve ate of the fruit of the Tree of Knowledge. A tree that had been forbidden by God. The bottom line being that Adam and Eve could do whatever they wanted to do but they were not allowed to know anything, and if they had not disobeyed, we doubtless would not be here.

The generations of man did not begin until Adam and Eve had been banished from the Garden, and since all subsequent human beings had been born into this Original Sin, they were doomed to perdition because they would forever fall short of the glory of this God.

He had other choice things to say about the Bible, but they were not germane to this story. Suffice it to say, that when the fruit was no longer forbidden, it lost its taste. That was his logic with Ilse. Unless love was added to the mix, sex was only sex. It lacked substance and therefore remained superficial.

In the end, it all came down to a matter of love. He would love her. He could do nothing greater than that.

Fifteen

The aftermath

The dust was in the process of settling in what became known known as occupied Europe. Of course, Herr Hitler didn't see Europe as anything but his. It was his by right of conquest and those who were conquered deserved to be dominated. This was all part of *Lebensraum.* The creation of living space for Germans, but only for those who were free of defects.

In order to accomplish this, SS second-in-command Reinhard Heydrich had established *Der Einsatz Gruppen.* These were special troops who followed in the wake of the invasion forces and rounded up the politicians and Jews. Some were killed outright while others were taken to concentration camps for further disposition.

These were the really bad guys.

It was unfortunate that many Allied soldiers were never able to differentiate between black and field gray. To them, a German was a German, and maybe that was only right. If anyone had to discern the difference between good and evil, maybe it should have been the Germans.

Besides, the act of invading one's neighbor for something as redundant as living space was an affront to all that might have been decent, if...in fact, decency was still a worthwhile goal for the world.

Getting back to the bad guys, even German regular army troops did not appreciate the Einsatz Gruppen, but they were soldiers of the Reich and the Reich was a police state. They did what they were told to do.

* * * * *

Gerhardt had often pondered the idea of Karl Mueller. The man represented an enigma. Gerhardt's relationship with Lisa was a good one except for her occasional forays with men like Josef, but those were few and far between, and no matter how intense those forays seemed to be, she always returned to him and was more affectionate than before.

Karl was another matter entirely. He was the lady's husband and little Heidi's father. Lisa had learned to love her husband since she had come to live with him. It was a strange situation that could allow a woman to love two men. If there was a problem, it was the fact that Gerhardt was privy to this while Karl was not.

The last few letters indicated that he might be getting wise, but he only spoke in vague generalities.. Both Gerhardt and Lisa believed that Karl might also be sampling French pastry. The kind that wore skirts that is. Karl was stationed on the French coast, but wasn't able to tell her where he was located or what he was doing. He was only able to tell her that he was part of an engineering detachment that was being taken care of by a young lady.

In one of Karl's more recent letters, he described her and went to great lengths to explain what it was that she did for him and his men.. Lisa never expected fidelity. After all, she wasn't being faithful to him. She only wanted him to be happy and when she returned his letter, she encouraged him to talk about her at greater length.

He did!

The girl's name was Yvette, and by the end of the letter, Lisa was certain that Karl had allowed himself to fall in love with the woman. The thought made Lisa feel funny, although it wasn't jealousy. It was more like sadness for a world in which people had to grab whatever happiness they could before someone came along and yanked the rug out from under them.

A month later, Karl told her that he was coming home for two weeks. Would that be all right?

Of course, she had written him back. She would be waiting for him. What he did not tell her was that he had an extra week that he spent with his parents. During that week, he made special financial arrangements for Lisa ...... and Yvette. Extraordinary as it might have seemed, the father did not question the wisdom of the son. After that, Karl took the train to Munich.

Karl's homecoming was not like the previous one. He was not a returning war hero this time, but Lisa lavished him with kisses and then they went to the cabin they had used during his last visit. The one thing different was his rank. He was now a Hauptmann or Captain.

From a personal perspective, Karl was an even better lover than he had been before, but he was often wistful and distant. Perhaps, he would rather have been with Yvette, but she didn't ask. Some things had to remain secret, but she guessed that he had come home more out of a sense of duty than a need to see her and his daughter.

That was probably good enough.

The two weeks brought them both back to the reality of the Fatherland. It was no longer the place they had been born into.

She did learn that he was billeted in a French village near the coastal city of Pas de Calais. Pas de Calais was the closest point between France and the English coast. It was only a few kilometers from the Dunkerque. It was from there that a large segment of the British Army along with French soldiers managed to escape certain capture while the Wehrmacht was forced to watch This was because Herr Hitler would not release the ground forces until it was too late. *Der Führer* had decided that *Der Luftwaffe* could pound the enemy into submission which they didn't.

Before leaving, Karl met with Gerhardt in the large receiving hall,. It was the Herr Hauptmann Karl Mueller meeting the Herr SS General Gerhardt von Leitner. Lisa was certain that Karl had been sizing the man up. The conversation itself remained formal although it managed to lighten some near the end.

The most impressive thing to Lisa was that Karl managed to carry himself with the confidence and dignity of a Prussian military officer. Near the end of the conversation Karl told Gerhardt, "I have wanted to thank you for making it possible for me to become a commissioned officer."

Gerhardt was taken back and replied simply, "Bitte shön, Herr Hauptmann."

After some more conversation, Karl thanked the General again for his time and begged his leave. That having been granted, Karl and Lisa left.

* * * * *

When Karl's train pulled out of the station, Lisa knew they had both come very close to absolute honesty, but somehow it had alluded them. Karl had told her that his assignment in France had been extended for two more years, a fact that pleased him greatly.

Her greatest surprise came when she returned to Gerhardt's bed. He had missed her and welcomed her back with all the gusto and ardor he could muster, and that was considerable. For the first time, she felt like she was returning to where she belonged.

* * * * *

Pas de Calais, France

It was a bumpy ride to the small hamlet just outside of Pas de Calais. Karl hopped out and hefted his bags out of the back.

He looked at the Sergeant who was driving and said, "Danke shön, Herr Sergeant."

The Sergeant nodded to the officer, "Bitte shön, Herr Hauptmann. Enjoy the day. It is going to be a good one." The sun was just making its appearance above the eastern horizon.

Karl nodded and headed toward the door. He thought about knocking first, but decided against it. She knew he was coming and would be expecting him. She had told him that her home was his home and he should never be timid about entering it. And so it was, that he turned the handle, felt the latch loosen its grip, and the door began to swing inward.

He was quiet lest she still be asleep, but in the corner, she was working quietly by the kitchen sink. She had heard the click of the door and turned. When she saw it was Karl, she brightened, and exclaimed, "Karl!"

He had set his bags on the floor first, and then she literally flew into his arms. After the first five or six kisses, he looked around and said, "Bridgette?" He was referring to Yvette's two year old daughter. Yvette had been widowed and her daughter orphaned by Hitler's expansionist policies.

Jean Bourdeaux, Yvette's late husband, was a soldier who took exception to Hitler's idea of *Lebensraum*, and did his best to do something about it.. Unfortunately, he died when he happened to be occupying the same space that an incoming shell decided to occupy.

Regardless of the French defeat, Yvette did manage to learn about Jean's death in a timely fashion, but she didn't have the luxury of being able to mourn her husband's death. Germans were all over the place and they had those brutes in black uniforms running around grabbing maidens and Jews and politicians and who knows what all. One thing the French peasants did learn how to do was tell the difference between Black uniforms and gray uniforms.

About three months after the dust settled, several gray tracked vehicles with those black crosses painted on the side rumbled into the village and stopped. The commander was a young Hauptmann. His name was Karl Mueller, and he spoke excellent French. He was actually nice to the townspeople.

He needed a base of operations, and managed to take over a vacant house. Yvette had heard about the nice young German and didn't believe there were any nice Germans. Young or old. In her way of thinking, the current generation of Germans were all a bunch of bastards. Like it or not, she ended up having a German command post for a neighbor, and she didn't like it one bit! She did a very good job of shunning Karl and his men.

Karl might have ignored her as well, but even a German like Karl had learned to appreciate the finer things in life and Yvette was definitely one of the finer things in life. When he went to see her, all he sought was a truce. He didn't expect to accomplish anything else. He had learned about the death of her husband, and from a German perspective, Jean Bordeaux had died a warrior's death, although Karl himself wasn't impressed with any kind of death other than old age.

Karl then did what no German had done so far. He humbled himself.

Once she had finally decided to listen, he offered her work. Work that he would be willing to pay her for doing. He assured her that he would make sure that her neighbors would not consider her to be a collaborator. She would be working for pay, and who among her neighbors could criticize her for wanting to support herself. After all, if they complained, let them put her to work. Since they hadn't, they probably didn't intend to.

In the end, Yvette turned out to be quite pragmatic. None of her reasons for not liking the young German officer had anything to do with him. She didn't like what he represented and for the first time, Karl began to look at things through another person's eyes.

This was France.....NOT Germany, and although France and Germany had been playing this deadly game since the Napoleonic Wars, what gave Germany the right to barge in and take over? Many of the young girls had been loaded aboard trucks and taken away. To where? Who knew? Maybe to brothels......to work camps......to wherever? She did not know. She had been spared because she had a child, but that was then. What if they came tomorrow or the next day. Would her daughter still make a difference?

Karl wanted to reassure her but he could do no such thing. He was an underling just as every other man in the Third Reich. Every man but Hitler that is, and he was in charge. To have promised her anything at all would have given her a false sense of security.

Just as soon as Yvette began working, things began to thaw between she and the young German officer. It actually took a month after the thaw began before they decided to take each other to bed.

His purpose in being there was to begin the fortification of the French coast and Calais was the closest point to the English coast.

It wasn't like anyone expected a counterattack anytime soon. After all, the English had been defeated rather soundly, but it was also assumed that Germany would be invading England and the engineers were needed to make things ready.

It was a good posting for Karl. He spoke French almost as well as he spoke German, and the townspeople respected the young German officer who explained that they should be happy not to have standard occupation troops in their village. The ones in the black uniforms. They were nasty people while he and his engineers didn't have time for such nonsense.

His relationship with the lovely Yvette couldn't have been better. Yvette understood how things were and she realized that should Karl leave, she might be forced to submit to someone she didn't want to submit to. Of course, neither was made of stone. Both had feelings and each managed to fall in love with the other.

Except for the existence of Lisa, Karl might have suggested that he and Yvette marry even though that might not have been possible under the Hitler regime.

Now, after spending a week with his parents and two weeks with his wife and daughter, Karl stood with Yvette in his arms and felt a familiar stirring in his loins. Yvette felt the result of that stirring and guided him toward the bed. Perhaps, they could accomplish the deed before her daughter woke up.

They had just finished when they heard Brigette for the first time. Karl smiled at Yvette and went to get the little girl up. For the first time, there was a purpose for living. His work was satisfying and he was living with a woman who loved him. He wanted it to last forever, and yet, he knew it wouldn't .

* * * * *

When Karl arrived at the cliffs overlooking the beach below, he observed the accomplishments and was impressed. The Germans were planning to build a defensive system and although an allied invasion was not expected anytime soon, it was generally assumed that building the defensive system would take a considerable amount of time and money.

Polish laborers were conscripted and sent south. French laborers might have been better suited but it had been decided to refrain from sending laborers to a place where they were indigenous to the land, language and customs.

Unfortunately, along with the laborers came the SS Guards. Karl became alarmed at having those SS types so close to the village. It could upset the delicate balance he had established. The SS was not interested in either cooperation or peaceful coexistence. They were interested only in control.

It was a dreary day in October, and Karl was at the beach when a Mercedes limousine drove into the village and sought out the Headquarters for the Engineering Battalion. Several curious villagers were watching as an SS General stepped out of the Mercedes. He was wearing a black leather coat and his trousers were tucked into black leather jack boots.

He opened the door to the small building and interrupted a woman who was in the process of cleaning. She whirled about and saw his imposing figure standing in the open doorway.

"Guten Morgen, Herr General," she said.

He replied in French, "And good morning to you, Madame, is it."

"Ja, Herr General. My husband was killed during the Battle of France."

"I am sorry, Madame. Wars are terrible," he replied in French. "You will even find Germans who believe that wars are terrible. And now Madame, can you tell me where the Herr Commander might be?"

She looked at the general strangely. He was an SS General who might not like war. Very interesting. Then she replied, "The Herr Hauptmann Mueller is down at the beach right now. He spends very little time here during the day."

In French he replied, "Very well, Madame. Thank you very much." And started to reach for the door. Then he turned, "By the way, Madame, would the Herr Hauptmann's given name perhaps be Karl?"

"Oui, Mon General."

"And your name.......would it perhaps be......Yvette?"

"Oui, Mon General. Are you perhaps ......clairvoyant?"

"Nein, Mein Frau. I am from Munich and Frau Mueller happens to be my secretary. Her husband speaks quite highly of you, and now.......I know why. It is because you are a very lovely woman who has decided that love is still a better option than hate. I commend you for it, Madame."

Her mouth dropped open with his disclosure, and he continued. "I am General von Leitner and the transfer of prisoners is now one of my responsibilities." He clicked his heels in typical German fashion. "It has been my pleasure, Madame. Perhaps I will see you before I depart. If not, Au Revoir, Madame.

She curtsied and replied in French, "It has been my pleasure, Mon General. Till we meet again."

He smiled and left. In his wake she couldn't help wondering

about the contradiction of it all. There were probably many good German officers, but they chose to remain silent while the bastards took over and now rule the roost.

* * * * *

Later, the General and Karl were walking along the beach and Karl, being the good officer that he was, simply walked in silence. If anything had to be said, it would be initiated by the Herr General. Besides, Karl still didn't trust those SS bastards, and like it or not, the Herr General was an SS officer.

Finally, the General stopped and looked out over the expanse of water that was the English Channel. "There is beauty in that body of water even on a cloudy, gray day like this, isn't there?" He asked.

"Jawohl, Herr General." Karl answered but his engineer's mind told him that beauty was only a perception and therefore, only the reality to the one who perceived it.."

Then, as though the Herr General had read his mind, he asked, "Tell me Herr Hauptmann, how do you view beauty?"

Without hesitation, Karl replied, "The majesty of mountains, the quiet beauty of a sunset, a woman's smile........." He drifted off dreamily as though he forgot where he was and who he was talking to.

"Your wife has a beautiful smile." The observation was sudden and unexpected, but not unappreciated.

Karl looked sharply at von Leitner, "Ja....that she does I have never fully appreciated it until this very moment, and yet, it took you to remind me."

"I think it is all a matter of appreciation, Karl." During their brief meeting at the mansion, they had been on a formal basis. Now the Herr General was dropping the formality.......at least on his end. The unspoken words between the two men would have admitted they shared the same woman. Perhaps, if the General were to remain at Calais, they might be sharing Yvette as well. Maybe that was the destiny these two men were to share, and maybe it wasn't. Maybe it only applied to Lisa. Well, the Herr General could have Lisa. He would release her from the marriage.

The General interrupted his thoughts, "Karl.....when you are back in Germany, why don't you wire Lisa to join you. You might find that the two of you have many things to discuss."

"I am going back to Germany?"

"Ja! But you will be returning here. There is much to be done here as well as elsewhere."

"What about the invasion of England?"

"I am not sure there will be an invasion of England. The Führer has decided to allow Göring's Luftwaffe to establish air superiority prior to an invasion."

"Are you suggesting perhaps, that the Luftwaffe cannot do this?"

"Probably not, but I will pretend that you didn't ask if you pretend that I didn't answer."

Karl grunted and a laugh almost escaped, but he managed to hold it at bay. The General continued, "We who believe ourselves to be pragmatic, have managed to persuade the Führer to at least defend the French coast from an invasion in the future. He believes that Calais is the likely place where it might happen. Do You?"

Karl wished the General hadn't asked, but he did and Karl would answer him honestly. "Nein, Herr General." His answer would place him in opposition to Adolph Hitler.

"If not, where, Herr Hauptmann?"

"Normandy, Herr General. I will admit that Calais might be a better place to defend, but Normandy would be a much better place to invade. That is only my humble opinion, Herr General."

"Danke shön, Herr Hauptmann."

"Bitte shön, Herr General, but I will be quick to add that we gave them a sound beating. It will be a long time before they can even think about an invasion, and I don't believe the English have the ability to mount a counter offensive against us. The best they will ever be able to do is glare at us from the other side of the channel, sir."

"I believe you might be right, Herr Hauptmann, but I will also add that America does have the power to oppose us, and if they ever enter this war, they might just be the force that balances the scales against us."

Karl regarded the Herr General strangely.

The General regarded the Hauptmann as well. "I have just spoken treason, and you may well decide to report it if you wish, but before you do, I ask you to understand the words in *Das Lied der Deutschen.*(The German National Anthem) I would like to believe that everyone has Germany's best interest at heart instead of their own agenda. Make no mistake about it, Herr Hauptmann. I am German first and everything else second. I will oppose **anything** that is not in the best interest of the Fatherland. PERIOD!"

Karl swallowed hard. What did that mean? After all, these words were spoken by an SS General, and he had already seen what *Der Einsatz Gruppen* were capable of doing. Was he really able to trust this SS General? After a few very long moments, he decided that whatever this General might be, that he was real and not synthetic. He responded by saying. "I fully understand, Herr General!" Karl did! Only too well.

Gerhardt drew his face very close to Karl's and asked, "Do you, Herr Hauptmann?" Then he closely studied Karl's eyes. Satisfied by what he saw, he muttered, "I am wrong!......You do understand!....Very well!......Danke, Herr Hauptmann!" He turned and walked back in the direction of his automobile.

Munich

Gerhardt had returned from his trip to the coast and things had seemingly returned to normal. Then, one day Gerhardt called her into the office and gave her a letter.

She just looked at it for the longest time. Then, she opened it and began reading, "It's from Karl."

"I know," he answered.

"He is going to Berlin, and wants me to meet him there."

Gerhardt knew that too, but said nothing.

"I wonder why," she mused. Then she thought of the French girl Yvette. Did Karl want out of the marriage?

This time Gerhardt decided to comment. "Maybe he feels that it is time for the two of you to inject some honesty into your marriage. Perhaps I should feel bad about that because I forced you to come to me."

"No Gerhardt!" She replied sharply. "If not you, it would

have been someone else. I was a woman poised at the edge of the abyss, and you literally shocked me back to solid ground. In a way I was fortunate that you came along when you did." She shook her head. "No Gerhardt, what happened...happened. We can't change it, and I don't believe either of us would if we could."

Once again, his eyes watered, but only one tear was able to fall.

Berlin

This time, she flew to Berlin, and was taken to the hotel by an official SS staff driver.

Now, as her car moved through the downtown area, it looked differently than it did the first time. Of course, that was when she had met Josef. She wondered if she would see him again. Then, she realized that it no longer mattered whether she did or not.

The car pulled over to the curb and Lisa realized that they had arrived at the hotel. The driver opened the door for her and escorted her into the lobby and to the registration desk.

The clerk looked at her and said, "Guten tag, Mein Frau. How may I be of service to you.?"

"Guten tag," she replied with a smile. "I have reservations in the name of Mueller, The Herr Hauptmann Karl und Frau Lisa."

He glanced down a list before saying, "Ach, here it is. I regret to inform you that the Herr Hauptmann has not yet arrived ."

"Danke shön, but I expected to arrive before he did. You see, he has just arrived from the French coast, and is in a meeting all afternoon."

He nodded his understanding, and gave her a key to the room. "Your room is 207 and I certainly hope you enjoy your stay."

"Danke schön." She said with a smile.

"Bitte schön," he replied with a flourish.

She had just taken a bath and dressed when there was a knock on the door. She went to answer it and when she opened it, there stood Karl. He was cool, confident, and handsome.

"Karl!" She cried, and without any further fanfare, they ended up in each other's arms. Then they kissed, and when they did, it was as two people who finally found that they cared for each other very dearly regardless of their emotional entanglements elsewhere.

Then, they looked each other over very carefully. *How he has changed,* She thought. *A boy left for the army and a man has returned.* She had seen him grow in stature with each homecoming, and now......the metamorphosis had been completed. Then, she noticed something new. His rank had been a Hauptmann. Now, he wore a different rank.

"Karl? Your rank! It doesn't look the same. What happened?"

He laughed. His laugh was relaxed and easy. He acted very much like a man who was at peace with himself. He answered, "It is because I am no longer a Hauptmann. They have promoted me to Major and placed me in charge of building the defensive wall at Calais." He was excited. She could tell, but before she would allow him to continue, she led him inside and closed the door. The neighbors didn't have a need to know.

Karl continued. "Ja, Mein Schatz, I am building." He shrugged. "Maybe it is not what I wish to spend the rest of my life doing, but I am building what I have designed. This is what I am trained to do, Lisa."

She smiled a thin smile. This was Karl's moment, and he was basking in it. She had plenty of time to think about who she was and who she wanted to become and she finally concluded that she was moving in the right direction. Her need to be experiencing the "thrill of it all" had not left her completely, but it was receding ever so slowly. Someday, she would be able to look at the irresistible force and tell him no.. She would do it politely, with a smile, but she would do it. There had been no lovers since Josef Hauser, but she hadn't been tempted either.

Karl told her all about Calais, about Yvette, and the new workers along with the dreaded SS Einsatz. He didn't like his country's way of handling *Liebensraum,* but he wasn't overly critical of it in the event there should be someone listening to their conversation.

Lisa couldn't tell him a lot about her job either, but she told him what she could. In the end, they went to dinner and decided to let it all hang out to dry. When all was said and done, neither shocked the other and both were glad to have it over with.

They dined and danced until late, and when they returned to their room, they only intended to hold each other, but........? Oh well.

When Karl left the next afternoon, it was agreed that they would remain married. They were willing to have it in name only, but the events of the previous evening turned the idea of a platonic relationship into a foolish folly.

Karl wouldn't be able to marry the French girl because she was a citizen of an occupied country, and marriage to the locals would not be permitted until *Lebensraum* went into the next phase. It was permitted for him to cohabit with the woman, but not to marry her.

Lisa could have married Gerhardt because her marriage to Karl had not been officially sanctioned by the Catholic church. The Reich yes.....the church no.

While they were waiting for Karl's train, he offered something that really caught Lisa off guard, "Marriage was created by man as a way of controlling the masses, and then the Priests decided to make it sound like God's idea. Maybe, we ought to rethink the whole process. I have come to believe that once two people love and commit to each other that they are married on a higher level and no earthly law can either sanctify or negate it."

It was so profound that she became speechless.

Karl left at 3:00 that afternoon, and Lisa had to wait until the next day to catch a plane to Munich..

That night, she decided go to a nice restaurant and night club, but she entered alone. That told the Luftwaffe officers at the bar that she might be available. It was like waving a red flag in front of a bull, and one particular officer, a Major, almost broke through her defenses, but in the end, she was able to smile prettily and tell him no. It took all of her resolve plus some that she didn't know she had but she did it.

Later, as she was going to bed alone, the lower part of her nature had some choice words for the better part of her nature, and she spent a restless night.

* * * * *

Christmas, 1940

Christmas of 1940 would go down as the best ever. Gerhardt threw the mansion open to the families of those who lived and worked in the mansion, and although the idea of Christmas had been played down in wartime Germany, no one tried to prohibit the idea and doubtless the prohibition would have been largely disobeyed anyway.

German families wanted and needed Christmas.

Ilse was now great with child and she looked forward to motherhood with the same glee that a child had when it looked through the candy store window.

* * * * *

And so, January 1, 1941 dawned clear and cold on a place called Bavaria and with the dawning of a new day also came the dawning of a new year. Many Germans prayed a fervent prayer for peace. In their way of thinking, there was no need for further conquest, and yet they were still hearing that death on a battlefield was a glorious death. One that should be savored rather than feared. Unfortunately, those who prayed for peace were vastly outnumbered by those who worshipped the war god.

At least one couple didn't buy into this way of thinking. That was Herr und Frau Liebert. They were looking forward to new life, and the thought of someday sacrificing that life for some foolish man's dreams of conquest made them both itch in places that couldn't be scratched in public. It also gave them the urge to vomit.

Finally.....On the 6th day of January, Peter Hansel Liebert entered the world howling in protest. He weighed in at 6 lbs 10oz, and was completely bald. The act of delivery was also an act of atonement for Illse Maria Liebert. God had finally smiled upon her, and although Max blew hot and cold about the idea of God, he didn't try to dampen anyone's ardor about the goodness of God. They could have their God. It didn't matter to him. On the other hand, Max couldn't help wondering about this thing called life. What was it? What was its origin. He had a bachelor's degree in anthropology and master's degree in philosophy, and still didn't know. Did anybody?

Now that Peter was here in the flesh, he would be expected to guide his son. How? What might he teach the lad? Then, in a sudden flash of clarity and insight, Max knew that his son would not grow up in Germany. Instead, Peter would grow up in America. Tears came to his eyes as he pondered whether he should share this with Ilse

Sixteen

The stark realities

1943

Friday, January 1

Gerhardt sat at his desk absently playing with the pencil in his hand. The war was beginning to go against the Fatherland, and yet the hierarchy still spoke of final victory. It was typical of the Führer to have unrealistic expectations, and the events of the previous three years had been mute testimony to the gross incompetence of the man, and now......he was poised on the brink of being swept over the edge of the abyss and he was taking the whole German nation with him.

Gerhardt stood and walked over to the full length mirror. The image looking back at him didn't appear to be evil, and yet, he had been a party to evil deeds. All done in the name of purifying the human race. It was enough to make him vomit. In fact, he had on several occasions.

Suddenly, there was a knock on the door.

"Come," said Gerhardt.

The door opened and Erik Halder walked in.

"I am sorry to bother you, Herr General, but there is a General von Hofer to see you. He apologizes for not calling first, but he tells me that he has a matter of great importance to discuss with you."

"It doesn't matter, Erik. He is an old friend and I would see him if all he wanted to discuss was the weather."

Erik smiled and backed out.

A few seconds later, the door opened and framed in the opening was Dieter von Hofer.

"Gerhardt!!!"

"Dieter!!!"

Both men came together in a crunch and hugged each other vigorously.

"I am so glad you came, Dieter. I am not feeling well this morning."

"Too much celebrating?"

"Nein, mein Freund.......I no longer have need of excessive amounts of alcohol in order to feel bad."

"Ach!" replied a sympathetic Dieter.

There were several moments of silence before Dieter finally asked, "The pretty blonde lady out front. Very classy . Very classy, indeed."

"You always did have an eye for the ladies, Dieter."

"Let us say that I appreciate the finer things of life. They don't always appreciate an old retread like me, but I appreciate them and that is all that matters."

Speaking of the finer things of life immediately conjured images of the lovely Baroness Maria von Hofer. A very lovely woman who had to be in her middle to late fifties, and still a beautiful woman.

He had been lost in thought and looked at Dieter, "Speaking of beauty, Mein Freund, how is Maria?"

"I believe she is fine, but I really don't know. You see, when the Allies finally realized that bombers could really carry bombs, I knew that it would only be a matter of time until they found their way to Berlin. And, since I consider Maria to be a priceless national treasure, I sent her and the household staff back to Schloss von Hofer. I have since been living the life of a bachelor, and it doesn't agree with me. Maria and I have always slept together unless plans were made to the contrary. I guess we are used to being together."

Gerhardt wanted to inquire about the lady's extracurricular activities, but such a question would have been be tasteless. After all, a true gentleman never discussed the more nefarious side of a lady's virtue with another gentleman, but Dieter was far too perceptive not to know what was on Gerhardt's mind. "Her eyes still wander occasionally, but her appetite has waned. She might seek an occasional diversion, but they are becoming fewer and farther between. "

"How do you feel about that?"

He chuckled. "Kind of strange. Back in the old days, when every man who hadn't been dead too long, still wanted her, I felt a smug satisfaction in being the man she preferred to sleep with. Now, I tend to wonder."

Gerhardt smiled and it caught Dieter by surprise. He had never seen Gerhardt smile. "Gerhardt, when did you learn how to smile?"

"That classy lady you mentioned a few
moments ago and I are what you might call, an item. She is my secretary, my lover, and my friend. I finally found someone I can love.

Dieter braced his friend's shoulders and said, "I am happy for you, Gerhardt. Are you married?"

Gerhardt managed only to shrug. He responded by saying, "Nein, Mein Freund, she is already married."

"Ach!" was all that Deiter managed to say.

Gerhardt knew there was a purpose for this visit and decided to broach the subject. "So......what brings you to Munich? A need to do penance at the statue of Horst Wessel?"

Dieter broke out in laughter......genuine laughter. Then he pointed up with his right forefinger and to his left ear with his left forefinger, and to his lips with his right forefinger. All signifying that the walls did indeed have ears.

Gerhardt stood and curled his right forefinger in a "follow me" gesture, and both men walked out of Gerhardt's office.

As they passed Lisa's desk, he pointed downward and Lisa nodded. The basement had been constructed like a maze. Those who didn't know how get around didn't have a need to be there, and located somewhere in that maze was a secret room that hadn't been discovered by the bad guys yet. It was a fairly comfortable room with two stuffed chairs, a couch and a daybed.

Once inside, a lamp was lit and Gerhardt pointed to the comfortable chairs and said, "Have yourself a seat. I will get us something to drink."

. Sitting on a coffee table was a bottle and two dirty glasses.

Gerhardt took the glasses and threw them into a waste container. Then, he reached inside a cabinet and extracted two more glasses.

"Have an excess of glasses?" Dieter asked with a chuckle.

Gerhardt shrugged. "I don't worry about the small things, Dieter." Then, he unscrewed the fill hole lid on the kerosene lamp and filled it from a can of kerosene that was setting in the corner.

Once that had been done, he handed a cup to Dieter and took one for himself. Then, he raised his cup and exclaimed! "To the Fatherland!"

Dieter responded with, "To the Fatherland!"

Both men drank.

After setting their glasses down, Dieter become very serious as he announced. "We have lost the war."

Gerhardt countered with, "Is this the great revelation you have brought to us Bavarian peasants from on high?"

"Just listen, Gerhardt and refrain from unsolicited attempts at humor."

Gerhardt nodded his acquiescence.

"I have studied the history of land warfare and found that during the American Civil War, the Confederacy lost its tactical ability to win the war after two events occurred in 1863. The first being the Emancipation Proclamation that was issued by the American President Lincoln on Jan 1, and the second being the loss of the Battle of Gettysburg on July 4th."

Gerhardt replied, "I have also studied the American Civil War, and agree with what you just stated. Now, what in the hell is your point?"

Dieter just looked at his friend for the longest time before saying , "Even though the Confederacy had lost the ability to win, they continued the struggle until April 7, 1865 when the situation finally became completely untenable and they surrendered."

Gerhardt became thoughtful, and Dieter allowed him to think and conclude. "You have just drawn a parallel, ja? It is the same with us, ja? We have lost the tactical ability to win because of the strategic blunders that Herr Schicklgruber has made, Ja?"

Dieter became tight lipped.

Gerhardt became very intense, "First, there was that debacle at Dunkirk where every man who got off that beach is a man who someday will oppose us." He held up two fingers, and said, "Two...The damned English again.. I told Hitler that he needed to invade that damned island. I told him that he needed to deprive the Allies of a staging point from which to launch a counter attack." Dieter only shrugged. "Mein Gott, Dieter we have had one bloody screwup after another. We have lost Africa! We are going to lose Russia, and the next thing we are going to lose will be Germany itself ." He took a long drink of his brandy, and then before he could get started again, Dieter held his right forefinger up.

"Pardon the interruption, Mein Freund, but lamenting the failures of Der Führer will not make these failures go away. They will only serve as a history lesson. I don't need that, and neither do you. We need only action. The entire general staff at the OKW (Oberkommando der Wehrmacht) may be in sympathy with your thoughts and feelings, but Herr Hitler is too well entrenched, and his inner circle is just as unrealistic as he is. No! We need something else. Something that will set us apart from the rest." He took another deep breath and stood up as though he needed to stretch his legs when, in fact, he often felt nauseous anytime he thought about the irreparable damage being done to the Fatherland. That was because of the acts of some really screwed up people who had thoughts of world domination dancing in their heads. He breathed three times deeply and exhaled through his nose, and then turned to face Gerhardt who was waiting patiently.

"Gerhardt, my brother belonged to an organization that I will not identify. That which you don't know can not be used to betray us, and the Gestapo has some really creative ways of extracting answers when they set out to get them." He paused only long enough to swallow. "No, suffice it to say that we are twelve men who are for the most part, Prussians and we are in the intelligence gathering business. Even the OKW doesn't know who we are. The Reich Main Security office doesn't have a clue. Our allegiance is to the Fatherland, and not to the Reich." His eyes seemed to snap as he said, "We don't give a damn about the Third Reich, and we firmly believe we will outlive the bastards."

Gerhardt sensed that he was hearing something important. Really important. Dieter continued, "It is the Fatherland that I love, and it is the Fatherland that I serve. I am allowed to move about freely throughout the Fatherland because I am a musician. I am in charge of morale. I can provide concerts to the people who, for at least an hour or two, can forget about their sons and husbands who are dying on the Eastern Front, and others who will die on the Western Front when the Allies finally get around to creating it. Then. and only then, will Fortress Europe finally prove to be nothing more than a house of cards."

"So what else do we do?" Inquired Gerhardt.

He sat down and removed his right shoe. Under the insole were six sheets of paper that he unfolded and handed to Gerhardt. "Take this and read it. Memorize it and burn it. Follow the instructions. I don't mean to undermine your intelligence, Gerhardt, but can you do this?"

Gerhardt was reading as Dieter had been talking, and he was overwhelmed by the content of what it was that he was reading. Intelligence was not the factor. Loyalty, simplicity, and perseverance was. Could he do it meant following the simple instructions.

Gerhardt looked back up at Dieter, "Ja! I believe that I can."

"Be sure Gerhardt. This life is not a rehearsal. This **is** the main performance. You either can or you can't. How say you?"

"Jawohl....Mein Freund......I can do it! I will do it"

Dieter heaved a big sigh of relief.

"Sehr gut, Mein Freund. Now then, let us have another brandy and join the rest of humanity."

Pas de Calais

It was a cloudy and cold night with a brisk wind blowing in off the Channel. The SS guard was huddling in the lee of a bunker and did not see the submarine surface several hundred meters off the coast. Even if the guard had been completely alert and scanning the horizon for enemy submarines, he might still have missed the surfacing of the submarine.

The guard continued to dally in the lee of the bunker. After all, it was damned cold and where were the officers? Where were the sergeants? He knew where they were. They were where it was warm.

Snuggled in their beds. That's where they were. A few minutes of dallying more or less would not hurt the Reich. He remained where he was and lit a cigarette. Two more hours and it would be his turn to get warm.

Meanwhile, four hundred meters off the shore, four rubber rafts were put into the water and each of the rafts were filled with British Commandos bent on a mission of destruction. They were going to light up the night sky and then try to get back to the sub alive.

The sentry ground out his cigarette with the toe of his boot and decided to give the idea of duty a go once more. He shouldered his rifle and began walking.

The lead raft came ashore in the light surf and the Commandos evacuated and carried the raft past the water line and ran, in a low crouch, to the rendezvous point. As each raft beached, its crew did as the first crew had done. Soon the entire force had been assembled.

Little was said as each man knew his job and each man was a veteran of many raids. Some successful, some not, but these raids were why Hitler decided to fortify the French coast. Tonight, the English were going to try and put a small hole in the wall.

At a command, they fanned out in different directions. Each with an assigned target to blow up.

The sentry was still cold and he stopped long enough to look out on to blackness of the water while wondering what enemy would even care about this God forsaken place.

Suddenly, his eye caught movement. He crouched and peered into the darkness once more. Again, he saw something, and wondered if Hans had seen anything in his sector. He needed to sound the alarm, but what if he was wrong? What if his imagination was running wild with him? He would be ridiculed by his sergeant, and maybe even his officer. No, he would investigate first.

A few minutes later, two Commandos heard something, and signaled the freeze order. Not long after that, the German sentry came into view. His rifle was at the ready. The Commando closest to the sentry inherited the job of eliminating him. The Commando had the advantage. He knew about the German while the German apparently had no knowledge of him.

When the time was right, the Commando sprung and his left arm went around the German's neck in a death hold, and with his right hand, he snapped hard on the German's head and heard the sickening sound of the bone breaking. The sentry's final thought was of his beloved Gretchen and their young son. As an overkill, the commando slit the German's throat.

In the next sector, Hans had no fear of ridicule. He too, had seen something, and sounded the alarm about the time his neglectful neighbor had died.

Suddenly, a siren sounded and floodlights illuminated the entire area. Before long, SS troops began to file out of the barracks and onto the waiting trucks.

On the beach, the British had set the charges and were returning to the waiting rafts. On a nearby tower, a guard was sweeping the beach with his spotlight and as the beam was moving to the left, it highlighted several men dragging a rubber raft. He opened fire hitting several of the man and puncturing the raft. About that time, everything began exploding all around him. Then, a bullet found him and the firing stopped.

On the beach, a Commando shouted, "I got the fuckin' Kraut! Now, let's get the bloody 'ell outta here."

* * * * *

Karl was sleeping soundly.

Suddenly, there was a loud pounding on the door. His eyes popped open, and he wondered why. Then the hammering began again. From his right, he heard Yvette say, "Karl, find out who it is, please.?"

Karl managed to drag himself out of bed and to the door. He opened it. Standing there was Hauptsturmführer Hauser, the man in charge of the SS troops. "Herr Major! There is an attack on the site."

"Attack? From whom?"

"English Commandos, Herr Major."

Karl was still groggy, but he said, "Let me get some clothes on, Herr Hauptsturmführer," and he went back inside and began dressing.

"Karl, what is it?"

"The English have raided the site."

"But why do you have to go?"

"I am in charge."

"But you are an engineer....not a soldier."

"Nein....I am a soldier first and an engineer second. Like it or not, Mein Schatz, but that is the German way."

She was tight lipped but remained silent.

When he finished dressing, he walked over and kissed her. "I'll be back as soon as I can." Yvette remained silent. After he left, she began crying. She would never see him again. Of that, she was certain.

Hauser was driving them and Karl sat calmly waiting. On the other hand, Hauser was obviously nervous.

"Ever been in a battle?"

"Nein, Herr Major." Josef Hauser answered. Hauser and Mueller had spent some time together, and the more Hauser knew Mueller, the more certain he was that Mueller was an enigma. The man had a beautiful wife at home and a beautiful mistress here. He even had a Knight's Cross that he had won in battle, and now he was sitting calmly as though they were going to get a bier instead of heading in the direction of the sound of gunfire.

When they came over the rise in the road, the beach lay in front of them, and the staccato sound of automatic fire could be heard along with the occasional explosion of grenades. Fires were burning everywhere. They were looking out upon hell.

The vehicle came to a stop and Karl got out. He picked up his rifle, checked to make certain that it was loaded and the action worked properly.. He didn't like automatic weapons. He always figured that automatic weapons made lots of noise and expended ammunition. That was why he used a rifle, and when he was in training, he had been good with a rifle. Karl looked at Josef Hauser, who hadn't moved yet.

Karl yelled, "Come on, Hauser. Do you want to live forever?"

Hauser forced himself to leave the presumed safety of the vehicle and as he did, he picked up his own weapon.

Just then, the SS Sergeant ran up and said, "Herr Major, Herr Hauptsturmführer....the English have raided and while they were in the process of withdrawing, we have cut them off and destroyed their rafts. We have them trapped at the water line. I await your orders."

Karl looked at Hauser who was paralyzed. *The damn fool is going to get a lot of good men killed if we don't get him the hell out of here.*

In the absence of a order, Karl spoke. "Let's go take a look, Herr Sergeant. You lead the way," and the Sergeant ran at a low crouch in the direction of the firing. Hauser followed in the wake of the two men who led. He felt the stab of shame for his cowardice and incompetence.

When they arrived at the scene, Karl quickly surveyed the situation and realized that the English were successful in their raid. The destruction was considerable, but that was now a fact that could not be erased. He needed to change the deployment of the SS troops. He told the SS Sergeant what to do and the Herr Sergeant moved out immediately to implement the Herr Major's orders.

Next, he looked at Hauser and motioned for the man to come and kneel next to him.

When Hauser was in position, he looked at Karl with a pained expression on his face. Karl had only contempt for the man. He said, "It's like this, Herr Hauser....As the senior man present, I will assume command. You are SS and I am Army. You are supposed to be in command, but I am not going to allow good men to die because of your ineptitude. Maybe all you're good at doing is fucking my wife, Ja?"

Hauser turned white.

"Didn't know that I knew that did you? Well, it doesn't matter. If she wants to fuck you, that is her business, although I must warn you.....her tastes have changed. She now prefers men!"

To the Herr Sergeant, who had returned, he said, "This place has a loudspeaker system. Find me a microphone, ja?"

"It is right here, Herr Major."

Karl chuckled, "German efficiency strikes again." He took the microphone and keyed it, "Silence!" Everything quieted. Even on the English side.

"Good evening, Englishmen," Karl spoke in English. "This is Major Karl Mueller. I am in command of the force that now opposes you. You have no way off this beach unless you know how to fly.

Therefore, you are best advised to throw down your weapons and surrender. You have thirty seconds to decide. After that, we will be forced to annihilate you."

While waiting, Karl changed the displacement of the troops to create a better field of fire. The Herr Sergeant had taken a liking to this engineering officer. He seemed to know what he was doing while his own officer didn't know shit. Karl asked, "I haven't been counting.

Has it been thirty seconds yet?"

"More like a minute, Herr Major."

Karl picked up the microphone and calmly announced, "Open fire!"

After that, all hell broke loose as the shots were fired just short of the phosphorescent waters of the surf. With one section shooting behind the Commandos and the other section shooting in front of them, it was hoped that the entire force would be caught in the crossfire. The annihilation of an armed enemy unit in a firefight was not quite the same as executing them, but the British Commandos had made their own choice as to when and how they wished to die.

Then, they did something completely unexpected. They charged. Just like the Light Brigade, they charged, and Karl looked at them with respect. They didn't cower in fright. They were doomed, but they were going out their way.

Karl barked orders into the microphone and his men quickly reacted accordingly.. His own rifle was at the ready, but the English were being cut down by small arms fire. Karl quickly surveyed the area and realized that some of the British were getting through. *Someone might get lucky,* He thought. *I had better be ready.*

Just as that thought occurred to him, a man wearing a British uniform came into view and looked point blank at the German officer. Without hesitation, he shot Karl twice at point blank range.

It was like being stabbed with a red hot poker and Karl immediately lost the ability to function and fell to the ground.

The Commando was going to take another shot when he felt a sharp pain in his throat. He looked at his assailant and saw that it was another German officer. Hauser stabbed him again and again but it became a moot point as the British soldier was already dead.

Hauser dropped by Karl's side, and looked at the Sergeant, "Get a medic over here......now!"

Karl looked up at the blurred image of Hauser. Pain grabbed him, and he struggled for control. He finally manage to say, "Whatever the hell you are, Herr Hauser, you are going to outlive me."

Tears came to Hauser's eyes, "Nein, Herr Major. Help is coming."

"Help? There is no help for the dead!" Karl managed to say through gurgles.

Karl realized that he didn't have much time. Things were ebbing fast, but dying wasn't really so bad. Suddenly, things became crystal clear to Karl and he motioned for Hauser to lean closer.. "Herr Hauser. We all have to die. Some just do it sooner that's all. I am loved by two women and have a lovely little daughter. I......" Pain grabbed him again and Karl grimaced. His breath now came in great gulps and he needed just a few more seconds. "Find out who...who you are...and be...that person. Don't sell yourself short.....ever! Tell Lisa that I died well, and tell....her that I love.....her......Tell her that, please?"

"Ja, Herr Major." Tears now streamed down the arrogant young man's cheeks.

"And......be.....kind....to.....Yvette.............." With The mention of Yvette, Karl Mueller breathed his last. The Medic arrived just in time to tell Josef what he already knew.

The Herr Major was dead.

Josef dismissed the medic and just looked down at Karl. His eyes were still partially opened and Josef closed them.

As he did, something happened. Something strange. The pall of death had been temporarily replaced by a radiance. It lasted for several seconds, and was viewed by several members of the SS force who had gathered around them.

Hauser looked up at them and said, "Here was a man. A real man, and Germany can ill afford to lose men like Karl Mueller. Now, all of you.....go someplace and do something, but...don't.... do... it...here."

His Sergeant barked out orders and everyone went to carry out their assignments. The Herr Sergeant remained behind. Josef looked up with a questioning look in his eyes. The Sergeant asked, “Do you wish for me to assign a burial detail, Herr Hauptsturmführer?”

“Nein.....Herr Sergeant. Take a detail and find a casket. If you can’t find one, build one.”

The Sergeant replied, “Jawohl, Herr Hauptsturmführer,” and walked in the direction of the warehouse.

Josef Hauser looked down reverently at the man who had thoroughly dressed him down just a few minutes before. Whatever Karl Mueller was, he was a good man, and he wanted the powers-that-be to know that fact. He wanted Lisa Mueller to know that fact, and if Yvette didn’t already know it, he would tell her as well.

When Karl’s face had became radiant in death, Josef had been certain that he had looked upon the face of God, and he reasoned that no man could ever look upon the face of God and deny Him. It was impossible. Josef started to cry and he crossed himself, and then began to recite the Holy Rosary.

* * * * *

Yvette was in the process of busying herself when dawn began to break. It had been hours since the distant sounds of shooting had stopped and still no Karl. In the absence of the facts, imagination had taken over, and Yvette continued nervously through the night while trying to steel herself against the news that someone was certain to bring.

She had loved her husband dearly, and almost died in sympathy when news of his death reached her. It had all seemed so.....so unreal. Now it was Karl.....wonderful Karl. A man who was actually the enemy, but Karl was no one’s enemy. He wore the German uniform because he was a German.

Karl knew the cause might not be right, but he believed in right.....that right would ultimately assert itself. He had told her often that the assertion of right might even require Germany’s defeat, but if a better Germany were to rise out of the ashes of defeat, it would all be worthwhile.

Now, her greatest fear.....the one that had deprived her of sleep....was that this wonderful man would not be able to participate in the rebuilding of his beloved Fatherland.

She walked over to a secret spot and removed the book that Karl used for his diary. He kept nothing from her and often read entries to her. Of course, his entries had been written in German, but she was now able to read German.

Tears came to her eyes once more, and since she had shed so many tears without knowing for certain, she wondered how many tears she might be shedding when she did know with certainty.

Her thoughts were suddenly interrupted by a knock on the door. She just looked at it—-the wooden structure that was the source of the sound—-she had wanted so much to hear that sound. Now that she did, she became terrified. She walked woodenly in the direction of the door, and realized that in two or three seconds, she would know for certain.

Oh God NO! Please God, make it not so.

She opened the door and standing there was the SS Hauptsturmführer who came to get Karl last night. The man called Josef Hauser. The bastard.

He just stood there—-dumbly.

She took one look at his face, and he didn't have to say a word. She backed up involuntarily and he filled the space she had just vacated. When he was completely inside, he closed the door—-softly. Her lower lip was now quivering.

It took a great amount of effort on his part, but he finally conjured up the ability to speak, and when he did, he started out very slowly, "Madame Yvette, I am truly sorry...." was all the further he got when she cried**, "OH MY GOD**!" And flung herself into his arms with a crunch.

After that, bastard or no bastard, she buried her head against his shoulder and wept uncontrollably.

Somewhere....during the night......on the lonely beach....with a dead man's head cradled in his lap..... Josef Hauser, an officer in Himmler's SS, became a human being once more.

As surely as he knew that the sun would rise in the east every morning, he knew that he would do right by Karl Mueller. He also knew that he would do right by Yvette. More importantly, he knew that he would do right by Josef Hauser.

As he stood holding the sobbing Yvette, he also knew that things needed to be done, but the newly discovered human part of him demanded that he hold on to this grieving woman for as long as she needed to be held. The Third Reich and all of its unrealistic expectations could go straight to Hell.

Munich

Max Liebert walked out of the message center and headed in the direction of Gerhardt's office. He carried a teletype message in his right hand. When he approached Lisa's desk, he asked, "Is Gerhardt in?"

Lisa smiled and said, "Ja."

The door was closed, so Max knocked twice, and the voice inside said, "Come!"

Max walked in.

"Hello Max, I haven't seen you all day. Where have you been?"

Max managed a weak smile as he replied, "I have been running some errands for Ilse. I hope you don't mind."

Gerhardt shook his head no, and then looked expectantly at the message in Max's hand. Max handed it to him.

Gerhardt read it and as he did, it drooped lower and with his elbow on the desk he cradled his forehead with his left hand. "Oh Mein Gott!" His tongue licked his lips as he looked up at Max. "Did you read this?"

Max nodded.

"This Josef Hauser......He brings tragic news in an eloquent manner. His message to Lisa......it sounds like he thought a lot of Karl."

Max nodded again.

"Would you ask Lisa to come in, Please." Max nodded. "And then leave us alone please?"

"I don't envy you, Gerhardt."

Gerhardt did the nodding this time.

Max stepped out of the office, and said, "Lisa, Gerhardt wishes to speak with you."

Lisa stood up and walked into the office. She started to sit in one of the chairs in front of the desk when Gerhardt said, "No dear.

On the couch, please."

Lisa did as he asked and when she was seated, he took her hand in his. "Lisa, Mein Liebe. I love you and would never do anything to hurt you. Do you believe that?"

"Ja," she answered quietly, but alarm now showed on her face. "Gerhardt...what is it?"

He exhaled a big sigh. "Lisa, there is no easy way to tell a person what I now have to tell you."

Another sigh. "Lisa, it's Karl."

As a reflex action, her hands came to her face. Tears began falling even before she heard the words that surely must follow. He began to speak again. "Last night, Karl's construction site was raided by British Commandos, and as the senior officer present, Karl assumed command of the German forces at the site. A British soldier managed to get through the defenses somehow, and shot Karl at point blank range. He died shortly thereafter." He stopped speaking because Lisa was now sobbing uncontrollably against his tunic.

By this time, everyone at the mansion had been informed of Karl Mueller's death, and a very subdued atmosphere ensued.

Let all future generations of the Deutchen Volk (the German people) know that their forefathers were not heartless. Misguided perhaps, but they did care, and they did cry. Quite often, and they cried far more than the allotted ......one single tear.

After a few minutes, Max returned to Gerhardt's office. He had Ilse with him. Ilse had also been through the loss of a husband and was now armed with several handkerchiefs and a heart full of love and compassion.

Lisa finally quieted, and she was still seated on the couch with Ilse at her side. Gerhardt stood, and said, "If you approve, I will go and tell your mother and father."

Lisa looked up through tear filled eyes and replied, "Ja...that would be good."

Gerhardt then appropriated Max to accompany him. They would go in Gerhardt's Horsch, and for a change, Gerhardt would do the driving. Riding gave a person time to think whereas driving did require the driver to keep his mind on driving occasionally.

Anna Rensler rode back with Gerhardt and Max while Gus drove the truck. Gus would have to drive back and take care of milking his cows. The news hit them both like a thunderbolt.

We walk through life with death as our silent partner, but the young always appear to be indestructible. Their purpose is to somehow vindicate the generation that begot them, and when they die first, we tend to view it as an affront to all that is decent and forthright.

When Gerhardt, Max, and Anna returned, Anna and Lisa went upstairs to tell a six year old girl that her Papa would not be coming home anymore. He had gone to live with Jesus instead.

der Bahnhof...Munich, Germany

The train pulled into the station, and passengers departed.

Awaiting the train was SS General Gerhardt von Leitner, SS Standartenführer Max Liebert und Frau Ilse, Frau Lisa Mueller, Herr und Frau Gustav Rensler, and Heinrich Sieloff, the mortician.

After the passengers had disembarked, the embarking passengers were told to standby. After that, the conductor walked to the baggage car and opened the door.

Inside, the flag draped coffin bearing the remains of Major Karl Mueller rested on rollers. The six members of the Honor Guard stood at attention with three men on each side of the casket.

The Honor Guard was commanded by SS Hauptsturmführer Josef Hauser, and was made up of SS enlisted men. Steps were put in place and SS Haptsturmführer Josef Hauser descended the steps with military precision.

Once on the ground, he gave the command for the Honor Guard to proceed down the steps. Once everyone was down, the steps were removed. By this time, a fairly good sized crowd had gathered to watch. It wasn't that death was an oddity to them, for by this time, many thousands of Germans had died on various battlefields. It was the act of actually sending a coffin home for burial. Most of the war dead had been buried near where they died.

With the nod of Hauser's head, the first two men began to pull on the flag draped coffin. Once, the coffin was securely in the hands of the Honor Guard, The Hauptsturmfüher did an about face and saluted SS General von Leitner.

Gerhardt returned the salute, the Honor Guard continued to

the hearse and placed the coffin inside. The Honor Guard then got into a limousine that was designated for the purpose of taking them to the Funeral Home.

The SS Hauptsturmführer then saluted the Herr General once more and walked in the direction of the hearse. As he passed Lisa, his face clearly showed anguish. When the hearse moved away, Gerhardt took Lisa by the arm and asked, "How are you holding up?"

She replied, "Just barely."

Lisa and Gerhardt had been living together for almost four years, and when one took into consideration the way they had come together, it was truly amazing that they had developed such a wonderful sense of honesty and closeness.

Karl Mueller had been a man of vision who should have died with grandchildren surrounding him instead of a motley crew of SS guards that were thrust into an unaccustomed battle situation. Gerhardt had stopped being threatened by the existence of the lady's husband three years before.

As Lisa slid into the Mercedes beside Gerhardt, he noticed a regal quality about her. She carried herself with both beauty and grace. She had all the qualities of a baroness, and a few months down the road, Gerhardt might just approach her about becoming the Baroness Lisa von Leitner. But, that was in the future. Today, it was all about Karl Mueller and that was as it should be.

* * * * *

Herr und Frau Heinrich Mueller arrived the next day along with two of their children. Two other sons were serving the Fatherland on the Eastern Front, and an ashen faced Heinrich knew full well that he might just end up not having any sons at all.

The decision to bury Karl in Munich had been arrived at during a phone call between Gerhardt and Heinrich. Munich was where Karl had been the happiest. Munich was where his body would be interred.

The funeral went as most funerals went. The dearly departed was eulogized, but since Karl Mueller was a holder of the Knight's Cross, he became part of the Nazi propaganda machine. A member of Gobbel's staff traveled to Munich for the purpose of speaking at the funeral.

Gerhardt could not stop this from happening, but when it came time for Josef Hauser to speak, he did so with such honesty and forthrightness that it preempted any attempts to create another Horst Wessel out of the death of Karl Mueller.

Josef described Karl as a very good human being. He described him as a man who led with skill, compassion, and courage. He did not describe him as a man who feared death, because Karl didn't look upon death as an enemy. Rather, Josef described him as a man who looked upon death as a necessary part of a process called life.

He described Karl as a man who looked upon the shortcomings of a man called Josef Hauser and didn't see shortcomings. He, like the Master, saw only potential. It didn't have to be said that Karl was not a National Socialist, but it was said that Karl believed strongly in the Fatherland.

It was also said that Karl Mueller believed very strongly in a God who was loving and just. That, in God's economy, nothing was ever wasted. Therefore, that which Karl Mueller was and is would live forever in the minds and hearts of those who knew and loved him.

When he finished, tears freely flowed down his cheeks. There wasn't a dry eye in the house. The man from Berlin had to reach for his own handkerchief. Tears even formed in the Herr General Gerhardt von Leitner's eyes.

At the cemetery, when the graveside rites were completed, Heinrich Mueller sought out the young SS officer.

"Herr Hauptsturmführer?"

Hauser turned and replied, "Ja?"

"I am Heinrich Mueller, Karl's father."

"Ach, Herr Mueller, it is indeed a privilege to meet you, and I am truly sorry that it has to be under such difficult circumstances." The two men shook hands.

"Difficult.....ja! Very difficult indeed, but not completely unexpected in time of war. The world now looks upon us as the great evil, and yet, we still sire men of compassion. Men such as you."

Josef was taken back, "Herr Mueller, I am such as I am because of your son. Before Karl, I was an arrogant sonofabitch who felt that he was God's gift to women. When Karl died, I became a human being once more. I don't know what I am going to do with my new found humanity, but I am certain that I will find a way.....if the Reich doesn't consider compassion to be weakness and execute me first, that is."

The elder Mueller seemed to ponder what Josef had just told him for the longest time before responding.

"Does the idea of death bother you?"

"Before Karl....Ja....After Karl....nein. He may have died on a lonely beach, but he died with dignity and grace. I should do as well when my turn comes."

"And, I as well," replied Herr Mueller. "Er....May I call you Josef?"

"Jawohl, Herr Mueller!"

"That's good. You're an SS officer. Keep up the pretense of being a good one. It's good for the morale of your superiors. Just remember one important point. It is always permissible to be different as long as your superiors never find out."

Josef smiled. It was the first time he had smiled since Karl's death.

Herr Mueller continued. "Josef, I am ashamed to tell you that I didn't really know the man you knew. Oh, I had met him on three occasions lately, but for the most part, I was on the outs with Karl. In the Fatherland, we fathers like to dictate. Especially men like me. Karl marched to the beat of a different drummer. He wanted to build things. He was as you described him............A man of vision. Now that he is gone, I am truly sorry that I didn't take the time to get to know him.. Don't be guilty of that, young man. When you love, love with patience.....love with kindness, and love them for who they are. Get to know those you love. Encourage them, teach them, but above all, love them."

Heinrich Mueller reached inside his coat and extracted a wallet. From the wallet, he extracted a business card. He handed it to Josef, and said, "Write your address down on something and give it to me. Take my card and don't be surprised if you hear from me. Now, let us retire to the Herr General's mansion and sample his hospitality. If you wish, you may ride with me.

"Danke, Herr Mueller, but I am riding with the Herr

Standartenführer Liebert and his lovely wife."

"Sehr gut. I will see you there."

The Mansion

In the Christian world, it is called a wake.

On this particular day, Gerhardt opened the mansion to all of those who attended the funeral. He spent most of his time at Lisa's side, but occasionally, he circulated.

It was during one of those circulating tours that Heinrich Mueller walked up to Lisa, and said "Hello Lisa."

Lisa, who happened to be holding Heidi's hand, smiled at her father-in-law. "Hello Papa Mueller."

Heinrich, who didn't know his granddaughter very well, knelt down and looked at the child, "Do you know who I am?"

"Ja."

"Who?"

"Grandpapa Mueller."

He looked at her with pride. "Is good, Heidi. Is good, ja?. Then he asked, "Can you give me a hug?"

She didn't hesitate.

She came into his arms with a rush, and his eyes misted, "Mein Gott. Why is it that we get too soon old and too late smart?"

It was a rhetorical question because no one within the sound of his voice had an answer. He spent quite a lot of time with her, and then brought her back to her mama.

Heinrich looked at Lisa with admiration before saying, "When it is convenient, I would like to speak with you in private." Lisa knew of only one room in the entire mansion that might be free of listening devices, and she took him there.

When they arrived, Heinrich shook his head and laughed. "If nobody I know is a Nazi, who in the hell are we hiding from?"

Lisa replied, "You'd be surprised."

She pointed to a chair and said, "Please, have a seat. Would you like a brandy?"

"Ja! I could use a stiff one."

Lisa poured them both a stiff drink.

Herr Mueller took a drink and placed his glass down. "And so Lisa, what are your plans now?"

She didn't change expression. "Other than the fact that Karl is gone now, I don't think much is going to change. I still have my work and things are quite comfortable here."

Herr Mueller's expression changed. "Look, let us not fence with each other. I know about you and the Herr General, and I also knew about Karl and Yvette. More importantly, despite the very unusual and tangled circumstances, your relationship with Karl had improved considerably over what it was when Karl entered the Army."

She nodded in the affirmative but made no comment.

"Therefore, things seemed to be working, but can I ask you a personal question?"

"Certainly,"

"It is a moot point, I grant you, but curiosity prompts me to inquire as to what you would have done had Karl survived this war."

"I won't mince words, Papa Mueller, but I fell in love with Gerhardt, and Karl fell in love with Yvette. You are quite right, though. It is a moot point, because I can't honestly give you an answer. To speculate would be useless."

Herr Mueller listened with fascination. "What in the hell did Karl ever do to deserve a woman such as you?"

She flushed indignantly and flared, "I beg your pardon!"

He backed up defensively and held his hands up. "I didn't mean that the way it sounded. You are one hell of a woman, Lisa. Somewhere along the way, Karl must have done something right."

She relaxed again. She even decided to smile..

Herr Mueller reached inside his coat and extracted the wallet again. He pulled out another business card. This one had writing on the reverse side. "Take this. On the back is the name of a bank in Zurich and a account number. Simply, go into the bank and tell them who you are. He will ask you to prove your identify so take what you need. Once he is satisfied, he will tell you how much is in the account. I won't tell you now, but it is quite substantial, and it is in Swiss Francs......not Deutschmarks."

"But..."

"But nothing, Lisa. I am not trying to buy your love. This is yours by right of inheritance. This may be treason, but Deutschland will lose this war. Mainly, because the man at the top isn't smart enough to wage one. This time, Deutschland might just be in ruins. I have some ideas and I am sure that your General has some as well. Perhaps, I shall talk with him before I leave. Now then, if you will guide me out of this maze, I will rejoin the rest of my family."

When Lisa rejoined the rest of the assembled humanity, she was preoccupied, and didn't see Josef Hauser until she almost ran into him.

She was embarrassed, and said, "I'm sorry, Josef. My mind was elsewhere."

Josef smiled a relaxed smile as he said, "It's perfectly understandable, given the circumstances."

It was an awkward moment, but Lisa managed to utter, "Danke shön."

Then she paused as though she were making a decision. Finally, she said, "I wish to thank you for the kind things you said about Karl."

He colored slightly with embarrassment. She noticed it and warmed to him. He said, "I meant every word, Lisa. Our last few minutes together were kind of strained, because of my gross incompetence and cowardice. He was forced to take command of my men away from me, but when he was shot and waiting for death to claim him, he told me to find out who I was and be that. He wanted me to tell you that he died well and that he loved you."

Tears began forming in his eyes, and Lisa found that she was bearing witness to a little boy who had finally grown up.

He continued, "He wanted me to do right by Yvette, and I will do that even if it kills me." He shook his head sadly, and said, "I am so sorry, Lisa."

In the middle of a mass of humanity, two people came together in a final embrace. When it finished, Josef clicked his heels, saluted, begged his leave, and left.

She turned and found Gerhardt looking at her. They both smiled.

Seventeen

When danger knocks.

Saturday May 1, 1943

The War was now going badly for the German Reich although the majority of Germans didn't really know this, because the knowledge of reversals in the field was given only to those with a need to know. Even the most ardent skeptic was forced to publicly remain an optimist.

Anyone who spoke out with a defeatist attitude was arrested by the Gestapo. Many were put to death. This was especially the case with high ranking officers. They were expected to be loyal to the cause. Reality was not to be tolerated even if it were a true reality. The Greater German Reich had become The World As Myth .

Those who were attached to the OKW or the Oberkommando der Wehrmacht knew that the realities of war had tipped the balance against them. Again, they were powerless to give their knowledge to anyone.

There has always been a feeling that the German people might have "done something" had they known, but then, that was only speculation. A revolt was not really possible because of the conditioning of the people and the continuing rumor that the "walls had ears."

A single person could not have effected a change and the Established Authority made sure that groups could not have gathered to discuss such a possibility. People who spied, pretended to be friend, and then reported what they had observed. Reprisals were swift, sure, and brutal. Therefore, people did nothing to upset the

Established Order of Things. They stopped trusting anyone.

The mansion

The phone rang. It rang again, and again. It kept ringing until Gehrhardt reached over an picked the receiver up. He spoke into the mouthpiece, "Ja?"

"Gerhardt?"

"ja?"

"Max."

Gerhardt turned the lamp on and saw that it was 3:30 AM. Max was neither a night owl nor an alarmist, and if he were calling, it would be serious. He became completely alert. He heard Lisa stirring beside him. "Very well, Max. You have my complete attention. What is it?"

"Ilse just received a call from her mother. The Gestapo has arrested her father about thirty minutes ago."

"The Gestapo? Did she say why."

"I heard Ilse ask, but the answer wasn't very coherent."

"Where are you?"

"In my apartment. I have an outside line, you know."

"Ach....I forgot. Are you dressed?"

"Ja!"

"Then, give me fifteen minutes and come knocking on my door. In the meantime, call Fritz, and tell him that we need him."

"Jawohl."

Gerhardt hung up.

"What is it?" Lisa asked.

"Ilse's father was arrested by the Gestapo. We don't know why yet, but we are going down to find out."

"Can you get him out?"

"Don't know. They are above the law, you know."

"What if it is all about Ilse and Gottlieb's attraction for her?" There had been other times when Gottlieb had gotten to Ilse, and each time, she cooperated. She also told Max each time it happened, and each time, Max had suppressed the need to kill Gottlieb. He had finally confided in both Gerhardt and Lisa, but it was Ilse who told the group that a woman could either have sex or she could make love, and she had cause to wonder if she had ever made love to Gottlieb.

"Hadn't thought about that yet," Gerhardt admitted, but added, "I'll keep it in mind, though."

Gerhardt had just finished dressing when there was a knock upon the door. Lisa, who had just slipped into a dressing gown, glided gracefully to the door and opened it.

It was Max.

Gerhardt put his hat on, joined Max and they disappeared down the hallway.

* * * * *

Gerhardt's appearance created a stir at Gestapo Headquarters, but order was restored once more with the appearance of Chief Inspector Heinz Gottlieb.

"How can I help the Herr General?" He inquired.

Gerhardt replied briskly, "Fritz Dorfmeier."

In order to keep the verbal fencing match going, Gottlieb asked, "What about him?"

"I am told that he was arrested and since he is the Herr Standartenführer Liebert's father-in-law, I thought you might be kind enough to tell us why he was arrested."

"I don't need a reason and you know that."

"Ja....I do know that, but you people are not in the habit of making random arrests just for the effect it has on the general population. You usually have a reason. I thought you might choose to share it with us."

Gottlieb thought for a moment before answering. "There have been some banking irregularities in his area of responsibility. He is being detained for questioning."

"Are you expecting to bring charges forth."

Gottlieb shrugged. "I don't know. It depends on what we uncover."

"I see," Gerhardt said dryly. His eyes never left Gottlieb's eyes. There was something else.....another agenda, but he wasn't sure just how to flush it out. Then, the subject of Ilse came to mind. What if Lisa was right, but why now? After all, it had been three years. Ja, why now?

"Can you release him to my custody?"

"Nein, Herr General. Not without the approval of the Reich Main Security Office. If they call and tell me to do so, I will. Otherwise....Nein, ist nicht!"

Gerhardt wheeled about and motioned for Max to follow him.

When they got outside the building, Gerhardt took a deep breath followed by another. He looked at Max and said, "Come, let us walk."

Downtown Munich was quiet in the early morning hours. A local police car cruised past them slowing as it did and then continuing on. Then, they cut across the Marienplatz and seemed to be headed nowhere in particular. Fritz, the chauffeur, followed slowly at a discreet distance.

The two men walked in silence, but this was not a leisurely stroll. No! They walked with purpose. Soon, Max stopped walking. When he did, Gerhardt stopped walking also.

It was Max who finally broke the silence.

"What is the man's real agenda, Gerhardt?"

"Lisa brought it up before we left, but have you considered that Ilse might be the root cause of the problem?"

Max thought for several long moments before admitting, "Ja....I have considered that.. I might have even feared it, and if I did, my thoughts helped to bring it to fruition."

Gerhardt looked puzzled. "I really don't accept that line of thinking."

"Whether you accept it or not has nothing to do with its existence. If it is, it is."

Again, Gerhardt just looked at Max.

Max decided to change his approach, "Look, Gerhardt......I think it is a very real possibility that Gottlieb wants to get his hands on Ilse, and he has no more regard for the sanctity of marriage than you did. You people just charge in like a bull in a china shop." His eyes met with Gerhardt's and remained that way. Max had no intention of backing down.

Finally, Gerhardt began to speak, "I-I never knew you felt that way. I wish you had told me."

"Would it have made a difference?"

Gerhardt, a master negotiator, was not used to being on the defensive, and he didn't like it. It took a long time, but he finally answered, "No, I guess it wouldn't have."

Max was actually furious although he managed to keep his fury under the surface. He took a deep breathe. "It's in the open now. I have finally voiced my opinion, and I am resigned to the fact that I am going to have to kill Heinz Gottlieb."

"No Max......I have killed and you haven't. I wouldn't be emotional about doing it."

"It's no use, Gerhardt. Neither of us can do it with impunity. They'll come after us. You for doing it and me for complicity. After we are gone, that pack of wild dogs would devour the girls."

"You are right, of course." Gerhardt said with a sigh of resignation. He looked away for just a moment and then asked, "Do you place me on the same level as Gottlieb?"

The question caught Max by surprise. "Nein, Herr General! You have class and Gottlieb is just barely above the bottom of the food chain."

"I should thank you, but I am not sure."

Max took a deep breath of his own and said, "Now then, short of killing Gottlieb, what can we do?"

Gerhardt looked like a light had just gone on somewhere. "Max, I don't believe there is an easy way out, so why don't we just play the hand dealt by Herr Gottlieb. Right now, we are only speculating, and that won't get us anywhere. He has arrested your father-in-law. If Ilse is the real target, sooner or later, Gottlieb will make his real intentions known. Just don't ever take the man lightly, Max. He was one of the most ruthless men to have ever worn a badge in Berlin."

Max shook his had sadly and Gerhardt made a gesture to Fritz in the Mercedes.

* * * * *

Max had just walked into the apartment when Ilse kissed him lovingly. Three year old Peter had just gotten up and was sitting in his highchair. Max sat down wearily at the table as Ilse studied her husband.

"So....what is it, Max."

"According to Herr Gottlieb, they have picked your father up for questioning in conjunction with some banking irregularities, and they only do such things at three o'clock in the morning. Gerhardt asked Gottlieb if he would release your father to his custody, and Herr Gottlieb said it was possible, but only if the Reich Main Security Office gave its approval. Otherwise.....Nein!" He stopped and sighed. His eyes met those of Ilse. *Such intelligent eyes on such a desirable woman.*

At that moment, she showed how perceptive she really was. "It is all about me, isn't it?"

Can I keep anything from this woman?

"It is only speculation, Mein Liebe, but both Gerhardt and I think we should consider the possibility."

"Damn!" Ilse said with disgust dripping off of each letter. "If that is true, what do we do?"

"It is your father, and you may voluntarily wish to go to him, but I would try to stop you."

"Why? If it's all about sex, I'll just go and have sex with him and have it done with."

"If I thought that would solve anything, I would take you to him right now and present you as a burnt offering, but it wouldn't solve anything and you know it."

"What do I know?"

"How often did Heinz Gottlieb visit you in Berlin?"

"Once or twice a month for two to three days at a time. One time for a week, but after that, it was over two months until the next visit."

Max considered what she told him. "Very well, Mein Schatz. Don't you see the pattern? He wasn't playing second fiddle to Otto. I am sure that he cleared each visit with Otto first, but he didn't have any single woman he attached himself to. You were simply a part of a pool of women whose purpose it was to keep Heinz Gottlieb sexually satisfied. Anyone of you would have bored him senseless, but all of you kept him happy and satisfied."

She looked hurt and he walked over and wrapped his arms around her. "Remember, I am talking about him......not me. You couldn't bore me in a dozen lifetimes. I wish only to give you love and he intends only to enslave." They kissed, but it wasn't the time for love. It was time for making a decision. She asked, "Back to my original question, oh wise husband, what now...my love?"

"Ilse, my love, first of all, we are only speculating as to his real motive. We really do need to have him tip his hand."

"What then?" She asked.

"We don't wait until then. We decide now."

"You are confusing me, O wise one. Stop using circular reasoning and talk straight."

He sighed. "Ilse, as a free moral agent, you are free to go to bed with any man you choose to go to bed with. As my wife however, your choices are more restricted. That means that you are free to go to bed with any man **we** decide that you should go to bed with."

"You are taking away all of my fun, you terrible man."

Max couldn't help but laugh at his wife's sense of humor. "Seriously Ilse, there might well come a time when it becomes necessary for you to bed another man simply because that is the only thing of value that you will have to pay him with."

She just looked at him curiously.

"Ilse! You may be a free moral agent, but we are not free to do as we please. Germany is still a police state. Germany is at war with everyone in the world, and I might have to decide that the only way to keep you safe is to get you out of Germany!"

Silence!

Heavy silence!

Then, after an long period of time, Ilse managed to stammer, "Out....of ....Germany?"

"Ja! Out of Germany. Since Uncle Adolph wants to rule the world, it has become necessary for him to fight the whole damned world. All we have to do is get you to one of our enemies and have you convince them that you really are a nice person, and not an enemy agent."

Peter began crying. "That brings up the matter of Peter. What do we do with him?"

"I shall miss you both terribly."

She picked Peter up and began cuddling him while making motherly noises. Then, she looked at Max. "Are you really serious about this?"

"I have never been more serious about anything in my entire life."

"I'll attend to Peter. After that, you and I need to have a long talk about this."

* * * * *

Two long talks took place. The first was between Max and Ilse. Then, Peter was placed in the capable hands of the governess, and they retired to the basement where the second meeting took place. This meeting included Gerhardt and Lisa. The first thing Lisa did was explain what it meant to become a whore for the Reich. That idea didn't do much for Ilse's already bad state of mind.

On one hand, she couldn't just disappear without creating grief for the families. Even if her death was faked along with Peter's, there was still the chance that the Gestapo would discover her alive at a later date.

Maybe they could take that chance, but how to go about it was the main bone of contention. Gerhardt and Lisa were both involved in Max's nefarious activities right up to their collective necks, but there were things that they didn't know. The only one who knew everything was Max Liebert.

On the other hand, when the Gestapo broke and arrested the principles of the White Rose resistance group, it was thought that organized resistance might have ceased altogether. It Hadn't!

They had just reached an impasse and were getting ready to leave when the door opened and shocked all four of them out of ten years of life.

Standing in the doorway was Erik Halder, the butler.

"I hope I'm not intruding."

Gerhardt found his voice before the others. "Erik, what are you doing here?"

Erik smiled. "I live here, Herr General. Did you think, perhaps, that I didn't know about this room?"

Gerhardt was astonished. "Frankly, I will admit to not even entertaining the thought one way or the other. That is the trouble of having domestics. After a while, you simply become part of the furnishings. I realize that is being arrogant, to say the least, but true none the less."

"If nothing else, I consider you to be an honest man, Herr General. What puzzles me the most is how an honest man has lasted so long in the SS."

"I can't answer that except to say that I haven't given my superiors reason to doubt me. Now then, how were you able to know that we were here and what we were discussing?"

Erik hesitated only slightly before answering. "The ventilation outlet in here is a blind. I can hear what is going on from another room, the location of which I will not disclose. You cannot tell what you do not know. Needless to say, I know when you are here and can usually determine what you are doing."

Lisa blushed. She had entertained nafarious thoughts with this room in mind, but in light of what Erik had just said, she was glad that she hadn't. .

Erik continued, "I heard you mention the need of the underground, Herr General. How then, can I help you?"

"Erik, I will admit to having my suspicions, but how are you able to operate after White Rose?"

"It is because of White Rose that we do operate.

"Why would you trust us not to betray you?"

"Well....you **are** an SS General, but no. I have known that you were sympathetic to the idea of decency ever since you helped Herr Ruhl to escape."

"I really didn't help him, but I did try to plant some ideas in his head. When he shot me, I wasn't sure."

"He wasn't sure that he hit you, but felt that he did have to make it look good."

"A little lower and I would have made a good looking corpse."

"Your shooting him was the real surprise. He was a moving target."

Gerhardt shrugged. "It was a reflex action, and I will admit to being a very good shot."

It was Max who finally interrupted, "This is all well and good, gentlemen, but there is no need for sentimentalities. Can we get down to business, please?"

Erik outlined a solution that was risky, but could be set up in just a few days. The idea of a faked death was dismissed by Erik just as soon as it came up. "The Geheime Staatspolizie (Gestapo) may be dumb but they are not stupid. I suggest we appeal to their dumbness by appealing to their greatest weakness."

"What is that?" Asked Gerhardt.

"The compartmentalization of the Reich Main Security Office which by the way, was implemented to avoid duplication, but what it was designed to eliminate actually happens more times than not. What we do is pick a day, any day, and have Frau Leibert and son be traveling in the company of her bodyguards. She will be followed by the Gestapo detail assigned to follow her, and when she gets close to her parents home, she will be intercepted."

"Her shadow will then become confused by the unfolding events and do nothing. They will not even close on you, and when the intersecting agents make off with mother and son, the real Gestapo agents will finally gain the courage to question the bodyguards who know nothing and therefore can tell nothing. At this point, my organization will take care of getting Frau Leibert and her son not only out of Germany but out of Europe as well. How we do this is our business and not yours."

"How about me?" Ilse inquired. "Don't I have a right to know?"

"You especially don't have a need to know. It is a dangerous venture but then....so is staying in Germany. You may think that you are only speculating as to Herr Gottlieb's real intention, but I know and your fears are not unfounded."

Gerhardt finally asked, "How did you come to possess Gestapo ID discs? It is capital crime to possess them."

Erik replied curtly, "Ask me no questions and I will tell you no lies."

Max had remained quiet throughout. It was really his show, but the less everyone knew, the better it would be.

Later that night.

Ilse had just tucked Peter in for the night and she joined her husband who was in a pensive mood. She walked to the kitchen and got them both a bottle of Beer. Max took note of that fact. She rarely drank.

"You might as well tell me what is bothering you, Ilse."

"You don't know?"

"You mean the escape plan?"

"You people acted as though I am going to pull off this charade with absolutely no problem and then just waltz out of Germany."

"Liebchen! I never meant to imply that it wouldn't be difficult."

"Danke schön, Mein Liebe. Is it possible that you **do, in fact,** acknowledge that it might just be a **little** difficult?"

He pulled her close to him, and she responded to his touch. Not that she was in the mood for love or anything of the sort. It was because she was basically a woman who thrived on the touch of a man. Not necessarily an erotic touch but a simple touch. It could give her peace or it could thrill her based on the intentions of the man doing the touching. Max could touch her anywhere he wanted to touch her, because she had granted him license to do so. This time, it was a reassuring touch, and it quieted her. She embraced him.

"Ilse," he whispered. "I didn't marry you to separate from you, but I have always lived with that possibility. I feel that it will all happen so quickly that I now have to look upon each moment as our last. You have brought meaning to a life that has spent too much time contemplating the mysteries of life and not learning how to live it. I love you Ilse Maria. You are my life, my love and my purpose for being. May you always be safe and may we find each other when this is all over."

The time for talking was no more and the time for touching and feeling and loving had replaced it. They would talk again, but first they would love.

* * * * *

And so, it came to pass, that three days hence, while on the way to her parents, Ilse's car was intercepted by a black sedan bearing three men wearing black leather coats and brandishing ID discs of the Gestapo, and she was placed under arrest.

Her child was with her and therefore taken also. The local Gestapo detail that was assigned to keep her under surveillance had been caught by surprise and predictably did not approach the false Gestapo agents. The encounter took no more than a minute, but during that time, the name "Berlin" had been used at least six times. It made an indelible impression on her bodyguards. Berlin being the sacred Mecca of all right thinking Nazi's.

The time it took for (1) the real Gestapo agents to approach the scene of the abduction, and (2) to find out what happened, and (3) for the bodyguards to be taken to Gestapo Headquarters for interrogation, and (4) the decision that was made to call Berlin for clarification, and (5) for Berlin to stonewall Chief Inspector Gottlieb who actually made the call, and (6) to finally realize that they had wasted time and allowed whoever took Frau Ilse Liebert to get away.

They didn't even have a make, model, and vehicle tag number of the vehicle involved. None of the roadblocks and check points had reported anything out of the ordinary.

A check of the airport revealed that two airplanes had filed a flight plan for Berlin and both were official government airplanes. An official at the airport remembered a woman and maybe a child on one of the aircraft. That led to the belief that a secret branch of the Reich Main Security Office was involved? Gottlieb slammed the phone down in disgust!

"Damn the idea of secrecy all to hell anyway!"

Inspector Franz Lehman looked at his boss curiously. "Has anyone gone to the mansion to confront the husband yet?"

Gottlieb looked at his subordinate dumbly as a light went off somewhere. He sighed heavily and stood up. Then he said, "Let's go!"

Both men left.

* * * * *

"She what?" Max Liebert asked incredulously.

Heinz Gottlieb carefully observed Max's face and seeing no telltale signs of anything, answered, "She has been abducted by three men who presented themselves as Gestapo operatives from Berlin. They presented proper identification and took your wife and child with them. I regret to inform you that we don't yet know where they have taken her."

Max could be every bit as intimidating as Gottlieb, but he didn't want to overplay his hand. Instead, he said, "Let me get this straight," he began. "Three men who presented themselves as Gestapo agents from Berlin took my wife and son while everybody stood around and watched them do it."

"Now wait a minute, Herr Standartenführer! I resent that inference you just made."

"I don't particularly care if you like it or not, Herr Chief Inspector. What I want to know is how those three men came into possession of Gestapo Identification discs if they weren't agents of the Gestapo. Just the possession of illegal discs bears the death penalty does it not?"

"Ja."

"Then, I strongly suggest that something is rotten. Really rotten, and maybe you had best get to the bottom of it." He was glaring at the Chief Inspector. He was still glaring as the Chief Inspector left.

* * * * *

Later, Max was approached by Erik. "You might be pleased to know that Frau Liebert has successfully made it to our first safe house which is not only outside of Munich, but quite a ways down the road, and because of your magnificent performance with the Herr Chief Inspector, they now believe that she has been taken to the Reich Main Security Office in Berlin for undisclosed reasons that will probably remain undisclosed."

Max gave Erik a tightlipped smile. "Danke, Mein Freund.....so far I am both pleased and saddened. Pleased, because it might just work, and saddened because your success is taking her away from me."

Erik nodded his understanding. "I will be able to monitor her progress until she leaves Europe. After that, it becomes much more difficult."

Max shook his head. "It is much more difficult to deal with from this perspective isn't it?".

Erik smiled an genuine smile. "Ja, because it is people that you love that are now within the pipeline."

"But, I love them all," replied Max.

"I know you do, Max. That is why I love you so much. You care. You really do care."

"Well, the waiting is difficult for whoever is doing the waiting. Is there anything I can do to make the waiting easier?"

"It is what your General can do for us that really matters."

Max raised his eyebrows, "Are you referring to Operation Missing Trains?"

"Ja, but tell the Herr General that I will speak with him at a time of my choosing."

* * * * *

"How can I be of service to you, Erik?"

"You have access to rail transportation schedules, do you not?"

"Ja. I even have manifests."

"Good!" The butler replied. "I have a plan that will require only train numbers and car numbers. The documents themselves are too risky to possess."

"Can you tell me what you plan to do with this information?"

"We are going to route random cars to the line that runs through to Zurich. We have already done it with isolated cars. When the opportunity presents itself, we will try to divert an entire train."

Because the border had been closed since the inception of hostilities, it wasn't possible for German trains to enter Switzerland without violating the neutrality of Switzerland, but this was a matter that had already been dealt with by Max and his organization. In his way of thinking, a little walking never hurt anyone.

"Sounds ambitious," Gerhardt mused. Then he added, "I would like to know how you do it, but then, I really don't want to know. I will work out something with Lisa. You and she can take care of the details."

"Very good, Herr General. Danke schön."

"Bitte schön, Mein Freund. Please advise if there is any other way I can help."

"Be assured that I will, Herr General, but as for now, I bid you Auf Wiedersehen."

"Auf Wiedersehen, Erik." He and Erik exchanged a final glance, and then, Erik left.

* * * * *

July 1, 1943

Gerhardt had not come to this decision lightly. Never before in his life had he felt this way, and yet, the possibility of facing it terrified him.

He was sitting alone in his office as he had done so many times before, and with the door open, he could observe her sitting at her desk. During the day, she was his secretary. At night, she was his partner and lover. He had made a specific point of being part of Heidi's life to the point where she now looked upon him as being a lot more than that strange man who sometimes came to see her.

She even called him Uncle Gerhardt.

As he looked at Lisa, he made his decision. He would never know if he didn't ask.

"Lisa?"

"Ja?"

"Come here, please."

She walked into his office with pad and pencil in hand and seated herself in her favorite chair.

"You won't need your pad unless you wish to take notes."

She sat back and relaxed. "What then, may I do for you, Herr General?"

"The first thing you can do is drop the Herr General. Before God and all the hidden microphones, I wish to tell you that I love you."

She smiled warmly and replied, "And I too, love you, but what brought this on?"

"I would like to take you to the finest establishment in the City of Munich for the purposes of celebrating."

"Celebrating what?" She asked.

He looked around then his eyes settled on the calendar. "How about the First of July?"

She couldn't help it. She giggled. "Kind of stretching things aren't you?"

"Well! Will you go with me or not?"

She shook her head in mock dismay. "Jawohl, my beloved. I love to go out. Should I dress respectably or shall I push the decency rules to the limit."

"Since you are the General's lady, perhaps you shouldn't push the threshold too hard." He held his right thumb and forefinger together and said, "You can push it a little, but not too much."

* * * * *

Later that evening after dinner and dancing, they were taking a walk and they were holding hands like lovers have always done. There was a casual informality that had existed between them since the first rocky beginning, but it was now being replaced by a sense that something was about to happen that would change them forever.

War was raging on two fronts and men were dying and yet........here in Munich, the illusion of peace and tranquillity still remained. There had been air raids, but nothing like Gerhardt had expected. Of course, the worst was yet to come.

They were caught in the lights of a police patrol car and the car stopped.

"Come here, Bitte (please)!" A voice spoke from the car.

Gerhardt and Lisa approached the police car.

The officer then recognized the uniform and high rank of the Herr General. "Excuse me, Herr General, but you are in violation of the curfew."

"Am I?" Gerhardt asked with a thin smile on his face.

The officer was silent.

Did the curfew extend to SS Generals? He didn't know, but his response was polite and professional, "Perhaps ja und perhaps nein. Perhaps it does not apply to SS Generals and their ladies, Ja? Perhaps, I shall retire to the station to check the regulations, ja? Perhaps, you will not be here when I return, Ja?"

"Perhaps not," replied Gerhardt.

The officer drove away.

* * * * *

This time, Gerhardt found a secluded spot and a place where Lisa could sit. After seating her, he knelt down on one knee and said, "I love you, Lisa."

"I know you do, Gerhardt, and I think I love you too, but what is love?"

"It's probably elusive, Lisa, but it is a feeling that stays with me long after sexual gratification. In truth, Mein Liebe, I don't know what love is. I only know that it is."

Maybe it was too dark to see her smile and maybe it wasn't, but she smiled anyway. "In lieu of whatever definition I might have given it, I will accept yours even if yours was no definition at all."

A silence ensued.

It began to become uncomfortable when Gerhardt started speaking, "Lisa, Mein Liebe, I have a question to ask you, and there are all manner of ways in which to ask this question. Many are much more eloquent than my way, but since I can be none other than myself, I will simply ask......will you marry me?"

Silence.

The silence continued.

The silence became maddening, and yet he knew there was strength in silence. For him to speak first would invalidate the question. He would not invalidate the question.

Regardless of how they had come into being, they had been a couple for four years. He now wished to give dignity and permanence to their relationship.

She cleared her throat slightly. A good sign. "Ah...Gerhardt....why do you want to marry me?"

"Isn't love a good enough reason?"

"To most people, ja, but you are not most people. You march to the beat of a different drummer."

"That is true, Lisa. I do think differently, but I have never seen you as anyone or anything other than who you are. If I had met you before Karl had married you, I would have given him a run for his money."

"And you would have won," she admitted honestly.

"Danke, Mein Liebe, but would I have beaten the man Karl had become when he died?"

"I honestly can't say, but my answer pays high tribute to the man Karl had become."

"That's why I love you, Mein Schatz. You are an honest woman who has probably never been intimidated by the fact that I am an SS General. In short, you are a very good woman. Maybe, you are too good for me. Whatever the case may be, I still love you and want you to be my wife."

She smiled again as she stood up. She placed her arms around his neck and kissed him. "In case you haven't figured it out for yourself, the answer is yes."

* * * * *

The i's had all been dotted and the t's crossed, and Gerhardt had three days to wait before the lovely Lisa was to become the Baroness Lisa Marie von Leitner. Yes, she would become a baroness.

His gift to her was the right to become a baroness. He had finally swallowed forty years of resentment and told her the whole sordid story. Strange as it might have seemed, somehow she understood.

Lisa was out doing female things with her mother and he was seated in his office being bombarded with happy thoughts when the phone rang. He picked it up and said, "Leitner."

"Hello Gerhardt. How are you?" No introduction was necessary. It was unmistakable. The voice belonged to Adolph Hitler.

Gerhardt sat up straight as though Hitler might be able to see through his phone. He formed his reply and spoke, "Mein Führer, I am delighted that you took time from your busy schedule to call me, and in response to your question, I am fine." He knew better than to inquire about The Führer's health, because the war was going badly.

Hitler replied, "I called to congratulate you on your forthcoming marriage. I understand that she is quite lovely. Your are to congratulated on your excellent taste in women."

"Vielen dank, Mein Führer"

Hitler rarely acknowledged gratitude. Instead, he said, "I have taken the liberty of providing a surprise for you. It should be arriving tomorrow. I hope that you can accept my gift in the true spirit of why I have given it. You will know what I mean when it arrives."

"I can do no less, Mein Führer."

"That is good, Gerhardt. Duty beckons to me once more, and I must leave you now. I bid you Auf Wiedersehen."

Gerhardt replied, "Auf Wiedersehen," but he spoke into a dead line. Hitler had hung up.

* * * * *

The next afternoon, Gerhardt had been informed that visitors were arriving by police escort, and the visitors were traveling under the highest priority.

This must have been the surprise Hitler had referred to, but who? When the gate called, he and Lisa stepped out under the side canopy and waited while the Horsch Limousine pulled slowly under the canopy.

An SS Haupsturmführer was riding in the shotgun position and when the vehicle came to a stop, he stepped out of the vehicle and saluted the Herr General. Then, he walked over and opened the right rear door. Out stepped a man Gerhardt hadn't see in twenty-five years. It was the Baron Frederick von Leitner of Vienna.

His father.

The elder von Leitner stood tentatively waiting to see what kind of reception he would receive.

Lisa carefully looked at the man she would marry on the morrow. The man hadn't cried since he was a small boy, and when he might have been inclined to weep, only allowed one tear to fall.

Now, it seemed like he stood rooted to that spot for at least two eternities. Suddenly, he raised his arms and approached his father. His face contorted as though he were about to cry.

"PAPA!" He cried out and then, Gerhardt and his father came together in a rush.. Both men had their arms wrapped tightly about each other and both were weeping unashamedly. It was not very German for a man to cry, but neither of these men were German. They were both Austrians.

The Hauptsturmführer had also assisted a woman out of the vehicle and when Gerhardt looked to see who it was, standing there was the Baroness Lydia von Leitner........his mother.

It didn't take long for the twosome to become a threesome and mother, father and son huddled in joyous reunion.

Lisa stood watching with tears of own streaming down her cheeks. She was proud of the man she was about to marry. Perhaps, this was the final touch. The man had finally returned to the human race. He was finally able to cry. He could forgive and was now vulnerable enough to love.

Finally, at long last, the huddle separated and Lisa heard Gerhardt say, "Come Momma...come Papa....I have someone special that I want you to meet."

Lisa dabbed her eyes with her handkerchief and stood prettily awaiting the magic moment.

Gerhardt took Lisa's hand in his. "Momma.... Papa, allow me if you please to present my future wife, Frau Lisa Marie Mueller. Lisa, allow me please, to present my parents, the Baron Frederick and the Baroness Lydia von Leitner of Vienna.

The Herr Baron von Leitner stepped forward, took Lisa's hand in his and bowed deeply as he kissed her hand. Lisa curtsied deeply. The baron then asked, "May I take the liberty of addressing my future daughter-in-law by her given name?"

She replied, "Certainly, Herr Baron."

"Young lady, do you refer to my son as Herr Baron?"

She shook her head no.

"Then, you shall not refer to me by that title either. If I may address you as Lisa, you may address me as Fritz. No one has called me by anything other than Fritz for longer than I care to remember."

"Very well, Sir......Fritz it is."

The Baroness Lydia didn't stand on ceremony. She walked right up to Lisa and embraced her.

* * * * *

The wedding itself was an anticlimax.

It was a small private affair held at The Mansion and was officiated by a priest although the marriage wasn't officially sanctioned by the church. Neither the bride nor the groom cared whether it was officially sanctioned by anyone other than the state.

When the pronouncement had been made, her new father-in-law officially welcomed the new baroness into the family. Since bombs were now falling on German cities and the war was being fought on two fronts, the idea of a honeymoon never came up. The newly wedded couple were no strangers to each other and as such, would simply go about their normal duties with one lone exception.....the parents of the groom were to remain at the mansion for an extended period not to exceed ninety days in order to give everyone an opportunity to become better acquainted with each other.

The parents of the bride were simple dairy farmers. The von Leitner's lived in a different world, but Fritz and Lydia were careful not to talk down to the couple.

In fact, Fritz and Gus got along famously. It was because of the simplicity of Gus Rensler that he and Fritz became fast friends. Fritz was trying to unwind while Gus wasn't wound very tight at all. It made for a great many humorous moments.

The man who had orchestrated it all....namely Max Liebert......simply became part of the proceedings. He listened....he laughed....but he didn't participate. His mind was elsewhere.

Eighteen

The New World

Sunday: August 7, 1943

The Atlantic

Ilse stood watching in fascination as the ship cut its way through a relatively calm sea. She had just witnessed a spectacular sunset and as darkness engulfed the ship she was treated to the phosphorescent glow of the bubbles as the bow cut its way through the water.

Ilse fought back tears as loneliness began to overwhelm her. Just the thought of her journey overwhelmed her. In the beginning, just the thought of leaving Max overwhelmed her.

Then, there was the thought of leaving her parents, her brothers, Gerhardt, Lisa and all that had gone into a life that she had come to savor. She had found peace and happiness in being with a man who was so intelligent that it was scary. She dearly loved Max Liebert, and when he suggested this insane scheme, she was certain that it would fail.

Now, as she looked at the ocean, she realized that she had already accomplished the impossible. The European continent was now behind her. Somewhere out in front of them was the New World.

What surprised her the most was how easy it had been to exit Germany. Obviously, they hadn't used an autobahn. That would have been impossible, but there were other ways.

Seven men were charged with the task of getting her out. The lead man was known only as Apollo, and the other men used nicknames as well.

Even when they were in Switzerland, travel was limited to the back roads. Unnecessary chances were not taken. The only conversation she had was with Apollo, and he continuously spoke reverently about a man he knew only as Aristotle.

Apparently, this Aristotle was fairly close to Hitler and had been feeding information and refugees to this underground organization since 1934. He was now considered to be a true German patriot by those within the organization. Those outside the organization did not have a need to know

It had taken three weeks to travel from Munich to Zurich. They had provided a small cart for Peter and the men took turns pulling the cart. Her greatest fear had been very short lived. That being the fact that they had been "abducted," and weren't able to take any of their personal belonging with them, but both she and Peter were supplied with warm clothing and good walking shoes. They even had the food that Peter was used to eating. Her benefactors had taken care of every contingency.

When they had arrived in Zurich, she had been taken to the residence of Kapitan Gunther Heilmann, a German speaking Swiss National who happen to be the Master of a ship that was owned by a Portuguese shipping company.

About a week after her arrival at the Herr Captain's residence, the Herr Captain arrived. She took an immediate liking to this ruggedly handsome but soft spoken man of forty-six. Captain Heilmann's only role in this operation was to assume responsibility of Frau Liebert and child and transport them from Zurich to the Poet of Maracaibo in Venezuela.

Then, came the surprise. She and her son would be issued documents of Swiss citizenship complete with Certificates of birth, passports and marriage documents. She would travel as the wife of Gunther Heilmann.

He then explained that as a Kapitan, he had spent a lot of time at sea, but four years ago, the rumor had been passed that he had taken a wife. Nobody had ever seen her, but a marriage license had been issued and when Peter had been born in Munich, duplicate documents had been filed in Zurich.

Even though no one had ever seen the mother and child, a check of the records would have revealed that they did, in fact, exist.

"Why?" She asked Gunther Heilmann. "Who am I that you would have gone to all of that difficulty without knowing that I would ever leave."

"Aha, but Aristotle did know. It was only a matter of time."

"**Aristotle....Aristotle**! All I ever hear about is **Aristotle**. Who in the hell is this man that he makes plans four years before they are needed?"

He looked at her thoughtfully for quite a few moments before answering. "I don't know, Mein Frau. His identity is a closely guarded secret."

Gunther Heilmann had just lied to the lovely lady. His basis was really quite simple. It was better for her to think he didn't know than to have her think that he didn't trust her.

At the same time, she remembered not knowing what to think. She had the distinct feeling that he did know, but didn't trust her. For that matter, could he trust her? She had been careful not to dress as Ilse Liebert had dressed or wear her hair the same as Ilse Liebert had worn it. She didn't even wear the same lipstick. For that matter, as Frau Ilse Heilman, she wore makeup. Frau Ilse Liebert had never worn makeup.

Her wardrobe had been replaced by the type of dresses that the Kapitan's's wife would wear, and this Captain was a man who definitely appreciated her as a woman. She could see it in his eyes, but he was an honorable man who would always remain in his place.

Ilse couldn't help wondering if he would ever step over that imaginary line if she were to tender an invitation for him to do so.

She and Max had discussed this possibility in detail. Max was realistic enough to know that getting her out of Germany was important for the continued safety of both she and her son. Max had repeatedly told her that she was even more desirable than Lisa. She had believed him, only because he had to reason to lie to her.

Of course, it wasn't news to her. She had known that from the four years she had spent in Berlin. She had also known that she could have had sex with a wide variety of men if she could have done so without being branded a whore, but she had also discovered the true nature of the male of the human species. They all possessed a wonder lust that didn't necessarily diminish with the advent of marriage.

Many men remained quite faithful to their wives, because it was their basic desire to be decent and honorable They would appreciate all woman but never covet a single one. She was *almost* ready to concede that Max might be one of these men. He had seemed to be totally devoted to her.

On the other hand, Max had learned to live his life *outside the box.* He did not venerate the institutions of the world. He gave only the appearance of following the rules. When it came right down to it, he realized that **all** institutions were only illusions in a world made up of illusions. Were men really dying on the battlefields? Was it really the German government's goal to totally eradicate the Jewish population in Europe? She had a difficult time accepting the concept of the World As Myth, but after four wonderful years of mentally fencing with this brilliant man, she had finally adopted his outlook.

Not that he had demanded that she do so, but that her arguments to the contrary had finally been exhausted. She never had to accept his way as the only way. She had been free to be whoever she had wanted to be. That was the sheer beauty of being Frau Liebert. She was his wife and yet she was free. His only proviso was that she always remember who she was, and take special care not to destroy her own illusion of purity and marital chastity. In the end, she had been informed that it was okay to be different as long as the nosy neighbors never found out.

Therefore, he approached her forthcoming adventure as he approached everything else in life.

He knew Kapitan Heilman to be an honorable man who had been married once and lost his wife in childbirth. The baby had died also.

Max was well aware that Ilse would be traveling as Kapitan Heilman's's wife, a fact that would place her in very close proximity to the Herr Kapitan. It would therefore be unreasonable for him to place unrealistic expectations upon his wife.

Max understood and accepted that way of thinking, and although he wasn't actually encouraging her to become the whore she had always wanted to become, he was encouraging her to be who she was.

Confusing?

Surely, but that is precisely what the illusion is supposed to accomplish.

Now, as she stood at the rail, she knew that someone or a lot of someone's were going to a lot of trouble on her behalf, and no one had made one single solitary mention of money. Maybe it didn't really exist once the illusion had been removed. She didn't know.

That brought up the question of risk. Make no mistake about it, if one managed to die in the illusionary world, they were dead, or at least they had ceased to exist within the illusion. Max had told her many times that the illusion of death was the greatest of them all. It simply did not exist. Unfortunately, this was the one point that she was the most uncomfortable with.

The idea of death was definitely part of her world. It was a fact that she had accepted with her first conscious awareness, and she didn't think it would go away anytime soon.

Back to the idea of risk. If one were to accept the idea of death as an absolute, then Kapitan Gunther Heilmann was risking his life on her behalf. Even if life never really ended, the illusion of separation was still far greater than her belief that the separation didn't exist at all. Confusing as it might have sounded to the uninitiated, this whole mental exercise was moral justification for the action she was about to take.

Meanwhile, high above the main deck, Kapitan Heilmann had ventured onto the port side bridge wing and quickly scanned that side of the ship for anything that was unusual. In the process, his eyes stopped on the figure of Ilse and her three year old son.

He knew this would be a difficult assignment, and now as he looked at her, he knew that it would not only be difficult.....it would be next to impossible. She was wearing a simple dress and a pair of ballerina slippers, but just looking at the woman was an erotic experience. The woman reeked of whatever it was that gave him his desire from every pore of her body. He grabbed the railing very tightly and took several deep breathes. He could not afford to lose his self control..........self control???? Who the hell was he kidding, anyway?

An hour later, Kapitan Heilmann walked into his suite, and into his bedroom. Ilse was either still out on the deck or was in her bedroom. He sighed again and prayed to whoever might be listening for continued strength. He couldn't help wondering if there was a duty watch at some Intergalactic Prayer Central.

He smiled to himself and was glad that he was still able to see the humor in things. The war was only an abstract reality to him, but Ilse Liebert was not. At that moment, Ilse's bedroom door opened and she stood framed in the doorway wearing something black, something sheer, something sexy, and something quite revealing.

"May I join you?" She asked.

His eyes had not left her as he answered, "Ja, but first, I would ask you to slip into something that is not quite so revealing."

She smiled a relaxed smile. This was something that was really quite different or was it? Then, she remembered how she had maneuvered Max into her bedroom. Normally, it would have been the other way around. Now, she was maneuvering herself into Gunther's bed, and she was quite certain that he wouldn't kick her out of it.

She knew how to make a man happy to be in bed with her, and if she did it right, he would be able to make her happy that she had chosen him.

She glided gracefully across the floor to where he was sitting on the bed. He had taken off his shirt and the upper part of his body was naked. He had sat down to take off his shoes prior to removing his trousers. She decided to sit quite close to him and she couldn't resist running her left palm over the hair on his chest. She was taking undue liberties with the gentleman, and if just the act of looking at her was an erotic experience, this had to be really quite maddening.

He fought for control and as he did, he said, "Please Ilse.....you don't have to be doing this."

She had moved her mouth to within scant centimeters of his mouth as she replied, "Ja....that I know and that is precisely why I want to do it."

"Your husband.....?"

"My husband is either Max Liebert of Munich or Gunther Heilmann of Zurich. I love them both. Which one do you happen to be? I can be completely loyal to either of you or both of you."

"Ilse, what about pregnancy? I have no protection against that. As far as disease is concerned, I have not been sexually active. For that matter, I do not know if my equipment still functions."

Her lips were so close to his lips that she had only to reach out and touch them with her own. Instead, she addressed his fears. "When Max and I discussed this very real possibility, he hugged me and told me that he would love that child as much as he loved Peter."

That was the Max that Gunther knew so well. She continued, but reached down to touch him first. He seemed to grow in her hands. "As to whether your equipment still functions, I believe that you have absolutely no worries in that department."

He closed the distance between their lips with the softness of a gentle breeze. He followed that kiss with several light kisses with each one lasting a little longer than the one before. He kissed her eyelids, behind her earlobes, on her neck, her nose, and then back to her lips.

Gunther Heilmann may have been out of practice, but he had learned how to love a woman. Someone had taught him right. She knew that kissing was the most erotic part of lovemaking and with the lone exception of Max, the rest of the herd believed strongly in the "inter" part of intercourse.

The men of the Reich were simply young stallions who seemed to attract the type of woman who wanted their lovemaking fast and hard.. Therefore, they hadn't bothered to learn if there was any other kind available.

Soon, Ilse and Gunther were laying down on the bed and the kissing had become more intense....more purposeful. These kisses were a clear message, one to the other, of what was coming. Clothing magically disappeared and Gunther began to kiss her in places where not even Max had kissed her.

What had begun as a latent desire had now become an absolute imperative. Ilse wanted this man, and although she knew she was going to have him, the idea of "now" had became the imperative. "Later" might have only been a few seconds longer, but "now" had become a better idea.

"Gunther.....please.....do it now!"

Gunther, who was in another world, actually heard her speak, and fulfilled her need. What ensued became the wildest ride either of them had ever experienced. In fact, they had two more rides that were almost as wild but not quite. In the end, she snuggled up next to him and slept like a baby.

In the morning, Gunther and Ilse walked hand in hand to the officer's mess for breakfast. Gunther carried the boy with his right arm, and when they walked into the galley, he received some knowing glances. He looked extremely happy.

After breakfast, he kissed Ilse and went to the bridge.

At this point, Ilse had absolutely no doubt about her choice, but if there were any lingering doubts, they would be dispelled before the morning had passed.

* * * * *

"Submarine.....surfacing off the port beam."

"Engines.....all stop!" Ordered the Kapitan.

"Engines all stop," echoed the helmsman.

Kapitan Heilman walked quickly to the port wing and raised his binoculars to get a better look at the submarine. He turned to the Chief Radioman who was standing right behind his Kapitan with clipboard and pencil in hand.

"Chief, send a signal to headquarters telling them that a German submarine bearing the markings U-1273 has surfaced off the port beam at a distance of about 600 meters. The deck gun is being manned and a boat is being lowered into the water. Their intention is to board us. The national ensign of Portugal is constantly on display as well as being painted on both sides of the funnel. The International Laws of Neutrality have not been violated by this vessel. Do you have all that, Chief?"

"Si, Mi Kapitan."

"Send it immediately, and ask for an acknowledgment."

"Si, Mi Kapitan." Replied the chief and he walked briskly in the direction of the radio room..

The First Mate trained the glasses on the rubber raft in the water. "It looks like the U-boat Captain and another man in a leather jacket along with some crewmen. They all appear to be armed, Sir."

"Arm the crew, Number One and standby. I am going to my office. When that Nazi fool arrives, I want his men disarmed and kept in the area of the Jacob's ladder. The Kapitan and the other person, whoever the hell he is, are to be brought to my office."

Ilse and Peter had been in Gunther's office when he walked

in and he told her to go into the chart room which was located next to the Captain's office. Ilse did so and was quite surprised that she would be able to see and hear what was going on in the office without being observed.

Minutes later, there was a knock upon the door.

"Come!"

The door opened and the mate escorted the U-Boat Commander and another man, presumably Gestapo, into the office.

"Now see here, Mein Kapitan, what is the meaning of meeting us with armed members of your crew?"

The words were not spoken by the Captain. Instead, they were spoken by the other man. In Gunther Heilman's humble opinion, the man was Gestapo. He decided to address both men, "Which one of you is the Commander of U-1273.

The other man, the one who was dressed like an officer in the German Kreigsmarine, spoke up. "I am U-1273."

"Then, I shall speak to you as the official voice of the vessel." His jaw set as he fought to control the anger that threatened to overwhelm him. "Kapitan, I am Gunther Heilman, the Master of *The Lisbon Lights*. Why do you board us with an armed boarding party? After all, I fly the flag of Portugal, and Portugal is a neutral nation?".

"You are not acting like a neutral vessel." Again, it was the voice of the other man."

"Herr Kapitan?"

"Ja, Herr Kapitan," replied the U-Boat Commander.

"Does this man have the authority to speak for you in matters concerning your vessel and its crew?"

The German Commander sighed heavily. "I regret to inform you that he does."

"And what is his capacity?"

"He represents the Reich Main Security Office?"

"Gestapo?"

The German Commander nodded.

The now unveiled Gestapo Inspector spoke and when he did, it was with unbridled authority. "That is all of the questions that I will allow for now. I need to see your cargo manifests along with documentation for all crew members plus any passengers that you might have aboard."

Kapitan Heilman's face looked like it had been chiseled out of granite, and he was deciding whether he might have a need to kill the bastard.

"Let me put it to you this way, Herr Kapitan and Herr Inspector. I am the Master of this vessel which happens to be displaying the flag and markings of a neutral nation. In this case, that nation is Portugal. I repeat this information for the benefit of our Gestapo Inspector as he appears to be a slow learner. I am sailing in a straight line course and moving at a speed consistent with neutral vessels. When a German U-Boat surfaces approximately 600 meters from my vessel, and a crew mans the deck gun, I have to assume the intentions of that vessel to be hostile. You are from a belligerent nation and I am from a neutral one. Bearing that thought in mind, and stipulating the aforementioned facts to be true and accurate, I can only assume that you are a pirate with a agenda separate and apart from that of your governing nation and its naval service.."

Gestapo asked, "Are you going to comply with my order or not?"

"What gives you the right to give me orders?"

"The fact that I am an armed vessel and you are not?"

"Then, I was right! You are a pirate."

"It doesn't matter. If you don't comply, I'll simply put a torpedo in you."

Suddenly, the German's eyes got bigger as he was now looking down the barrel of a 9mm Luger. "Your submarine might just do that, but neither of you will be giving the order."

He reached over and pushed a button. The door opened, and two armed mates entered. "Relieve them of their weapons and stand-by."

The Kapitan picked up the phone and waited for two or three seconds.

Then, he said, "Bridge? Give me Mister Mendoza." A short wait followed by, "Mister Mendoza? These are my orders and they are to be entered into the bridge log. Make ready to get underway. Do so in the shortest time possible and when you are ready, set a collision course for U-1273. I wish to ram the bastard. Call and tell me when this has been accomplished. Preferably, just prior to the moment when you push the collision alarm."

Mr. Mendoza replied, "Si Mi Kapitan," and Heilman hung up and looked at the German submarine Kapitan, his eyes blazing.

"What the hell is so damned important that you are willing to risk your own lives as well as the lives of your crew."

The German Commander now looked at Gestapo for the very first time. The Kriegsmarine was definitely not unopposed in the Atlantic. The war was beginning to go against the U-Boats as well as the rest of the Reich and Captain Heiner knew it.

He looked carefully at the Swiss Commander of the Portuguese vessel and knew that the Herr Kapitan had been there and done that. He couldn't kill without feeling bad about it, but he would kill. Of that, Kapitan Kurt Heiner had absolutely no doubt. He looked daggers at Gestapo while he asked, "Well, Herr Inspector, tell him what is so important that I have placed my vessel at risk."

Silence.....followed by......more silence......and more silence until they all felt the sensation of movement. The ship had gotten underway.

"Well, I am waiting, Herr Inspector. You told me that your orders came straight from the Reich Main Security Office in Berlin."

The Gestapo Inspector quickly found his voice. "Do you mean to tell me that you are going to back down to this Swiss bastard?"

The German Kapitan backhanded the Gestapo Inspector hard in the mouth. "You do not refer to the Master of this vessel in that manner. Besides, he has a gun and we have none. Are you perhaps.....bulletproof?"

The phone rang and Gunther Heilman picked it up, and said, "Ja?"

After a few very long moments, he said, "I don't care what kind of evasive maneuvers he takes. If he fires on us or hits us with a bow shot, he can't stop us from killing him. He can't even submerge fast enough. He had better give his soul to the Lord, because his ass now belongs to us."

"After making the hard turn, increase your speed to flank." After a moment, Heilman placed the receiver on its cradle.

"It's your move Herr Kapitan." Captain Heilman now looked very much like the man who had just drawn to an inside straight and had gotten the right card.

Captain Heiner was now thinking like a man who needed to be back at the helm of his boat. "My name, Herr Kapitan, is Kurt Heiner, and I am the Commander of U-1273. The Herr Inspector is only a passenger, and as of right now, he is excess baggage. He does not, I repeat, does not speak for my vessel. I do! People like him have been self will run riot just about long enough. They don't give a damn about human life, and you can say the same thing about me if you wish, but the people I shoot at do understand the risks they are taking. Neutral vessels do have the right to expect unimpeded passage. That order comes to me and the rest of the fleet directly from Der Führer by way of the Herr Admiral Doenitz."

The ship had just made a hard turn to port and with it, came the feeling of acceleration. At that moment, another voice was heard. It was the Herr Captain's hand held radio. "Herr Kapitan! The merchant ship is going to ram us. What is going on?"

There was no panic in the officer's voice, but there was a definite sense of urgency.

Kapitan Heilman couldn't help smiling. "Your First Officer asks the first intelligent question that I have heard since your arrival. So.....what **is** going on?"

"Very well, Herr Kapitan, you are not only holding all the aces but the trump card as well. I am sorry about this whole mess. We will not attack you and you have my word as a naval officer. He extended his hand to Heilman who accepted it, but his acceptance was not without its conditions or questions. Unfortunately, the rule of the day was first things first. He picked up the phone, "Number One, can you abort? If so, then do it.....NOW!"

Suddenly, the ship lurched hard to starboard. Collision alarms sounded, but there was no impact. The phone rang.

The Kapitan said, "Ja?".

"It was that close, Mi Kapitan, but we missed them. The entries have all been made."

"Very well, Number One. You did remarkably well. I will not forget this."

The First Mate thanked his Captain and they both disconnected.

He hung the phone up again and addressed the German, "Germany hasn't been a very honorable nation. Why should I accept your word of honor?"

The German Commander was now very much in charge. "Please do not blame our military for the bad habits of our political leaders."

The Inspector now looked at Kapitan Heiner with absolute contempt, "You incompetent fool. You speak treason and it will be severely dealt with when you return to Berlin."

Kapitan Heiner only gave the man a wry smile in return. Kapitan Heilman saw the smile and couldn't help wondering how arrogant this fool must be to think that he could make a threat like that with complete impunity. Obviously, Kapitan Heiner felt the same way.

"Herr Inspector, I am the Commander of that U-Boat, not you. I will make all decisions concerning its operation, not you, and I will not tolerate any insolence from you. Therefore, when we return to the boat, you are to be confined to your quarters."

"You'll pay for this outrage!"

"We'll see who pays for what," replied Captain Heiner dryly.

They moved from Kapitan Heilman's office to the Jacob's Ladder where Kapitan Heilman ordered his men to return the weapons to the German seamen. Once that had been completed, Kapitan Heiner ordered his men back to the rubber boat. . When his men had all negotiated the ladder, The Herr Inspector was ordered down into the raft. Kapitan Heilman had fully expected that Kapitan Heiner was going to push him off the ladder, but something else happened instead.

Maybe Divine Providence intervened, and maybe not, but as the Herr Inspector stepped over the side, he missed the next step and in clear view of the many witnesses, he fell to the raft head first, his head impacting with one of the oar locks first and then one of the wooden seats. He didn't even break his fall on one of the crewmen. When he stopped falling, his body lay in a heap. The senior man in the boat examined the Inspector and yelled up to his Kapitan, "He is dead, Herr Kapitan."

Heiner looked at Heilman and said, "It is at times like this when I am certain that God is still in control of His universe."

Heilman only shook his head in wonder. Then, he requested that the Germans return to the main deck so that statements could be taken from them.

After the paperwork had been completed, it was unanimous. The Herr Inspector had missed a rung in the ladder and had fallen headfirst into the rubber boat, and broke his neck upon impact. Death was instantaneous.

A log entry was made into the ship's log, and then on separate log pages for Kapitan Heiner.

The body was to be returned to the submarine where it would be buried at sea. After all of that had been completed, the Germans made ready to depart once more. When Kapitan Heiner was the only man left to go, he turned and shook Captain Heilman's hand again.

Kapitan Heilman shook it vigorously, and said, "I am delighted to see that the Kriegsmarine of der Wehrmacht is still using competence as the basis for promotion to command ranks."

Kapitan Heiner shook his head sadly, and replied, "Not in all cases, Herr Kapitan. Of course, a sailor must still know how to sail, but when political reliability becomes the sole basis for promotion to command rank, it doesn't speak very highly of the culture that employs such a practice."

Kapitan Heilman was thoughtfully considering those remarks when Kapitan Heiner added, "You shall have no more trouble from my vessel. I cannot speak for the rest of the fleet, but I am willing to wager that you shall have no more difficulties"

"When exactly did you pick us up?" Asked Kapitan Heilman more as a matter of curiosity than anything else.

"We have been shadowing you since you left Lisbon," Captain Heiner admitted honestly.

"You specifically chose to follow us?"

"Jawohl," replied Captain Heiner.

"Did the Inspector say why?"

"No! Only that he had orders from Berlin to check this particular vessel. When I protested, he backed me down. His breed is very good at that sort of thing. They use what is called *Implied authority*, and men like myself are either too frightened or too impressed to do anything other than obey. It is the German way, Herr Kapitan."

Heilman shook his head. He was thinking of Premier Antonio Salazar's repressive regime back in Portugal when he said, "You

Germans aren't the only ones who do things like that."

The German sighed heavily and said, "I don't think either of us is going to change the world, but I feel good about what happened here today. It tells me that a sense of justice still prevails. I would mourn the loss of a human life if that life was worth mourning, but it wasn't. Now if you will excuse me, Herr Kapitan, I must be returning to my boat. Auf Wiedersehen."

The two skippers embraced and Kapitan Heiner started down the ladder.

"Auf Wiedersehen," said Kapitan Heilman thoughtfully to himself. It had been an interesting day.

* * * * *

Ilse didn't crowd Gunther for the rest of the day, but she was really quite proud of him, and when he told her what Kapitan Heiner had to say, they determined that it was possible that she could have been the object of a hunt Unfortunately, they didn't know. Furthermore, they didn't know to what extent the Gestapo was willing to go, but vigilance became the order of the day for every day that was left on the journey.

It also made her heart beat faster when she thought about what might have happened back home in Munich. What if the Gestapo had broken the chain. What if she were heading in the direction of safety while her family and friends suffered.

When she broke down and told Gunther about her fears, he comforted her by suggesting that she not borrow trouble. As long as she didn't know, why fear the worst? That's precisely what the Nazi's wanted her to do. In order to defeat them, she had to believe that everything back in Munich would still be the same as it was when she left.

* * * * *

The rest of the trip was free of incidents, but that didn't stop the vigilance, and the abandon ship drills were held so often that Ilse felt that she could abandon the ship in her sleep.

One time, he actually stopped the ship and they really did

abandon the ship. That way, Gunther was certain that everything would work. He was a very careful man who already had the respect of his crew before the incident. After the incident, his crew would have followed him to hell and back.

If Kapitan Heilman had his druthers, he'd have druther put into the Port of Veracruz in Mexico rather that the Port of Maracaibo in Venezuela. It was safer and closer to Ilse's final destination of Berkeley, California, but the vulgarities of war and the narrowness of the Neutrality Laws precluded the idea of stopping at the Port of Veracruz even to drop off a passenger.

That brought him back to the idea of Maracaibo, and when they arrived, he was not able to dock until he had paid off the Established Authority. Once that had been accomplished, the ship was docked and tied up at the assigned pier. As soon as the ship had been secured to the quay, he established what the U.S. Navy refers to as a port and starboard watch schedule and then, he made certain that the crew was armed and knew the Rules of Engagement. In other words, could they shoot and if they could, were they allowed to kill anybody?

The irony of it all was that this was a neutral port. He doubted if they would have had to take these precautions had they docked at the port of a warring nation.

Once he felt that everything had been taken care of, he took Ilse and Peter ashore and checked into a hotel. After that, he sent a wire to Juan Miguel Garcia, a local businessman with connections throughout Latin America and the United States.

By reputation Juan Miguel had an eye for a dollar, peso or whatever was available, but he was also an honest man who preferred honest money. It was a fact that made him a breath of fresh air in an otherwise stagnant room. He was neither naive nor was he stupid. He was tough to deal with because he dealt with thieves and black marketeers. He had helped a good many Jews escape from the Nazi death camps and further assisted them in finding a new life in the new world. In that regard, there were a good many right thinking people in the world. There just weren't enough of them.

Within the hour, the phone rang in the hotel room. Gunther answered it in Spanish. It was Juan Miguel. He was in the lobby. Gunther took Ilse and Peter down to the lobby to meet Senor Garcia.

When she saw Juan Miguel Garcia, something got stuck in her throat. Perhaps, it was a lump. Juan Miguel was a strikingly handsome man. He was wearing a white linen suit with a black shirt that was open at the collar. His hair was black and he wore a pencil thin black mustache.

He greeted her first and then flattered her by kissing her on the hand. She surprised him by speaking to him in Spanish. She had learned Spanish in school and was fairly conversant with the language.

Juan Miguel took them all to dinner that evening, and then bid them good night. Gunther and Ilse retired to their hotel room for their final night together, and when Ilse woke up in the pre-dawn hours, she contemplated her relationship with Gunther and how it had affected her relationship with Max.

The truth of the matter was that she didn't know, but she wasn't about to question things at this late date. Max had insisted on her leaving Germany, but he was going to ride it out until the end of the war for the sake of some noble cause that he had been unable to discuss with her. She dearly loved Max but enough was enough.

When Gunther woke up, she gave him something to really remember her by.

* * * * *

After the transfer had taken place Juan Miguel took her and Peter to his estate where they stayed nearly three weeks while they were preparing for the trip north. The need for her to fend off his advances had been greatly exaggerated in her mind as he remained friendly and cordial but he made absolutely no overt overtures in her direction. In short, he had been a perfect gentleman.

Then, came the day for departure, and they loaded into a land rover and left the estate to travel via a heavily armed convoy to a marina on the Pacific coast of the Republic of Columbia. The roads were bad but Juan Miguel didn't complain as he had traveled them many times before. The border crossing was routine. In fact, in Ilse's way of thinking, it was much too routine. Money was the lubricant that made it happen.

From the Colombian border to the marina was a monotonous

journey, but when they finally arrived at the marina, she found that it was in a cove that was concealed from discovery from both the seaward and landward approach. In fact, one had to actually be looking for it or discovery might have been impossible.

Thoughts of gun running, smuggling, drug dealing and slavery managed to crowd her imagination, and prompted her to wonder, *Is this much secrecy really necessary?* She kept her thoughts to herself.

Not many boats were in the small harbor. Perhaps a dozen at the most, and one of those boats managed to get her attention. She believed it was called a schooner, but she wasn't sure.

After all, she was from Munich, Germany, and Munich was very much in a landlocked place, but that didn't stop her from being fascinated by the sea and the ships that men had used to sail the seven seas.

This one was a sleek vessel with fore and aft masts and polished hardwood and glistening white. It looked like it was moving and yet, it was still docked in the harbor.

She was not surprised when they went to that particular ship and boarded her. Juan Miguel smiled at her and said, "This will be your home for the next two weeks. How do you like her?"

"Like her...I love her. She is so graceful, so beautiful. I didn't see a name. What do you call her?"

Juan Miguel smiled, "You won't believe this, but she is called *The Ilse Maria.*"

"But how.....what?"

"It is very simple, Senora Liebert. She doesn't belong to me. She belongs to your husband, and if you lived in a country that honored community property laws, she would also belong to you."

Ilse looked all about her as a sense of great awe began to envelope her. Who was this man she had been married to? He wore the uniform of a SS Standartenführer, carried papers that were signed by Adolph Hitler himself, and came and went much as he pleased, but just who in the hell was he really? The idea didn't hurt her. Not at all. Where she came from, the walls really did have ears and the success of a secret really did depend on how few people knew it. Even wives couldn't be trusted. Therefore, she wasn't angry at Max for withholding all of this from her, but how did this son of a Munich baker manage all of this?

The balance of the morning and the first two hours of the afternoon was spent loading baggage and additional provisions aboard the schooner.

When all was completed, Juan Miguel took some money out of his pocket and gave it to one of the men. She assumed that he was the man in charge of the workers although she didn't really care.

After that, he led her back aboard *her* ship, and Ilse became overwhelmed by the sheer size of the vessel. The crew, which had been aboard for several days, were introduced to the pretty German lady who happened to be the wife of the owner. *Everyone* seemed to know Max and everyone seemed to love him to the point where each would gladly lay down his life for the lovely lady and her son.

At that moment, she too, wanted to wrap her arms around Max Liebert and never let him go. *I am very sorry, Juan Miguel, but you are <u>not</u> Max Liebert, and as such, will not have the same privileges that Gunther Heilman had.*

To her great relief, the matter would never come up and before the next two days had passed, Juan Miguel would finally confirm her suspicions. Max Liebert was in fact ....Aristotle.

As she walked about on *her* deck, she was filled with wonder and love for man she had chosen to be with. The other men in her life were just other men in her life.

As the trip wore on, she had decided that if Juan Miguel approached her, she would bring him into her select circle, but he didn't approach her until later. Much later.

Nineteen

The beginning of the end

1944

It might have been accurate to state that 1944 was the beginning of the end for the Third Reich except that Max Liebert would have disagreed with that statement. The beginning of the end actually started on January 30, 1933, the day that Adolph Hitler became Chancellor of Germany.

That was the day when he traveled to Zurich, Switzerland to convene with Gunther Heilman, Juan Miguel Garcia, Konrad Ruhl, and Erik Halder. These men were concerned about Adolph Hitler, and what would happen when his power became absolute. They also knew about the legal talents of a certain Gerhardt Ludwig von Leitner, and his fascination for Hitler. Max correctly suspected that von Leitner might have been fascinated with the sheer audacity of Hitler rather than foster any kind of love for the man. No one ever suspected that this refugee from Vienna's Mannerheim (A men's halfway house) would be able to come from nowhere to become Chancellor of Germany.

Nobody but these men, that is.

At that moment, these men pledged their lives, their fortunes, and their sacred honors to form the ***Black Guard Legacy,*** but unlike the signers of the American Declaration of Independence, these men had to remain anonymous. Theirs was a different world than the American colonists faced in 1776. It was just as dangerous, but different.

Max Liebert had degrees in both philosophy and anthropology, but his real expertise was in the field of international banking and finance. In that area, he had become an absolute expert and because of his expertise, he was placed in control of the Legacy which by 1938 had grown to over thirty million in British Pounds Sterling. Quite a feat for the son of a poor Munich baker.

Actually, Max had become a modern day Robinhood. He had become quite adept at diverting transient cash from *Point A* to *Point Z thus bypassing all points in between.*

In truth, that was what was happening at the beginning of this story except that Hitler got into the act and placed Max in charge of the investigation. That was tantamount to placing the fox in charge of guarding the hen house.

Konrad Ruhl and Max knew each other, but they played their adversarial roles to the hilt. Ruhl, as a member of the Black Guard Legacy, was quite prepared to die. The unexpected ingredient in the stew was the sudden emergence of SS General Gerhardt von Leitner as an ally. As a result, the Herr General was able to give a sense of reality to the escape of Konrad Ruhl. Ruhl had followed the same pipeline to America that Ilse had. He was the man that Max had sent Ilse to meet.

Max now looked back upon it all and wondered why the Powers That Be In God's Universe had chosen to endow him with such marvelous mental capabilities. In addition to all that had been said about him, he had no problem learning any language he chose to master. Max was, in fact, a true genius who was several light years ahead of at least 99.9% of the humans on this planet. Hitler was a genius also, but what separated him from men like Max was his grip on reality. Hitler had none. His dream of *Lebensraum* (living space) did not take into account the rights of ownership.

This war would probably become known as the *Forces of Good* Vs the *Forces of evil* when it should really have become known as the *Forces of Those Who Wish To Remain Free Vs The Forces of Those Who Can Be Led.*

Max reflected that his fellow Germans had really gone off the deep end when they decided to follow Herr Schicklgruber, but that was a harsh judgment he had just heaped upon his countrymen. No one outside of Germany would ever know what it was like to be a

German during the time of the Third Reich. Even an ethnic German who had grown up outside of Germany would never know what it was like to be of this generation of Germans. The world would condemn them but they would not know. They might also appreciate what a blessing it was to have Hitler in power instead of someone like Himmler or Göring.

Hitler was definitely the right man to lead Germany through a time of oppression and dreams of world domination. Under anyone else's leadership, Germany might have won. No, that was not true. There was no might about it. Under competent leadership, Germany *would* have won, because a competent leader would have always consolidated his base before initiating further expansionist moves.

For instance, a competent leader would have conquered Britain before taking on the Soviet Union. Instead, a mighty armada was being assembled on English soil while the Red Army was not only fighting back, but looked very much like it was winning.

March 1944

The mansion

It was a restless Max who now wandered through the mansion with its three floors and labyrinth of rooms. *Did any man need this much room* was a question he often asked himself. He had just received word that Ilse and Peter were in California. It had literally taken months to get the word back to him. In the meantime, he had feared the worst. *Praise Be To God!* Tears came to his eyes. The human part of Max wanted to hold her and kiss her and make love to her just one more time.

The Higher part of him realized that she was a Child of the Universe, and his role in her life was more of a custodial one. He happened to be the lady's husband, but what did that mean? Ownership? He certainly hoped not..

He found himself on the second floor which was the floor his apartment was on, but he found himself walking into the nursery instead. Normally, he would have stopped to play with Peter, but his son was in America with his mother. Maybe, someday he would join then..

Bridgette Gunderson, the nurse, had been at The Mansion for going on five years, and had planned on leaving when she got married, but Gerhardt talked her out if it by convincing her that she might be safer where she was when her husband returned to duty. Then, after her husband's third leave, she became pregnant, a normally joyous occasion, but prior the baby's birth, her husband had been killed at Stalingrad. She had been devastated, and everyone feared for her baby, but it was a normal birth. The baby was a healthy little girl that she named Maria Louisa.

Now, Bridgette had two children to occupy her day. Heidi had turned seven and Baby Maria was now two years old.. Bridgette was now very grateful that she had listened to Gerhardt. Her days were full, and although the loss of her husband still hurt, it had been reduced to a dull ache.

When Max walked in, she turned and smiled. "Hello Max. I am so glad you decided to pay me a visit."

He returned her smile as he replied, "Actually, I just turned up here. It was not by design. I had nothing else to do so I just wandered around aimlessly."

"Well! I will say it again. I am glad for your company." She then looked at the sadness in his eyes and felt an empathy for him. He had experienced a loss also, but his was a different kind of loss. He didn't know the fate of Ilse and young Peter. As terrible as it was, at least she knew that Eduard would not be coming home.

In Max's case, the sadness was attributed to his loneliness. He was not able to tell anyone outside the circle what had really happened, and Bridgitte was outside of the circle.

Bridgitte offered him a seat and Max accepted it.

Two hours later, Max stood up, thanked her, and left.

Unknown to Max, Bridgette had designs on him. Max was the real reason she had remained at The Mansion. If the Gestapo had abducted Ilse and her son, she was probably dead. The fate of the boy might be the same, but chances were that he would be would be integrated into the Nazi's Perfect System.

She would see Max again at dinner time. Maybe she could wear something that might cause him to notice her in a different way..

* * * * *

One of the upstairs maids always took care of her daughter during the evening meal, so when Bridgette came to the dinner table, she was wearing a black velvet sheath dress with a scoop neck, a tight bodice, and a skirt that hugged her hips snugly. She wore a pair of black heels.

Max rose to his feet and seated her. She smiled prettily as she thanked him. For some reason, unknown to Max, he found himself sneaking looks at her all during the meal. His dinner companions did not fail to notice this....especially Bridgette.

After dinner, Gerhardt and Lisa decided to do their own thing which left Max to keep Bridgette company. He would occasionally make physical contact with her and instead of shying away, she seemed to be encouraging him. He didn't mind being encouraged, but he resolved to remain an honest and honorable man. When they arrived at her suite of rooms, she thanked the maid, and the maid departed after giving Max and Bridgette a strange look.

Bridgette went to check on the sleeping form of her daughter and then returned to Max. Max might have been a genius but the services of a genius were not required to determine what she wanted from him.

She walked straight to him, placed her arms about his neck and kissed him. His normally demented mind had wondered what it might be like to kiss this young lady.

Be careful of what you pray for because you might just get it.

Well, he hadn't been praying. Not exactly, but wondering was a form of desire that was a form of prayer. He was taken back by the kiss, but he wasn't backing away from it. In short, he was giving as good as he was getting, and things were about to unravel when he mustered the courage and strength to finally push away.

A hurt look immediately appeared on her face. "You don't want to kiss me?"

He was just catching his breathe as he answered,

"Bridgette, I am married!"

"Ja, that I know, but Ilse was taken by the Gestapo several months ago. Do you really expect to get her back?"

He sighed heavily. *Oh my God!* He thought, but he made a

quick decision. One that he might regret, but he made it anyway. "Bridgette! I have something to tell you, but can you keep a secret?"

"From the Gestapo?"

"From anyone.....everyone. You must tell no one, because if you do, people may die."

"I would not wish to be responsible for another person's death."

"Does that mean that you don't want to hear the secret?"

"No! It means that I will not tell."

"Danke! Now then, Ilse is still alive. We were able to stage her abduction by using fake Gestapo agents."

"But....but....where is she? I have not seen her."

"She is on the west coast of the United States. A city called San Francisco."

"I have heard of it. It is a long way from here, Ja?" It was a question. Not a statement.

He shook his head yes. "Ja! That is correct. It is a very long way from here."

"If she is still alive, do you intend to join her?"

"Ja. When the war is over."

"But.....what if you can't?"

"I must try." Max looked down and away from her.

She said, "Max, look at me." He did, and she continued, "I have lost a husband, and you still have a wife who is a long way from here. You still may never see her again. You have to face that as a very real possibility." She paused for both breathe and courage. "I have a daughter who needs me, and I am not looking for a husband. Not yet anyway. You kissed me like a man who wanted to kiss me, and I think you know how I feel about you. I only want someone to hold.......someone to love.....someone to make love too.....I have even found out how not to become pregnant, and you must also know that I have made love to another man since my husband died. I needed someone, so I reached out and grabbed him. I will not do that again. I am not ashamed to say that I have chosen you. If you reject me, I will be disappointed, but I will get over it." She stopped talking and waited.

Her honesty.....her frankness....her forthrightness, everything about her overwhelmed him. He had always attracted intelligent, perceptive women and Bridgette was no exception.

His delay caused a tear to form in her eye and then she saw him smile. He pulled her close to him and said, "Only a fool would reject you, and my Papa did not raise a fool."

They kissed again.....and again.....and again.

* * * * *

It was a short but very intense affair if that was what it could be called. For the next ten days, each fed a fire that didn't seem to be extinguishable. Of course, the fact that neither was reaching for a fire extinguisher might have had something to do with it.

Then, when only ten days had passed, they both brought an end to their out of control express train. Max didn't really care about Ilse's sexual odysseys. They were hers and if she needed them, so be it. The truth of the matter was that every time he was making love to Bridgette, he was making love to Ilse. It didn't matter to Bridgette in the beginning, but as time started flitting by, it started to bother her, but not badly enough to quit. On the tenth day, she told him that maybe they should halt the affair. Max, being the gentleman that he was, didn't dispute her decision. She did suggest that they might decide to spend a few days just holding each other.

Max wasn't certain that he could hold her and kiss her and not make love to her, but that theory did not have to be tested. There was a man in the house. A man who had been there for years, but had always been on the periphery of her life. A man who secretly harbored a love for the woman even though she had been the wife of another man.

A man who grieved with her when she had lost her husband, and felt joy when her baby was born. A man who felt that he was not worthy of her, and therefore had never presented himself for either acceptance or rejection.

That man was Frederick Heinekin AKA Fritz Heinekin, Gerhardt's driver. Fritz was a big man but not a fat one. He was the kind of man who usually drove for Generals, Admirals and high government officials. He was officially an employee of the SS, and he wore a uniform, but there was no rank displayed upon it. Instead, there was a patch identifying him as a driver and bodyguard.

He really was a nice looking man, and not really inexperienced where the ladies were concerned, but to him, Bridgette was someone who was really quite special. She needed someone to take care of her, and when he went to pick a dozen roses from the rose gardens, he was hoping she might consider him for that honor.

It was thirty minutes after Max had left her, that she heard a knock on her door. When she opened it, there stood Fritz.

"Why Fritz," she exclaimed. "How nice of you to call."

Her smile lit up the room. She was still saddened by the joint decision that she and Max had just made, but there was something about Fritz that brightened her.

Then Fritz took his right hand from behind his back and exposed the roses. He cleared his throat and said, "I would like you to have these, Bridgette."

"Why....they are beautiful, Fritz. Thank you so much."

She knew they came from the garden, but what mattered was that he picked them, wrapped them, and presented them to her. What was it that Max had just told her?

You need a man who will hold you and not wish that he were holding on to someone else.

"Fritz, please come in. Can I give you a cup of coffee or tea?" Fritz only want to be with her, and talk with her. He didn't need coffee or tea in order to do that. Maybe some other time.

In God's economy, nothing is ever wasted. People who perform services tend to become invisible, and Fritz had been no exception. He knew his place, but he also wanted Bridgette. In the end, he would have both his place and Bridgette.

It could be said that they were meant to be together, and anything that had happened in their lives prior to that moment was incidental and preparatory to the moment.

Even though she had made love to Max the night before, it wouldn't have bothered Fritz. Without knowing or realizing it, he had already taken his feelings to another level. When he looked into her eyes, he could see all the way to her soul. He wouldn't have been bothered by anything as superficial as the carnal needs of her body. He too would find wonderment in her physical charms, but always on a higher level.....with deeper meaning.

June 20, 1944

Listening to the local government radio station was like listening to a Grimm Fairytale. Correction: The Grim Fairy tales were better, but short-wave radios were illegal to possess. There was one at The Mansion anyway. As far as they could determine, the personnel at The Mansion had committed enough crimes against the Reich to warrant executing each of them many times over, so what was another broken law more or less?

Apparently, Marshal Stalin had been running around the Kremlin threatening murder and mayhem if Eisenhower didn't get the Western Front up and running. What Stalin didn't know was that the American President Roosevelt didn't care how many Russians it took to defeat the Third Reich.

Every German that got himself killed by the Russians was one less that the Americans had to face. Max Liebert had become quite adept at analyzing the world political scene. He clearly saw things that seemed to baffle other people.

Most German soldiers were not afraid to face the English or the French. They were not afraid of the Russians either. The problem was that their commander ......namely Hitler......was crazy

It was next to impossible for the German army to fight the Russians and their Führer's bad decisions at the same time. Germany still had good generals, but they were no longer in charge.

On June 6, 1944, the allies finally gave Josef Stalin something to cheer about, but the invasion didn't happen at Pas de Calais like Hitler's astrologer told him it would. The Allies invaded the beaches at Normandy instead. In fact, several hours after the invasion had begun, Hitler finally got up from his nap and told his Generals to do something. Anything! It was if they hadn't been doing anything at all.

Old German soldiers were like old soldiers everywhere. When the shooting was over and it was time for the stories to be told, the story would grow with each telling. The German machine gunner who faced the Allied soldiers on the beaches didn't wait for Hitler to wake up.

That was for the commanders to do.

German machine gunners were like machine gunners everywhere. They simply opened fire..

* * * * *

The air raid sirens were becoming a routine occurrence in Munich. It seemed like the Allied bombers were trying to destroy the city building by building, and although the Allies hadn't touched The Mansion yet, many days and nights were spent in the basement. Gerhardt had a part of the basement reinforced to withstand a direct hit. (He hoped.)

August, 1944

It was a hot August afternoon, and Lisa's parents decided to make the short trip from the farm to The Mansion for a visit. Gerhardt even took time out from his activities to visit with his in-laws. He had come to really like them. No! He had come to really love them. Gerhardt von Leitner had discovered a real capacity for love. He and Gus often replayed battles from the Great War. They never did get around to calling it World War I. To them, it was, is, and always would be The Great War.

The Renslers always timed their visits so they came between milkings. This time, it was three o'clock when Gus stood, stretched, pulled out his pocket watch and announced that it was time to go. Anna picked up her bag and kissed everyone in route to the door.

The air raid siren hadn't sounded yet which led people to believe that they had somehow been granted a reprieve for the day. Then, as Gerhardt was closing the driver's side door, the air raid siren sounded and everyone groaned.

Gerhardt said, "It's not a good time to be on the road. Why don't you join us in the basement?"

Gus shook his head vigorously. "Nein! The cows, they don't wait for nothin. They get milked when they need to get milked. I go to the cows, Ja?"

Both Lisa and Gerhardt tried to dissuade them, but to no avail, and shortly, they were watching the truck move slowly toward the main highway.

* * * * *

In the beginning, the U.S. Eighth Air Force had taken a terrible beating from the Luftwaffe. B-17 losses had been tremendous, but the Americans stubbornly persisted until improvements were finally made.

The greatest improvement was the addition of the P-51 Mustang to the attack force. The P-51's had great range and maneuverability, and acted as a protective shield for the B-17's, in route to the target.

In the beginning, they engaged any German fighters that came up to meet them until the German fighters were no longer the potent force they had once been. This allowed the P-51's to seek other "targets of opportunity." And so, when the B-17's were beginning their bomb run, the P-51's were released to do their own thing.

* * * * *

On this particular afternoon, a Mustang was flying along the east side of the Starnberger See when he looked down and spotted a vehicle that was painted the same color as German military vehicles.

That color was called field gray.

The fact that it didn't have black crosses painted on the sides might not have concerned the pilot at all. American ground forces were fighting these very same Germans a few hundred kilometers from this place, and he might have determined that every Kraut who bought it here was one less that might cause problems for the Americans soldiers at the front.

He lined his fighter up on the target and just as soon as the truck was in the cross hairs, the pilot opened fire.

According to Hans Reinek, a neighbor, the initial burst was short as it hit the road just behind the moving truck. In any respect, Gus and Anna seemed to be oblivious to the impending danger. The fighter pilot nudged his nose slightly upward, and began firing again. The tracers showed the bullets walking through the wooden cover of the truck bed. The wood continued to splinter until the 50 caliber bullets struck the cab. The first bullet that struck Anna Rensler was the only one that struck her, and that was the one that killed her.

Gus had been hit three times.

The truck swerved to the right and impacted a shallow ditch. The sudden stop caused both occupants to be thrown from the truck. The neighbor came running as fast as his legs could carry him and he yelled a curse at the fighter as it flew past the wrecked truck, but it did no good as the pilot couldn't hear. This was the impersonal side of man's inhumanity to man.

As Hans approached Gus, he realized that Gus was not only still alive, but he was crawling steadily in the direction of the fallen body of his wife.

"I am coming, Anna. Hold on, Anna, I am coming," He kept saying that over and over. Hans went to Anna first, but he quickly realized that the woman was dead. Then, he thought about seeing what he could do for Gus, but Gus seemed to be oblivious to his presence. Gus was only concentrating on Anna, and he seemed to be getting weaker.

Then Hans saw the blood. Gus was bleeding to death, and before Hans could get to him, the right hand of Gus touched the left hand of Anna Rensler, and with a mighty effort, the big man raised the upper part of his body off the ground and spoke with an uncommon eloquence, "Mein Gott.....Mein Anna....Mein Schatz....Du ist die Einzige.....Ich liebe dich." (My God...My Anna...My treasure.....you are the only one...I love you.)

After that mighty effort, he slumped back to the ground.

Gustav Rensler had joined his wife in death.

Hans Reineck, who had already lost three of his five sons to this bloody war, crossed himself and began to cry. After a few very long minutes, he began to shout to God and anyone else who had a notion to listen, "Mein Gott....Mein Gott.....Have you completely forsaken us? Tell me what to do and I will end this bloody war right now."

Unfortunately, it would require a few more months and a lot more blood before the war would mercifully come to an end.

* * * * *

For some reason, bad news always travels fast, and Gerhardt had just come up from the basement when an ashen faced Erik approached him.

"Herr General, there is a Herr Hans Reineck at the side entryway. I am afraid he has some very devastating news for us."

Alarm came to Gerhardt's eyes. "O Mein Gott! Not Gus and Anna too!. Please tell me it is not so. Please."

The look on Erik's face told him he could plead all he wanted to, but it wouldn't change a thing.

A woman's voice from behind him asked, "Is something wrong, Darling?"

There was never an easy way to announce the arrival of the Angel of Death. He always seemed to strike like a thief in the night. This time, she didn't have to be told. This time, she knew. Gerhardt gently placed his arm around his wife's shoulder and whispered, "Come.....my darling. The angels are waiting for us."

* * * * *

The funeral might not have happened at all had Gerhardt not been a high ranking officer in the SS. The civilian death toll had grown much larger and those not killed by the bombs were made homeless by them. Many seemed to lose their sense of reality and continued to wander about in a dazed state until they met their fate.

Graves registration was much too busy to be concerned about two bodies, but when the SS General pointed his 9mm Luger at them and inquired if they desired to be thrown into a sewer as opposed to being buried in a grave, they saw the wisdom of paying proper respect to the remains of the Herr General's in-laws.

After the funeral, Gerhardt, Heidi, and Lisa stood quietly at the graveside. Heidi had turned seven in March, and was old enough to understand what had happened. When she had been told, she looked up at him through tear filled eyes, and asked, "Papa Gerhardt, why did Grandmother and Grandfather have to die?"

Gerhardt looked down at his stepdaughter and then knelt beside her. "Heidi, Mein Schatz. Some very bad people have done some very bad things to some very good people, and the friends of the good people are fighting back. It is too bad, but your Grandfather and Grandmother just happened to be in the wrong place at the wrong time. Besides, God has a much better place for them to be."

She looked at him through tear filled eyes and inquired, "If they are in such a good place, why are we here?"

Good question! Do I have a good answer? A reward for a life well lived? Come on, Gerhardt. You don't believe that crap yourself. Don't try selling it to her. On the other hand, why do we live and what happens to us when we die?

Then, he sought refuge in the only answer that Christianity could offer. "Heidi, we must live here before we can live there. Those are the rules. A long time ago, God made a rule that was broken, and because of that broken rule, we live in a state of wrong. We can still live in that state of wrong, but to do that, we have to live without God. It is the same as being dead. A spiritual death. It is our choice, but God had given us another choice. That choice is Jesus. If we choose the love of God, we can live in the light of His Love and Grace which allows us to live. You may not understand this for a while yet, but Grandfather and Grandmother chose to live in this Grace.. We will all be rewarded in Heaven, but we have to live here before we can live there."

She considered these words for the longest time before looking back up at him and saying, "That is good, Papa Gerhardt......I think."

* * * * *

Now, the three people who were the closest to Gus and Anna stood looking at the two caskets that were ready to be lowered into the graves. Lisa was holding up remarkably well, and so was Heidi although she had already lost her father to this war.

Suddenly, Heidi broke away from the two adults and ran toward the two caskets.

Gerhardt yelled, "Heidi!" But, Lisa shook her head instead, and Gerhardt backed off. Heidi then kissed each casket and uttered her own good-bye to each one.

She told each of them, "I'll see you in Heaven."

After that, she returned to her momma and Papa who, in turn, went to each of the caskets and did what the child had done before them.

And, it shall come to pass that a small child shall lead us out of the wilderness.

* * * * *

October, 1944

Somewhere in Northern England

It was a simple U. S. Army staff car that was being driven by an American Army sergeant. In the back of the car was a British Brigadier and an American general.

The American general asked, “How much further is it to this place?”

“Not far,” answered the Brigadier. “Just as soon as we catch sight of the North Sea, we should see the cottage.”

Just then, the sea came into view and the Brigadier pointed. “There it is now.”

The general asked, “What kind of man is he?”

The Brigadier struck a thoughtful pose before answering. “Physically, he is a bloody good looking bloke. Built something like a Greek god.. He has a quiet reserve about him that could easily be mistaken for German arrogance.”

He paused slightly and then continued. “You know, sir....even though the Reich is now facing certain defeat, you would be hard pressed to find a German POW who doesn’t think he is a far better soldier than the soldiers who are now defeating his country.”

The general smiled in agreement. “He might just be right. The idea of Blitzkrieg is great for offensive warfare, but it can’t defend against someone like Patton who thinks that he is the reincarnation of every great general who ever lived. Personally, I think that he and Guderian will have a lot to talk about when this bloody mess is finally over and done with.”

The Brigadier then asked, “About Josef Hauser, did you want to know the kind of man he is or the kind of man he was?”

“How about both?”

The Brigadier cleared his throat and the general told his driver to stop. “Josef Hauser was actually SS Hauptsturmführer Josef Eduard Hauser from somewhere near Frankfurt. In case you don’t know, his SS rank is roughly the equivalent of our Captain. That fact made him a minor player in Heinrich Himmler's scheme of things, so they had employed him as an officer courier, a fact that allowed him a lot of free time. When you see what the man looks like, it won't surprise you to know that he has seduced an amazing number of women, and unlike Casanova or Don Juan, he never had to take flight from a second story window. He also quietly informed us that he never parted company with any woman who was not satisfied. In fact, he was driven by this wanderlust."

"During the course of his travels as a courier, he was in Berlin awaiting a new assignment when he met the wife of a German Army officer who just happened to be in the company of an SS General. The General was not the officer who happened to be the lady's husband. Needless to say, the lady and the General got their communications all bloody fouled up and the lady ended up in the arms of Josef Hauser."

"By his own admission, Josef Hauser was probably not valued very highly in Hammer's organization, so when the opportunity for a change came about, he grabbed it, but he still didn't wish to end up on the Eastern Front in a Waffin SS unit. By a stroke of luck, he found himself attached to that very same SS General and was told to take some Polish POWs to Pas de Calais on the French coast and report to an Army Engineer by the name of Karl Mueller. *Major* Karl Mueller."

"Hauser admittedly had a lot of contempt for the Major. First, because he had heard the Major's wife's passionate outcries, and secondly by the fact that the Major had such a quiet demeanor. To make matters worse, in the mind of Hauser, the Major was living with a very pretty French widow. Hauser finally admitted to resenting the Major because the Major had everything he lacked. Fortunately, for Josef Hauser, he was an incompetent leader, and on several occasions, Major Mueller covered his mistakes. That caused Hauser to question why? Even the most hardened Nazi might have questioned kindness on the part of the intended victim."

"In any respect, general, this adversarial relationship finally came to a head one night when one of our Commando units conducted a raid on the Major's facility. Hauser was awakened by his sergeant and, fearing a fire fight, he went and woke the Major who realized that this might become a bloody balls up for the Germans if competent leadership didn't rise to the occasion and take over. Therefore, the Army Engineering Major relieved the SS Officer of his command and told him to stay the bloody hell out of the way. It all came under the heading of getting it done first, and worrying about the paperwork later."

"As a result of this change of command, our blokes faired rather badly. In fact, it became a bloody balls up for them. Not one of our blokes survived, but during the suicide charge, one of them got close enough to shoot the Major at point blank range. Hauser, who tagged along for good measure, finally found his courage and made our bloke pay supremely for the privilege of killing his Major. I guess that Hauser used a knife and used it rather savagely. Once again, general, a man who might have kept us bottled up on the beaches of Normandy died instead. I shudder to think of how much potential Germany had if only they had had the right leadership."

"I agree with you, Brigadier," said the general wistfully. "So how did Herr Hauser manage to find his way to England with the lovely French lady and her daughter?"

The Brigadier answered, "He had the audacity to sneak over to a marina under the cover of darkness with the lady and her daughter and steal a sailboat. As incredible as it might sound, he had no knowledge of how to sail the boat, but he managed do so and he reasoned that if he just sailed away from the French that he would manage to find the English coast. He did, and how he managed to avoid the British and German patrol boats is still beyond the experts." Then, he stopped for an instant as though he were remembering something. "I almost forgot something, Sir. They are expecting her second child very shortlly, and I will need to move them to a hospital compound." He stopped as though he were making a mental note so that he wouldn't forget again. Then, he returned to his discourse..

"Now then, Hauser told me a tale about his kneeling on the beach with the dead Major's head cradled in his lap and managing to find that he was a human being after all. His next duty was to take the Major's body home for a military funeral which placed him in close proximity to the widow and her General, but for reasons completely unknown to him, he was treated well by everyone including the late Major's father. In fact, the father brought him into a plot to get everyone out of Germany. Hauser still doesn't know how everyone else faired, but he managed to get Yvette and her child safely out of the range of the Gestapo."

"Are they?" Asked the general.

"Are they what?" Inquired the Brigadier.

"Safely out of the range of the Gestapo?"

The Brigadier shrugged. "Who knows. The Gestapo is made up of the lowest elements in German society. It, like the Mafia, doesn't need a national government in which to operate, but we are protecting them as best we can. The best that killing him would accomplish is to somehow soothe the fractured ego of some demented bastard out there someplace. His presence is a closely guarded secret and will remain that way. I understand that his sketches were invaluable to us when we were we planning the invasion."

"Yes," agreed the general. "That plus all of the hours of debriefing he withstood. I personally have never met the man, and look forward to the privilege. Which brings me to the point of the trip."

The Brigadier agreed and the driver drove on to the cottage.

An hour and a half later, the two general officers emerged from the cottage, and Josef was accompanying their return to their car. The American general looked at the former German SS officer and decided to make a frank inquiry, "You have a very lovely wife, but as I understand it, she literally hated your guts in the beginning. How did you manage to pull it off?"

A smile of understanding and compassion came to Josef's face. "I did it the same way Karl did it. I earned it. I don't remember when it was that she stopped looking at me like I was a fool and began to see a man of real value. In fact, for the very first time in my life, I managed to win a woman with the strength of my character rather than my sexual prowess."

The general chuckled. "So, if I can manage to pry a little further, which came first, the sex or the character?"

"My ego tells me to lie, but alas, I cannot. Yvette is a very tough lady. She had to be tough. Nein Herr General, I could have been the composite of all the great lovers who have ever lived and she still would not have swooned before my advances......No Sir! It had to be character or not at all."

"Then I congratulate you, Herr Hauser. I don't know what

you have lost, but I dare say that you might have gained for more than you have lost."

"I heartily agree, Herr General."

"Then, I must be going now." He reached out offered Josef his hand.

Josef took it and said, "Auf Wiedersehen."

The general replied, "Auf Wiedersehen," and left.

* * * * *

Re: Hi Glenn

Hi Glen,
Thanks for your last email. You have demonstrated some of your writing genius your description of the place you would like to talk to me. If I did not understand how writer
thinks sometimes I might have thought you were coming on to me Glen LOL. Anyway, it is nice to dream, isn't it? Life is all about dreams.
I am on my way to Toronto tonight and then I pick up my younger daughter there and we head out to Brooklyn by the overnight bus. In the meantime a blizzard is brewing up at this end. I hope it does not affect my trip.
This week has flown by pretty quickly. Her it is Saturday. I am busy cleaning up the house to make sure it is left spic and span. I hate coming back to a dishelved house.
I've washed all the dishes, made the bed, will soon take out the garbage and then I will be able to relax.
I hope you had a good week. I hope your singing career is taking off to more seniors homes or perhaps someother places for e.g. the Legion Hall meetings.
What is your current writing project? I am trying to write a play about a teenager leaving home for the big city. When she gets there she begins to see the real world. It's all about work and very little play. Sounds not so interesting eh? I'll jazz it up.
My older daughter Maiko has been asked to sing at the Legislature for International Women's Day celebration. The Minister of Status of Women always throw a receptions and giv out some bagged Subway lunches with tea/coffee or juice by way of honouring women's achievements over the years. My daughter is quite excited to do this. She will be backed up by a guitarist.
I am looking forward to my trip to relax and not think about my work and stuff just
let it all hang.
I will not be checking my Zaadz mail so I won't communicate until I am back in a couple weeks.

and yourself. It's all about the journey, not the destination, that the secret lies. Talking about secret - have any thoughts on the Book of Secrets written by the Australian Writer, Rhonda Brynes - I have not read it yet but I think I will buy the DVD.
Take care

Mayflower

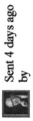

Sent 4 days ago
by

Twenty

It'll be over when it's over!

1945

The German world was steadily crumbling around the edges, but there was still a semblance of order. The German soldier had a lot of pride and the idea of some gum chewing sloppy undisciplined American beating him on the battlefield was an affront to his sensibilities. Perhaps, the Japanese felt the same way, but the truth of the matter was that as of January, 1945, the last great German offensive of the war had been entered into the record books as an Allied victory.

The German Ardennes Offensive or the Battle of the Bulge as the Allies called it, was embraced by the German High Command because the idea of unconditional surrender didn't sit very well with anyone who was German.

The American President Roosevelt was highly respected by the Oberkommando der Wehrmacht (High Command). It was he who kept prodding Stalin to stay in the war and not make a separate peace. Roosevelt rightly concluded that a separate peace might have forced the allies to seek an armistice instead of unconditional surrender. Therefore, a precarious balance had to be maintained between Stalin and Roosevelt, and that balance was none other than Winston Churchill.

Then, along came the Ardennnes Offensive, which was intended to rip a hole in the Allied lines large enough for the Germans to advance all the way to Antwerp, a fact that would have set the Allied time table back considerably.

History tells us that the Americans had visions of going home for Christmas floating dreamily in their heads. Nobody is quite sure if that was the prevailing mood or not. All anyone ever said was that we were caught by surprise and nobody elaborated. Besides, the After Action Reports make dry reading

The military historians tell us that the Germans made some rather deep penetrations against the unprepared American lines in the area of the Ardennes Forest, but the attack bogged down because of difficult terrain, limited roads, and bad weather conditions.

Of course, these bad same conditions also hampered the Allies. It was probably too bad that wars could not have been fought on each military commander's tactical boards, because moving a piece on the board was one thing, and moving the unit represented by that piece was another matter entirely.

Entire divisions were surrounded and swallowed up by the Germans. Chaos prevailed. The Germans even had men who masqueraded as American soldiers. At the junction town of Bastogne, the 101st Airborne division was completely surrounded by the Germans.

It was at this point in time that the Americans demonstrated something the Germans didn't think they had. It was raw courage and persistence in the face of a gun being pointed at their collective heads.

Brigadier General McAuliffe, the Commanding General of the 101st Airborne Division became a hero when he replied to the surrender demand given him by General von Lüttwitz, the Commander of the XXXXVII Panzerkorps.

He said, "Tell `em....nuts!" The German Commander had to be told that the word used was American slang, and it didn't mean yes.

General Patton's Third Army then rushed to relieve the beleaguered 101st Airborne Division, a feat that was termed as being downright miraculous.

The Americans might have exposed a soft underbelly that bothered their Soviet Allies, but if one were to use the analogy of a boxing match, the Americans seemingly acted like a fighter who had looked at his bloodied opponent and came to the wrong conclusion.

In the collective American mind, the opponent was finished, and probably wouldn't answer the bell for the next round. In reality, the opponent had plenty of fight left in him..

Just remember, the Germans were on the ropes, but they were in no way finished. They were still on conquered soil, they still had a strong fighting force available, and they had been able to mask their intentions from the Allies who opposed them.

The civilians in the area still feared the Germans, and were able to give German spies valuable information about the American state of mind.

When you come right down to it, the Ardennes Offensive was a gamble that Hitler and the High Command had to take. *Unconditional Surrender* didn't quite fit into their way of thinking. Unfortunately, from the German perspective, it was a gamble that lost.

By mid-January of 1945, the Germans were withdrawing from the area of the Ardennes Forest. In the east, the Red Army continued its relentless advance across Poland by first capturing Warsaw, and then by liberating Aushwitz.

On March 6th, while the noose was being tightened about the Nazi monster's neck, the Germans actually had the audacity to mount what would turn out to be their last offensive of the war. In fact, it was a counter offensive that had been designed to defend the oil fields in Hungary.

Wednesday, March 7, 1945

The Mansion - Munich

So far, The Mansion had been spared by the bombers and the fighters, and the teletype still sent messages that told of German successes in the field. Gerhardt mused that the Herr Propaganda Minister had less and less to talk about.

How much longer can this war last?

Lisa chose that moment to walk in the door. He looked up and smiled at her, and she kissed him. She noticed the teletype and asked, "What is this? Marching orders?"

It was remarkable that humor could still be found in the midst of all this death and destruction, but Lisa determined that the ability to laugh in the face of danger was better that cowering in the shadows.

Garhardt smiled at her humor and replied, "Nein, Mein Schatz! We have mounted a counter offensive in Hungary."

"Does it mean anything?" Asked Lisa.

He shook his head. "No!"

"So then, what is the real story?"

"We have lost.....completely and absolutely. The American 7th and 3rd Armies are advancing in our direction and the Russians are advancing on both Berlin and Vienna. We still talk about victory, but how? We have nothing left to fight with other than our bare hands."

A dark cloud settled over Lisa's face and Gerhardt was about to ask her what was wrong when she volunteered. "I know that you have predicted defeat from the very beginning, and for that reason, maybe I should be happy for you, but I am saddened for my country. My Germany. So many people have died for a perverse cause, and had you not brought me into your life, I might have believed in that cause myself. I now fear that we will pay a terrible price for pursuing this cause."

Gerhardt pulled her close to him and held her tightly.

"Lisa, my beloved, I will do my best to protect you and Heidi, but we have Americans approaching from one direction and the Soviets from another. It would be bad enough to have to worry about the Allies, but we also have to concern ourselves with SS Einsatz Gruppen, the Gestapo, and other secret organizations like the Werewolfs. I fear they will be killing lots of people in order to cover up the evidence. Then, they will have the audacity to sneak out the back door while the Allies are coming through the front door."

"So, what do we do?" She asked.

"Like all brave Germans, we will make a run for it, and when we approach the Allied armies, we will surrender to them. We shall also be grateful that the closest Allies are American and not Russian."

Saturday, April 7, 1945

It took a month to the day for that to happen, and when it did, they weren't making a run for it. Instead, they had planned to leave the mansion and go the Rensler farm which had been unoccupied ever since Lisa's parents had been killed.

The farm house stood at the very edge of the village which lie at the very edge of the farm itself. Gerhardt determined that it might protect them for a while.

Therefore, Gerhardt and Max loaded the trunk of the Mercedes with the clothing and personal items needed for survival. Gerhardt then had mixed emotions about what he should wear, and although being an SS General gave him status, it might have been better if he were an Army General instead.

He quickly disregarded that idea because if he were a Army General, he would be out there facing those Allied Armies. So far, he had spent the entire war in Munich with a warm body sleeping next to him every night. It beat the living hell out of the way he had spent the last war.

The order had finally come telling them to burn everything, and/or anyone who might expose the more nefarious activities of the SS. Gerhardt scoffed. He hadn't waited for orders. He had already burned everything. He bid Erik and whatever staff that remained good-bye and left.

Max had already made escape arrangements with Erik and his organization, but at the last minute, decided to stay with Gerhardt. The final order from Berlin was a recall order for Gerhardt to report to Berlin. *To do what? Go into the street and fight Russians?* Gerhardt disobeyed that order.

And so, it came to pass that they left the estate in the Mercedes with Fritz at the wheel and two other men, two women and two children riding as passengers.

The trip was short but difficult.

People who hadn't been dislocated by the bombs of the American 8th Air Force were becoming dislocated by the advancing armies of the invaders. It was clearly the intent of the Allies that no German would be able to look around after the war and say, "We were tricked."

Nope!

Their intention was that the Germans would not only know that they were beaten, but that they had been beaten very badly.

Everywhere he looked was evidence that Germany was, in fact, a beaten nation. Refugees had been steadily streaming from

Austria in the direction of the American lines.

On this particular road, people seemed to be coming in the direction of the city in order to avoid becoming collateral damage or damage incidental to contact between warring factions.

As the advancing army approached, the entire area became subject to collateral damage. The countryside, the buildings, the villages, the cities and all of the people became possible collateral damage.

They encountered the only roadblock just prior to entering the Village of berg.

Fritz asked, "We might still have some clout. Do you want me to stop, Herr General?"

"Ja," replied Gerhardt. "After all, we have women and children aboard. Allow me to do the talking."

The Mercedes came to a stop and an SS Unterführer (Lieutenant) sauntered up to the Mercedes. An officer on roadblock duty meant only that he was raw meat and intended only as a sacrifice to the Great God of War

The officer noted the Nazi flags, and the fact that a General officer was in the vehicle. Then he recognized the General.

He snapped the Nazi salute and said, "Heil Hitler."

Gerhardt responded dryly, "Heil Hitler," and then he said, "Guten tag, Herr Unterführer. Is your roadblock intended to stop the Germans or the Americans?"

The young officer looked flustered. "I need to know who you are and where you are going." The General then told him the names of everyone present in the vehicle, after which he said, "As per orders from SS Headquarters in Berlin or what now passes for SS Headquarters, I have closed my headquarters, burned everything, and am in the process of delivering the women and children to what I hope is a safe haven, after which we men will be heading in the direction of the sounds of battle rather than away from them. What we will accomplish, I do not know. Perhaps, we will find someone to order around."

The young officer was writing everything down and then, he looked up and signaled someone to raise the gate. After that, he rendered a standard military salute and said, "Go mitt Gott, Herr

General."

Gerhardt returned the salute and replied, "And, peace be with you, my son, and please believe me when I tell you that."

Fritz accelerated the Mercedes through the roadblock.

Lisa said, "Why don't we just quit and stop the killing?"

Gerhardt sighed and replied, "You know the answer to that one as well as I do. As long as Adolph Hitler lives, people will die."

The rest of their short trip was uneventful, and although the small villages were spared the devastation that had been suffered by the cities, they were not spared the deprivation.

Fritz drove the car around to the back of the building where the entrance to both the house and the barn was located. There was a door on the right side near the front that had been intended to be used as an emergency exit. Gerhardt breathed a little easier.

When everything had been unloaded from the vehicle, Fritz walked up to the Herr General and saluted.

"Stop that Fritz. I am only days away from being a former General in the SS. The Americans will make certain of that."

"Until then, Herr General, I pay you the respect that you deserve."

Gerhardt snapped to attention and returned the salute. "Now then, Fritz. What can I do for you?"

"I've been talking with Bridgette, and she agrees with what I am about to suggest." Gerhardt nodded and Fritz continued, "This house will be very crowded and I know a place that is near here. We can leave when it gets dark. Maybe, it will give us a better chance at survival."

"Do you even know if this place is still there and unoccupied?"

"Nein Herr General, but you didn't know if this place was still here when we left the Mansion. The place I refer to is an unlikely place.. Maybe it will be good enough."

Gerhardt nodded. "Very well, Fritz. I shall not hold you back."

When darkness fell, Fritz, Bridgette and the baby left the Rensler farm. Gerhardt couldn't help wondering if he did the right thing.

Saturday, April 28, 1945

Most of life is driven by events and does not necessarily happen as a result of careful planning as much as we would like to think so. There might have been a perfectly right time for the small group to emerge from the dwelling and run happily in the direction of the invaders.

Conversely, the invading army was not rushing happily in the direction of those who might wish to surrender to them. Invading armies were always more careful once they were on the enemy's sacred soil. Every German now had to be considered as hostile, and were approached accordingly.

Most villages and small cities had Burgermeisters who were wise enough to realize the wisdom of hoisting an honest white flag from the tallest steeple in town. The word honest is used, because some Burgermeisters flew a white flag as bait for a trap. Not many did that, and those who did paid a very high price.

Twenty-one days had passed without incident and although there had been traffic on the road in front of the Farmhouse, nobody had stopped. There were no signs of life that might have induced the Gestapo to stop, if in fact, the Gestapo was out patrolling at all.

Gerhardt somehow knew that this day would be the last day in this safe haven. When the leading elements of the Allied army got close enough, they might just blow this house apart rather than risking a single American soldier's life. Approximately 200 meters from the north side of the house was the beginning of the Village of Berg. An alfalfa field occupied the field between the farmhouse and the start of the village.

Max was on watch at the front window when he heard the sound of engines. No sooner did he hear the sound than three personnel carriers turned into the driveway. When they came to a halt, a whistle was heard and Black suited SS troops began filing out of each carrier.

Max yelled, "Shit! We're trapped!"

Then he backed away from the window to avoid being seen although it wasn't likely as the living quarters was on the second floor over the barn below.

Gerhardt yelled back, "What was that you said?"

"I said we're trapped."

Gerhardt replied savagely, "Like hell we are!"

He quickly rounded Lisa and Heidi up and briefed them both. In conclusion, he said, "We don't have time to pack anything, but don't despair....I have some extra clothing, food and water in the Mercedes. Now here's the plan........," and they listened.

The SS troops did not know if anyone was in the house or not. Consequently, they were in no hurry to enter it.

That gave Gerhardt and his group time to go down into the barn level. At the bottom of the stairway, they were greeted by semi-darkness, but they could see the Mercedes, and they hurried to get into the vehicle

As soon as everyone was inside, Lisa and Heidi were told to get down and stay down.

After some very long minutes, the back door opened and footsteps were heard going up the steps and down the hallway into the main living area.

The main door to the barn was on a counter weight. All Gerhardt had to do was snap the latch, and give the door a push. He looked at Max and gave the signal to start the engine. Just as soon as it caught, Gerhardt pushed on the overhead door and the spring loaded counterweights literally threw the door open much to the surprise of the six SS troopers standing there.

Max floored the accelerator as Gerhardt threw himself back into the Mercedes, and with tires squealing, the Mercedes plowed into the six troopers without as much as a second thought.

Max gave the steering wheel a hard turn to the right as he headed toward the road. He couldn't remember if there was a ditch there or not, but with three personnel carriers in the way, he would have to chance it.

Gerhardt picked up his sub machine gun and commenced firing just as soon as the Mercedes cleared the corner of the house.

SS troopers who were loitering paid the price of being exposed. Others hit the dirt and began returning fire but the car was moving fast enough that bullets seemed to bounce off the side of the vehicle.

Both Gerhardt and Max had forgotten that when they

received this vehicle, it was reputed to be bullet proof. Once the car hit the road, it fishtailed wildly until it finally found purchase and began speeding south.

As Max watched the distance open between them and the vehicles they left behind, he breathed a sigh of relief.

Now, where in the hell were the Americans?

Suddenly, a rocket shell landed in a field next to the car. A second later another one hit the road in front of them. Another look told him that he sighed with relief too quickly. Behind them was a open vehicle with a recoilless rifle mounted where a machine gun was normally mounted. Whoever was doing the shooting obviously knew what he was doing.

Max began fishtailing to avoid giving the marksman a target to shoot at. Suddenly, there was another explosion and the Mercedes swerved wildly and just missed a good sized tree and then plunged into some bushes and came to a halt with the front wheels hovering above the water of Lake Starnberger.

Gerhardt shouted, "Everybody out!" and everybody got out. It was a short run to the ruins of a burned out cabin and they all headed for it without being told. Both Max and Gerhardt carried what amounted to a small arsenal.

When everyone had gotten undercover, another rocket exploded and they were reminded rather abruptly that they were still not safe.

This time, Gerhardt reached down to his side and pulled back a bloody palm.

"Gerhardt!," Lisa screamed.

"It appears that I have finally been blooded in battle," Gerhardt spoke quietly, and then he looked for the location of the weapons carrier, and noticed that it might just be within range of his Mauser.. He picked up the Mauser and checked the action. After that, he went to the corner closest to the weapons carrier. Lisa was about to protest but it died in her throat. She watched as her husband carefully sighted in on the sharpshooter.

As Gerhardt looked through the sniper scope, the shooter was taking the time to put more rockets in the hopper without considering that his own life might be in danger.

His job being done, the shooter stood to stretch before getting back into position. At the apex of his stretch, his body lurched in its death throes and fell limply back on the vehicle bed.

At least thirty SS troopers who had evacuated the carriers took cover out of respect to whoever fired that shot.

Nobody wanted to be second.

Back in the burned out cabin, Gerhardt came running back and dropped down beside Max, Lisa and Heidi. The red stain had gotten larger.

"Gerhardt! Let me do something about that wound."

Gerhardt looked at her incredulously, and replied, "And what, pray tell, are you going to able to do, Doktor von Leitner?"

"I don't know, Gerhardt, but I need to do something."

He reached over and braced her shoulders with his two hands. "Lisa, mein Schatz! You need to listen to me. You too, Max! There are at least thirty soldiers out there, and they intend to kill us. All of us, and the allied army is probably just beyond our ability to see it. Think of that! An entire army is approaching and all these idiots can think of is us. Germans wanting to kill Germans! Why? Because they think we might know something that would incriminate them."

He took another look and saw a soldier running across the open ground. He picked up his rifle, led the man and pulled the trigger.

The man fell.

"That is my point precisely." He said and almost immediately, he softened and reached for her.

"Lisa.....my beloved. The romantics have always told us that life sometimes compresses the years into days, the days into minutes and the minutes into moments just prior to the end, and tell me my darling.....is the end of now......the end of everything?" He shook his head. "Nein, Liebchen. It is not the end. It is only the beginning, and for you an even better tomorrow."

Lisa sobbed, "Gerhardt! I have lost my first husband, my parents, and now......must I lose you?"

He reached down his side and pulled back a bloody hand. "Lisa, I am already dead! Must you die too? I mean, there is you and there is Heidi, and how about you, Max. You have a wife and son waiting for you in San Francisco. This is **not** a noble gesture on my part. I am slowly bleeding to death, and the bleeding cannot be stopped. Why can't my death mean something? I am dreadfully sorry to have to say this, but those men out there are the worst that Germany has to offer to the rest of the world. Better they die here."

Max and Lisa looked at each other, and back at Gerhardt. He looked at them and then said, "Now, go people, and go **now**!!!"

Through tear filled eyes, Lisa embraced him and said, "I love you, Gerhardt."

"And I have loved you since the first time I saw you. That is precisely why I took such extreme measures. May God bless you, my beloved."

They embraced one more time and then Heidi embraced her Papa Gerhardt. At eight years of age, she was now witnessing one of life's most cruel and yet more tender moments. He and Max embraced, and then all four of them managed to embrace. Max then took Heidi and Lisa by the hand and started to leave the ruins. Lisa turned for a final look and nearly broke down. Then they moved into the trees and beyond the sight of Gerhardt.

From this point on, no one knows what really happened except that somehow, Gerhardt went on the attack and managed to kill twenty-four of the SS troopers. That was all who faced him, because six men went after Max, Lisa, and Heidi. The following was what he thought would be the final entry in his diary:

Saturday, 28 April 1945

Don't know how much time I have so will make this quick. Max, Lisa & Heidi have left, and it is lonely. Very lonely! Have been watching them get ready to close in on me, and at least six of them won't be around to make the final charge. Shooting them was like shooting ducks in a shooting gallery.

Now to the really important things..... Lisa. I love you more than my life, and I might just be proving it.

I lied to you.

This wound is not bad enough to kill me. It only looked that way. The truth of the matter is that I am a soldier. I trained to be a soldier. I learned the craft well and I have a medal to prove it. Soldiers fight. Sometimes soldiers die. It's as simple as that.

Lisa, my beloved, all of us could not have reached the American lines and you know it. I only hope you and Heidi can make it.

I ask only two things of our God, assuming there is one. First, that He grant you and Heidi safe passage, and second, that He grant me the courage to fight and die like a man.

May God be with you, my beloved.

Gerhardt

Max was carrying both Heidi and a sub-machine gun. Lisa was carrying a sub-machine gun, Both were running. Behind them, the sound of small arms fire followed by explosions could be heard. This was followed by more small arms fire.

All too quickly, the firing stopped, and Lisa began sobbing. Her sobbing continued as they continued running. They didn't know who if anyone was following them.

After a few minutes, they stopped to catch their collective breath, but their respite was interrupted by the sound of a bullet ricocheting off a tree. Someone had lousy aim.

Max quickly looked around, and said, "No time to argue. You and Heidi continue following the lake shore. I will divert them in the direction of the road. Now go!"

Lisa caught her breath and, just like that, Max was gone. She needed several hours of crying time, but right that moment, survival had the higher priority.

Suddenly, she had become very lonely and the quiet that ensued had become unbearable. Heidi looked to her mother for guidance and direction, and seeing neither of those, looked in the direction of a small grove of trees and decided to lead her mother in that direction.

Lisa followed her daughter dumbly. They had just reached the cover of the trees when another bullet careened off the side of a tree. Heidi hugged her mother tightly while her mother only had Heidi to hold on to.

Then, they heard it.

A low rumble of an engine growling and a metallic sound like chain being dragged on the ground.. She moved in order to get a better look. Then, she saw it. *Der Panzer!*

Panzer being the German word for tank, but it wasn't a German panzer. It was painted a different color, and instead of the big black cross, a white star was painted on the side.. *You can tell the Americans by the white star they paint on the side of their vehicles.* Those were Gerhardt's words.

Then, she saw the men. All carrying weapons at the ready.

These are the men who have defeated the thousand year Reich. I wonder what manner of men they be?

The Panzer has stopped!

The men stopped, and one of them was pointing in her direction. Something on the top of the panzer, a gun, swiveled around and before long it was pointed in her direction.

My God, they are going to shoot.

One of the men took something in his hand and began speaking. It was a microphone. He began speaking in perfect German.

"MY NAME IS JOHN SCHNEIDER, FIRST LIEUTENANT, UNITED STATES ARMY. I AM SPEAKING TO WHOEVER IS IN THOSE TREES. COME OUT AND COME OUT RIGHT NOW OR I WILL SIMPLY BLOW YOU OUT OF THERE! DO NOT HESITATE! YOU HAVE UNTIL I COUNT TO TEN! "

"EINS (ONE)"

She did not hesitate.

Whoever these men were, they apparently had no desire to kill her. At least, not yet, anyway. She reached into her skirt pocket and pulled out a white handkerchief that she began waving over her head as she stepped into the open.

Up on the Sherman tank, a sergeant said, "Look Lieutenant, it's a broad....and a little broad!"

Lt. Schneider smiled. The sarge was a good man. He wasn't the kind of man one necessarily invited to an afternoon tea party, but he was a good man to have around if you decided to go and fight a war instead.

"Sergeant Kelly!"

"Sir!"

"Take these men and provide an escort for the lady and her child . Show her that American soldiers can also be polite and helpful."

"Yessir!" The sergeant barked, and he immediately rounded up the other six men and headed in her direction.

Fifty meters from Lisa's position, a man stood in the tall grass and began to take aim at her. Lieutenant Schneider, a combat hardened veteran, had ventured part of the way with his men and was continuously scrutinizing the countryside.

As fate dictated, it was the Lieutenant who first caught the movement at the corner of his peripheral vision. His instinct immediately told him that any man aiming a weapon was not a friend, and he fired his Thompson just prior to the moment that the unknown assailant fired. The result was that he died and his shot missed Lisa by scant centimeters.

It was over in seconds, and the Lieutenant went running in the direction of the woman while the other soldiers of Dog Company fanned out with their rifles at the ready.

The Lieutenant got there first. The German lady was shaking her head and crying. "Danke shön," was a phrase that she kept repeating over and over.

Lieutenant Schneider took her gently by the arm and said, "Please, sit down on the grass." She looked up at him through tear filled eyes and unruly strands of hair. He had spoken to her in German. He must have because she knew very little English, and she had understood every word he had spoken.

He handed her a canteen of water and said, "Vasser.(water)" She drank only after she had given her daughter a drink first.

A man with a red cross painted on his helmet came running up, and the Lieutenant ordered, "Look `em both over, Doc," and then, to the sergeant, "Who was our snake in the grass, sarge?"

"Dunno, Lientenant. Man in civvies. Leather coat. Might be Gestapo."

"At the use of the word *Gestapo,* she looked up."

In German, she asked, "May I see who you are referring to,

Herr OberLieutenant?"

In German, he replied, "Ja. You may see him, but we will bring him to you," and he barked orders to his sergeant.

She returned to her feet and said, "Nein, Herr OberLieutenant. I am capable. I will walk." He nodded and she did.

Shortly, as she looked down upon the pall of death, she was puzzled. The would-be assassin was unknown to her. A total stranger!

Lieutenant Schneider asked, "Do you recognize him?"

Lisa answered, "I have never seen this man before in my life."

"Why then, would he want you to be dead?"

She looked up at the lieutenant, and answered frankly, "I really do not know. I was my husband's secretary, and perhaps he and his people thought that I might have knowledge of things that he didn't wish to have revealed."

"Do you?" Inquired the Lieutenant.

"It is possible," Lisa admitted frankly.

"Maybe we should start over. I am John Schneider, First Lieutenant United States Army and the Commanding Officer of Dog Company, and you are?"

She handed the Lieutenant a waterproof packet which he began to open, and she answered, "I am Lisa Marie von Leitner, the wife of SS General Gerhardt Ludwig Baron von Leitner." She paused briefly and then added, "Perhaps I should amend what I just said. I am probably the widow of the Herr General."

"You are a baroness?"

"Ja. I am a baroness, but only because I married a baron. I am not an aristocrat. I am the daughter of a Bavarian dairy farmer." She spoke those words with pride.

Lieutenant Schneider bowed slightly, "Very well, Baroness, for you, the war is over. I will have you and your daughter escorted to the chaplain's vehicle where you can ride in safety."

"Can't I walk with you?" She inquired with a small voice.

"I am flattered that you might want to, but as of right now, a state of war still exists between your country and mine. We are in your country, a fact that means that every German citizen is a possible enemy. There might be shooting and I cannot and will not subject you to that possibility."

She was then taken back to the chaplain who tried to engage in conversation with her, but he was unable to speak German and she did not speak English.

The column moved steadily forward for about thirty minutes before it stopped again. This time, Lieutenant Schneider came to her, and said, "Baroness,, I apologize for his intrusion, but we have come to a burned out building, and I am wondering if this might be the place where you parted company with your husband."

She looked and recognized it immediately. "Ja...Jawohl. This is the place! May I see Gerhardt?"

"It is a nasty looking place, Baroness. I don't think you should see it."

"Nonsense! I have seen worse. Now, lead on, Herr OberLieutenant."

He did and she walked back into the place where she saw Gerhardt for the last time. Despite her brashness with the Lieutenant, she treated it as though it were a sacred shrine. Then, she saw his crumpled body, and ran to his side. She knelt down, and realizing that he was dead, began sobbing.

Both Lieutenant Schneider and Sergeant Kelly found it hard to keep there own eyes dry. They thought they had become hardened to the horrors of war, but there were times like this, when it became much too real......too human.

The man wore the rank of an SS Gruppenführer which was equal to a Lieutenant General in the American Army. He was a very high ranking officer indeed, and probably possessed many secrets.

It had cost them twenty-four men to kill him, because that was how man bodies Sergeant Kelly had counted. He also wore the Iron Cross First Class, and the Lieutenant wondered when and how the man had won it.

This was not the Germany of his parents. What kind of country was able to spawn this kind of people, and what drove a man to attempt to assassinate a woman in plain sight of the enemy? What secrets did the Baroness possess? There were too many questions and not enough answers.

His attention returned to the Herr General. Then, he saw the book lying just beyond the Herr General's reach. A pencil was lying near it. He surmised that the General had been writing when death claimed him.

He walked over and picked it up. He glanced at the grief stricken woman who was kneeling beside the dead body of her husband, and stuffed the book inside his own jacket.

If it was a diary, maybe it would shed more light than many hours of interrogation. For the first time since he had gotten involved in this damn war, he began to think like a lawyer. Then, he spoke to the Sergeant once more.

"Sergeant, I want that body given special attention. I don't care how you do it, but get it done."

Lisa had overheard and inquired about what he had told the Herr Sergeant.

"I told him to give your husband's body special attention. It will travel with us in the ambulance."

She began to cry once more, and regardless of how it might have looked to his men, she embraced him." He held her tightly.

She didn't know it yet, but the man who now held her was really quite special. How special was a fact that was still yet to be determined

A lot of questions still needed to be answered, but for her, the terrible war had finally come to an end.

Epilogue

1958

March

Since their parting on the banks of the Starnberger See, Lisa and Max had gone their separate ways. Each not knowing the fate of the other until this very same fate had finally intervened on the streets of San Francisco. It was a chance encounter that prompted an immediate reunion. One that angered the motorists since the reunion took place in the middle of a busy street..

They were two long time friends. Long enough not to care about a few angry motorists.

Max made an immediate decision and requested that Lisa and her husband come to the Big House on the Hill the following Sunday for dinner.

And so, the following Sunday found Colonel and Mrs. John W. Schneider approaching the Big House. John Schneider whistled softly, and said, “So this is how the other half lives.”

Lisa agreed with her husband. It was every bit as big as The Mansion back in Munich. In fact, it might have even resembled The Mansion. She didn’t know for sure. She only knew that it was big.

John pulled into the spacious driveway and parked his car. Then, he got out and walked around to open the door for his wife. He had done that since the very beginning. He would not allow her to open her own doors or be seated without his assistance. She had gotten used to it, and wouldn’t have known how to act if he had stopped doing it. She was definitely spoiled.

John looked apprehensive. "I don't see any signs of life. Are you sure this is the right place?"

She smiled weakly and replied meekly, "I certainly hope so."

Her took her hand and said, "Come my love, let us go to the front door and find out."

John pushed the button for the doorbell, and stood waiting with Lisa standing at his side.

Suddenly, the door opened, and framed in the open doorway stood Erik Halder. He was definitely an older version....maybe 75 or so, but still standing tall and straight with a full head of white hair and a sparkle in his blue eyes.

He smiled.

Her face contorted as though she were going to cry. Then, she exclaimed,

"Erik!"

After that, there was no holding either of them back as their bodies collided in an embrace of happy reunion.

John watched as his wife and the man she had spoken about so often engaged in a tearful embrace that seemed to last forever.

He didn't mind.

Not at all. These people had been a part of her world at a time when just the act of living had to have been a precarious adventure wrought with dangers, but she had spoken of that time as a happy one even in the light of the personal tragedies that seemed to plague her.

Erik and Lisa finally released the hold they had on each other, and each just looked at the other.

She finally spoke. "My God, Erik...how I have missed your presence. You represented a quiet strength even when we were surrounded by chaos."

He maintained his quiet demeanor, "I thank you for that, my lady. I, too, have missed you. You were Gerhardt's good right arm in more ways than one."

Then, Erik glanced at the tall man who stood just behind his wife. He wore the uniform of a full colonel in the United States Army.

"I hope you don't mind my reference, Herr Oberst." He had just referred to John's rank in the German vernacular.

John replied in German, "Certainly not, Mein Herr. I think I know the whole story, and I am not threatened in the least by the mention of Gerhardt von Leitner. From my perspective, he was one hell of a man."

Erik smiled and Lisa decided that introductions were in order, "Erik, allow me to introduce my husband, John Schneider. John, this is my very good friend, Erik Halder."

Each took the other's hand and squeezed firmly. Their eyes locked in contact and spoke only of wonder and friendship.

Finally, Erik said, "Come, let us retire to the stube. Americans refer to this room as a den, but I am still more of a German than I am an American.

When they entered the stube, four men and two woman stood waiting for them, and when the threesome entered the room, they applauded.

Colonel and Mrs. John W. Schneider stood red faced as they received the applause.

Standing there were Max and Ilse. The Lord and Lady of the Manor. As always, Max didn't give one the impression that he was in charge of anything at all. That is, until he opened his mouth. Then you knew.

Ilse was still Ilse, but she had become a better Ilse. In fact, she looked beautiful. She was wearing a white dress with a tight bodice and a skirt that flared out and matching white heels. Her eyes sparkled when she smiled, and spoke only of happiness and contentment.

When she left Germany, she didn't know that it would be almost three years before she would see Max again, and although she had her flings, no one could displace Max as the number one man in her life.

One of her flings had lasted two years, and managed to self-destruct without any outside help. She attributed it to loneliness and not knowing whether she would ever know the fate of her husband.

Lisa embraced her symbolic sister first. After that, she embraced Max.

The next man was a surprise. A man that she hadn't seen since 1936. He was none other than Isaac Nusbaum. In truth, he had been Ilse's partner during her two year affair, but he backed away when she told him that she would not divorce Max in absentia and marry him.

In her way of looking at things, he was making an unreasonable request of her. After thinking about the matter long and hard, he had agreed with her.

Lisa embraced him as a friend, and not as a lover from many years before.

` The final couple was a complete and total shock to her. They were Josef and Yvette Hauser.

Josef and Lisa then embraced each other as they had never done before. They had not seen each other since Karl's funeral. His beautiful eulogy still rang in her ears.

She looked deeply into his eyes, and saw that the metamorphosis was complete. He was no longer the shallow human that used to thrill her in bed. No, there was now depth and a calm assurance about himself and she was willing to bet that no small amount of the credit went to the lovely lady standing at his side.

"Yvette?" She asked meekly.

"LISA!" The next few minutes were devoted to their embrace.

Yvette was the first to compose herself well enough to speak. "Lisa? Why is that we seem to be sharing men?"

Lisa immediately swung around and looked at John, and he responded defensively by saying, "Not me! I've never seen the lady before in my life."

Yvette quickly amended, "No, no, I meant Karl and Josef."

Lisa pondered the idea for a few moments before replying, "There are no coincidences in God's universe. Therefore, nothing occurs by accident. I also need to point out that both Karl and Josef became better men after you came into their lives. The next time you look into a mirror, you need to ask that woman who she really is, because by the look in your husband's eyes, he thinks your really something special."

The last man was unknown to her, but she had heard of him the first week she spent with Gerhardt. His name was Konrad Ruhl, and he was the man that Gerhardt helped to escape. He was also the one man that Max trusted to run the San Francisco station.

Lisa then did the honors by introducing John to everyone and after that, the wine glasses were distributed and filled.

Erik stepped forward and raised his glass. "Ladies and gentlemen.....Damen und Herron....it is wonderful that we all somehow managed to survive the Third Reich, but it is with sadness that one of our number, the man known simply as the Herr General is quite conspicuous by his absence. Of course, I am referring to Gerhardt von Leitner." He raised his glass even higher and said, "To his lasting memory."

Everyone drank and then, after an awkward pause, John Schneider began speaking. "I really haven't said much until right now, but I would be remiss if I didn't add something to these proceedings and fill in some of the blanks, so to speak.."

"First of all, I need to say something about the man we just toasted. The man known as the Herr General. Maybe it takes an American to really appreciate the kind of man Gerhardt von Leitner really was. He was in every respect, a true German aristocrat. A patriot who always kept Germany's interest in the foreground of his mind. He lived his life with absolute honor. He even ended his life with honor, because he knew that he was far too highly placed not to be forced to pay dearly for the crimes of the Third Reich. The War Crimes Commission would have made him accountable for knowing something without trying to do anything about it. They might have even executed him."

"When the war ended, someone discovered that I not only had a law degree from Yale but that I had total command of the German language."

"Therefore, I was promoted to Captain and sent to the War Crimes Commission as an investigator. At this point in time, I was still in possession of a dairy that I had picked up laying next to the body of Gerhardt von Leitner. Lisa didn't see me pick it up and I didn't tell her about it until much later."

"Since I read and speak German, I didn't need an interpreter, and what I found was hours and hours of very interesting reading. Some of it was very sensitive. So sensitive that I decided not to turn it over to the Commission. What it did though was exonerate Max Liebert and Lisa von Leitner of any wrong doing."

"He had made what he thought was a final entry, but he apparently went on the attack and somehow managed to kill all of the men he faced, and he was able to scribble another paragraph."

"At the time, I didn't know Max, but something told me that the pretty young baroness was very important to me. Important enough to care if she was making it in a chaotic world where being a baroness might have gotten her only a few more dollars for thirty minutes of sex in a brothel."

"Things were chaotic in Germany, and although it was our intent to de-nazify Germany, you would have been surprised at how many Germans remained loyal to Hitler or at least, the idea of Hitler. There was no money and it wasn't safe for people like Lisa."

"Right then and there, I drove to Munich, found her and requested that she return to Nürnberg with me. She wanted to know why, and I told her that I cared enough to want to see that she remained safe. I also tried to assure her that I had no ulterior motive. I remember that she looked at me dubiously, but came with me anyway."

There was laughter around the room.

John continued his monologue. "The War Crimes Trials lasted until October 1, 1946, and by that time, I had convinced first myself, and then her, that our futures lie with each other. As for the diary, I gave it to her, and when we finally decided what we should do about his remains, we had the body cremated and the diary with him. Then, we returned his ashes to the Baron and Baroness von Leitner in Vienna."

"Shortly thereafter, we were married and she became an American Army officer's wife without any of the perks that she had as the wife of an SS Gruppenführer."

"We have had our moments like any married couple, but I have never regretted my decision, and I was able to treat Heidi like my own daughter. Thank you for listening."

Lisa blew her nose and took his hand in hers. "John, I have been fortunate. So very fortunate. I have been married to three wonderful men, and since you are number three, I can only tell you that I am very tired of burying husbands. Therefore, it is my heartfelt desire that you bury me this time..................about fifty years from now. I love you, John."

She raised her face to his and he kissed her to the applause of the assembled guests.

* * * * *

The following month, Lisa and her husband traveled to Okinawa for John's final duty assignment prior to retirement. It was during that time that she met a Marine Corporal, and was prompted to tell him her story.

When Lisa told it, she predicted that I would someday write and publish her story. It took me 45 years, but I finally did it.

Therefore Lisa, I really did this for you...

Ich liebe dich, Mein Schatz

Grüss Gott

Otto Behrman